Restless Heart of Evil

A Dangerous Worlds Adventure

Written by Marc J Wilson

Illustrated by Elmundo Garing

Dangerous Worlds gamebooks
© Marc J Wilson 2014

To the Appucine Lofts

River Devani

To Mirror Marches

N E S W

1. Gates of Heaven
2. Bractianine Gate
3. Wailing Crags
4. City Gaol
5. The Mezzaluna
6. Elven Quarter
7. Gate of the Leaping Lion
8. Cemetery of Innocents

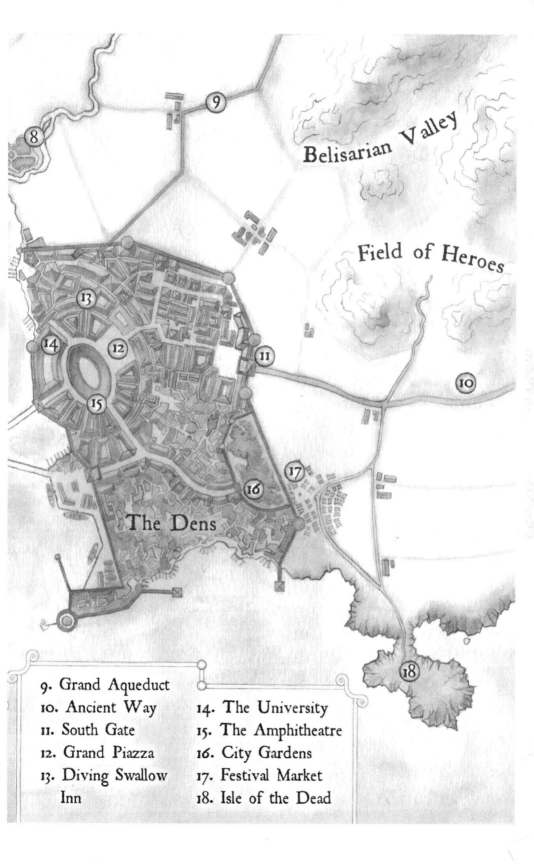

Belisarian Valley

Field of Heroes

The Dens

To the resilient playtesters – a grateful thanks

Diana Wicker
Alexander Torofiev
Oli Tridgell
Stefano Ronchi
Yves-Arnaud Jouret

Rules of the Game

This is a diceless system, so in a traditional sense, random chance plays no part of your adventure. There are times when rolling dice may be impractical; on public transport or on holiday for example, and so this was a conscious decision, reached by the author after some soul searching.

Dice or not, this is an adventure in the finest traditions. You tailor the character to your own needs, choosing Attribute enhancements and Gifts, fully enabling you to build a hero fit to face the deadly perils to come.

These Attributes, and occasionally your Gifts and Trappings, will usually have a direct effect on combat. Again, no dice are rolled, but how healthy - and deadly - you are, and what you are carrying, will tilt combat in your favour...or not. Fighting in this age of careless bloodshed is quick, brutal, and often fatal. Choosing to fight an opponent of superior size or ability can have disastrous effects, so choose your battles wisely.

This is a points based system: **You have 7 points to spend.**

Increasing an Attribute by one level, costs 1 point. Likewise, buying a Gift costs 1 point. Your points must be fully spent before commencing the adventure. You cannot choose to alter your Attributes or Gifts along the way unless directed to by the text.

ATTRIBUTES

Agility
Agility determines your general physical ability; to run, to climb, to leap and to dodge, and so on. Some sections will query your Agility level, and the outcome of a physical feat may depend on it…

You begin with a default Agility score of 7.
You may increase your Agility score by up to three levels, to a maximum starting total of 10. Unless specified in the text, you may not increase this attribute higher than the starting total.

Dexterity
Dexterity determines your general skill, and also your combat abilities. This is the main Attribute leveraged against during combat, but a high level will also assist you in hand-eye actions such as catching, shooting and throwing.

You begin with a default Dexterity score of 7. You may increase your Dexterity score by up to three levels, to a maximum starting total of 10. Unless specified in the text, you may not increase this attribute higher than the starting total.

Fortitude
Fortitude describes your state of health, your endurance, your mental and physical resistance, and is used to mark 'wounds'. Being injured in battle or otherwise will reduce your fortitude. Having very low fortitude will also affect your Agility and Dexterity.

You begin with a default Fortitude score of 12.
You may increase your Fortitude score by up to three levels, to a maximum starting total of 15. Unless specified in the text, you may not increase this attribute higher than the starting total. If it reaches zero, you are dead.

GIFTS

You may purchase up to **four** Gifts, **each costs 1 point.**

Silver tongued

You have a natural ability to convince, persuade, and talk your way into otherwise denied opportunities, and out of trouble.

Skullduggery

Criminal skills picked up during your life of questionable morality. Lock-picking, pickpocketing, and assimilating with people of a dubious background come easy to you.

Survivalist

Hunting, tracking, foraging and building shelters are essential for a life outdoors. You are also adept at reading the stars, navigation, and identifying flora and fauna.

Arcania

A skill only attained by years of conscientious study, you've gained insights into forbidden knowledge, symbolism and languages. Though no sorcerer, you have a theoretical understanding of magical lore.

Martial prowess

Years of saving your own skin has given you razor sharp reflexes in a combat situation. You are an expert at avoiding blows and striking first, with deadly force.

Intuition

Some say you are touched by the gods… others maintain you're caressed by forces of darkness. You have an uncanny knack of avoiding danger by chance. Some admire this gift, others will fear it.

Acrobatics

You have honed your skills over the years to be an expert at climbing, jumping, and other physical feats and tricks.

Hyper senses

Your finely tuned senses are keener than those of the common man. Eagle-eyed and rabbit-eared (at least in allegorical sense), you have the nose of a blood hound and taste buds more discerning than that of an Emperors cook.

Iron willed

Something in your constitution renders you utterly stubborn to outside influence. You cannot be lulled or coaxed. Your spirit always remains your own, and you rarely break under pressure.

Stealth

You are a master of the shadows. Silent movement and concealment are easy for you. Your footsteps make not a sound, and you melt easily into most backgrounds.

FATE

There is one set of variables which you are not able to determine. Only your deeds and actions during your adventures can influence your **Fate,** in the eyes of fickle and capricious gods. There are three levels of **Fate.** A section may question what level you enjoy, with the results based on your favour with the Gods…such is their want.

Level 1 : Favoured

Your life is protected, to a degree, as the Gods hold you in high esteem and deign fit to watch over you.

Level 0 : Unwatched

You are one of the anonymous billions - flotsam whose prayers and devotions appear to go unheard, and unheeded.

Level -1 : Marked

You irritate the Gods with your wasteful, selfish, or murderous actions. A score is scribed through your name in the Eternal Scrolls.

You begin the adventure as Unwatched.

KEYWORDS AND NUMBER REFERENCES

You will be required along the way to record actions and encounters. These come in two forms, **Keywords** and **Number References.**

Keywords

These are hints and clues, which you will be prompted to note down along the way. They may promote an additional encounter or task, or they may cement your fate, either in this adventure…or the next.

Number References

Occasionally you will be asked to record a number, or collect an item which is numbered. When prompted by the narrative, you will commonly be guided to turn to that section number.

THE 'WATCH TEST'

During the course of your adventures you may be prompted to take a **'Watch Patrol'** test. The local militia – colloquially known as 'Watchdogs' are known for their mendacious temperaments and bestowers of casual violence upon hapless civilians. Your deeds may bring you into conflict with these law enforcers, so take care to restrict any criminal deeds to the mute shadows, or your watch total – and chance of arrest – will greaten.

You begin the adventure with a Watch Total of 0.

TRAPPINGS

Your **trappings**; what you have, and what you are carrying, will need to be recorded throughout the adventure. There are no 'maximum numbers of items' mechanics. The text in relevant sections will guide you if a decision is required. Like most Adventure Gamebooks, certain items of equipment can have a profound effect on both your Attributes, and encounters along the way.

You travel light, and begin the Adventure with a **fine sword**, a **dagger, 50 silver scuda, a finely crafted wheellock pistol with ample munitions** and **two ancient volumes** as requested...

DANGEROUS WORLDS ADVENTURE SHEET

DEXTERITY

AGILITY

FORTITUDE

FATE

TRAPPINGS

GIFTS

NOTES

The Restless Heart of Evil

A Survivor's Tale

Better dead, than a meaningless life untouched by the caress of wisdom. It wasn't always this way. Expanding your understanding of the Gods, old and new. Of the stars in the heavens and the shadows in the depths. From the mundanity of trade accounts, of ledgers and banking formulae, to the forbidden mysticism of ancient rites and manuscripts, crackling with capricious lore. Pouring over the practicalities of rudimentary mechanics to absorbing the mysticism of alchemy and astromancy; 'sea-sponge' is what the Professor called you, when first he led you into his studies and libraries, and reintroduced your empty soul to learning.

Your mother died in childbirth. A handsome young girl with high cheekbones and a kindly smile. You owned a portrait of her once, in a delicate silver locket, taken from your father's grasp, as he hung stiff from the noose. But you long since surrendered possession of this icon - sold cheap for a night of mead and menace. And now you can't really picture her at all, just a sadly fading blur remains.

The world about you was shattered forever, before manhood was reached. Your father's ship sank in the Straight of Claws one night during a storm, consigning the cargo, your father's finances, and any hope you had for a prosperous life to the deep. So it was when you found your bankrupt father's body, swinging stiffly in the desolate shell of your former home.

Soldier, mercenary, outlaw. Murderer. Slave. Your story twists this way and that. Through times of plenty, and times of sorrow and indifference. Sobbing with pain and bleeding to near death in muddy battlefield trenches, to watching numbly as homesteads were put to torch. Memories of weeping women, sodden, cursing you in the freezing rain. From rolling in gold, marvelling at fantastic treasures and toasting business ventures with fine wines, to fleeing from debtors, monsters - creatures of the night - and vengeful victims of your many awful crimes.

One adventure too far. A strange land. Capture, sentencing, and a slow death of slavery toiling in a Black Elf galley. Beaten and bitter, you were able to sullenly reflect on your childhood of relative joy, the abrupt interruption of unjust blame, and your descent into hollow greed and purposeless violence. With every beat of the drum, every lash of the whip, and every stroke of the oar, you silently begged your mother for forgiveness, your heart aching with longing and shame.

Wretched and half-dead, and commanding a paltry price - quarter that of a side of ham, you were lined up with the dregs to be sold at a distant slave market. But a diamond of desire must have twinkled in your eyes as the passing man stopped a moment to glance at you. Broken and bloody, scorched by the sun, and barely able to lift your head, you were only able to croak 'Wasteland' through cracked lips, in response to his enquiry of origin. Lifting your chin with his fingers, he looked pitifully upon you, and motioned for his attendant to pay the pittance to secure your soul. Thus you entered the service of Professor Hieronymus Kroos, famed antiquarian of Maasenborg.

Docking once again in the city of your childhood, beset with an angry fever, you were gradually nursed back to health - fed on thickly buttered slices of rye bread, and bowls of clotted ewes cream. Never destined for the drudgery of domestic duties, the Professor was delighted to find you literate and modestly educated, with an aptitude for foreign tongues, gained on your myriad adventures. He listened, rapt, and smiled encouragingly as you laid bare your brutal and turbulent existence - leaving little except the darkest and most painful periods out of your reminisces. So began your education, as you were taken under the wing of the polymath scholar and pioneer. An insatiable student, you drank in the wonders of science, astronomy, and cartography, eventually becoming a trusted servant, and latterly friend and confidant - running the more mundane aspects of the estate whilst the Professor endlessly roamed, sometimes travelling hundreds of leagues for a particular volume of this or that, or item of interest.

Near half a year has passed since the Professor left for Deva, along with Adz - a Norsiczan retainer of immense constitution - at the behest of an acquaintance and fellow explorer of note, Artur Keijzer. His promising to return in one hundred days, you reluctantly remained in Maasenborg, conducting routine business on his behalf. But these last unaccounted for months have left you anxious, unable to sleep and your senses polluted with a sense of foreboding. And so the letter requesting your attendance in the Middenlands brought relief, and also served to ignite the smouldering coals of adventure in your heart. Methodically you packed up your kit bag, secured your purse and sharpened your blade, ready for another journey into the unknown.

Standing now on the deck of the creaking old carrack, the westerly winds cool in the long summer evening, and the sun set low, casting a blazing light over the docks and warehouses of Maasenborg, you bob out of the harbour into the wide open seas, and onwards, to Deva.

Tidings from the Middenlands

My dearest friend Sigasünd.

I trust you are in good health, and knowing you well, expect you will not be entirely surprised, nor deterred by the contents of this letter. I write with great haste, for the carrack 'The Boogenhofen' leaves the port of Aedes to Maasenborg imminently, and Captain Hessler has made plain he intends not to delay on my account. He has been paid well enough to be reasonably trusted to deliver this to you, with the promise of more, once you are transported here, to Deva, on the return voyage.

I confess that I am excited, though anxious, and am in some trepidation of events to come. For these last several months I have been in the company of Artur Keijzer, who you will not need reminding is an explorer and fellow antiquarian of great renown. Together we have travelled across the Midden hinterlands uncovering tremendous discoveries and artefacts - from the remnants of the (formerly!) lost city of Tylos, all the way to the Black Gulf. I have for you a fine helmet of exquisite craftsmanship, inlaid with pre-ancient Elven inscriptions; in fact I am very close to deciphering...
...alas I digress, and must hurry as the pilot is hailing the helmsmen to haul anchor, and the captain is already pacing the foredeck, glaring out to sea.

To the point. We have found two artefacts of irresistible power, pieces of an Elven triptych with the potential to open...certain gates...which defy common laws of time and distance. Keijzer - in a foolish display of impulsiveness that belies his wisdom, has contrived to unlock one gate we discovered, here, near Deva, and has made off for the Lagoon of Sorrows in search of the third and final piece of this ancient puzzle. For my part I am headed to the city, where you will join me...as I am carrying the triptych which appears to unlock a gate somewhere in the nearby environs. I am not at all sure whether to simply cast this object into the sea and be done with it. An object of such power does not unearth itself after thousands of years without rousing the attention of malignant forces - of this we can be depressingly certain. Please take care to wrap up my affairs ...take what you need from our workshops and laboratories, but travel light. Bring with you a keen blade and even sharper wits - not to mention good fortune. Also take from the library the Bel-Aliad papyrus, volumes three and four, and keep them from prying eyes. I anticipate they will reveal some secrets I previously disregarded as mere folk lore.

Adz hails you. He is taking care of me in his own oafish manner, and together we enjoy reasonable health, though Adz complains endlessly of the summer heat, and bids you bring with you a chill wind from the Sea of Shards...
I am being bellowed at by the bosun. Godspeed.
Yours etc.
Kroos.

Turn to 1.

1

Unknown friend,

Should you recover this flotsam from the waves, and enrich yourself with the golden ducats sealed within, I oblige you locate the volumes owner, Kroos of Maasenborg, who will provide many times more for safe delivery of the same. As for me...I am of no importance, and if you are reading this then I am now surely drowned. Pray for my shade. Sigasünd...

You lay down the trembling quill, and glancing at the volumes; sealed in wax against the sea and indented with gold ducats, you consider whether these will be your final words. You can only hope your attempts at flotation - the tethering to inflated skins - will keep them from the depths, should the tumultuous sea finally consume this ship. You wager the gilding of the gold is enough to attract the greedy shipping plying these waters, and hope for a keen eyed captain to take an interest in this particular cargo...

After weeks of unremarkable progress, aided by gentle prevailing winds, matters took a turn for the worse after an unscheduled brief stop at the small headland port of Aedes. The winds transformed, and have latterly descended into a swirling maelstrom. 'The Boogenhofen', for two days since, has been brutally punished with every wave. Angry white horses have boiled up from the sea and threatening to splinter the timbers with every teeth-grinding kick. Crew have been lost. Those that remain are of dire constitution and frayed of nerve. Green of gills and tired of spirit, you fall into a fitful rum soaked slumber...and so it is with much surprise and relief that you awaken the next morning. Drenched in vomit and sticky with perspiration, you utter a grateful oath as the ship limps closer the rich Midden port of Deva - a mere days sailing away.

Turn to 456.

2

You clamber up onto the roofs of the buildings lining the way, and gingerly begin to make progress across them. From your elevated position you are able to follow the route of the Avenida to the Piazza. In the streets below all manner of sin is being inflicted on its weaker denizens. Lumbering undead contest with roaming gangs of thugs in inflicting terror upon the hapless proles. Perhaps without a care, or perhaps in acknowledgement of the End of Days, sounds of rapine can be heard down dark alleys, punctuated with stifled gasps and screams. You glance down in disgust as you see a charred corpse being gnawed by two figures, only compounded with the realisation the rewarded diners are half starved members...of the living - taking a grisly advantage in this all-comers feast.

As you near the Piazza Arborea, you call out to Adz and Professor, competing with the shouts and screams of the city. Palls of smoke drift across your vision as powerful winds fan the flames of the slum fire.

'Seven Hells!' you cry, 'How can anything be achieved in this inferno!' The gaps between rooftops widen as you near your destination. It's perhaps one hundred paces to the Piazza, which will have to be reached at street level. Nothing is emerging from its direction except for a succession of fiends, dead Stygians and reanimated corpses. A powerful ear shattering howl fills the night sky, sending birds careering into the broken clock towers and spires. You look at your hands and attempt to stem the rigours before you climb back down into the street. The Beast - the Master of the Pit - is holding court, on a throne made of the dead branches of the Tree of Life. When he speaks, the city trembles.

If you wish to leap down and hurry to the square in case Adz and the Professor are still nearby, turn to 118.
If you think it likely that they would have retreated to the Diving Swallow, turn to 120.

3

You hurtle toward the relative safety of the forest as fast as your legs will carry you. Splashing over the sodden green carpet of the bilious plain and thick lichen-like surface, causes you to stumble and slip. The Bone Dragon soon swoops, and with a mighty roar consumes you in a hell-like furnace of blazing flame. **Lose 4 points of Fortitude and 1 each from your Agility and Dexterity.** If still somehow alive, you conquer the unspeakable agonies of your scorched flesh, and turn to face the gargantuan beast - which has now landed before you, poised to strike with its immense claws.

If your Dexterity and Fortitude combined total 12 or more, turn to 263.
If they total 11 or less, turn to 244.

4

You creep up to the filthy grey clad figure who remains soundly asleep in a nest of straw. 'Wake up, dear little prince,' you whisper into his ear, a knife at his throat. The figure groans and reaches down to give his arse a deep scratch, screwing his face up as he rubs his sleep filled eyes. You hear Adz snigger, before the man suddenly feels your hot breath, and the cold steel held tightly against his skin, Opening his bloodshot eyes in wide surprise, he struggles so much that you are driven to press the blade deep into his flesh. Even this doesn't quell his vigour. The man looks drugged. Or else a fanatic - long beyond the fear of death. Adz pulls him to a corner and pummels him into submission with his mighty fists. Soundly beaten, the figure slumps like a leaking sack whilst you and Adz attempt to question him. The man offers you nothing, save curses and blood filled spittle, absorbing your blows and threats.

'Kill me now!' he screams with determination, 'For I will have but hours of impatient rest before the tree falls and I am embraced by the eternal life of The Master. Ignorant fools! This mortal body is of no consequence to me now,' he mocks, smirking. He points a grubby finger at Adz, 'And as for you, you fat Nhortlünd pig, The Master will make a quick meal of you!' Adz growls and smashes his fist into the man's face, causing it to break like a pottery vase. Nudging the man's body with your boot yields no response.

'Sorry, Siga,' Adz apologies, turning out his palms, 'you heard what he said about me.'

Turn to 168.

5

You ease the door open - as much as you can ease a 200 year old lump of marble - without making anything more than a nerve jarring scrape, and carefully step down into the tomb. Sarcophagi in various perilous states are strewn over cracked marble slabs, the contents looted from the empty coffins generations ago. Only two remain intact, the two small white coffins of the tragic Moretti children. A glum sadness grips your heart, and you feel momentarily so apathetic, that you feel like lying down and sleeping. You sigh heavily, sitting down to stare at them despondently, depression weaving through your empty veins.

If your Fortitude is 8 or less, turn to 19.
If your Fortitude is 9 or more and/or you are carrying a PYGMY TOTEM, turn to 273.

6

Enraged at the constant harassment, and cornered like wild quarry, you feel forced to fight. You make good in dispatching the keenly deserving Militiamen. No one else will suffer their malignant attention. Alas your efforts are all for nought. For unseen, a burly citizen-hero lands a sucker punch with an improvised cudgel and you sink to your knees, nauseous with concussion. The last thing you remember are the hostile glares of Devan locals, and the accusatory eyes of the dead watchdogs surrounding you on the cobbles. As you draw your last breath, you curse this sorry foreign land.

Your adventure is at an end.

7

'Hold hands!' you urge cheerfully, 'Never let go - follow me like a chain of ducklings - don't dally, only look at your own footsteps - but never let go.' You look round at the chain of children, bright fires of hope burning in their eyes, and you've never been more afraid.

'Bless you, Siga,' coos the High Priestess, 'Your name will be sung loud, if dawn ever breaks again... and if not, it will be sung in The Everlasting Garden, by Aloevopias flowers and jewelled butterflies.'

'Dawn will break again for these children. I promise it,' you state confidently. You feel light-headed with the commitment, and somehow almost totally free of self-control, as you lead your little gaggle out into the alleyway, and toward the docks.

Turn to 281.

8

You catch sight of a stout earthenware jug hurtling toward your skull, and duck sharply, grimacing as you see it shatter heavily on the floor beyond. Sensing the crowds distaste for your delaying tactics, you decide to change your tactics.

Turn to 58.

9

Moretti looks skyward and howls at the heavens, 'Why must I kill again!' he screams, and with an agonizing effort clambers ignited onto the battlements, and leaps from the tower. Rushing to the edge with Adz, you look down to see him thrashing through the thick mud, leaving a trail of smoke as he endeavours towards to sea. The tower lurches sideways as the supporting wooden innards give way, and a heavy grinding noise suggests total collapse.

'Here we go again,' says Adz with a grin, as you both leap over the edge of the towering inferno and plummet into the thick mud below, landing with a wet smack.

If you want to run down the Vampire, turn to 394.
If you decide to leave him to surely blaze to his demise, turn to 388.

If you want to run down the Vampire, turn to 394.
If you decide to leave him to surely blaze to his demise, turn to 388.

10

You curse with frustration as you lose sight of your quarry. Old injuries blaze painfully as you gasp for breath. Exhausted and bested, you have little choice but to continue back to your lodgings.

Turn to 243.

Turn to 243.

11

You approach the mythical beast carefully. 'Am I to ride this creature, as do the Gods?' you mutter, in wonder and awe. As you go close Pegasus whinnies and snorts, its hooves digging up furrows in the sodden turf. It appears nervous, stressed even. As it lowers its graceful head you can see in its giant dark eyes a palpable look of disappointment. With a final interrogative stare, the unfathomable beast turns and gallops off across the plain, taking to the air before wheeling and disappearing into the descending night, leaving you quite alone.

You stand crestfallen and abandoned in this warped land, contrite at your many ill deeds, which the Pegasus has harshly judged. The orb feels like a lead ball. A burden. A curse. Night falls, and you sigh deeply as you begin the long trek back to Deva.

Turn to 121.

Turn to 121.

12

The panes high above shimmer and shift with lightning speed. Fractured prismatic images of two dimensional shapes begin to fill the air above you. Alternating between lighting fast and frozen inanimate, and blinding you in a rapid riot of colour, the **Stained Glass Heroes** wake from their slumber. As you stand dumbstruck, your ears are assailed by a pin-sharp screeched warning.

'Intruder!' goes the arcane Elven cry - along with other cries so high-pitched they're barely audible. High up in the stinking city above, untold numbers of dogs foam, snap, and howl in agony.

The figures shift and bend as fast as light itself. Coloured light falls upon you from a source unseen, and on impact with your boiled leather armour and worldly trappings, a million fragments of beautiful razor sharp shards explode forth, lacerating exposed areas of your soft human flesh - **lose 2 points of Fortitude.** As more cracks form in the ceiling, moonlight bursts in, causing another storm of shattering glass. **Lose another point of Fortitude.**

It's clear that if you remain static for much longer you will be lacerated to mere slivers, such are the chaotic explosions, caused by the rays of illumination from the intruding world above.

Will you choose to run forth, and slice open this foulest of wombs before The Master of the Pit fully awakens? If so, turn to 82.

If you decide that your small soft body and toy-like sword are no match for such a creature, nor present a suitable shield against these glass automations, then you flee this place, back whence you came. Turn to 270.

13

You walk forward - for you now realise there is no way back - towards the next row of glyphs, separating the Goddess Sanromai and the dread God Menax; deities of Love and War. You tread on the illuminated flagstones, ready to receive the next fateful test. Once again, the leaden and unseen voice demands answer to its eternal question.

The number of conquests bequeathed to the world by Pentarc, the first Primarch's guiding hand'

If you know the answer to this question, turn to the relevant section.
If you don't, but are Favoured and / or have the Gift of Arcania, turn to 100.
If you don't know the answer, and not Favoured nor have this Gift, turn to 66.

14

Breaking away from the dust cloud of locals trooping back to the city, you hike up a thorny slope and along a dusty path leading to the Belisarian Valley, striving to keep your quarry in view. As you descend a treacherous course, cursing your punished limbs, the path spirals sharply into the nape of the valley. Scanning the silent landscape there is no sign of Ingmar - the bone dry terrain yields no tracks. You take a draft of water and wipe a hand across your dampened brow, considering your next move. Looking around you on the valley floor, there are clear signs of terrible conflict. Gleaming white bones jut forth from the earth, and rusted and broken weapons of great antiquity lay strewn over the ground. A haunted place. No carrion birds wheel in the sky, no scavengers scurry amongst the vast collection of lost souls. The dead who lie here were picked clean centuries ago, and remain now a mere historical footnote. You notice a path winding around a steep slope, which you suppose leads toward a collection of small caves you notice embedded in the hillside.

If you want to search the caves, turn to 101.
If you want to investigate the battlefield remains, turn to 137.

15

You feel someone lurch into you with a heavy force, winding you, and dropping you to your knees. You put your free hand over your face, protecting yourself from the melee for the spilled pastries, when you hear gasps, and notice a pool blood expanding around your knees. You only have time to glance up at a blurred vision of a Stygian assassin melting into the crowd, before you notice, with a degree of melancholy, the stab wound to your lung. You have but breathless moments, to reflect on the regret that your life has ended in such a ridiculous fashion. Devan sandals scuff the dust around you, grabbing pastry crumbs. Drowning on your very own blood, you sink into the tender embrace of the End of Days.

Your adventure is at an end.

16

You stumble through the masonry choked streets as if in a dream. The clouds of debris conspire to create an ethereal landscape in which dust covered wraiths stagger, panic-stricken, through the night. All around you the begging for futile mercies. The answers in bestial violence. You follow Adz as best you can in this near dark. In a world devoid of light save the red-orange glow of the flame, you tumble down a narrow alleyway, and into a deserted piazza. Central in the piazza is an amalgamation of covered wagons, bolted together to form a train of sorts. The horses that used to draw it lay dead and partially devoured on the flagstones. Through the gloom you can make out the carved signs atop the former attraction, 'Friar Bartók's Befamed Curios.'

Adz, panting with fatigue, stops momentarily and gazes at the wooden steps leading to its entrance. A fearful curiosity seems to grip your friend as he notices, like you, the door is slightly ajar. Periodic banging and grunting sounds from within cause the hairs on your neck to rise, as you stare into the shadows beyond the doorway. Blood turns to ice in your veins as your eyes drift to an object discarded, or dropped, near the portal. The professor's staff. The unmistakable spirals of the milkwood shaft, and the worn pommel, dulled by thousands of leagues of travel. Adz sees it too.

'Siga...' he begins, before you cut him off. A pit of despair forms in your stomach. 'I see it also...'

If you want to enter the wagon train of curios, turn to 30.
If you decide to continue your search toward the university, turn to 367.

17

You wait for the Ogre to swipe at you with its ham-like hands. Quick as a flash, you pivot and step outside the beasts swinging arc. Predictably, it lumbers forward under its own momentum, and as it does so, you leap mightily - plunging your blade between its shoulder blades. A deafening roar fills the square as the miserable abomination drops to its knees. Like a delivering angel, you grasp its filthy hair and decapitate it, sending it back to End of Days. As its despicable head bounces across the marble flagstones, impressed onlookers alternately shriek with horror and sigh with relief. Both emotions settle down into a degree of awe, and for a moment you greedily bask in it.

Turn to 200.

18

As the masses begin their return to Deva, along dusty paths and through parched olive groves, you catch site of an ungainly figure struggling atop a small, and seemingly stubborn tempered mule. As you shield your eyes against the sun, you peer through the hazy air and...yes, there's no mistaking the raspberry splotched skin even at this range. It's none other than Ingmar Kops, one of your fellow passengers from the Boogenhofen. A curious youth at any time, his innate peculiarity is highlighted further today, clinging as he is to the mane of his unruly mount, and moving opposite to the crowds. Moving towards the Belisarian Valley...

If you want to follow the young man, turn to 14.
If you choose to follow the crowds back to Deva, turn to 397.

19

Lacking the necessary vitality to resist the magnetic pull of doom, you lay down wearily in the dust, bitter with regret about all that befell you in your violent and tragedy afflicted life. So heartbroken and consumed with despair are you, that you don't even move a muscle as two beautiful and abominable creatures slide back the lids on their coffins, and creep out to greedily feast from your veins. Staring motionless at the tattered fresco of the tomb, you consider for a moment that this is also your final resting place, and with a huge sigh you exhale your final breath.

Your adventure ends here.

20

As you approach, one of the Elves moves to block your way. However, upon noticing your proudly displayed Victory Laurel from the wrestling ring, a Devan junior officer nudges him aside and winks at you.

'Great display in the ring brother…from one wrestler to another,' he says. 'You won me a tidy sum you did - in you go.' Ushering you forward, he glares suspiciously at the Elves as he escorts you inside, and to a choice seat near the front of the stage. Patting you warming on the shoulder he leaves you to take in the show.

You take in the vista of the sweeping arena, and are able to pick out a few key figures; the Duce is here, resplendent in his personal box. Like a finely-dressed toad - his jaw jutting out in constant defiance. Heads of several of the religious orders are here too, and many of the Council of Fifty, who feign to rule this City-state.

Delicate yet powerful melodies resonate throughout the arena, as the Elven ensemble begins their passion play with a beautiful musical introduction. There's audible scoffing within the crowd, which grows into outright guffawing as the all-male warrior troupe take to the stage bedecked in various historical outfits. It seems what passes for serious storytelling in the land of Elves, only raises hilarity in Deva. You can't discern a reaction from the proud elves - all of whom seem apparently lost in the play, wearing utterly inscrutable expressions of complete seriousness. The ages are covered, highlighting episodes of Elven intervention and guidance in the world of man. The Devans seem either to smirk or yawn in equal measure. A distinguished figure steps forward.

'That's Aegnor – leader of these fairies,' scoffs a drunk from the row in front. The leader of the Elves steps forward and directly addresses the crowd, and in particular the Duce, who matches his steely gaze with his own. He begins,

'Never again dear cousins; never again can we, jointly, allow evil to penetrate these lands to the extent of the past. After **two hundred and twenty eight** peaceable years of the White King's reign, we are again at the gates of armageddon friends, and they buckle against the vanguard of darkness. Disorder needs *no* invite! No invitation to enter this world, and it does not need assistance from meddlers in the black arts. Dear cousins of common cause, we have watched from afar, but can watch no longer. We have come to help you protect yourselves. Yes, I say this now, and I beseech you to heed my words. Only by joining as one can we hope to eliminate the threat - only as one can we hope to bolster the gates, and make them bulwarks against evil. Portents of the most ruinous form have been scryed in the Crystal Pools, and it is said these threats are *imminent.*'

Aegnor again regards the confused and mocking crowds somewhat urgently. 'Friends,' he pleads, 'we must address this without delay...we have seen that under this very city...' You sit forward to listen keenly, it becoming harder to pick out what is being said with the onset of cat-calls and booing. '...there are gates which are opening...' The boorish pig in front of you rises to toss a used flagon at the stage, but you firmly pummel him back into his seat, '...we locked these gates eons ago!...they are not the playthings of humankind!'

It's chaos in the amphitheatre, as people rise to make off - when suddenly The Duce cries out in pain and sinks into his velvet throne clutching an arrow sunken into his breast. Suddenly one of the crowd rises and shouts 'The elf! There upon the colonnade!!' and points to an Elven figure making off from the scene to the north, bow in hand. Pandemonium ensues as elves and men alike try to comprehend the situation, both reaching instinctively for their weapons. As you scan the shadows high on the colonnade, you see another figure, this one black-clad, returning an unshot arrow back into their quiver before darting off to the south.

If you give chase to the assassin headed north, turn to 208.
If you want to pursue the figure making off to the south, turn to 69.
If leap onto the up to the private box and assist The Duce, turn to 235.

21

Like the ground surrounding the orb, the forces of nature are strong around the stairway. Its twenty or so steep and spiralling steps to nothing. Tall grass bends in the grass, brushed gently by a breeze of unknown origin, and gay blooms drape themselves wilfully beneath the steps. Unlike the circle around the orb, the line between the contrasting terrain is blurred, but taking no chances you toss an apple core onto it. When it's not vaporised, detonated, or sucked mercilessly into some other twisted realm, you step - still with some lingering trepidation - towards the finely hewed steps. They appear constructed of finest marble and the smoothness and condition of them belies their timeless age. Reaching the top step your heart sinks a little, when confronted with a mundane drop back down to the plain. You mutter testily and spit to the bottom, watching the dry white gob hit a dazzling bloom. Galiael clutches your hand. His eyes wet with tears of ecstasy, he stares into the middle distance, eyes wide with wonder as he encourages you onwards. 'One more step friend,' he says excitedly. Reluctantly you prepare to take a leap and fall several spans to the soft earth - it's a quick way to get down from here you reason - and step with the elf. You boot makes contact with a surface unseen and you exhale, incredulous as a spirals of wispy blue and silver vapours circle in front of you, forming a portal four or five spans in circumference. 'A g...gateway of the Old Ones,' the elf stammers in broken Midden-speak, white with awe. For a moment you think he is about to faint, and so you clench his sleeve ever more tightly. The portal tendrils accelerate with power unseen, and the blue and silver mask dissipates until all that remains is a watery mirage...and from that mirage a rippling vision appears. Across the boiling seas and the cloud bursting mountains, beyond soaring Warrior Kings and past its immense citadel, the unmistakable Land of the Elves. Galiael gulps nervously, and stamps his boots to compose himself.

'My Prince!' he barks loudly and bows deeply, his features now etched with a steely determination. You gawp at the figures framed within the Portal. A ruler, no doubt; clad in the deep emerald green armour of High Dragons. Mages and Nobles too, their tall helms festooned with arcane symbols and gilded with gold and encrusted with gemstones. No ordinary collection you muse... and nor likely a chance meeting either. They stare back you with confusion, and a degree of haughty mistrust.

Do you have the lozenge of tongues? If so, turn to 256.
If not, turn to 225.

You stumble down the hillside for what seems an eternity. The pernicious terrain endeavours to spoil your efforts at every stage, turning up deep gullies, sheer rock faces and impassable knots of bracken. Even as the comet hangs low in the sky and illuminates the landscape, it does so in stark highlights and shadows, its blistering heat taxing your reserves of energy. Your efforts are in vain, and soon the realisation hits you that you will neither reach Deva, nor have time to put sufficient distance between you and the comet by discarding its beacon. Sighing deeply, you light up a cheroot, and sit atop a craggy outcrop and await your fate. As if sensing your melancholy a bold a weasel approaches, and you delight in sharing a last meal with the little fellow, before the two of you are immolated in the atomic impact.

Life's adventure – for both you and the weasel – ends here.

'Hold fast there, dear friends,' you command, stepping into the moon's silvery light.

'Get out of our way strangers! This has nothing to do with you. Gods! Whose side are you even on?' One spits into the dust, and collectively they attempt to posture threateningly.

If you stand aside, turn to 404.
If you want to draw your weapons, turn to 119.

The riverside is a teaming mass of imbibers, over-indulging in sumptuous and exotic foods, not to mention the arrays of fine beverages on offer. Smells waft through the hot summer air, gamely competing with the foetid stink of the river. Added to the locals are a vast array of students, poets, minstrels and dancers, who perform either on improvised stages, or else wander the crowds for coppers. You pause to buy a flagon of chilled Purple Hand Ale, and wander the site until you find an empty bench in the shade on which to sit. **Deduct 1 silver scuda from your adventure sheet.** No sooner have you sat down to enjoy your drink, when some shabby velvet curtains open from the adjoining stage, and a nervous young minstrel appears, and begins his frankly terrible repertoire. He doesn't even reach the chorus when some young, and very drunk lordlings, begin to heckle him, putting him off with jibes and tossed food. Rolling your eyes at this behaviour, do you:

Finish your drink and head on your way? If so, turn to 40.
Stroll over and tell them to leave the minstrel be? If so, turn to 48.

Foolishly - in the face of such conditions - you stand to fight the figures pouring out the darkness. In the confusion of the gloom, you fight only a short while before you are overwhelmed and rendered limb from limb, as the hungry fiends feast upon your corpse. The comet fragment, torn free of its bag by gnashing undead claws, sinks anonymously into the mud.

You never live to see it draw down the comet - its progenitor - and its detonation in an apocalyptic explosion. An explosion which breeches the walls, and brings down the gatehouses - serving only to expedite the fall of the city and the demise of all within, your friends included. Whether this is a blessing or a curse, is for the Gods to decide.

Your adventure ends here.

Bearing its huge teeth as it bears down on *you*, you leap to one side - avoiding the swing of its plated arms. In an instant you raise your blade and thrust it with venom between two mighty shoulder blades. With a bellow, it thrashes around in agony, still attempting to grab you. Darting this way and that, you finally land enough blows to still the beast, whilst avoiding major injuries.

As you slump to your knees with battle fatigue, seconds after you catch sight of Adz slaying the Rhino-man. Through the gloom you witness him struggling to retrieve his mighty axe from the creatures armoured hide. It brings a smile to your lips to see your friend swear and curse as he tugs it free of sinew and bone.

Turn to 367.

27

In the near dark, and dizzying environment, you swing the great weapon with maximal force, smashing it into where you imagine the **Rock Elemental** to be most vulnerable.

If your Fortitude is 8 or greater, you smash it to oblivion and press on. Turn to 438.
If it's 7 or less...turn to 436.

28

Dispensing with all thoughts of desecrating your dead friends body in full view of this all-knowing and lawful creature, you collect your own belongings and tentatively climb onto its back. With a powerful cry, and little forewarning, the mighty white winged stallion soars into the sky and blazes a path to Deva. The creatures magical energies have beneficial effects on your being, revitalising the worn fibres of your aching body. **Restore 4 points of Fortitude and should you need to, restore you Dexterity and Agility to their original totals.** Hours pass by, but it feels like fleeting moments. For such is the exhilarating joy you experience flying through the cool night sky, atop this mythical creature.

'How many men have done this before me?' you mutter to yourself indulgently, drinking in the Gods-eye view of the Devan landscape. Even though night, the moonlight paints the canvas of the landscape in hues of green-grey and purple. Tiny hamlet fires, and wayside torches twinkle like amber beads. You factor it must be an hour or so to dawn when Deva comes into view. Oranges first - of the blazes ripping through several districts - and then the looming black walls, pointed spires, crenellations and ships masts. To the west, the ocean, and its endless black expanse.

As you near the great city, the beating of Pegasus' wings becomes irregular and he throws back his mane, distracted by something unseen by your comparatively weak vision, far down below. A league or so from Deva, the mighty steed begins to wheel and descend as to land. Close to the ground you see the source of his unease. The soul gnawingly sad spectacle of the Cemetery of Innocents. The tragic resting place of unblessed and orphaned infants. Barbs of pity pierce your heart, as you peer down and see a writhing mass of tiny figures. They crawl like mewing kittens, flesh tones tainted with sickly reds and greens. Bawling in terror, they claw at the dry earth, shockingly awoken from their eternal slumber.

If you allow Pegasus to land, turn to 485.
With Deva in sight, if you press Pegasus to continue onwards, turn to
199.

29

'Siga, what are you looking at?' asks Adz, as you look suspiciously at the rear wall. 'This building is smaller on the inside that it appears from the outside,' you reply, rubbing your palms against the boards feeling for a lever or catch. 'It wouldn't surprise me if....aha!' You press against an imperceptibly raised area, and with some satisfaction hear a click, as a section of the rear wall swings open revealing a narrow concealed doorway. Together with Adz, you tiptoe down the stone steps into a tiny passageway.

'Where do you think it leads?' asks Adz. Raising a finger to your lips you motion for the big man to follow you as you squeeze down it, following dim coloured lights far into the gloom. After several minutes you encounter a wrought-iron grill set into the floor. Shafts of multi-coloured lights emanate from it, and peering down you see can just about make out a huge room filled with coloured glass, and a very audible beating sound. Adz grips it with his sausage-like fingers and heaves and tugs to no avail. 'It won't budge, Siga,' he explains, red-faced. You press on, and after a minute or so arrive in a dark circular chamber with no apparent exits. Tiny pinpricks of light pierce through the chambers ceiling and so Adz hoists you up to investigate. Your investigative fingers locating the edges of something solid, you press upwards, and look up through the gap to see the occasional boots and sandals of people passing through small square. Blue blossom dances around the flagstones, blown down from the proud tree in the squares centre. You lower the false flagstone and ease yourself back down into the chamber with Adz assistance. 'Let's get out of here, come on,' you urge with friend who nods in agreement. No sooner have you turned back toward the warehouse do you hear exclamations from the direction in which you came.

If you make good your escape back to The Swallow, via the false flagstone, turn to 161.
If you hold fast, and await the approaching voices, turn to 218.

You nod in affirmation, extracting a grimace from Adz who tiptoes - as best he can - toward the wagon train. You follow close behind, catching a ghastly glimpse of the shredded horses. Blood still runs in thick red deltas to the sewers below. Horse's blood, you tell yourself. Only the blood of beasts. As Adz climbs the three little wooden steps, you reach from behind and prod open the door with the tip of your sword, silently questioning your reasoning. The wagons seem to form a long corridor, comprising of 'curios' behind fine tin mesh, and a walkway to the centre. Adz stops in the near pitch black darkness and sniffs.

'Dung,' he says, pursing his lips. You smell it too, the unmistakeable stench of animal waste. Your own bowels threaten to move as a loud bang resounds in the darkness followed by a grunting. A snort. A pungent mist floats through the wagon. Something is breathing, deeply.

'I don't see him,' you whisper hoarsely to the Adz, who opens his mouth in reply, 'Wait...!' The big Norsiczan is abruptly cut short by a thunderous sound of stamping hooves and wild grunting; a huge figure charges through the wagon train and crashes into him. The force of impact breaches the walls of the carriage and sends both crashing into the piazza beyond in a riot of splinters.

'Gods be damned!' you exclaim in shock, looking out to see Adz tussle with a huge humanoid-rhino figure of enormous bulk.

'I...' you are about to hail your stricken friend when another unseen foe smashes you through the hole in the wagon to send you tumbling to the gore stained flagstones. **Lose 2 points of fortitude.**

Dizzied from the force and shock, you stagger to your feet, with scarcely enough time to collect your weapon. Defying all laws of nature, a huge **Armoured Ape** bashes its way out of its prison - reanimated by the call of the Master - and holds you in its cold bloodthirsty gaze eyes. With a primal roar it beats its plate mailed chest and hurtles terrifyingly toward you.

Do you raise your weapon and face it head on? If so turn to 401.
If you want to chance leaping aside, and striking it from the rear, turn to 26.

31

Together, you peer into the dank gloom of the sink-hole. Noxious vapours - probably sealed for centuries - rise from below and spiral unpleasantly around your nostrils. Adz is already stripped to the waist, attempting to squeeze through the narrow fissure and cursing hotly.

'Seven Hells, Siga! I can't fit my lithe figure through this impossible gap!' You see the problem plain and simple – Adz' giant frame, huge head and barrel chest will never squeeze through.

'I'll go on alone,' you offer, 'You go and find a sledgehammer and work the stone...make a bigger gap. Catch me up.' Adz makes to protest, but relents, reluctantly thinking on the same lines as you. Time is of the essence, and so sliding through the gap, Adz hands you your sword, armour and other trappings, along with an improvised torch he fabricates quickly. With encouragements and blessings, you leave your giant friend and descend into the darkness.

Taking a glance over your shoulder you see his optimistically expectant face, and smile nervously. Whispering a silent prayer to any Gods caring to listen, you immerse yourself into the chasm. After fumbling blindly through a narrow passage way for a few moments you emerge into a cavern of sorts. The way is illuminated by tiny shafts of light, beaming down from the many cracks in the mantle, guiding your way through the darkness and the dust. The surfaces of the stone react to the light and glimmer with an uncommon resonance - this is of timeless origin, and no doubt this is part of what was the ancient Elven city. You tread carefully further into the dimly lit opening and see a stone-hewed spiral staircase leading downwards. Another narrow entrance - almost entirely caved in - is, or was, embedded into the wall to your left. From beneath the rubble you see a pair of legs protruding, and a low groan. The boots of the trapped individual push slowly against the surface as they attempt to free themselves.

If you want to pull away the rubble and help free the buried person, turn to 481.
If you choose to ignore this, and descend down the steps, turn to 427.
Or if you'd rather squeeze through the partially collapsed doorway, turn to 317.

You carefully tether the horses before continuing, the bridge will certainly not bear their weight, you can be sure. As you walk toward the bridge, it seems to quiver fearfully as you approach. The foot-boards buckle upwards as it shies away from your presence, and it creaks loudly. Almost in a state of bemusement you press down your boot on the first board, to test it.

'Oooh, Ow!' the bridge exclaims, be-sorcelled by unseen forces. You stamp down with greater force. The bridge protests once again with pained cries of unknown origin, but holds firm. You turn to Galiael, who remains impassive, evidently awaiting your next move.

If you wish to press on across the bridge, turn to 133.
If you decide against using the bridge, and instead ease your way behind the waterfall, turn to 471.
Alternatively, you could go back and follow the woodland trail, if so, turn to 224.

Clawing at the fragments of knowledge embedded in the hidden recesses of your mind, you are somehow able to conjure up the answer to the question. The first of the Elven Primarchs, Pentarc, was responsible for the conquest of *one hundred* kingdoms. You shout out this answer to the dark places high within the chamber, and step forward with confidence.

Turn to 100.

You pull out the Iron key and show it to Adz, who inspects it for a few seconds, before declaring confidently, 'It's a warehouse key, see the three teeth on it - look.' He points to them and rolls his eyes at your obvious ignorance. 'All warehouse keys look like that - I worked the docks long enough to be sure of that.' He shakes his head and laughs at you, incredulous that you wouldn't know that - despite you never having worked, like him, as a stevedore. Big Norsiczan oaf, you think fondly, playing the fool.

If you want to tell Adz the story behind the key, and head to the city docks to investigate, turn to 409.
If you insist on doing as the professor said, in picking up supplies from the market, turn to 205.

Dust fills the chamber, and deafening sounds disorientate you, as the figure tears itself from the rock face with a thunderous roar. Stepping back anxiously, you are roughly knocked from your feet as quickly shifting rock form barrels into you - **lose 1 point of fortitude.** In the darkness of the dust and debris filled chamber, you have no alternative to fight the **ROCK ELEMENTAL,** as it twists and spirals around you. Again and again it smashes into you, with a chaotic and violent force.

If you have an Iron-tipped Club turn to 27.
If you don't, but your Fortitude is 11 or above, turn to 436.
If you don't have an Iron-tipped Club and your Fortitude is 10 or less, turn to 153.

Before you can react, the maddened elf flies toward you. 'I am sorry my friend!' cries **GALIAEL** in Midden-tongue, as he lands a shocking strike, chopping down on your collarbone. You collapse in agony onto damp mossy ground - **Lose 1 point from your Dexterity** until further notice, and **4 from your Fortitude**. Gasping with pain and stricken from the blow, you claw at your weapon, desperate to defend yourself from this murderous fiend. Rolling painfully to a combat stance, and gravely wounded by the elf, you have no alternative but to kill him before he kills you.

Turn to 109.

If you have the word LUDOVICO on your adventure sheet, turn to 132.
If you don't, then you have little choice but to depart with Adz back to Deva to join up with the professor. Turn to 131.

You reach for the hand. Your head swims with blood and you feel your pulse halt. All goes black, all goes silent. For a fleeting moment you imagine this is the passing to End Of Days, when you suddenly smell the mineral aroma of blood, and feel the pernicious heat of flames. Upon opening your eyes, you find yourself in the midst of a battle! You fling yourself to the ground as galloping warhorses career past, foaming with terror and rage. You reach for your sword, and just have enough time to unsheathe it before a huge ruby-red barded destrier kicks up sods of wet earth, blinding you. As its hooves thunder down on top of you, all you can do is curl into a ball - sure of deadly impact, and expecting a skull crushing braining. But the hooves pass through you, indeed the stallion passes through you, and charges off into the massed ranks of faceless men. You lay back panting with fear and confusion on the muddy battlefield, only to see the silhouette of a huge figure towering over you. He leans and twists his body slowly, which allows light to fall onto his drawn looking features, and impossible bulging eyes.

'I am Menax, I thirst for souls of the fallen, and my desire is never sated,' he says unsteadily, his maddened eyes fixed fast on the middle distance behind you. 'Keep your soul, for now, and I will call for it when you fall in battle, as I do for all liars who claim to act for valour. My labour is to cause brother to fight brother, lest the living ever outnumber the dead and my dry mouth becomes a desert.' You gape at the terrifying figure in a heady cocktail of fear and awe - are you truly in the presence of a God? Can Gods be so? **Write the name MENAX on your adventure sheet.** The figure grinds his teeth, and turns away, causing blood to seep from his eye sockets. He looks at the battle playing out in the tapestry, and screams a clarion call...
Turn to 247.

39

You sprint off away the city walls toward the river. From behind you on the Appucine road, and all around you in the darkness - the low moaning of the restless dead. Not stopping for a second, you tumble through smallholdings and vegetable plots as you dash down toward the river bank. You clatter along a small jetty of rickety planks towards a little fishing coracle, and cutting its bindings and jumping aboard, you fumble at the oars and set it off onto the river. The sounds of footsteps on the duck-boards behind you and the splashes of unseen followers cement your wise decision not to dally outside the city walls. Feeling a degree of calm, you ease a course downstream toward the city.

The river chain is unmanned. No doubt its sentinels pressed into service elsewhere at this desperate time, or else dead, and you are able to slip beyond it and past the towering gatehouses flanking the river into the east of the city. The unlit and otherwise silent Dens line the river bank, offer nought but occasional shrill cries. Internally celebrating the ease of accessing the city, your spirits sink a little as the hairs on your neck stand to attention with uncanny reliability. A pocket of dense fog tumbles across the surface of the Devani River, and emerging from its chill embrace looms an ancient galley. Covered in weeds, barnacles, and the filth of the river bed, you gasp at the sight of its baleful crew. **Ancient Mariners**, bound by miserable essences of distant drownings, issue silent cries as they eagerly jostle with each other and force their way to its prow, and access to you!

If you have the Gifts of both Stealth and Survivalist, you fancy your chances of evasion - by silently entering the water and swimming to shore. If so, turn to 60.
If you don't, you begin to furiously rummage around in your knapsack hoping one of your collection of arcane objects may help you ward off these spirits. Turn to 268.

40

You draft your cup, and wiping your mouth with the back of your hand, you toss it into the choked river, disturbing the cloud of bloated flies hovering on the thick surface. Moving on from the wastrels of wine and song, you leave the festival – **and if you haven't already** - head onwards to:

The Diving Swallow, and await the professor, turn to 361.
The Stygian Fayre, turn to 226.
The Grand Market, turn to 376.

You step over the threshold into the massive octagonal chamber and discover the source of the kaleidoscopic light display. High above and entirely dwarfing you, stand tall lead stained windows, each depicting a towering figure of legend which encircle the circumference of the vault. From cracks in the deformed and deteriorating roof structure, rays of moonlight from the world above force their way through, and are magnified from the mundane to the bedazzling as they're absorbed by the coloured glass of this hidden place. Like blazing fiery tailed comets, beams of brilliant light bounce in all directions. The glass impressions of heroes of yore are highlighted magnificently - reunited with fundamental energy after eons entombed in the pitch black subterranean underworld. Their colours are saturated and life-like.

Seconds later, and with eyes now accustomed to the illumination, your spirit sinks, and is met duly with the unsteady quivering of your bowels. In the centre of the chamber, imprisoned by a dense cocoon of black and decaying roots, a massive fluid filled sac - twice your height and just as wide - expands and contracts with every booming heartbeat. Contained within the wobbling pink membrane, is the fast emerging form of the blackest of horrors, the likes of which you have met only in nightmares. Glistening of darkest red, and tainted with the polluted blood of rebirth, this true shape of evil uncoils its powerful blackened limbs and stretches its sinewy digits outwards, caressing the delicate and near-transparent walls of its confines.

A sickening liquid filled smack echoes through the chamber as a blackened root uncoils itself from around the birthing membrane, and falls listlessly to the floor. Looking up in desperation, you see other roots noticeably slacken and drop - the miasma of sour vegetation filling your nostrils. With every bond released, the beating 'thub-thub' sound - the restless heart of evil - resonates louder and with increased frequency. Your soul fills with dread most foul, as the beat seems to match that of your own racing heart.

You look upwards to the expectant and illuminated faces of **Stained Glass Heroes**. For eons these silent guardians have held determined vigil over The Master, and now a petty combination of fundamentalism and simple-minded ignorance have unwittingly conspired to unlock its bulging prison. Leaping aside as another blackened root falls - splitting open beside you like a ripe fruit, and under the seeking gaze of this pantheon of inert guardians, you would smile wryly at your misfortune, if your grim features were not etched with terror.

If you are in possession of a Ring of Kindred, turn to 231.
If not, turn to 12.

42

You thrust at the Ogre, losing your balance. With surprising speed it clenches the shaft in its huge hands and tugs the weapon from your grasp. With a deafening howl it swings the blunt at you, smacking painfully into your hip. **Lose 2 points of Fortitude.** Drawing your knife you dart forward for the kill, as the Ogre is spun by the momentum of its strike.

Turn to 292.

43

You race down the stairwell, leaving behind acrid smoke and cracking timbers, evil flames licking through the narrow windows. A rare shaft of light burns through the grey mist, as the late afternoon sun illuminates the tower. You witness a man you presume to be Moretti leap from the crenulations into the mud flats below, their skin bubbling and engulfed in plumes of smoke. Dragging Adz, you struggle quickly through the thick tidal mud flats after your howling quarry, now licked with flame. The shaft of sunlight expands and bathes the bay in sunlight, electrifying the white mists. Moretti stumbles and splashes into a shallow gully thrashing desperately and sobbing all the while. Treading carefully, you trudge as close as you dare, weapons drawn.

If you decide to finish him off so can search his body before it's consumed by flame, turn to 204.
If you want to tell him how you killed his granted his children eternal rest, turn to 240.

44

The young woman pouts at you and begins to weep sourly, berating you for a coward. With this display tugging at your sentimental persuasion, you are about to change your mind, when the wolfhound pads back into the room. 'How did he...it...open the door?' you wonder, before Captain Hessler, the Bosun, and several other crew members enter the cabin.

Surveying the scene, the Captain snorts with dissatisfaction, glaring at the young woman, who scowls in return. 'You and I had better have a little chat,' he murmurs to you, not taking his eyes off his prize.

If you agree to go with him, turn to 87.
If you'd rather take your chances in this confined environment and attack now, turn to 149.

45

You hurtle toward the relative safety of the forest as fast as your legs will carry you. You splash over the sodden green carpet of the bilious plain but the thick lichen like surface causes you to stumble and slip. The **Bone Dragon** soon swoops, and with a mighty roar rakes you across the back with its massive talons. **Lose 3 points of Fortitude.** If still somehow alive, you conquer the unspeakable agonies of your torn flesh, and turn to face the gargantuan beast which has now landed before you, poised to strike again.

Turn to 392.

46

You manage to evade capture, and eventually the sounds of struggle dissipate. As you move through the dark streets, a band of thuggish looking Militiamen give you a customary filthy look, but you avert your gaze and hurry past them. One of them spits, calls out and laughs. A few seconds later, you hear one of them shout something you can't quite make out. Whether at you or some other misfortunate you aren't quite sure, but either way you increase your pace, and are relieved to make it back to the Diving Swallow.

You eat some leftovers from the kitchen - **regain 1 point of Fortitude.** You consume it in solitude, as it seems other patrons are already in their beds. Once satisfied, you tread heavily up the rickety stairwell to your bed. To the soft coos and chirps of the avian residents, you sink into a deep and relaxing sleep.

Turn to 125.

47

Guards at the entrance - human and Elven - seem to compete in hostility as you're rudely prodded away at with the tip of a halberd. 'No uninvited guests!' the Devan soldier barks. You make to protest but he curls his mouth into a sneer and you can see his fingers tighten around the shaft of his weapon. Sighing, you have no option but to trudge back to the Diving Swallow.

Turn to 243.

48

With a reassuring nod to the young singer, you confidently stroll over to whisper some dark words into the tugged ear of the loudest fop.

If you back up these words by revealing the hilt of your dagger, turn to 318.
If you think verbal threats will suffice, turn to 357.

49

The legions of the dead, drawn in thick knots by the magnetism of the master, turn with primeval instinct at your battle cries. As you plough through the soft corpses like a scythe through ripe wheat, you can't help but wish Adz were here, to see this majestic spectacle. Despite the circumstances you're unable to stifle a wild belly-laugh at the thought of his sorrowful face when...if... you regale him of the tale. Inspired by the vision of your comrade in arms, and against all odds, you hack a path toward the Master.

His gaping bestial maw emits a paralysing roar - a roar of terror! In confusion and panic he lurches to and fro, trying to shift his massive bulk through the hordes of the dead, to the foul sanctuary of the smouldering crater. Despite your valiant efforts, the dead are too many, and you fall to the blood-red marble flagstones of the square, stricken by the many savage wounds inflicted. You feel your heart quiver and fail - the spectre of impending death circling overhead. But your mind lives on a few more breathless moments. Drowning on the blood rapidly filling your lungs, you have the fortitude to claw at the drawstrings and unveil the comet fragment from its bag. For a fleeting second as you twist upwards to face the heavens the child is superimposed upon the parent, and you are superimposed against the dark shape of The Master, as you hurl the beacon toward the epitome of darkness.

You do not live to see the calamitous detonation, the blinding white holocaust which leaves no stone in the square unturned. For a duration no greater than that of the hummingbird's heartbeat, you are entwined with The Master, melded together as one in the inferno.

But then, to the Pantheon for you, and your place at the Table of Heroes. To the Pit for the fiend. The unnavigable, inescapable pit.

Such are the whims of the Gods.

Your adventure, and your mortal soul, ends here.

50

You steady your arm and pull the trigger, sending a puff of acrid white smoke into the air. You scarce have time to avert your eyes, when a veritable hailstorm of multicoloured glass fragments burst through the cloud of gunsmoke - the Crystalline Lion shattered into a million tiny pieces. As you pick shards of glass from your face you look over at Galiael. He has smashed the other Lion with a single blow, and shrugs his shoulders and smiles. Evidently these creatures were as brittle as they were beautiful. With some distance left to cover, you brush yourself free of glass, and press on upwards toward the summit.

Turn to 441.

51

With a violent tug, the unseen hands grasp at your sodden leggings and drag you momentarily under the surface. With all your might you pull yourself free and desperately gasp for air. Raising your blade high you beat down into the water, chopping violently at the submerged and long dead Elven bones. You swallow a mouthful of brackish liquid as you bob underneath the water whilst breathing rapidly.

If you have the Gift of Survivalist, you can attempt to control your breathing and struggle through the pool. Turn to 147.
If you do not have this Gift, turn to 453.

52

You tread carefully down the narrow passageway to the Captain's cabin, as the ship rolls and creaks in the in the early morning swell. Tapping your knuckles softly against the timbers of the stout door yields no reply - as you had hoped. Unexpectedly, a sneeze from within peels out. A delicate little emission...undoubtedly the sneeze of a woman! Before you can consider your next move, you glance toward the tight little stairwell leading to the galley and hear a clatter of pots, and footsteps approaching.

If you want to try handle and slip inside quickly, turn to 283.
If you'd rather wait outside to await the approaching footfall, turn to 276.

53

Whether plain desperate, or fuelled by sorcerous malevolence, the Crystalline Lion springs toward you. You scarce have time to strike, but you manage to land a blow with the creature mid-air. As your tempered steel connects with its crystal hide, a hailstorm of multicoloured glass fragments burst forth, as the creature shatters into a million tiny pieces. You pick shards of glass from your face you look over at Galiael. He has smashed the other Lion with a single blow, and simply shrugs his shoulders and smiles. Evidently these poor creatures were as brittle as they were beautiful. With some distance left to cover, you brush yourself free of glass and dust, and press on upwards toward the summit.

Turn to 441.

54

Utterly shattering the Skeletal wretches, and with the world as you know it collapsing all around, you give up any effort to remain on your feet, and jump headlong down the narrowing passageway. You slide with great speed, ushered along by the increasing gradient, the smooth wet rock and the veneer of slippery green vegetation. A nauseating stench fills your nostrils as the cavity meets with a flood drain filled with the filth and animal detritus. Blinded in the darkness and picking up speed, you feel a sense of exhilaration as the sounds of falling rock give way to sounds of crashing breakers and the cries of unroosted gulls. As the aperture of exit becomes wider - and closer - you see pinpricks of light sown into the tapestry of a clear nights sky. The ground gives way beneath you, and you shoot out of the rocky tube into the cool air at great pace, before plummeting a great distance until you meet with a slap, the welcoming embrace of the sea.

Gasping for breath as you emerge from the salty depths, you swim through the dark brackish waters of the port to a nearby boon. Hauling yourself up exhausted, you brush off the worst of the muck, and for a few moments to gaze up at the constellations above. In the fabric of the night sky the twinkling stars shine like diamonds, unending and undying. So much for the chaotic and pointless lives of the this world's denizens. Murdering and rutting and wriggling. Grasping for wealth, for nourishment, for a hot piece. How the Gods must be ashamed of their wayward and wasteful creations. You look across the inky waters to the city of Deva; the screams punctuating the night air, the many fires burning. Plumes of blue-black smoke spiralling up into the ether. You look at the wharf-side and see the opportunistic. For already gangs of armed men wander, looting and pillaging, risking even the unseen terrors of the night in pursuit of their material goals. As another tremor rumbles through the city the screams grow louder, accompanied with bestial howls not of this earth. No doubt danger stalks these now cursed streets. The Master, now apparently free from his arboreal prison, is no doubt tearing a channel through the city in ways you try hard not to imagine. The dead will be risen, and other abominations will no doubt be drawn to its baleful presence. You look to the nearby ships, on some of which crews scurry like ants, working the rigging with a determined intensity. For a moment you consider evacuating the city, leaving behind the crucible of fire and blood...and then you remember. The Professor will be waiting for you, with your old and trusty pal Adz. Casting an envious glance at hoisted sails and raised anchors, you dive once again into the waters and swim to the nearby north quayside.

Dripping wet in the moonlight, you take care to avoid the roaming bands of freebooters by hiding behind some barrels, as you ready yourself, and your gear, for the next chapter in this eventful evening.

If you wish to head directly back to the Piazza Arborea, in the hope of Adz and the Professor still being there, turn to 341.
If you think it best to cross the city to the Diving Swallow, and hole up there awaiting their return, turn to 120.

55
Your shot falls a little outside the bullseye, but the Dwarf's luck is even worse, with his bolt ricocheting off the target and clattering to the tiles. Relieved, you come to face a grizzled old captain, bedecked as is customary in these parts, with an expansive doublet and collar. He greets you with a nod of affirmation. He raises his richly oiled arquebus and takes aim. You do the same, stemming the tremors in your hand.
Add one for each of these Gifts you possess: Iron-Willed; Hyper Senses; Martial Prowess - and combine it with your Dexterity total. Minus one if you have visited the Festival of Wine and Song. Is the figure 9 or above?

If it is, turn to 294.
If it is not, turn to 181.

56
Brushing the worst of the muck from your hands, you prostrate yourself somewhat self-consciously before the pantheon of Gods - twelve in total. Their stern frozen faces display no warmth, simply a cold indifferent, stasis; silent Gods deaf to the petty intrigues of the mortal realms. Nevertheless, you compartmentalize your natural affinity for

rational doubt, and issue your silent appeals. A man not used to praying, you fumble for the words - struggling to know who to appeal for help, and with what devotional promises to offer.

If you pray to the Elven Gods, turn to 496.
If you pray to the Gods of Man, turn to 358.

57

After a thorough soaking you emerge from the cascading waters intact, and a nervous examination confirms you are still in possession of your limbs, eyes, ears nose and mouth. Galiael by contrast looks exhilarated, with reddened cheeks. The elf is gently panting as if recovering from some ecstatic experience. You frown at him, but he smiles disengagingly - some Elven secret or other on his lips. Booting a stone and mouthing a silent curse at the inscrutable nature of Elves, you plough on.

Turn to 441.

58

Lurching toward Rollo you grasp his stout legs with hydra like speed, and send him toppling to the canvas. Sensing your chance, you clench the big man's neck in the crook of your elbow and squeeze with all your might. The bulging-eyed champion's purpling tongue hangs limply from his drooling mouth, but your arms are aflame with fatigue.

If your Fortitude is 12 or higher, turn to 77.
If your Fortitude is 11 or lower, turn to 112.

59

You find the fortune teller, a wizened old crone of indistinguishable age, her sour face covered with a rash of mushroom like growths, attended by her contrastingly fulsome young granddaughter. You secretly chide yourself for partaking in such nonsense, but in high spirits you hand over the 2 silver scuda necessary for a reading. **Make a note of this on your adventure sheet.** The wagon has a deep purple velvet interior, reeking of mistwood incense. There is a glass ball on the table between you, with wispy coloured vapours swirling within it. The old woman's face is a mask of ugly concentration, and she sighs heavily, placing her claw-like hands upon it. A period of silence passes, the crone's face looking increasingly tormented…

'Strange,' she moans, '…thirty-four…I see the number thirty-four…but I…' she trails off and begins to groan loudly, her eyes rolling up into her sockets. In a demonic voice she spits, 'MY CHAINS WILL BE BROKEN…MY PRISON WILL CRUMBLE…DAY WILL BECOME NIGHT…' The voice becomes higher and turns into a piercing shriek as the old crone pulls her hands, smoking, from the glass orb. The old crones granddaughter pulls back the curtains and lets out a startled cry. 'Get out - leave, now!' she demands, and with the smell of burning flesh and brimstone filling your nostrils, you hastily make off.

Shaking your head in nervous bemusement, and **- if you haven't already-** you can now head to:

The wrestling contest, turn to 275.
The circus, turn to 379.

Or, leave the Fayre, and - **if you haven't already**:

Head to the Grand market, turn to 376.
Head to the Festival of wine and song, turn to 363.
If you've already done all these things, or would rather just head back to your lodgings and wait for the professor, turn to 361.

60

With the wailing Mariners left behind, and keen to escape the pernicious mist wreathed river, you swim wearily, and silently, to a deserted riverbank. Hastily clambering up onto a tall rooftop, a spitting black cat soon joins you, evidently harbouring the same principle of safety from a great height. Together you peer down into the streets below. Feasting ghouls stalk the blood splattered cobbles, running down those foolish enough to expose themselves alone. You wince helplessly as you witness dozens of innocents fleeing in useless terror, only to be caught, and torn asunder. You look on in horror as you make out the distant Grand Piazza and straining to see, you make out a figure holding ghastly court. The abominable figure of The Master sits, resplendent of his perverse throne of skulls. Shuddering, you glance around you. No doubt you would have to leap down into the streets and move some three hundred twisting paces before you reach the square.

The fragment of the comet burns brightly within the confines of the bag it's stored in. Orange light creeps though the worn stitching, and the blackened bag is hot to the touch. You glance at the cat, busy now cleaning its balls, and feel a twinge of envy.

If you want to head directly toward the square, even though the streets are still dark, turn to 254.
Or if you choose to wait until sunrise before venturing into the open, turn to 472.

61

'Speak!' you command, towering over her. The assassin stares at you mutely for several seconds. Only then does it appear that she is seemingly holding her breath. You shrug in confusion of the bizarre situation, too late to realise that she has somehow released a form of odourless and poisonous gas, without you having the wit to realise. Crestfallen, and resigned now to your inevitable demise, you ruefully shake your head that you could be taken in by a pleading woman. The cat-like **Assassin** smiles mischievously at you, until you finally slump to your knees unconscious, never again to see the rising sun or the tempestuous oceans.

Your adventure ends here.

'What is this? Some kind of grenade?' one asks. 'A naphtha device I'll wager,' adds another.

Holding the comet fragment aloft, it blazes orange and emits spirals of golden smoke. 'You are all wrong,' you explain quietly, before detailing its true origin - its celestial course, and its purpose - saving the city - and who knows, maybe the world as they know it. The men gaze in wonder at the twin sights, the parent and child. You can almost see their renewed hearts pounding beneath their cuirasses. A bottle is passed round, and under the warm glow of the burning sky, each man swigs generously from it...each man muttering an oath afterwards. As the bottle reaches your lips, you drink lustily, the burning liquid an appropriate foil for the bright little star. As you wrap it in soaked leather rags and place it once again inside its bag, you stare hard at each of the men.

'So what is it, best-of-men?. To die in your bed, shit-stained and decrepit, or in the service of some cuntish lord? To die for gold, to die pointlessly - for some soon to be forgotten border? Or is it to seize the chance to sit at the Pantheon table - the Heroes table - and have your name written into the lists of the glorious dead! What will it be comrades, to seize this chance to be a hero today? Or to die tomorrow? With me men, over the barricades! Let us light a rocket under the arse of this ugly bastard - and send him back to pit! Tomorrow is for the dead, tonight is for The Living!'

'The Living! The Living!' the men roar, emboldened by your words. With fearsome war cries in a dozen tongues, and under a blood red and fiery pre-dawn sky, you clamber over the barriers and charge headlong into the masses of undead.

Turn to 309.

You impetuously leap down into the cloying mud, and begin to hack at the beast. The slimy abomination moans with dull idiocy as he reaches out with childlike imprecision, grasping at your legs. Two or three savage strikes are all that are required to split the Troll in two ragged halves. Much pleased with the quick battle, you gradually notice a burning sensation on your arm. In the shower of gore, some of the Trolls disgusting and corrosive stomach liquors splattered over you. You rub cooling – if stinking – mud over the sore, sullenly reminding yourself to be more careful should you ever have the misfortune to meet one of these creatures again. **Deduct 2 points of Fortitude** due to the burns inflicted at close quarters. Soothed, you mount the steps once again and tread a mucky path through the foul pantry, and head on up the inner staircase

Turn to 386.

Snatching the silver from you, the bosun ushers the children aboard. 'Step aboard, my little princes and princesses,' charms the man, with a deferential sweep of his arms. The gaggle of little ducklings eagerly descend the slippery green steps down to the overladen rowing boat, still holding hands tightly. Their bright faces turn to face you, wide innocent eyes burnished with childlike hope.

'Look Sire!' the little raven haired girl shouts at you with pride, 'We're all still holding han...'

On the Captain's command, the bosun rises from the row boat and with a sturdy boot, kicks the little raven-haired girl from the vessel. A hollow 'plop' is all you hear, as your heart stops, and your chest contracts with horror, as she disappears into the dark waters of the harbour. 'Plop. Plop, plop...plop' - one after another the orphans are kicked or shoved overboard to their deaths, as the crewmen roll with harsh laughter. You are powerless to act, as the captain leans over the ships railings and mocks you from afar.

'You think 20 silver scuda buys anything but a cold drink for your rats? Ha ha ha!' He bangs his fist on top the carved wood of the rail-top, with cruel incredulity, before turning back to matters on board.

You sink to your knees and sob bitterly with contrition at your petty minded miserliness. What good have you of silver and gems in a land with no economy? In a land crawling with the dead - risen from their tombs. You feel the air pressure sink all around you, and your soul darkens with depression as an unseen hand seems to tug at your boots, tug at your cloak, slowing you down, and bringing lethargy to each step. You feel weaker, older, and less able to struggle on this earthly plane - with all its horrors and violence. **Reduce your Fortitude by 2, lose the Gift of Iron Willed –**

if you have it - and if possible decease your FATE by 1 level, as the Gods strike a score through your name in the Scrolls.

If you're still alive, you face no choice but to hurry to the Diving Swallow, and the hope of a chance to perform some heroic action, to save your soul. Turn to 120.

<hr>

65

You creep past the hound, which opens a lazy eye, observing you for a moment before returning to sleep. Padding softly to the curtain, you clasp the velvet drape and draw it back...revealing a surprised and somewhat ravishing young women, bound at the ankles, in a fine but tattered red dress. She gasps, clutching the curtain to her breast before scowling at you suspiciously. 'You're not one of the crew.' she challenges, in educated tones. This assertion is confirmed by your dumb-stuck expression, and her countenance rapidly changes. 'Brave warrior,' she urges breathlessly, leaning close. 'I have been abducted by these impudent pigs, they mean to return me to my abusers,' she pleads, tears welling up in her deep dark eyes. 'Please...take a message from me to Tancredi, son of the House of Toggia. He will reward you greatly...tell him I am returned to Deva, he will know where to find me.' With that, she immodestly reaches deep within her amble bosom pulling out a small folded note, causing you to avert your eyes. Blushing, you turn around and have just enough time to ponder where the wolfhound has disappeared to...when she presses into your palm and kisses your cheek.

If you agree to take the note, turn to 180.
If you decline and return it to her, turn to 44.

66

As you step further into the massive chamber, the rock face groans with seismic shifts. Huge splintering cracks appear in the supporting statues of the Titans, and beads of rock fall from their labouring brows. Staring high up into the vaulted ceiling, you can see the struts bow alarmingly. You walk forward - for now you realise there is no way back - towards the next row of glyphs, which separate the Goddess Sanromai and the dread God Menax, deities of Love and War. You tread on the illuminated flagstones, ready to receive the next fateful test. Once again, the leaden and unseen voice demands answer to its eternal question.

'The number of years blessed by the reign of The White King'

If you know the answer to this question, turn to the relevant section. If you don't know the answer, turn to 152.

67

You dodge a swinging arm from Bruno, and force your way past the two fops, giving each a glare, and a boot in the rear to match, before melting into the crowd. You brush past any attempts to restrain you before the Watchdogs arrive - their shouts ringing in your ears.
Add +1 to when prompted to take a 'Watch Patrol' test.

Where to next?

Your lodgings at The Diving Swallow, turn to 361.

Or, **if you haven't already visited these locations**:

To see what's going on at the Stygian Fayre turn to 226.
To head to the Grand Market, turn to 376.

68

Concealing your pistol, you weave through the thronged masses towards the tourney grounds in the east of the city. If anything, the crowds are greater now than earlier in the day, and the sun hotter, hanging low in the sky. The combination of heat and sweating humanity reminds your toil in the galleys, and you begin to yearn for the grey drizzle of The Wasteland. The marksmanship tourney is set to take place in a colonnaded arena, roped off from the gathering crowds. To deter common riff-raff and wayward adventurers, there is a high entry fee of 10 silver scuda. You can see other entrants milling around; some dandy looking gentlemen, some men of martial appearance, and most noticeably a finely attired Elven noble, accompanied by several retainers.

If you wish to compete in these tournament heats, and have the money, deduct the fee from your adventure sheet, and turn to 116.

Otherwise...

You could quench your thirst down at the Festival of Wine and Song, which runs all day into the night, turn to 420.
You can choose to head off to the Plain of Heroes for the Military Display, turn to 413.

69
If your Fortitude is 11 or higher, turn to 255.
If your Fortitude is 10 or lower, turn to 10.

70
Leaving the wrestling tent you can now head - **if you haven't already-** to:

The fortune teller, turn to 59.
Investigate the animal show, turn to 379.

Or, leave the circus, and - **if you haven't already**:

Head to the Festival market, turn to 376.
Head to the Festival of wine and song, turn to 363.
If you've already done all these things, or would rather just head back to your lodgings and wait for the professor, turn to 361.

71
You descend down the steps, warped by the quakes and caked in debris. You enter another circular chamber - again, with more steps lead further down into the catacombs. Stepping into the centre of the chamber you hold your torch aloft to investigate before making to press onwards. A grinding sound is emanating from the one patch of rock and you carefully step forward to the source. Thrusting the torch toward it you can see the rock face shifting before your very eyes. You watch it, incredulous, for a few seconds as it begins to morph into a humanoid figure, and the grinding

grows louder - into deafening cracks and splinters as the Elemental hues itself from the granite veins of the earth.

If you want to wait until it binds into a substantial form, turn to 35.
If you choose to make a quick exit, and hurry away toward the steps, turn to 438.

72

The Watchdogs give you a cursory glance, and one of them mutters a rude regional joke at your expense. Just when you think they're going to swagger past you to ruin someone else's day, one of them halts. In a sudden moment of apparent recognition, he stops his comrades. 'That's the Nhortlünder criminal we're looking for!' he shouts. Clattering into an arrest formation, they level their halberds at you, and one of them barks, 'Halt scum, in the name of The Duce!'

If you do as they say, turn to 476.
If you think fleeing the scene is the best option, turn to 103.
If you decide to put up a fight, turn to 286.

73

You quickly wrap your sleeves around your hands and beat out the fuse, the last sparks extinguished with barely a finger width of wick remaining. You sigh with relief, and afford yourself a nervous laugh as you leap down from the cart. The Elves have cut a swathe through the Stygians, with Adz' help, but not before the crows managed to cut many deep wounds into the Tree. Axes hang embedded in its trunk, and a lone saw wobbles, mid-stroke, its teeth embedded deep into the trees woody flesh. Tears of midnight blue liquid ooze from the trunk as its branches begin to list weakly. The last of the cultists is dispatched by the one remain elf, and on seeing the Trees wounds, he drops his sword and sinks to his knees weeping, head shaking forlornly. The Devan locals, joined by the arrival of the watch, look on at the scene agog.

You step forward and awkwardly place a hand onto the elf's shoulder, as blue blossom begins to cascade to the cobbles from the Trees once proud branches. Adz looks up in wonder as a blizzard of petals fall to the earth, carpeting the whole square in brilliant azure. The elf turns to you, tears searing his cheekbones, 'Our time here is done. Soon this whole city will be consumed...' Shaken, you are about to reply, when you hear raised voices entering the square. Turning toward the commotion you see one of the Council of Fifty, and his retinue, approaching the soft blue blossom carpet around the Tree. Reaching down, he grasps some of the petals in his pudgy fingers, and stares open mouthed at the scene, opened mouthed at you, and opened mouthed at the Militia, who look at their boots abashed. He makes to ask what in God's name is going on, when the earth lets out a faint beat from deep beneath the cobbles, and just, you think, the slightest of tremors.

'Shhh!' the senator barks to no one in particular, but everyone freezes in silence regardless. Another 'thub-thub' sound. Another tremor. You watch the senators jester, wringing his hands - the bells on his fools hood tinkling softly with every beat of the earth. 'Hush, I said!' the senator shouts glaring at the horrified fool. 'It's not me... it's not me!' the miserable jester whimpers, close to tears, grabbing his little bells. 'It's the earth,' he says white with fear, 'the earth is moving.'

Turn to 227.

74

As you move to press the fight against the bemused extremists, the Elves struggle to pass by the melee. 'By God, what are you doing, you fools!' screams the elf in total horror. As you break off from the combat in surprise, the Elves hurtle desperately towards the fizzing gunpowder laden cart. With a loose feeling in your bowels, you wince as the cart thuds into the tree and halts, the fuse crackling to completion...

Turn to 197.

75

As you make your way to The Diving Swallow, through the dense crowds, the late morning sun casts short finger like shadows on the cobbles, some of which seem to dance and flicker malevolently. Shaking yourself free of a sense of foreboding you press on, turning a corner straight into a sweating and belligerent looking watch patrol.

Take a 'Watch Patrol' test:

If your 'Watch Patrol' score is 1 or more, turn to 72.
If your 'Watch Patrol' score is 0, turn to 447.

With an almighty killing blow you bring your sword down on its thorax, and smash the undead beast back to the dust. The Dragon collapses into a mess of loose bones and you stand panting with effort, face glowing with satisfaction. Possessing of the Orb and your spirit newly invigorated with each and every success, you jog to the tree-line. As you rush onwards towards the forest, you feel strangely empowered by magical energising forces coursing through your views. The fickle Gods must now be looking down on you, despite your wicked deeds. You feel strangely bestowed with physical resolve and steely determination. **Restore 3 points of Fortitude, and should you need to, restore your Dexterity and Agility levels to their origin levels.** Though in possession of the softly glowing orb, you are many leagues away from Deva, and quite alone in consideration of your next action.

If you possess a mechanical owl, turn to 311.
If you don't, you have little option but to depart directly on the return trek to Deva. Turn to 121.

Satisfied Rollo is a dead weight, you dump him to the canvas and stagger to your feet exhausted. The crowd gasp in awe at your powerful display. The Ringmaster leaps into your limelight and pushes a **Victory Laurel** onto your sweating brow. 'The show of the day!' he gushes. **Make a note of this on your adventure sheet**. You politely brush off attempts at signing you up permanently, as you gingerly nurse your cuts and bruises.

The beaten Champion eventually rouses and eases himself up off the canvas. 'Friend,' he croaks, 'the likes of an opponent like you I have never before met - you have my respect.' You grasp his outstretched hand and hold it aloft to soak in the cheers of the thrilled audience. **Write ROLLO on your adventure sheet.** Collecting your winnings - **add them to your adventure sheet -** you walk proudly from the tent.

Turn to 70.

The lock releases with a satisfying click. Together with Adz, you slip quietly inside and out of the blistering midday heat. The two storey warehouse appears to be empty, except for a few sacks of decaying lemons which fill the air with citric vapours, and something else...

'Black-powder,' confirms Adz, sniffing his nose like a discerning cook. 'Look!' the big man exclaims, and you follow Adz eye-line to a dark space underneath the ladder leading to the small loft. Kneeling down you rub your fingers through the sulphurous grains and dab a tiny amount on your tongue. 'Unspoiled too, this is fresh...' Adz grimaces, and furrows his brow, 'This place squarely reeks of it, wherever it is now there must have been a lot of...' Adz halts abruptly, and clenches your arm tightly in his mighty grip. Pained, you turn to protest when he looks upwards and flicks his head twice, his other hand pressed against his lips in a motion of silence. From the loft above, you hear the faint sound of rustling, and what appears to be someone sleeping. Whoever lays above farts loudly and groans with relief. When again you hear sounds of slumber, Adz leans in close and whispers, 'Climb the ladder, Siga, you know how heavy footed I am.' Passing your sword to Adz, you grip your dagger in your hand and scale the ladder.

If you have the Gift of Stealth, turn to 4.
If you don't, turn to 237.

79

You scarce reach the corner of the next intersection before howls of animalistic satisfaction shake down your spine, as you hear the ghouls break through the flimsy barriers into the orphanage. You clench your palms to the side of your head as cries most terrible fill your ears. Screams and squeals that are an affront to any and all noble Gods looking down fill the air, as unimaginable carnage is inflicted on the tender innocents within. Somewhere in the Garden of Hope, Heliopas - Goddess of Healing - lays down Her pestle of herbs and wild-flowers. Her pale blue-green eyes mist with tears and her mouth tightens. For Heliopas feels the pain of all Her children, and casts scorn at those who inflict pain - or those who suffer its infliction - upon them. For your turned cheek, and averted eyes, this deity sees you as a coward. You feel the air pressure sink all around you, and your soul darkens with depression as an unseen hand seems to tug at your boots, tug at your cloak, slowing you down, and bringing lethargy to each step. You feel weaker, older. Less able to struggle on this Earthly plane, with all its horrors and violence.

Reduce your Fortitude by 2, and if possible decease your FATE by 1 level, as the Gods strike a score through your name in the Scrolls. **If you're still alive, you reach the harbour side. Turn to** 281.

Flustered by the naked attempt on your life, you rush to avenge the cowardly act quite forgetting the erratic nature of Devan workmanship. You curse, and yell in pain as you twist your ankle on a loose flagstone. **Reduce your Agility score by 1.** Even angrier, you seek redress - issued in blood.

Turn to 115.

You make your way to the Mezzaluna - a sweeping crescent in the more salubrious area of the Merchants Quarter. Looking though the tall gold-gilded entrance gates, you can see it overlooks finely tended gardens and dainty water features. The entrance to the crescent looks heavily fortified, and professional looking soldiers guard both this, and the Mezzaluna within - you can see periodic patrols of the same. A stockily built guard prods your fingers from the gates and motions for you to stand away.

The little square adjacent to the entrance is clogged with beggars, the desperate and dispossessed waving petitions and shaking pathetic wooden begging cups. Away from the main entrance however, you see a forlorn and looking character in a tatty jerkin, sat on a bench underneath a shady cypress tree. He has the impassive look of someone used to waiting a long time, and has the same Lemon Tree insignia sewn onto his threadbare tunic, as the one you handed over to the shadowy stranger on your entrance to the city.

If you want to engage him in conversation, turn to 439.
Or if you wish you head off to the soon-to-begin military show, turn to 413.

Bellowing an oath to the Gods soon met, you burst though the blizzard of sparkling razors, toward the wobbling sickly pink sac of pus. Enraged so by the total evil facing you - threatening you, threatening all you care for - that your screams shatter the shards in the very air. Strangely invigorated by a million cuts, stitching a patchwork design across your body, you leap with all your might, blade raised high aloft. Blinded by brilliant white light as you soar through the air, you may as well be an eagle in the sky as all time freezes.

Across the eternal sea, an unseen hand scores the last words into your scroll. Flashes of memory. Brotherhoods; images of lives lived, and love ones lost. Sun-cracked and shackled to an oar. Screaming in smoke filled battlefield agony, chest racked with sobs and waste deep in Friesburg mud.

Pleading to your mother joins the legion of other forlorn voices, 'Mama! Mama save me! A father dead. Swinging like a wax mannequin from the noose.

Dimly aware as though as in a dream, your blade slices through the butterfly-wing thin membrane effortlessly...as you rise up into cotton clouds. Whatever was, has fallen, and continues to fall for all time down the never-ending pit. A mother's smile never seen, but a voice heard and gentle, a tender and reassuring caress felt. A melodic and lilting hum, soothing you as you sleep. 'Settle down, little one. Always kicking, so full of life!' Love felt from a life as yet unborn. Love requited, love to be felt again. The proud tousling of wayward hair, 'My beautiful boy, Siga, what a handsome boy you are!'

Your adventure ends here. Your story, about to begin again.

83

Following Galiael through the soaring archway into the soft golden light, you enter the temple. The fine structure seems immaculately preserved. Smoothly polished marble clads the walls, indented with fine murals of topaz, sunstone and sweetwater pearl. The ornate torches burn brightly, with a supernatural intensity, illuminating the magnificent dragon lectern with a halo of silver fire. You look to your Elven companion who kneels stiffly before the imposing altar and trembles with unrequited piety. Old wounds nag at your consciousness, pain from your joints, your teeth and your scars - a warning from an old acquaintance. You rub your tired and dusty eyes with a cracked palm and...you freeze. Dropping your hand slowly you see that temples pews filled with apparitions, row upon row of ethereal spirits, the translucent long dead Elven worshippers. Their cowled heads are bowed in deferment to the ancient Elven gods and as one they begin to murmur an unholy requiem. Galiael spins round and gasps in horror, muttering a silent oath. As one, the **Ancient Wraiths** stand and pull back their hoods revealing eyeless masks of bitterness and pain. No temple of such great age could be in such a pristine condition, and this evil-tainted structure is at best a construct of dark sorcery, and at worst the very manifestation of Elven hell. You glance at the torches, and the ragged wraiths, and consider firing the whole accursed place.

If you want to hurl a torch into the densely packed pews, turn to 258.
If you have the Gift of Stealth, you can try to creep back out unnoticed, turn to 383.
If you think it best to attack these Ancient Wraiths, before they attack you, turn to 141.

'Yes, Brother, yes!' the fanatic squeals with unconfined enthusiasm, clasping your shoulders in his hot sweating palms. 'I knew you were a sensible and right-thinking man the minute I clapped eyes upon you,' he continues excitedly. Then, with a twinge of paranoia, theatrically looks around him, wary of dissenters. Leaning forward and winking conspiratorially, he pulls you close and whispers into your ear. 'When the midnight wolves howl, be in the tavern named 'The Hundred Sixty Six' - after that famous regiment of *men* who stemmed the greenskin tide. The leaders will speak...join us, brother, we are legion...we grow daily with every foul outrage and humiliating insult cast upon us by...by the...' He can't bring himself to say it.

'The Elves?' you continue helpfully, relishing the spasm of pain that runs through the crazy malcontent, at the merest mention of the word. **Write down 166 on your adventure sheet.** When prompted at **midnight**, you may turn to this reference. You ponder now, how to spend the rest of the short voyage.

If you choose to call on the awkward young Casconqian man, turn to 474.

If you want to investigate Captain Hessler's cabin - and the female noises within, turn to 52.

If you've already done both of the above, or just decide to save your energies for adventures yet to come, you rest up in your bunk. Turn to 220.

You hack wildly, blindly, until all is still. Wiping the gore from your blade on the tattered rags of the dispatched wretches, you press onwards through the narrow passageway. All the while your instincts point toward continuing descent, despite the spatial confusion of your confines. The metronomic beating sound echoes off the walls, adding to your sense of disorientation. After a score more paces the flames from your torch reach out and illuminate a wide alcove to your left. How deep you can't tell without investigating. An infrequent sobbing sound appears to be coming from the darkness. Though every time you strive to listen more closely it ceases, so that you are not at all sure whether your mind is playing tricks on you. Directly ahead further down the passageway, you can see a faint light.

If you wish to investigate the alcove, turn to 289.

If you decide to press on toward the light source further down the passageway, turn to 438.

Lost and utterly alone, your heart burns with shame as you listen to the terrible screams of the abandoned children, as the unseen beast enters the dwelling. You clutch your futile hands to your ears as you try to blot out the horrible sounds - none so worse as the sound of babes murdered. **Decrease one step of FATE if possible,** as the Gods most noble avert their gaze from you in justified disgust. Aghast with horror and with eyes and lungs filling with burning and acrid smoke, you face no choice but to scramble up onto the rooftops. Flames sweep across, and through, the improvised dwellings - sending blazing awnings and washing soaring into the sky like doomed phoenixes. From your elevated position you are able to follow the route of the Avenida toward the Piazza. In the streets below all manner of sin is being inflicted on its weaker inhabitants. Lumbering undead shambles, contest with roaming gangs of thugs to inflict terror upon them. Perhaps without a care, or perhaps in acknowledgement of the End of Days, sounds of rapine can be heard down dark alleys, punctuated with stifled gasps and screams. You glance down in disgust as you see a charred corpse being gnawed by two figures, only compounded with the realisation the rewarded diners are half starved members... of the living.

As you near the Piazza Arborea, you call out to Adz and Professor, competing with the shouts and screams of city, palls of smoke drifting across your vision as winds fan the flames of the slum fire.

'Seven Hells!' you cry, 'How can anything be achieved in this inferno!'

The gaps between rooftops widen as you near your destination, its perhaps one hundred paces to the Piazza, which will have to be reached at street level. Nothing is emerging from its direction except for a succession of fiends, dead Stygians and reanimated corpses. A powerful ear shattering howl fills the night sky, sending birds careering into clock-towers and spires. You look at your hands and attempt to stem the rigours, as you climb down into the street. The Beast, the Master of the Pit is holding court and his throne is made of the dead branches of the Tree of Life. When he speaks the city trembles.

If you wish to leap down and hurry to square in case Adz and the Professor are still nearby, turn to 118.
If you think it likely that they would have retreated to the Diving Swallow, turn to 120.

The captain motions for the other crew members to leave, and alone leads you to the ship's hold. He seats himself on a barrel, and motions for you to do the same. Hessler regards you keenly for some moments, his steely grey eyes boring into you, as he rubs the dark stumble on his chin. 'You've got some fire in your balls – entering my cabin. Let's hear it then,' he says, circling his hand and prompting you to speak. 'I know you've got a story and I want to hear what it is - from one old adventurer to another. I have a melancholic attraction to hopeless pursuits.'

If you decide to lay bare your mission to Hessler, and tell him everything, turn to 151.
If you decline to reveal your mission, and put on a pretence of mundanity, turn to 238.

88

You fix you gaze intently on the Orb. Remembering passages from half read texts, and heeding examples of spell-casting witnessed on your life's travels, you think it prudent to dispense of your armour and any metal concealed on your person. Laying these down carefully and steeling your mind tight with concentration, you reach deeply into the caverns of your soul. Clutching the Elvish scroll you hesitantly begin to recite the words, the undulations of the arcane tongue causing your dry mouth to stick. Gusts of wind appear from nowhere and a huge hole is ripped through the mists to the heavens above revealing the black sky bejewelled with a thousand twinkling stars. As the winds of space roar through your soul, you near completion of the recital, both invigorated and terrified by the unfathomable forces at work.

Combine the total of your Fortitude, plus two for each of the following:
Your Fate level is 'Favoured'.
You possess the Lozenge of Tongues.
You have the gift of Arcania.
You are carrying Artur Keijzer's notebook.

If your total is 10 or more, turn to 239.
If your total is 9 or less, turn to 463.

89

Remembering what the minstrel said, about apparently seeing Hobgoblins in the Stygian animal caravan, you linger around unobtrusively for quite a while until the crowds thin out. Sensing an opportunity you surreptitiously creep into one of the covered pens housing the beasts, at the rear of the circus tent. The enclosure reeks of dung and sweat. You look into various cages - a mangy looking mountain lion, a rather forlorn looking unicorn, and a half dead giant spider seem to be amongst the star attractions for the easily impressed city dwellers. As you silently creep through the pens, you notice a cage at the far end of the pen, with a heavy leather tarpaulin covering it. As you approach stealthfully, you can hear sounds of scratching and hoarse barking from within. Something pricks your senses - a taste on your lips and a thick stench of ...a familiar smell, garnered from your time in the eastern steppe, clearing the Vaults beneath Kaban of...

'And you might be?' The animal master suddenly appears as if from nowhere. A thickly bearded man, carrying a whip in one hand and a heavy cudgel in the other, he advances carefully towards you, with some degree of menace.

If you hastily beat a retreat, turn to 179.
If you stand your ground, turn to 320.

90

With some embarrassment, you regale Adz of your encounters with the fair Contessa. Rapt, Adz listens on excitedly as you describe her alluring physical attributes. 'Gods, Siga, who would have thought an ugly scarred lump like you could attract such a hot piece! My loins are stirring at the thought of it!' He lets out a booming laugh and pats you with unintended force across your shoulders. 'We'll have to start calling you "His Eminence" soon, you giant lovestruck fop.' He effects a mockery of a finely educated man, and teases you mercilessly until he runs - not before time - out of steam, still chuffed with his own humour. 'So, are you going to deliver this note then?' he asks, drafting his ale.

'Wait,' you say, 'There's something else.' Taking a slug of ale, you recount the story of the Moretti family, the vampiric children, the possible link to the other events and the exiled patrician, to Adz - who listens on excitedly.

'The market can wait,' he declares. 'Let's go and hunt down this fiend. If his hunting lodge is only ten leagues away we can get there and back before nightfall - come on, Siga, it'll be like old times – Let's go and get some mounts from Hessler!'
You look at the giant lump, excited as a child at the prospect of a bit of adventuring, and can't help but think to humour him. Considering that the professor, from experience, will probably take longer than a day before he's ready to set out - you have the time.

If you want to attempt to deliver the Contessa's note, turn to 162.
If you agree with Adz about seeking out the Moretti hunting lodge, turn to 262.
If you insist on doing as the professor says, in picking up supplies from the market, turn to 205.

Exposing yourself to their dubious mercies, you are unceremoniously dragged through the streets, attracting the mockery of any Devan citizens out at this hour. **Deduct 2 from your Fortitude,** as you are periodically pummelled by your captors and eager spectators on your way to the gaol.

If you are still alive you are thrown into a dank hole, to lick your wounds and reflect on your foolishness. An age seems to pass by as you entertain yourself trying to make out the desperate etchings carved into the pitch black cell walls. Suddenly the door swings open and a sergeant grabs you, and roughly pulls you out into the antechamber housing these miserable prison cells.

If you have the word ELFKIN on your adventure sheet, turn to 290.
If you don't, but have a Silver Bow, turn to 385.
If not, but you have the Victory Laurel, turn to 416.
If you have none of these, turn to 189.

Old wounds flare up as you tear through the streets, their resurrection causing you to puff and wheeze. Even so, a fleeting moment of satisfaction elates you, as you suspect you've lost them...before you hear a loud grunt, and feel a dull crack to your knee. **Lose 1 point from each of your Agility and Fortitude** as the Watchdogs pole-arm smacks into it. With their superior local knowledge of the twisting alley ways they have encircled you! Picking yourself up from the cobbles - your knee throbbing from pain - you count three of these bullies. Their sneering faces turn to smirks as they confidently approach.

If you submit their superior numbers, and surrender, turn to 165.
If you think it better to fight your way out of the situation, turn to 261.

Unaccustomed to resistance, you evidently take the bullies by unawares, as their narrow eyes widen with surprise and fear.

If your Dexterity is 7 or more, turn to 340.
If your Dexterity is 6 or less, turn to 269.

Bringing the horn to your lips, you empty your lungs into one almighty exhalation. A deafening low tone blasts out across the night skies, sending roosting birds for many leagues flying in terror. The Giant Cadaverous Birds flap their tattered wings chaotically, their cries melding with the sound of the horn. Bones, talons, disgusting parodies of feathers, tumble to the earth far below as the creatures begin to disintegrate in the face of this sonic boom. Elated, you unsheathe your weapon and guide Pegasus headlong into the remnants of this undead puppets, chopping and hacking with scarce controlled glee.

Enemy vanquished, Pegasus begins a spiralling descent and once landed throws you from his back with a violent buck. The equine flyer holds you for a moment in its huge mournful eyes, before turning his head away. You make to remonstrate with the unfathomable beast, but he gallops up into the darkness of the night sky. Abashed, you recall the pitiful sight of the undead infants some distance back and suddenly feel guilty earth. But it's too late to turn back now only four hundred paces from the Gate of the Leaping Lion. A tiny figure in the dark, and outside the city walls, you feel chillingly vulnerable and alone. Further along the road, the huge city walls rise up before you like a sheer black cliff, its timeless gate sealed shut from the outside world. Further away to the east, five hundred paces away, the river flows into the city. You factor it's protected by chains and locks, but in these times...who knows what lurks there.

If you wish to approach the city by road and via the gate, turn to 351.
If you favour an attempt to re-enter Deva by river, turn to 39.

Anustüg- the sixth day, MMDXXXI

You bid farewell to Captain Hessler and the crew, and bound down the gang plank to the bustling wharf side. The sea docks are alive with activity. Stevedores glisten in the mid-day heat as they go about their labours, unloading an array of cargo. Furs and salted fish from the wilds of Norsicza, spices and exotic birds from the distant Daab. Traders and merchants gesticulating and shouting in a cacophony of tongues - a riot of sights and colours and smells that overloads your senses. By comparison the distant Wasteland seems bleak and grey. You miss it already.

You look up at the massive harbour, which was carved out of solid rock, eons ago, by the Elves - before they departed the Midden lands for the last time for their home across the Vastness. Some delicate, if weather beaten, embellishments still survive - exquisite carvings of old Gods staring out over the shimmering ocean.

As the sun beats down, you push your way through the seething harbour crowds, wafting away hawkers pushing their wares in your face. You have little choice but to allow yourself to be carried along by the meandering crowds. It's some effort to keep your footing on the loose cobbles as people push and shove. You feel eager and malintentioned hands brush your purse - but a few steely stares at your close neighbours prevent any bloodshed.

Suddenly, you hear a shout of 'Make way for the Duce!' A surge of bodies part as a fat nobleman, mounted on a huge destrier, canters towards you. Eager not to be trampled beneath the oncoming hooves, people jump for safety in a tumble of limbs. You curse as you catch a stray arm to the face and lose your footing, crashing into a fellow traveller sending them spilling to the ground. Pulling yourself to your feet, you turn to offer your apologies to see a thin figure, bedecked in a dark grey hooded cloak. As you pull the stranger upright, his limp gloved hand reaches out to cobbles, towards a medallion dropped in the collision. Still apologising, you bend down to pick it up, briefly glancing at it; a gilded disk with the emblem of a lemon tree on it. Quick as a serpent, the stranger snatches it out of your grasp. Without thanks, let alone further discussion, the man melts away into the crowd, ushered away somewhat shifty looking group he seems to be travelling with. One of the group casts a parting glare over his shoulder as they disappear from view, into the masses.

You spit into the dirt; and cast a wry smile at the rudeness down of these Middeners, and their foreign ways… when you freeze. The hooded cloak, and gloves in the blistering heat..? That smell… you didn't notice it at first, but odour lingers even after the old man has vanished. The stench of death. The hairs on the back of your neck stand up as your heart seems to stops beating. The noise of the crowds seems to dim, and the colours fade. Stray dogs begin to claw desperately at the ground, and the sounds of wailing mothers rise beneath your boots. In a dreamlike state you gaze upwards and the sun, which seems to drop and let out a tired groan.

A silhouetted figure suddenly appears before you, its hand reaching out toward you. Instinctively you sweep the hand away and grasp the figure around the neck, squeezing tightly, your finger nails digging into flesh. Suddenly you gasp as you feel your heart beat into life, and with a dizzying crash, all the colours and sounds of the city accelerate back to life, leaving you choking a terrified looking - and ridiculously attired, pamphleteer.

'P...Please Sir..!' he gasps breathlessly, before you release him to collapse into the dirt.

'Sorry friend,' you apologise, as you pull him to his feet, his legs scrambling in the air as if he makes to flee. 'What do we have here?' you ask, motioning at the pamphlets. The frightened pamphleteer peevishly dusts down his garish outfit, and gives you a cool look - no doubt taking you for an illiterate - before cautiously handing one to you. It's a proclamation about the Summers End festival currently under way in the city.

Festivala di Deva

Seigiorno Morni

The Grand Market of exotic itemes
The Stygian Fayre, Beasts of Beyond
& Feats of Strength
Festival of Wine and Song

Pride of Deva: Witness our Vigour
on the Plain of Horeos!

Seigiorno Set

Gentlemen Targeteers Delighte
Dr Dolls Wonderous Scientifical Proof
Elven Mysteries

Riposorno Set

Grande procession: Masked Parade
around the mighty and indefatiguable walls
of the City of The Leaping Lion

By Order - Duce
Leader of the Coundil of Fifty

You thank the young man, causing him to wince as you offer him your hand - a token of apology for throttling him. He tentatively reaches out and limply shakes your hand, before he waltzes back off into the crowd - nervously glancing at you all the while. How strange these events, and how inevitable - trouble has an easy time finding you - you muse with a joyless smile - and she's a reliable mistress. 'The Boogenhofen' arriving ahead of schedule, despite yesterday's storm. Naturally, your first port of call will be The Diving Swallow, where your master, Professor Kroos, is lodged.

Turn to 449.

96

Possessing not the specialist talents required to navigate a course through this tainted and dizzying landscape, you quickly become lost. Stumbling for an indeterminate amount of time, you eventually reach a donkey trail which you resolve the follow, and some hours later you meet the coast - which to best estimates appears to lead to the south of Deva. The trail winds around a steep coastline, and looking out to see you see a nearby dark pine clad islet. No torches illuminate the darkness, and it appears uninhabited. Below you stands a wretched fishing hamlet of a handful of dwellings. This also wreathed in darkness. The orb glows with a fierce luminance, and is hot to the touch. Above you, you hear the roar of the comet, and its impending heat begins to cause your skin to tingle.

If you think it best to discard the orb and head for the safety of the islet, turn to 313.
Or, if you persist in a last ditch attempt at reaching Deva with the orb, turn to 22.

97

You plod off down the road with a troop of refugees, looking enviously at the torches from nearby islands. The fires of fishing communities, isolated from Deva by narrow channels, protected by swirling currents...if you could reach...

Suddenly terrible screams ring out from dawdlers in the rear. You spin round instinctively, dark and tattered figures emerging from the gloom are no returning citizens, but the shallow buried former residents of some recent atrocity! Their hands covered in filth and muck from the fields, these maggot ridden zombies tear into stragglers, their gaping jaws open wide, groaning in unholy turmoil. Like bewitched sheep, some of the refugees are simply unable to move, offering no resistance and unable to comprehend the horrors with engulf them, until their assailants long green-black fingernails puncture the soft pink flesh of their exposed limbs.

Seven Hells are unleashed on the unsuspecting column, and casting a glance behind you to the sealed city gates, you know now what you must do. The fires of the fishermen await - surely the only chance of salvation rests upon their protected shores, not in the open and indefensible spaces of the countryside. With re-entry into the city nigh-on impossible you sprint down through lemon groves, and gently undulating fields until you reach the coastline. The cool salty mists of sea refresh you , as you search feverishly for a vessel. Happening across a secluded cove you come across a trio of small row boats tethered together at a dilapidated jetty.

Casting your eyes heavenward, you mutter some silent prayers to any Gods listening and jump aboard, unfastening the ties. As you row slowly and methodically toward a small rocky islet you look toward the distant majestic Devan harbour - the last vessels exiting through the mighty Elven gates. You can only hope Adz and the Professor are aboard one of them, you can only hope they have abandoned you, as you have abandoned them.

Still alive you promise to the sky, to the sea, and to the stars in the heavens, that you will atone for your flight and be reunited with them once again.

Your adventure - but not your life - ends here. Still in possession of your soul, and with the trappings of this mortal realm, you are alive to see the morning, and live on to one day continue your adventures.

98

'Ho, a fine night for mischief eh best of men!' you whisper to them conspiratorially. 'Elven scum!' you spit. 'Think they own the place, eh friends?'

'We are many, brothers!' they reply cheerfully, 'come join us, this will teach them. We'll get our message across loud and clear!' he boasts with a proud smile.

Turn to 404.

99

You wink to the crestfallen student as your shot hits the mark. Eventually you're called forward into another pairing. This time you face a laconic scout, bearing some kind of Casconqian insignia on his tunic.

Steadying your hand, you look long down the barrel. **Is your Dexterity 8 or above?**

If it is, turn to 122.
Otherwise, turn to 207.

100

'Pentarc gifted the world with *one hundred* conquests!' you shout, up into the gloom. Your heart feints to stop completely during what seems an everlasting pause. Nervously glancing up at the faltering ceiling of this chamber, your fears of premature burial are allayed by the perceptible nods of these massive statues. Beckoning you onwards, the titans grimace with fatigue at their eternal burden; holding up the impossible weight of the city high above. You tread carefully toward the third and final row of be-glyphed flagstones, which like the others, shine with uncommon radiance. Between the Gods Tanath, and Naed - the Creator and the Destroyer - you close your eyes and step across their threshold. The statue of Tanath turns its head to you with a massive grinding sound, and its eyes seem to widen in mute appeal.
  'For how many years has the White King has reigned in glory?'

If you know the answer to this question turn to the relevant section.
If you don't, but have a Bronze Diadem, turn to 429.
If you don't know the answer, and are not in possession of this item, turn to 152.

101

You haul your aching bones up the steep hillside path toward the caves, satisfied to see Ingmar's donkey tethered to rock at the mouth of the largest. You creep as best you can along the rocky trail, patting the miserable looking beast as you pass. From inside the cool, dark aperture you can hear halting incantations and louder curses. An inexperienced young man struggling to recite ancient lore. Shaking your head at the fool, you reach for your weapon instinctively, and hurry through the neck of the cave and into a raised cavern.

Ingmar is clad in a dark robe emblazoned with celestial runes, arms aloft and voice rising into a crescendo, as an ancient crested **Skeletal Centurion** rises from the cavern floor. It's a pitiful sight. Jerking as if on puppeteers wire, unstable and inexpertly bound to this mortal realm. Its jaws open and close in comical fashion, as its eyeless sockets seem to implore a return to the earth.

'Damn Fool, boy!' you angrily shout, startling the amateur necromancer, who spins round in horror. 'Depart this place, for I cannot guarantee protection from my host!' he replies dubiously. With this, control is seemingly lost and the pathetic skeleton dances awkwardly toward you, gladius raised.

If you have a Mirrored Shield, Turn to 201.
If not, you collect a rock from the caves surface and raise it high above your head. Turn to 335.

102

If you have the word BROTHERHOOD on your adventure sheet turn to 329.
Otherwise, turn to 221.

103

Sensing a lack of both reason and empathy in these watchdogs, you turn on your heels to flee the scene.

Combine your current Fortitude and Agility totals, and add 2 if you have the Gift of Stealth.

If the result is 17 or more, turn to 435.
If the total is 16 or less, turn to 476.

104

Rollo leans against the ropes and drafts a mug of beer handed to him by a lackey. The adulation of the crowd lionising Rollo melds with mocking cries and catcalls aimed toward you, as you climb up into the ring. The stifling air is thick with sweat, the stench of piss, and the metallic smell of spilt blood. As you look around at the dark indolent faces of the spectators you remind yourself these odours are not uncommon to you. The cacophony dims to a respectful murmur as you strip to the waist, revealing an iron-hard frame covered in a patchwork of scars. From across the ring, Rollo purses his lips in disdain and cracks his knuckles. A cymbal crashes and a huge cheer rings out - the fight has begun. Choose your tactic in this physical contest.

If you choose to pursue the bruiser aggressively, hoping a flurry of telling blows will demoralise him into submission, turn to 249.
Should you decide to grapple him to the canvas and sap his vital energies, turn to 58.
Or if you decide to keep the old bear at bay, and dance rings around him, striking from distance, turn to 177.

105

As you step further into the massive chamber, the rock face groans with seismic shifts. Huge splintering cracks appear in the supporting statues of the Titans, and beads of rock fall from their labouring brows. Staring high up into the vaulted ceiling, you can see the struts bow alarmingly. You walk forward - for now you realise there is no way back - towards the next row of glyphs which separate the Goddess Sanromai and the dread God Menax, deities of Love and War. You tread on the illuminated flagstones, ready to receive the next fateful test. Once again, the leaden and unseen voice demands answer to its eternal question,

'The number of conquests bequeathed to the world by the first Pentarc, the first Primarch's guiding hand'

If you know the answer to this question turn to the relevant section.
If you don't, but are Favoured or have the Gift of Arcania, turn to 33.
If you don't know the answer, and are not Favoured nor have this Gift, turn to 152.

106

As you approach the crypt you notice the door is slightly ajar. A damp chill circles evilly around your feet, emanating from within. You can't make anything out through the gloom. Thunder begins to roll in the heavens above. The steward hands you a torch and waits expectantly, his mouth agape and hands trembling.

If you want to burst through the door in the hope of catching whatever lurks within by surprise, turn to 326.
If you want to creep in without making a sound, turn to 5.

107

You turn the handle once more - the door opens with low creak. The main chamber of the tower contains a large table, set out with eight chairs, and places laid with fine, but unused, crockery. Adz rubs a finger along a plate and inspects the thick dust thoughtfully. Torches flicker in their fastenings, giving off a gloomy glow, casting strangely shaped shadows of the mounted trophies adorning the walls. As you pad carefully on the old floorboards you consider this place has not seen company for some time. A quick inspection of this level uncovers nothing of interest, except for the steps leading up in a circular fashion to the next level. Adz presses a finger to his lips and points upwards. Looking up into the dimly little stairwell, you can hear the faintest sound of sobbing from above. You shrug your shoulders. Adz grins.

You carefully ascend the steps to the next level, turn to 386.

108

In an instant you draw your pistol and level it at the nearest thug. In a puff of acrid smoke the man crumbles to the ground, screaming, and clutching what's left of his face. Your blade glints keenly in the moonlight as it soon dispatches the next Stygian footpad to a miserable death - gurgling to the reddening cobbles. You can hear shouts, whistles and the clank of approaching armour and torches. You take a quick glance about you - Pepin is nowhere to be seen, he must have gone to fetch the watch, naive child! The dark cloaked old man needs that split second to bound onto a water butt with astonishing athleticism, and with one leap clamber up onto the roof of the single story house.

If you try and follow the old man, turn to 324.
If you want to quickly search the bodies, turn to 308.
Or flee the scene by darting down an alley and make your way to meet the professor, turn to 233.

109

Half crazed with twin emotions of duty and regret, Galiael mutters his apologies as he lurches toward you. Fine words mean nothing to you. The elf must die.

If you have a pistol you can attempt to get a shot off. If this is your choice, turn to 307.
If you have a throwing star, you can hurl it toward the maddened elf, turn to 252.
If you have neither, or if you'd rather feel the soft kiss of Elven flesh on the cold steel of your sword, turn to 312.

The watchdogs obviously feel the need to exercise a bit of bravery in tackling a lone stranger. They begin circle you menacingly, their rough faces pinched tightly with menace. Surely they wouldn't just attack you for no reas... Oof! You curse your lack of concentration, as one of the bullies strikes you with a sneaky punch to the gut. Tempers bubble in your veins, and grasping your assailant by the throat you smash a chunky fist several times into mouth - turning his snarls to whimpers.

One of the others - obviously now doubting their wisdom in tackling you – shouts, 'For mercy, assist the City Watch! We have cornered a thief!' You hear corresponding shouts, and two burly looking artisans emerge from a workshop, clutching improvised weapons in their sweaty hands.

If you continue the fight, turn to 6.
If you wish to surrender, turn to 91.
If you'd rather make a swift exit and try and flee, turn to 123.

Tracing your steps back to the exact spot the orb had been held in statis, you tentatively turn the two dials protruding from the owls back. One for the distance to Deva, and one for direction. The mechanism gives a little whirr, and the artefact vibrates into life. Two copper eyelids open and its talons extrude to a level which exactly matches the diameter of the orb. With a satisfying 'clunk' you attach the orb, causing the machines head to spin on its axis and hoot with what you take for pleasure, and with that you release it to the heavens and watch it flutter towards Deva.

Sparking up a cheroot - using the lingering flames from the vanquished dragons fiery breath - you clamber a little way down the hillside and take a position atop a rocky outcrop. Watching the little fellow through Hessler's lens for as long as possible, its shimmering feathers disappear into the night sky, as you wait tentatively for the inevitable.

The comet; a huge ball of blinding white light, soars through the air above you, bathing you in its searing heat as it thunders through the sky. Seconds later - a huge detonation, which sends shockwaves up the hillside, and untold tonnes of debris up into the air. The cataclysmic explosion engulfs what you take to be the very centre of the city, whence the Master holds grisly court.

Still, lingering doubts nag at your conscience. You can only hope your friends survived, and that evil was vanquished by the comets impact...

Whatever the outcome, this adventure ends here.

112

Unable to retain your grip a moment longer, you grunt with exhaustion as you're forced to release the champions thick neck. Enraged, Rollo pulls up his mighty frame and staggers to his feet. He releases an almighty roar and swings his hammer like fist, knocking you to the canvas and claiming victory. **Lose 2 points of Fortitude.**

Defeated, you spit the blood from your mouth and hand over the silver you gambled – **Make a note of this on your adventure sheet.** With a splitting headache and an uneasy sense of balance you fumble your way from the tent.

Turn to 70.

113

You strike with primitive blows in the dark confines of the tight alley. No finesse is required in this contest of the living and the dead. At times close enough to smell its stinking breath and feel its bristling hairs, you quickly break the beast and hack it into myriad parts – leaving nought but a bloated steaming sack, leaking its liquors into the gutter. After sending this slave of the night back to the earth, you decide that clambering to the rooftops is your only hope of navigating a course to the Piazza.

Turn to 2.

114

Adz is ahead of you already. Great Axe swirling through the air to the sound of a Norsiczan battle-oath - you can only admire his bravery. As you step to face a spitting Hobgoblin alongside three quivering militia men, you notice the Duce exit the stage. Flanked by an armoured column, he disappears back into the Palace, leaving his beloved populace to scatter like ducklings. You push aside the ashen faced Watchdogs and unsheathe your sword. The **HOBGOBLIN** bares its teeth and barks loudly, and springs toward you.

If you still have your pistol and wish to let off a shot, turn to 433.
If you want to rummage about your person for a magical item, turn to 117.
If you'd rather you combat ability win the day, turn to 446.

115

Batting aside the would-be assassins trembling dagger, you ruthlessly skewer the man, embedding the hilt of your own weapon against his ribs.

Wiping the assassin's blood from your blade, you consider how his crow-like corpse starkly contrasts with the shining alabaster flagstones. You're brought back to your senses by a growing din of fury. Shocked locals shout angrily at you, unwelcome intrusion of death to their banal days. Never mind that an attempt was made on your life! You note one or two do-gooder citizens peeling away sneakily - presumably to fetch the watch.

Add +1 to when prompted to check for 'Watch Patrol'

If you wish to search the hooded Stygian corpse, turn to 192.
If you want to lose yourself in the crowds at the Military Display on the Field of Triumph, turn to 413.
Or, if you were given a location by the Freelander merchant, you can – if you haven't already - turn to this now.

116

The tournament is taking place in a colonnaded square near the Gate of the Leaping Lion. This is a more upmarket area of Deva, as is evident by the well-to-do competitors and spectators, more than a few of whom seem slightly inebriated, shouting out encouragement to their champions. You pay the entry fee to a martial looking gentlemen with fine white whiskers, who chalks your name on a large board, and you guides you to the shooting stalls. Surveying your opponents, you can immediately separate the wheat from the chaff. You're drawn first, against a nervous but chatty young noble. He wishes you good luck with some bonhomie, blushing as his fraternity egg him on with cat calls. Emptying some powder into the pan and selecting an untarnished shot, you step to the mark.

You squint, and take aim. **Is your Dexterity 7 or above?**

If it is, turn to 99.
Otherwise, turn to 207.

117

You furiously examine your trappings for something to quell the Hobgoblin's spitting fury, but you dally too long. The beast takes a gigantic leap and secures its fangs around your arm. **Lose 2 points of Fortitude and 1 point of Dexterity**. Shaking it free, you painfully roll away and ready yourself for its next attack.

If you still have your pistol and wish to let off a shot, turn to 433.
If you'd rather you combat ability win the day, turn to 446.

118

Easily swatting the shambling corpses aside as you go, you sprint past the clumsy fiends towards to your destination. Blood flows down through the cracks in the cobbles, creating a sticky red delta, forming islands of the dead laying stricken or twitching. Steeling yourself for the vision of hell that awaits, you rush through the portico into the Piazza bellowing war cries as you go - and so you emerge for an audience with the Master of Pit.

A legion of undead. A score or more black clad Stygians, pallid faces stiff with mortis. Some standing, others limbless or headless - thrashing around as if in a nightmare. A nightmare this is, for alongside the Masters disciples are the risen bodies of The Brotherhood, the watchdogs, and dozens of others filling the square. They all wear the mask of undeath, their blue lips pulled back tautly revealing sharpened incisors and blood shot eyes.

In the middle of this assembly of damnation, stands the huge hulking figure of The Beast - The Master of the Pit. Its glistening ebony skin is pulled tight over its thick muscled frame, still wet with the slimly liquor of birth, its horned head is the size of a barrel, embodying the worst of mankind. Its prominent chin and arching brow give it a moon-like idiocy, though this is tempered by intelligent and irrepressible gaze. Oily black teeth, each the size of field-spike, fill its drooling mouth. The Tree is no more, only a gaping sink hole remains where is once proudly stood, for eons. A pulsing and unnatural blue light radiates from below, from which evil source you can only imagine.

Skidding to a halt on the flagstones, greasy with blood, you freeze in momentary terror as you regard this vision of hell. Frozen in your tracks, the reanimated occupants of the square turn as one to face your unwelcome intrusion. In an unholy chorus, which causes your bowels to quiver, the legion of the dead howl with fury, and spring to defend their master. Realising the overwhelming odds stacked against you, you about turn and run as fast as your legs will carry you, the undead host snapping at your heels.

If you want to flee in the direction of the Diving Swallow, turn to 120.
**If you think it best to flee to the docks, in the hope of finding them
finding sanctuary on board The Boogenhofen, turn to** 393.

Perhaps the Professor and Adz have joined the multitudes fleeing this
charnel house of a city?

If you think so, you head to the nearby South Gate, turn to 462.

119

'All collaborators must die, the battle for resistance is nigh,' the leader
utters in a dead voice, and the five of them reach for concealed knives and
cudgels. You exchange a quick glance with Adz, who grins at you as he
clenches his great axe in his giant hands. Drawing your sword, you mutter
an oath as you head straight for the leader, as another strives to intercept
you. The other three circle Adz, who is smiling, wild-eyed, and recanting a
Norsiczan blood-litany. You must fight the leader, and a nervous looking
Brotherhood member, whilst Adz takes on the other three.

If you focus your attention on the leader, turn to 445.
If you want to deal with the nervous foe first, turn to 395.

120

Through burning streets you race. Horrors unimagined assail you on
every street, at every junction and square. You deaden your soul and dull
your senses to the vain appeals of the innocent and the helpless, bearing
witness to crimes most foul. By the time you near the Diving Swallow your
features are etched with lamentation, and your eyes are wide - exposed so
to the suffering of Devan's citizens, by the undead and their acolytes.
Upon reaching the door and knocking with haste, Evassa welcomes you
with relief, and leads you down into her cool cavernous cellar. The space
has hastily been converted into an improvised war room. Barrels and crates
are haphazardly pushed up against the walls, and in the centre of the room
several smaller tables have been adjoined into one. A large map of Deva
and its environs lays unfurled across it. As you descend the stone steps the
conversation halts abruptly, and all eyes turn to you.

Eight figures stand around the table; the professor - pale and watery
eyes glisten with joy at your appearance.

'Oh my trusted friend, I'm so glad you are safe.' You smile reassuringly
and regard the other seven. Hessler, Sea Captain and scoundrel is there -
which surprises you considering the means at his disposal to flee this
chaos. Surprise gives way to curiosity as you take note of the two Elves

present; Aegnor and his champion Galiael, impassive in appearance and gesture. Pepin, the messenger boy, wide-eyed with youthful excitement. A martial commander you do not know, and two adjutants complete the retinue. Your heart stops as you take note of Adz' absence.

'What of Adz, master?' you ask, sick to your stomach and steeling yourself for the worst. At first the Professor says nothing, his lip dangling apologetically as he turns his palms to you in silent apology. 'Tell me master – please,' you insist, with an uncharacteristic quiver.

The professor's mouth opens and closes, as he struggles for the words. 'Adz is alive, my dear pupil. Alive and resting in his crib. We waited for you, Siga, we waited as long as we could...' he trails off.

'Why is Adz in his crib and not here, taking his place at the table,' you press, anger rising up from within you.

'Oh, my dearest Siga!' the professor wails, his bony chest heaving mightily, 'It's my fault...I fell, I was sure I was about to die...in a flash there was Adz, fighting like a Titan and roaring like the King of Bulls. He saved me, Siga.' The professor swallows hard and averts his eyes, with palpable guilt. 'He suffered a terrible wound...oh, Siga, poor Adz, poor Adz is blinded!'

The words melt behind you as you fly up the stairs to the room you share with your old friend. You burst through the door, fair knocking the door room its hinges. Adz lays stricken, a doe-eyed servant boy is mutely fanning him, and mopping his fevered brow. Across his face lays a blood mottled bandage, a red smear soaking through. Dismissing the sullen boy, you shuffle closer to this wounded giant, and sensing your presence Adz breaks into a wide grin, steadfastly concealing his undoubted pain.

'Don't blame yourself,' Adz muses. 'It's my fault - my fault for having such broad shoulders and this big ugly head. Curse that hole! The three of us should have gone down that subterranean pisshole together.' He reaches clumsily for the nearby plate of gnawed mutton bones and chews on one, and suddenly props himself upright, with apparent concern. 'You're fit of body and mind, Siga - not blinded like me, are you?' Taking his hands, you smile an unseen smile and, and reassure him of your well-being.

'What has happened?' you ask emptily, 'What happened on this night? Adz cracks a comforting smile, recounts the events of this long night.

'Not long after we parted did we hear the first screams, some bitch or something I thought at first, giving birth or dying of the pox, one or the other, and then her husband - not 20 minutes dead, trampled by a furrier's cart - lumbered into the square. Well, his Excellency and his fine and upright men, they did scatter so! The ground shook, and shook harder, and the beats grew louder. It was then that the crows, those black Stygian who lay dead around the tree, started moving.' The old Ox grimaces, and takes a sip of fortified wine before continuing, 'Before we knew it the dead had returned. Like in Budazan- do you remember?' You shudder at the memory, all those years ago - another city, another plague of undeath.

'Then those fanatics starting shambling around, one of them caught a bodyguard and took a chunk out of his neck, like this,' Adz clenches his big jaws open and shut with unnecessary theatre. 'Well, that was it - chaos reigned. I got lost in myself I must admit and starting swinging and chopping, and all murder broke out - before near the whole square sunk into the ground with an unholy thunder.'

'Go on,' you urge, as Adz pauses in reflection.

'Before we knew it, we were surrounded, everyone else had buggered off leaving me to it. Stupid really, I should have thought first of the professor - there were too many of them for just me, it was over-confidence, if you like.' A maudlin look drifts over what is left of Adz' face, 'I'm sorry, Siga, I abandoned you. I failed the professor. If it wasn't for those Elves showing up we both would have been done for. Who would have thought it, eh, saved by an elf.' With that thought running through Adz' mind, and with your soothing words of protestation your old friend sinks into a fitful sleep.

You kiss his forehead and rearrange his blankets so, before you depart back to the cellar, to this improvised council of war.

Turn to 440.

121

Through the embracing darkness you stumble, down through the forested hillside. Sweet smelling pines and cypress trees are intermingled with scars of crystalline disease. The moonlight casts capricious shadows against this bizarre terrain, disorienting you to the point of utmost confusion. All the while the orb glows with increasing luminance.

Do you have the Skills of Survivalist and / or Intuition? If so, turn to 234.
If you do not, turn to 96.

Pulling the trigger causes a cloud of blue-grey smoke to erupt around you. It clears to cheers, as the spectators applaud another pin-point shot. Your opponent shrugs and ambles off, leaving you rubbing shoulders with the final barrier to your progression into the evening sessions. You face off against a dashing Devan gentleman, who regards you with some disdain - declining to acknowledge your offer of a handshake. You resolve to defeat this arrogant dog. An ominous breeze picks up causing the canvas on the target to ripple in the wind. Attuning your senses to the conditions, you take aim once again.

Is your Dexterity 9 or above and/or do you have the Gift of Hyper Senses, and / or Martial Prowess?

If it is, you win through to the final rounds. **Write the word TARGET on your adventure sheet.**

Either way, turn to 207.

Add together your current Agility and Fortitude totals, adding +3 if you have the Gift of Stealth.

If your total is 17 or less, turn to 6.
If your total is 18 or more, turn to 243.

Ducking her murderous attack, you pivot and land a telling blow. Your tempered steel slices into her breastbone, extracting a shrill scream and sending the bitch folding to her knees. Crying in agony the Stygian woman assassin yields to your mercy, rising slowly on one knee and laying her blade over it, with due martial etiquette.

'Sir,' she tearfully begs of you, sobbing through heaving breaths. 'You *must* believe me, I am not acting cohesively of my own mind, but as an automation – I am being controlled by evil forces!' She winces in agony clutching her temples. 'Please...' she begs, 'You must help me to break this curse, and help me too reveal the true puppet masters.' With the woman looking at you with imploring eyes, you regard the pathetic figure.

If you finish her off without delay, or are Iron-Willed, turn to 422.
Or if you wish to listen to what she has to say, turn to 61.

On your cot, you dream a deep and reassuring dream. Sitting in the family parlour, your mother smiling fondly at you, as sit in the golden glow of the hearth. Content and joyful, you proudly show her a mechanical toy owl you have been repairing…pride emanates from her warmly…her heart beating loudly, roots forming a chain around her neck. 'Thub-thub!' goes her heart. Never so happy…never happy at all…it isn't real…this isn't…

Bang! BANG! BANG! You're abruptly shaken from your sleep, dripping in sweat and trembling. Another loud BANG! BANG! For a few seconds of confusion you don't know if you're still dreaming a dream. No, a nightmare. A nightmare about a beating heart and wooden chains…or if someone is indeed banging on the Swallow's stout oak door. Another BANG! BANG! Someone calling your name snaps you back into reality. You instinctively fumble for your pistol, and trip disorientated from your bed.

Another two knocks, and someone shouting. 'A message from Professor Kroos - you're to come urgently! You descend the stairs, meeting a concerned looking Evassa, and motion for her to step back. You creep across the foyer, and as you swing the door open with your weapon drawn, a drenched young messenger boy takes a step back, 'I...' he stammers - nervously glancing down at your blade - 'I have a message for you. You're to follow me to Via d'Leopardo, to Artur Keijzer's house - the Professor will meet us there. It's burning'.

You rub the sleep from your eyes, and order the messenger to wait a little while you collect your things. Figuring it's the middle of the night, you decide it would be a good bet to wear your sword and pistol. (Assuming you still have them). Soon the pair of you are padding softly through the empty and sodden pre-dawn streets.

Turn to 405.

126

'By **Pentarc's hundred conquests**! What are you doing, you fool!' Screams the elf in total horror, as he struggles to get past you. Suspecting you've made a mistake, you release him from your grasp, as he hurtles desperately towards the fizzing gunpowder laden cart. With a loose feeling in your bowels, you wince as the cart thuds into the tree and halts, the fuse crackling to completion...

Turn to 197.

127

Beaten and bleeding, you are dumped in a dark cell for a period of time you can't fathom, hoping you can talk your way out of the situation, or hoping the professor can come up with a way to release you. The city fathers, however, have no tolerance for common murderers - especially during the Festival - when it paints Deva in a bleak light. You are subsequently hung, quietly and somewhat sadly, in a bleak and anonymous yard, before your corpse is tossed down the Wailing Craggs. A lucky death, by comparison - considering the fate that befalls the city, and your friends - the professor and Adz, shortly after your death.

Your adventure, and your life, is at an end.

128

You struggle with the burly and thickly muscled animal master in the tight confines of the pens. A cacophony of howls, roars and chattering explodes as the animals go wild with fear at the violent struggle. Eventually prising the whip from his sausage-like fingers you draw it across his neck and wrap the leather tightly around. A dry purple tongue protrudes from his gasping mouth as he desperately digs his fingernails into your cheeks. **Deduct 1 point of Fortitude.** You grit your teeth in pain and exasperation, but you are too strong, and holding fast - you finally witness the last vapours disappearing from his empty lungs.

Turn to 486.

129

Do you have the Gift of Stealth? If so turn to 213.
If not, turn to 187.

You join the line of perfumed and finely attired Devan citizens. None of them show much interest in you, save a few disdainful glances, and whispered titters, no doubt at your expense. Some time passes before you reach the front of the queue. One of the Daaban guards smiles at you, and politely declines entry.

'Friend,' he begins in a thick desert accent, 'I do not think you can afford to buy from my Master, covetous glances are nothing to him, only your silver will buy what your eyes desire to see.' He nods down towards your pouch and motions with his hand, beckoning you to open it up for inspection.

If you want to open your pouch for a rather demeaning inspection, turn to 170.

If you'd rather not, you can opt to:

Head to the Stygian Fayre turn to 226.
Head to the Festival of Wine and Song, turn to 363.
Or, if you've already done all these things, or would rather just head back to your lodgings to chat to Evassa, turn to 361.

After an uneventful journey back to Deva you arrive within the city walls in the early evening, as night falls. After returning the horses to one of Hessler's men, you make directly for The Diving Swallow. You converse with Evassa, who informs you the Professor hasn't yet returned from the university, but that near the whole population of Deva is taking to the streets for the final celebration of the festival - the masked procession. Distant firecrackers explode to cheers in the distance, as the revelry begins. Hearing exciting calls from the street outside, and peering through the near opaque inn windows, you can see streams of people, garishly dressed - some masked, some entirely garbed as troubadours, clowns, or wild beasts from the forest. Some carry drums and symbols which that bang enthusiastically; others have whistles or flaming torches. All seem animated with anticipation, and not a little merry on local brews.

'We're late for the party, Adz. Come, stop scratching your balls and lets us go and join in the...fun.'

Tonight is the final night of the festivities and the culmination of the three day Deva festival. You may at this time have some clue of events to unfold, or an idea of where you may want to be.

You may now turn to a paragraph number provided earlier.

If you don't have a reference to turn to, you have little option but to take to the streets and join the party. You understand that the procession takes a route parallel to the city walls, and ends in the Grand Piazza in front of the Palazzo.

If you want to join the procession around the walls, turn to 298.
If you want to head directly to the Grand Piazza, turn to 173.

'Like old times, Siga. Me and you, and trouble coming along to make three!' You frown at Adz' simplistic excitement, who consequently looks a little crestfallen, as you inform him that this journey to the Moretti hunting lodge is a reconnaissance trip, and should on no account turn descend to the fine red mist of a killing spree. He sinks back into his saddle and scowls.

An hour passes slowly, as Adz recounts stories already told a hundred times, when Gallo gestures for the three of you to leave the main road and head to the coastal path. There is a palpable change in the weather once you near the marshy shoreline, and a depressing grey drizzle falls into a sea, motionless as a millpond. Adz becomes uncharacteristically quiet as you pull your cloak tight against the chill, silently cursing the lack of warm clothing.

You travel the winding coastal path for more than an hour in silence - Adz face is a mask of thunder as droplets roll down his brawny forehead. Gallo is also silent several spans ahead, wrapped up against this dank micro climate. A thick mist soon descends and visibility becomes poor, your guide becomes but a wraith in the near distance. Looking down onto the path, you notice with some horror that sea water is gently lapping over the stones.

You hear Gallo's horse whinny to the front, and seconds later Gallo gallops past you, shouting something unintelligible to you in his thick brogue, causing your horse to snort nervously. Adz manages to control his mount and sidles up to you cursing. 'This is queer place, Siga! Do you see how we are losing the path?' he says, pointing a huge finger at the submerged hooves of the horses. 'What shall we do?' Your eyes follow the guide's shadowy form, as the coward disappears into the mist and out of view.

If you want to head back to the city, turn to 131.
If you want to push on along the coastal path, turn to 332.
If you want to head inland, but still in the direction of the lodge, turn to 460.

133

The elf shows no signs of moving, and so you bite your lip and tread carefully on the first rung of the bridge. The rickety crossing emits a forlorn sigh and noticeably quivers. Some looser threads on the frayed bindings snap under duress. Looking nervously over your shoulder, you exchange glances with Galiael, who smiles warmly - a barely perceptible nod encouraging you onwards. Taking another step, and with the bridge letting out a gasp of pain, you look down into the boiling swell below, sure that you're about to plunge to your doom into it. But another footstep, and another...the bridge cries and winces, but remains intact. With an exhalation of relief you leap the last four slats to the solid earth on the other bank, much pleased at having survived the ordeal. With no little pleasure you relish the spectacle of Galiael crossing, an illusion of Elven grace masking the reality of mortal fear. Patting him on the back with a wry grin, and with your pulse still racing, you quickly ascend through rocky outcrops to the plateau itself.

Turn to 441.

134

You fight a rearguard action as you back into the nape of an alleyway. The frustrated Ghouls tangle and squeeze against each other, furious at being denied immediate access to your sweet, tender flesh. With the singular combats more equal, you feel growing confidence that you may dispatch these slaves back to the pit.

If your Agility and Fortitude combined total 13 or less, turn to 219.
If they total 14 or more, your resolve swiftly crumbles, leaving you no option but to flee. Turn to 198.

135

You pass the Bravos manning the barricade to a cat-calls and insults. One mutters some prayers towards you, waving a shamans amulet. Rites for the dead. You turn to face the demons alone. One of the men places a hand on your arm, 'Don't be a fool!' he hisses, 'For it is suicide!' You shrug his hand off and glare hard at him, until he breaks his gaze, and muttering, he spits into the gutter. A respectful silence suddenly descends at you mount the barricade, and at the summit, you cast your eyes out at the sea of tormented dead separating you from the Master of the Pit. Under a portentous and fiery pre-dawn sky, you leap down into the square, and run headlong toward your destiny.

If you are Favoured, turn to 49.
If you are not Favoured, turn to 402.

136

You travel upstream, carefully following the river though the wooded vales. Sounds of crashing water falls into earshot, and glancing at Galiael he wordlessly confirms the same, with a barely noticeable nod of his proud head. The bubbling waters fall diverge from the trail as you approach the waterfall, which itself towers above a rocky cliff face. You grimace as you stare hard as the cascading waters, and Galiael spits in disgust. Contrary to laws of nature and science, the unclean hand is at work here. For the tumultuous waterfall is flowing up the cliff face! Its nature defying waters bubbling forth from a foaming lagoon at its foot. A ledge of smooth rock seems to wind its way behind the waterfall to the other side. A rickety and worn bridge spans the width of the lagoon. Its threadbare ropes frayed perilously thin, it swings in the light breeze, creaking uneasily. There appears to be no way forward but to cross the river at this point.

If you decide to ease your way behind the waterfall, turn to 471.
Alternatively, you could go back and follow the woodland trail, perhaps losing valuable time, turn to 224.
Should you choose to test the precarious looking bridge, turn to 32.

137

You wander through the endless dead, their bleached bones cracking underfoot, as you search through the battlefield canvas. The sun beats down mercilessly into the exposed valley, the lack of shade soon makes every step a punishing one. Your eyes burn with fatigue, dazzled by the glare blasting the valley floor. **Lose 1 point of Fortitude** due to exhausting aspect of your endeavours.

Booting a shattered skull with something approaching frustration, you are just about to abandon your search when you see a brilliant reflection poking through from the dry earth. You sweep away the dust, and with your knife carefully excavate a brilliant **Mirrored Shield** - its unblemished surface defies its apparent age.

Regarding its location, you notice with interest that not another skeleton lays within several yards of its former bearer, and just outside of that range a veritable mound of bones encircle it. **You may add this to your adventure sheet if you wish.**

You curse and spit, in a fashion, through your cracked lips, as your water skin yields its last drop. Not wishing to surrender to the heat and end your days amongst the dead of the valley floor, you seek shade in one of the hillside caves.

Turn to 101.

138

You push past the local thugs, who are busily engaging the terrified and frantic elves. Striving to reach the cart, you witness the other Stygians beginning to gouge the tree with axes and saws. Dizzied by these bizarre and sudden events you athletically attempt to jump aboard, to snuff the fizzing fuse-wire...

Add together your current Agility and Dexterity totals, adding 3 if you have the Gift of Acrobatics.

If the total is 15 or less, turn to 373.
If the total is 16 or more, turn to 73.

139

You thrust your blade into the sickly green carpet of the plain, and cock the silver arrow into the arcane Elven bow. Taking a moment, you shake your arm to rid it of the fearful tremors threatening to engulf you, as the enormous dragon bears down. You release the arrow which parts the air with supernatural force, thudding into the tattered flaps of skin on the beasts belly. Within the blink of an eye, an explosion within the Dragons ribcage sends electric blue bolts of energy fizzing through the clear air. The beast roars, and spiralling wildly, careers into the soft grass of the plain creating a huge furrow before you. Even so, the malicious forces binding the beast to this earthly plain spitefully conspire to empower it in one last murderous charge. Shaking sods of earth from its bleached bones, it lumbers toward you.

Turn to 185.

140

A crack rings out through the valley and the driver is engulfed in a cloud of white smoke. You hear a swooshing sound, followed by the thud of something hitting you square in the chest - you've been shot! Falling from your horse you bounce painfully along the bone dry track. **Lose 5 points of Fortitude** combined, from the shot and the fall.

'He shot me! you thunder, 'The weasel shot me!' Like an avenging demon Adz races his mount toward the cart. You hear the driver yelp in terror as the horse gallops across the hard earth, its rider holding aloft a huge battle-axe. Furious, Adz strikes, cleaving the driver in two - the bottom half of the unfortunate man left seated where he died - the head and torso falling into the grass with a wet slap. The coaches door swings open and a young man jumps out, shrieking at the sight of the bloody remnants of his driver. 'You killed him!' he wails incredulously.

Picking yourself up, you stagger wheezing to the scene. Adz stands over the man's bloody corpse like a hungry dog, clutching his great axe. 'How much did my father pay you to drag me back to his dreary villa?' the young man demands in quavering tones, 'did he pay you extra for murdering my driver?' Adz pulls a face and raises his furry eyebrow.

'You mistake me for a watchdog,' you counter without emotion, 'I am not here on your father's business, but to bring a message from your love, the Contessa.'

'Oh,' he says, and looks suddenly crestfallen, 'I...I abandoned hope of being reunited with her,' he says quietly, lips trembling. He breaks the seal and reads the note. Sighing and exhaling heavily as he pours over the words with deep concentration, before gently folding the delicate paper and tying the ribbon. He looks somewhat stunned, placing his hands on his head and puffing out his cheeks. He looks up sourly from his note. 'Will you kill me too?' he challenges angrily.

Curiosity overrides any need to apologise to the young man, and gnaws away at your sense of high adventure. You wrestle the notion of inquiring about the note's contents, stealing it even. But you resist the temptation to pursue it. Considering your mandate, and other numerous obligations, you turn without another word, and head back to the way marker to reunite with your guide.

Write TOGGIA on your adventure sheet, and turn to 37.

141

As you race for your weapon a cacophony of shrieks fills the temple, causing you to scream in an agonising duet. Frozen in a rigid state of terror, you can do nothing as the Wraiths continue to shriek into your face – each rushing in to emit their timeless and overpowering spite. Your last dying blink of memory is that of Galiael; pantaloons soiled, with rivers of tears staining his cheeks. So comedic is the sight that it almost cause you to la...

Your Adventure, and your life, is over.

142

'Get them back inside the city,' you mutter quietly to the guardsman, as you begin to pace backward toward the gates, never taking your eyes from the shambling figures emerging from the pitch-black countryside. 'Get back into the city!' you shout at the groups of refugees, as the figures come within umbrella of illumination from the gatehouse torches.

The dark and tattered figures are no returning citizens, but the shallow buried former victims of some recent atrocity. Their hands covered in filth and muck from the fields, these maggot-ridden fiends head directly for the knots of terrified citizens, gaping jaws open wide, groaning in unholy turmoil. You grab and shove as best you can, but like bewitched sheep, some of the refugees are simply unable to move; unable to comprehend the horrors with engulf them, until the blackened fingernails of the undead, puncture the soft pink flesh of their exposed limbs. As the gates are levered shut with a resounding thud, you lean against them with the wide-eyed soldier. The appalling screams from beyond eventually die down, until only pitiful groans remain.

Your comrade turns to you, chest heaving and green with fear, his mouth dripping with vomit. 'By the *Gods*,' he whispers into the night, 'What is to become of us?' He's clutching your arm. Whether by instinct or design, who knows.

'I know not what you will do on this long night, friend,' you reply, shaking your arm free of his grip, 'but I know where I must go.'

Pushing through the crowds, you head for the one place Adz and Professor may have headed for: The Diving Swallow.

Turn to 120.

143

Doubtfully, you turn to question the steward, when suddenly the child springs up and sinks its abhorrent fangs deep into your neck. The steward screams in terror, grabs the torch, and bounds back up the stairs, sliding the door back sealing the tomb. Plunged into total darkness you blunder towards the steps, stumbling over debris littering the crypt floor, whilst bellowing curses at the cowardly steward.

You feel the tear of agonising pain, as teeth rip through your wrists as veins are punctured. After minutes of desperate thrashing you slump to the cold earth, surrounding by echoes of childlike and taunting laughter. You slip painfully into unconsciousness, only to rise later that night as one of the living dead.

Your adventure ends here.

144

You cleave a swinging tentacle, sending it flying into the gelatinous mud with a satisfying smack. The Marshlights - animated with excitement - buzz all about you, distracting you with mischievous delight. A thick tentacle smashes down on your thigh, sending you toppling face down in the stinking mud. **Lose 2 points of Fortitude**. Another tentacle wraps around your ankle and you feel yourself pulled towards its gaping maw with irresistible force. Wriggling only serves to encourage the foul beast to tighten its grip. Your eyes close and you consider what End of Days may be like, before it shudders and relaxes. Looking up you see Adz smiling lustily, retrieving his mighty ax from the gibbering mound of dead blubber. Much abashed at your unimpressive performance, you offer your apologies as he looks on with contentment and good humour. **In the struggle you have lost your pistol, cross it off your adventure sheet. If you did not have a pistol, cross off a non-monetary item of your choice.** Eventually, you manage to remount the horses, and after a little while manage to decipher a course to your destination.

Turn to 264.

145

Overcoming the soul sapping negativity of the tomb, you cleave the ghoul into two equally disgusting parts. Near heaving from the foul odour it emits, you prop the torch up in a nearby coffin. It eerily casts your shadow up into the game portrayed on the tattered fresco of the tomb ceiling. Nervously, you grip a wooden stake in one hand, and your sword in the other, as you use your boot to flip the lid from the coffin. Sadness bites your soul once again, as the golden light illuminates the angelic features of small boy, aged not more than 4 or 5 years of age. A little colour remains on his porcelain cheeks, and blonde curls dance down his cheeks. With a heavy heart you pause, something about this doesn't feel right. Suddenly, the boy inhales and wakes, and with imploring eyes and a trembling lip, tearfully whispers, 'Please, don't hurt me!' Shaken and now trembling yourself, do you:

Question the steward - who has advanced into the doorway - if he is *really sure?* If so, turn to 143.
Thrust the stake into the child's breast without further consideration. If so, turn to 482.

146

You place a calming hand on Adz arm, reckoning these two door-keeps as formidable opponents.

If you have the Gift of Silver Tongued, turn to 480.
Otherwise, you can choose to ride to a high point, and wait to intercept his coach when he comes out. Turn to 206.
Or, head back to the way marker and reunite with Gallo, turn to 37.

Leaving the sunken pool behind, you cross the threshold into a massive chamber beyond, lit with dim eternal flame of unknown origin. A vast space of immense craftsmanship - its high vaulted roof is decorated with exquisite frescoes depicting scenes of ancient Elven citadels, towering peaks and heavenly constellations. Six huge pillars support the hall, each topped with a huge statue depicting one of the Gods of the Ancients. The expressionless titans support the weight of the cavern struts on their mighty shoulders. Names you recall from your studies of the Undying; Tanath, Sanromai, Illias... As you peer up through the gloom, their carved faces appear strained, their jaws twisted with effort, and their stone veins - thick as your arm - pumped full with the blood of their labours. Directly across the hall is another entrance, from which beams of coloured light blaze. As you step forwards you see that three lines of flagstones form between each of the three ranks of Gods, and these indented with carved Elven glyphs. The glyph adorned flagstones shine brightly, releasing the radiance from their mineral core.

Drawing on your modest appreciation of the ancient lores of the Undying Ones, you attempt to decipher them - with some haste, as the 'thub-thub' grows louder and ever more ominous...

You walk carefully forward toward the first line, separating the God of Dreams and the God of Wild Places. Almost inevitably, a booming voice rings out throughout the chamber in an ancient tongue. With your learned mind, you can just about make out the question asked,

'How many Gods serve in the Heavenly constellation?'

If you know the answer to this, turn to the section sharing the number. Otherwise, you have little choice but advance with caution into the room. Turn to 105.

Taking the silver from you, and pocketing the necklace, the Bosun ushers the children aboard. 'Step aboard, my little princes and princesses,' charms the bosun, with a deferential sweep of his arms. The gaggle of little ducklings eagerly descend the slippery green steps down to the overladen rowing boat, still holding hands tightly. Their bright faces turn to face you, wide innocent eyes burnished with childlike hope.

'Look Sire!' the little raven haired girl shouts at you with pride, 'We're all still holding hands...' Your spirits rise when the children are lead aboard, struggling with the crewmen to still clench hands.

'Thank you for your contribution to our wares noble, Sire!' The captain mocks from afar, leaning over the ships railings. 'You think 20 silver coins buys anything but a trip to the nearest slave market - it'll be chains that hold these children together, not their hands! Ha ha ha!' He bangs his fist on top the carved wood of the rail, with cruel incredulity, much mirthed with his own humour. He makes to disappear below, before turning back and shouts pointing at the eldest of the girls, 'Oh, except this one, she'll entertain us mightily on our voyage!'

You sink to your knees, his laughter biting at your soul, as you sob bitterly with contrition at your petty minded miserliness. What good have you of silver and gems in a land with no economy. In a land crawling with the dead - risen from their tombs? You feel the air pressure sink all around you, and your soul darkens with depression as an unseen hand seems to tug at your boots, tug at your cloak, slowing you down, and bringing lethargy to each step. You feel weaker, older, less able to struggle on this Earthly plane - with all its horrors and violence. **Reduce your Fortitude by 2, and – if possible - decease your FATE by 1 step,** as the Gods strike a score through your name in the Scrolls.

If you're still alive, you face no choice but to hurry to the Diving Swallow, and the hope of a chance to perform some heroic action, to save your souls. Turn to 120.

149

Sensing an opportunity you unsheathe your blade and flash it dangerously. With surprising speed the Captain levels his pistol at you, and the wolf hound springs up, baring its teeth with a snarl. As more crew members pile into the cabin, you are forcefully disarmed and led to the hold. Sat on a barrel, Hessler inspects and questions you about every one of your possessions, before handing them to the bosun, who deposits them into a large sack. You are still expecting to walk off the ship, alive but poorer, when your hopes are dashed. Led onto the deck by mocking crew members, you have barely any time to consider the swirling maelstrom surrounding you before you're heaved over board, to be consumed by the deep.

Your adventure, and your life, ends here.

Decrease your FATE level by 1 step, if possible.

Smiling warmly to disarm the figure stood at sword tip, you suddenly spring forward - quick as a serpent - and entirely pierce the throat of the elf before he has chance of even the merest squeak of protest. The reddened steel of your blade drips with foulest murder as Galiael lays dead in front of you - a spring of warm blood bubbling forth from the mortally inflicted wound.

Staring down at the lifeless figure, you numbly recollect distant memories of prior crimes; other victims of your brutality, far more deserving but no less calculating. Your only companion dead by your own hand. Alone on this soul wrecking and desolate plateau, you slump down sighing heavily with fatigue. Old injuries appear like unwelcome guests, bearing gifts of aches, pain, and sorrow. Now aware that the only realistic salvation of Deva likely opens a door to your own condemnation, you consider once again your fleeting existence. To answer the call of the sea, and run from this place - to start again; a familiar exit - animal like and cowardly, and one that guarantees uncertainty and promises nothing. Or to seize this Orb, and invoke the magic bound within it - reckless and almost certainly deadly, but the only chance to save the Professor, Adz, and quite possibly your eternal soul at the Table of Heroes. Under a baleful and unearthly sky you must make your decision, with dejection gnawing at your soul.

If you return to the Orb, with the intention of using it in salvation of Deva and your friends, turn to 355.
Should you decide to flee this place, and live to see adventures yet to come, turn to 371.

151

As you recount your past and present adventures to the Captain, he listens rapt, his glossy eyes twinkling in the candle light, only occasionally interjecting to request a detail of this or that.

'You were in Budazan... when they burned the city?' he asks with incredulity. 'I lit the fire,' you reply automatically, deadly, staring at an exposed and twisted nail in one of the barrels. A period of silence descends in the hold as you both struggle with the nightmares of the past.

It seems we have a lot in common...Siga. My days are being chalked off keenly by the Neverborn's agents, as they wait eagerly for my arrival. But how I envy you. If I was ten years younger...' The captain shakes his head, as if dismissing a foolish notion. 'No, no - my time is past...but, should you ever need a fast escape in a leaking old carrack, you'll know where to find me.' With that he offers his hand, and you toast your new found bond with a half flagon of best rum. 'Stay away from the other two passengers,' he suggests before he leaves, 'They look like trouble to me, but paid richly for their short passage.'

Whether you heed the captains words or not, you can now - **if you haven't done so already** - choose to:

Call on the awkwardly aloof young man, turn to 474.
Pay a visit the wild-eyed 'extremist, turn to 451.
If you've already done both of the above, or decide hole up in your cabin for the rest of the voyage, turn to 220.

152

As you falter, and struggle for an answer within your scrambled mind, the six Titans let out a bone-chilling sigh and relax their shoulders. With a cataclysmic crack, the supporting struts explode under the weight of the rock above, and you are consumed under a thunderous mountain of debris.

Beneath the gaze of the Undying Gods, you have failed to gain access to that which they imprison. Though dead, you are unwittingly a hero, sealing forever the Masters tomb from the pernicious and avaricious men-folk above.

Your adventure, and your life, ends here.

153

Avoiding even the pretence of stemming such a force of nature, you drop to your hands and knees and scamper across the chamber floor with furious vigour. Time and time again this creature, born of the hardest mineral, careers chaotically about the chamber, knocking you sideways. Seemingly without intention, however, as it spirals out of control -

oblivious to your presence. You crawl towards the stairwell protecting yourself the best you can.

Lose 1 point of Dexterity – as the gargantuan force crushes your outstretched digits. Wincing in pain, and sucking your mightily throbbing fingers, you finally make it to the stairwell leading downwards.

Turn to 438.

154

You approach a figure you mark out as the bosun of 'The Firefly', he's sweating profusely, with hair tied in greasy braids as he works feverishly alongside the toiling sailors.

'Friend!' you greet him, gripping his arm tightly so as to distract him from his labours. No time for niceties on a night such as this.

'What is this?' he replies angrily, attempting - though failing - to release his arm from your steel grip.

'Take these children,' you insist, 'They are orphans and have *no-one*, in this world to protect them. Would you leave them to perish?' With a great tug the bosun releases his arm from your grip and turns to his captain, for direction. The captain spits overboard and raises an eyebrow, a thin smile creeping out from beneath his beard. What will you offer by way of passage?

The High-Priestess's 20 silver coins - keeping the necklace for yourself. If so, turn to 64.
The High-Priestess's 20 silver coins, and the necklace. If so, turn to 148.
The High-Priestess's 20 silver coins, the necklace, plus whatever silver you are carrying. If so, turn to 328.

Make the necessary adjustments to your notes, before continuing.

155

Deciding not to dally, you stride forward out of the dark, unnoticed by the ethereal. With a savage cleave, you bring down your blade through its wispy form. A desperate deafening shriek fills the cavern as it rises up into the air above you. Spiralling and swooping, its stretched effigy of a face is a mask of torment. In agony, you slash your blade once through the trailing essences. The blow scores an electric blue mark through them, and illuminates the dark surroundings with brilliant sparks. The scream turns to a gasp of, relief? Of pleasure? Of deliverance from statis, and the dispatching of a tortured soul? Stillness once again reigns over the subterranean chambers. Only the constant and metronomic 'thub-thub' reverberates through the silence.

If you have the Gift of Hyper Senses, turn to 210.
If not, you depart down the passageway to the light source, and the steps leading down towards it, turn to 438.

156

You start to back away, whilst slowly drawing your weapon. In a flash the brilliant creature leaps toward you, blinding you as the lights dazzle and bounce from its glassy hide. You feel a searing pain as its razor sharp claws connect with your chest. **Lose 2 points of Fortitude.** As you tumble backwards onto the trail, the Crystalline Lion postures to pounce again.

If you have a pistol and wish to fire at the beast, turn to 50.
If you don't, or prefer to level your sword in readiness for its next attack, turn to 53.

157

You realise too late the man's murderous intentions, and though you try to pivot away from the blow, you feel a searing pain as the blade slices a deep gash into your shoulder.

Lose 1 point of Fortitude. Additionally, reduce your Dexterity by 1 unless prompted to restore it by a future paragraph.

Crying loudly in pain, you fumble to reach your dagger, pulling it from your jerkin and turning to face your foe. The amateurish **Assassin** looks flustered and anxious, isolated as the crowds part and the shouts ring out. Regardless, he seems determined you shall not see the day out…

If you are Iron Willed and/or your Dexterity is 7 or more, turn to 115.
If you are not Iron Willed and your Dexterity is 6 or less, turn to 80.

158

You arrive back at the Diving Swallow, Adz stows away the supplies the professor requested, and you both await his return from his studies. Sitting with Adz in the shady atrium, soothed by the pleasant avian chorus, and tongues sated by refreshing and powerful sherbets, you both soon sink into delicious snooze.

Adz shakes you roughly from your slumber, 'Siga, wake up, it's nightfall already - we've been asleep for hours!' Refreshed, you stretch your bones, restore **2 points of Fortitude,** and rub the sleep from your eyes. Talking to Evassa reveals that the Professor hasn't yet returned from the university, but that near the whole population of Deva is taking to the streets for the final celebration of the festival - the masked procession. Distant firecrackers explode to cheers in the distance, as the revelry begins. You hear exciting calls from the street outside, and peering through the blinds you can see streams of people, garishly dressed - some masked, some entirely garbed as troubadours, clowns, or wild beasts of the forest. Some carry drums which they bang enthusiastically, others have whistles or flaming torches, all seem animated with anticipation, and not a little merry on local brews. 'We're late for the party, Adz. Come, stop scratching your balls and lets us go and join in the...fun'.

Tonight is the final night of the festivities and the culmination of the Devan Festival. You may at this time have some clue of events to unfold, or an idea of where you may want to be.

If you have the word TREE written on your adventure sheet, turn to the reference noted.

If you don't have a reference to turn to, you have little option but to take to the streets and join the party, despite lingering thoughts about plot and intrigue. Shrugging your shoulders, you exit the Diving Swallow troubled and ill at ease. You understand that the final festival procession takes a route parallel to the city walls, and ends in the Grand Piazza in front of the Palazzo.

If you want to join the procession around the walls, turn to 298.
If you want to head directly to the Grand Piazza, turn to 173.

159

At the merest nod of your head, Adz smashes his meaty fist into the doorkeepers face with a sickening crunch, dropping the man to his knees. The **Half-Orc** blinks twice. Its slack jaw opens and closes in a moment of dull realisation, before he grabs an iron studded club. The creature bellows a battle cry and lumbers towards you. Adz' opponent has surprisingly clenched him around the knees, and is cursing the big Norsiczan through the stumps of his broken teeth. He takes the two of them tumbling down the steps onto the baked earth below. You're barely able to draw your sword, before the bastard-spawn swings his club with malicious intent.

If the total of your Dexterity and Agility is 13 or less, turn to 347.
If the total of your Dexterity and Agility is 14 or more, turn to 265.

You usher Pepin to stand behind you as you draw your sword. Rain drips down the blade, as you take a position in the centre of the alley way, steeling yourself to meet the approaching strangers. A few seconds later a group of **Stygian Footpads** hastily turn the corner - you instantly assess the situation.

'They've seen us now,' one spits to the other in a harsh whisper.

'They'll have to die,' says another – the old man you knocked over at the gate!

The heavens open, and raindrops smash like grapeshot against the cobbles as the three crow-like figures advance with wicked intent.

If you have a pistol and wish to use it, turn to 108.

If not, and the total of your Dexterity and Fortitude exceeds 15, turn to 299.

If not, and the total of your Dexterity and Fortitude is 14 or less, turn to 216.

Troubled, you confide in Adz your gravest fears. 'Well, it certainly seems this Elven tree is at the centre of several plots - for whatever reason.' His eyes twinkle with excitement.

'Let's strap on our gear and disguise ourselves for a stakeout! There will be so many fantastical outfits out on the streets tonight for this masked procession, that no one will give us a second glance. Maybe Evassa has something we can wear...?'

Some minute later and you're inspecting each other in fits of laughter. Adz is covered in an old bearskin, sewed together so it fits him like a gown, and dons a ursine mask, its mouth stretched in a comical smile.

'What a sight!' you exclaim clapping the big oaf on the shoulders, 'Where are your cubs, mother bear?'

'You can talk,' he retorts, 'You look like a Desert King's Mother-in-Law!' He has a point. You consider your own outfit, mimicking a long dead desert lord, complete with flowing robes and a skeletal mask that fits disconcertingly well to the contours of your face.

Together you head back out into the thronged streets, following the procession as it passes though the city until it travels through an area near the Piazza Arborea. On the intersection of the Elven and Merchant quarters, you break off and consider the positions for your covert surveillance. The square seems empty, except for the beggar sound asleep on one of the two benches at the neck of the square. A light flickers from a three story tower within the walls of the Elven compound overlooking the square, and you notice the shadow of figure periodically casting a glance out. The walls below are a combat of rude graffiti and fresh whitewash.

There is a tiny colonnade to the east of the square, were lemon sellers set up during the day, now cloaked in shadow. Three merchant carts are tied up for the night near the centre of the square, one of which is covered - a few spans away from the tree. You hear voices and footfall from behind you, as others approach the square...

If you want to wait where you are - in the entrance to the square, turn to 337.
If you want to take cover under the shadowy colonnade, turn to 470.
If you want to dart behind the wagons, turn to 293.
If you want to settle down on the other bench and affect the role of sleeping revellers, turn to 339.

162

It takes you more than an hour to locate the House of Toggia. Fed up of Adz' constant complaints of the heat, of the din, and of the crush, you are eventually directed to an impressive private residence, in a tranquil corner of the metropolis. Soaking in sweat and with your dry tongue stuck to the roof of your thirsty mouth, you thump, irritated, on the bold vermilion door. At first there is no answer - a delay Adz meets with a heavy sigh. You turn to snap with exasperation at the great steaming figure, when you faintly hear soft slippers padding toward the door on the other side.

'Yes. Who are you?' demands a manservant opening the door and immediately narrowing it in suspicious disdain. Adz' hefty boot is already planted in the door frame before you speak, sparking flickers of panic in the doughy serf's eyes.

'Where is your lord, best of men?' you inquire cordially, sweating heavily, 'We have a message which requires his attention.' The man coughs nervously, never taking his eyes from Adz' thick leather boots, before replying in wavering tones.

'I will deliver the message upon his return...if you would be so kind.' A wide smile spreads across your face, disarming the fearful servant and causing him to smile thinly in return.

'Oh yes,' you say matter-a-factly, 'we will be so kind...as to break your fingers slowly!' With speed belying his hulking frame Adz grabs the man's digits and squeezes tightly. The servant emits a porcine squeal, filled with shock and pain as you press your callused palm over his mouth and whisper harshly, 'Where is he? Do not dally with your reply as this hot sun bothers us so!' The man's chest heaves with relief as you pull away your hand, and affects a theatrical splutter,

'At Heaven's Gates!' You look quizzically at Adz who merely shrugs. Taking your knife and showing the man the grey-blue steel expedites the completion of his answer, 'The pleasure houses at the six league marker... on the coastal road to the north...'

'You've done well, friend,' commends Adz, patting the flinching man on the cheek. 'Come on, Siga,' he says eagerly, 'Let's go and acquire some mounts from Hessler.'

If you have LUDOVICO written on your adventure sheet, turn to 223.
If not, turn to 362.

If you have LUDOVICO written on your adventure sheet, turn to 223.
If not, turn to 362.

163

Tethering the horses, you creep through the bracken around the base of the tower. Sickly yellow lichen clings to the black granite, seemingly binding the leaning tower to the earth. As you circle down to the shore to reach the stone steps, you peer out over the featureless tidal flats - the low tide is somewhere leagues out to sea, hidden by the dismal mist. With some effort you trudge through the stinking mud and reach the steps leading to a seaward entrance. Adz nudges you encouragingly and you clamber up to investigate, and are somewhat surprised to find a wide door ajar and creaking in the breeze. Creeping inside the circular tower, you enter into a stinking long abandoned larder, rotten food adorns the shelves, and insects buzz around a gleaming white marine skeleton laid out on the wet tiled floor. You glance though to the main chamber, and see stairs leading upwards.

'Is that...a seal carcass?' asks Adz, doubtfully pointing at the remains. You're just about to answer, when you hear a low watery gurgle from behind you...as an estuarine **MARSH TROLL** rises up from its muddy kingdom!

If you want to jump down, and dispatch the beast before it can fully emerge, turn to 63.
If you would rather tackle it from the solid foundations of the tower steps, turn to 364.
If you choose to flee toward the inner staircase, turn to 386.

164

You clamber up the scrub choked slope and hail Captain Hessler, who responds agreeably. After exchanging pleasantries, you inquire about his thoughts on the drills.

'I'm not here to drink in this fine show of folly, for I've seen enough armies of dead men marching. As have you I dare say?' He fixes cold, steely gray eyes on you, whilst he seems to ponder a release of information. His face softens, and his lips crease into a narrow smile. He turns and points far out to the empty horizon, and swings the looking glass in its pivot toward your grip. 'I'm here to get a better look at *them*,' he says, guiding the lens for you as you stoop to peer through it. Twinkling on the shimmering horizon, you can make out the diagonal silver sails of a squadron of three Elven Warships. 'Bad for business. Well, bad for my businesses anyway...' Hessler mumbles ruefully. 'As for these lot,' he spits with disdain, 'they're as interesting to me as their 50,000 long dead comrades over in the yonder Belisarian Valley, and will surely end up the same at some point. That's the soldier's life, eh? High odds of a violent end. A fool's path.' His dog looks up at you quizzically through his spectacles, causing you to avert its gaze. 'Ruined his eyes,' says the captain, reading your mind. 'From reading too much romantic poetry. The damn fool.' The Captain seems to notice someone in the crowd and excuses himself, citing some unsealed dealings to be addressed. He bids you a cordial farewell, and shakes you by the hand, leaving you none the wiser about the strange beast.

If you have a Dragonfire Gem on your adventure sheet, turn to 280.
If not, you set off back to the city, turn to 18.

165

Isolated and alone in this foreign city, you hold your arms outstretched and drop to your knees, hoping for a chance to explain the situation. You are summarily arrested, maintaining your innocence all the while. Disregarding your protestations, one of the Watchdogs manacles you with careless violence, and presses your face into the dust as you feel your possessions torn away from you. **Have you killed anyone from The Watch the beginning of your adventure?**

If you have, turn to 127.
If you haven't, turn to 473.

166

You approach the entrance to the shuttered tavern, down a narrow alley way. Locating the doorway, you knock three times on the door, which creaks narrowly open, spilling orange light onto the darkening cobbles.

'A noble cause...?' asks a voice from within.

'A Brotherhood of Man,' you reply. The door opens fully and the burly looking doorkeep stands aside with a nod of greeting. You descend the stairwell into the packed hall, which has been cleared of all furniture, piled up to the rear against shuttered windows. There is a convivial atmosphere, the boisterous crowd uniform in its views, and emboldened by close proximity of fellow malcontents. You chortle conspiratorially as someone tells a bawdy joke about why elves ears are pointed so.

Listening as the speakers froth and bluster, it's apparent these people hold a personal grievance. A perceived slight, a trade account lost, an opportunity spurned - and attach all blame to the Elven quarter. As the unadulterated wine flows the atmosphere darkens, as the leading demagogues whip the crowd up. You step into the shadows as the extremist from 'The Boogenhofen' takes to the stage and launches into an over-exaggerated account of Elven influence in The Middenlands. The crowd shake their heads furiously at the legion injustices being ignored by the authorities, and some shout out threats, 'Kill that stuck up Aegnor...who does he think he is making demands!' 'Burn down their warehouses...I have a torch and I am ready!' 'Chop down that bloody precious tree of theirs...'

The threats are abruptly interrupted by a loud bang at the entrance, and shouts from outside, 'The Duce has escaped death by assassination! Martial law is declared. No unofficial gatherings after dark!'

'Militia...someone has betrayed us!' the speaker cries, as the crowd stampedes towards the shuttered windows. Not wishing to be caught in this compromising situation you join the fray as they push and shove to clamber out of the windows. Several city militiamen have taken up positions in the street and grab at stragglers, pummelling them to the floor with heavy cudgels. Write **BROTHERHOOD** on your adventure sheet.

Batting people aside, you try to evade the clutches of the watch. **Combine your current Fortitude and Agility totals, add 2 for each of the Gifts of Stealth and Acrobatics which you have.**

If the total is 14 or less, you are captured, turn to 91.
If the result is 15 or more, turn to 46.

167

You join the terrified citizens in scrambling from the area, forcing your way through, and over, the smaller and weaker unfortunates, crushed to death beneath the stampede. It's a melee of elbows, knees, and fists as the rabble flee for their lives. **Lose 1 point of Fortitude** in the violent crush, from the many sprains and gouges you acquire.

You eventually squeeze up one of the many conduit lanes leading from the piazza, and slump to your knees with some other cowards, gasping for breath in a doorway.

Turn to 186.

168

Together with Adz, you strip the corpse, finding nothing of interest, save some Stygian tattoos which mean nothing to you. Searching the warehouse also yields no further clues to this cults plans. Adz mutters with disappointment, resigning himself to the mundanities of collecting supplies for the Professor's imminent trip to the hills.

If you have Intuition or Skullduggery, turn to 29.
If not, you clap Adz on the back and accompany him to the market, turn to 205.

169

You collide into the far wall and feverishly pad the walls for the exit as the world tumbles down around you. Choking on dust and blinded by the same, you cry bitter tears of frustration as your search reveals nought but stone after solid stone, with no aperture of safety found. Desperate, as the dull pain of thudding stonework numbs you, you prepare to embrace the now inevitable End of Days. And then...a gap! Your hand brushes through the empty air and not a entombing rock-face! With scarce time to think, you throw yourself headlong though the portal, as the lintel collapses behind you, sealing the void with a mountain of solid rock.

The once flooded passage way you crossed now shudders with tremors, and has sunken markedly. A quick glance reveals a slimy residue of moss, and a couple of foetid puddles are all that remain of the pool, now drained by the shifting earth. From the gallery of tapestries from which you came, torches still appear to burn brightly. You can hear ancient ethereal voices beckoning you inside, but the dust filling the air obscures your vision. As another giant tremor knocks you off balance and causes you to leap from a deep chasm formed scarce two paces away from you, you must urgently decide on your escape route.

If you want to follow the now drained passage way, turn to 461.
Should you choose to retrace your steps, through the gallery, turn to 287.

'My humble pardons, master,' apologises the Daaban, 'I mistook you for a common man - I bid you enter.' He flashes a smile at you, and with an extravagant sweep of his arm he pulls back the curtain. You step inside, out of the burning sun, and into the cool interior of the tent. Multicoloured flames flicker from ornate candelabras, the pyrites and sulphides fizzing and melding in the thick air with the pungent spiced perfumes on offer. The tent is so full of merchandise it's difficult to register where one section begins and another ends, rich but trivial treasures from every corner of the world adorn trellising hung from the supporting structure of the tent.

A small, but incredibly fat figure, regards you keenly from a plump purple velvet upholstered sofa. A wide golden-toothed smile adorns his welcoming face, under an enormous gilded turban.

'Ask me whatever you may wish, brother,' he coos in honeyed tones, 'I am but your humble servant.' You look at the goods in disdain, your nose turned and scowl plastered across your face.

'Pftt,' you snort, 'Trinkets. Trinkets for caged birds in gilded cages,' you scoff as you gently toss them aside. The merchants smile becomes thin.

'I see, man of the Nhort. Well, let us then dispense with pleasantries.' With this the man reaches underneath the counter and pulls out a finely woven sheet, which he unfurls on the counter top, revealing several items.

'These are objects are only for connoisseurs such as yourself. Pay heed to my words, for they are the truth, under the all hearing Gods.' You glance down at the objects on display, and listen as the merchant describes them.

Wooden Pygmy Totem - "A lucky talisman, ensorcelled by cheerful spirits" - 15 silver scuda.
Dragonfire Gem - "Mined deep within a Dragon's lair, the bearer feels not the burning lick of flame" – 18 silver scuda.
Lozenge of Tongues - "From gobbledegook to reason, for the seasoned traveller" - 12 silver scuda.
Calcified Horn - "Said to sweep evil birds from the skies" - 20 silver scuda.
A small mechanical Owl - "Carries the celestial seed" – 25 silver scuda.

You may purchase anything you wish to buy. **If you the Gift of Silver Tongued, reduce the above prices by 3 silver scuda each. Make a note of this on your adventure sheet,** and decide your next action.

To head to the Stygian Fayre turn to 226.
To head to the Festival of Wine and Song, turn to 363.
Or, **if you've already done all these things**, or would rather just head back to your lodgings and rest. **Turn to** 361.

171

All it takes for you is a deft side step and a strike of deliverance, to send the former guardian to End of Days. Rinsing the gore from your blade in the cool mountain-born waters of the aquifer, you hurl the to the rocks below, and look on impassively as it bursts like a tossed watermelon upon them. With little difficulty, you're able to squeeze past the broken grills and enter into the city. Any other protectors of these irrigating tunnels are long since fled, or dead - or worse.

You navigate a course further into the heart of the city. The shrieks and howls echo through the tubes, setting your teeth on edge, as nerves threaten to get the better of you. Through tiny apertures, you occasionally peer down into the streets below. Feasting ghouls stalk the blood splattered cobbles, running down those foolish enough to expose themselves alone. You wince helplessly as you witness dozens of innocents fleeing in useless terror, only to be caught, and torn asunder. You look on in horror as the pipeline runs parallel to the main square, and there, holding ghastly court, the abominable figure of The Master sits, resplendent of his perverse throne of skulls. Shuddering, you move on to seek out an exit point and presently the tunnel terminates, reaching the central pump-house, some three hundred paces from the square.

The fragment of the comet burns brightly within the confines of the bag it's stored in. Orange light creeps though the worn stitching, and the blackened bag is hot to the touch.

If you want to head directly toward the square, even though the streets are still dark, turn to 254.
Or if you choose to wait in the abandoned pump-house until sunrise, before venturing into the open, turn to 472.

172

Screeches and cries ring out through the dark night skies, melding with the whinnies of your mount, and your own hoarse roars. The battle rages across leagues of countryside, and far away from the Cemetery. You feel a curious sense of exhilaration as you hack and slice at the ragged puppets, whilst clinging tightly to Pegasus' mane. The carrion animations offer little threat, and eventually you are able to dismember them, and send a tumble of bone, talons and feathers scattering to the fields and olive groves far below. **Lose 1 point of Fortitude as your arms throb with fatigue.**

Turn to 248.

You fight your way upstream against the masked revellers touring the city walls and head for the Grand Piazza. Drunken dandies and anonymous whores abound. Their poxes and disfigurements thinly disguised under the all-seeing nights moon. Lit from torches adorning all four of the grand colonnades lining the square, you see harassed looking slaves making final preparations for The Duce's speech. They move in frantic human chains, swilling down the vomit caked flagstones and brushing filth into the heaving gutters.

'I wonder what the fat man has to say tonight?' Adz muses, rubbing his chin with a calloused palm. You can only wonder. Since an assassination attempt on his life yesterday evening, and the ensuing mayhem which pitted man versus elf, the Eternal Ones have been expelled to their ships and forced to lay anchor in the open seas outside the harbour walls. The main bulk of the city's populace; the ignorant and the reactionary, have welcomed this populist news with dull witted elation, and a ridiculous sense of victory and archetypal pettiness. Older, wiser, heads have silently expressed grave concern. The immolation of an eons old relationship to play to the fickle tune of the mob. As the square fills up, you take note of the very heavy presence of Militia, and representatives of all the Mercenary Companies, who, no doubt, are eager to reposition themselves in the new Devan order. A large stage has been erected in front of the Palace to the south of the square and the thronged masses push and shove as the Duce, limping and flanked by armoured knights, exits the Palace to trumpet blasts and deafening cheers from the intoxicated crowds.

You grit your teeth, and listen to the shameful charade as it unfurls, elbowing and cuffing anyone who steps within your personal space with disproportional violence.

The grossly fat leader of the council of fifty waddles across the gilded stage. He hands a lackey a sweat soaked rag, shooing of the manservant with a dismissive flick of the wrist. After a preamble, saluting the populace and assembled dignitaries, it's not long before he gives the crowds what they want...

'From what do they now protect us? It is not from our enemies, of that we can be sure. For did they not sit mute in the shadows as we fought against Bractia and the City-states of Lyrr? What did they say to us in our times of struggle? Yes, they said, 'We cannot intervene'. We cannot intervene! Your house is set ablaze during a drought, you struggle to quench the flames, whilst your neighbour sits on his well, bucket in hand and says, 'I cannot intervene!' The Duce wipes a bead of sweat from his brow and licks his lips greedily as the crowds boo loudly, as if at a carnival show. The puppeteer continues, 'We have graciously allowed them to trade freely in this fair port of ours, for generations, collecting not one silver scuda in the process, for they have cited long forgotten treaties absolving them from contributing - in their role as protectors! Their swollen treasury speaks weasel words of false friendship…do you know what it says my friends..?' The whipped up crowd gleefully shouts out, 'I cannot intervene!' and cheers heartily, full of drink and menace. Adz tugs on your sleeve to leave, sensing as you do, a riot. As you turn to leave, a Stygian driven cart hurtles from a side lane, into the square and headed straight into the crowds. Screams once again ring out across Deva, and with a dull crack the cart hits one of the stone-hewed lions guarding the fountain and splits in two. The cries of surprise escalate into screams of horror as four **Hobgoblins** escape from between the bent bars of their now splintered cage. The crowd stampedes, and the shouts and whistles of Militia and Mercenary Captains to ring out across the city. Adz pulls you away and the pair of you beat a hasty exit from the square, batting any terrified revellers foolish enough to cross your path to the cobbles. Catching a look over your shoulder you see the frenzied Hobgoblins rending and tearing at the defenceless meat on offer. Like demons, they spit their plague tainted bile at the armoured forces now flooding into the square from all quarters of the city.

'What the seven hells, Siga!' Adz exclaims as you take cover, catching your breath behind an upturned vegetable cart. Suddenly, a huge explosion rips through the hot night sky and large plume of grey smoke - and blue petals - rises into the orange sky from the direction of the Elven Quarter. You look down at your hand, clasped tightly on the pommel of your sword, and your white knuckles represent exactly the feeling in the pit of your stomach.

If you want to head across town toward the sound of the explosion, turn to 250.
Or if you want to stay in the main square and assist in dealing with the Hobgoblins, turn to 114.

174

With primal fury, the creatures snapping jaws angle into your neck, and only a blocking arm prevents contact. You yell angrily as its teeth sink into your arm. **Deduct 1 point of Fortitude.** You clench the hellhound's rank fur, and with your foot in its groin, you flip the beast headlong down the stairs. 'I said heel, you mutt!' you scream at the slavering canine, with your weapon held aloft, poised for the kill.

Turn to 296.

175

As your final shot thuds home, cheers ring out and people huzzah at your triumph. A crowd of well-wishers surrounds you, which the self-important little organiser squeezes his way through, and thrusts the prize - an arcane Elven **Silver Bow -** into your hands and motions you to hold it aloft in triumph. People rush to congratulate you, and you can't help but enjoy the eulogies about your stellar performance. The voices die down and your new found friends take a half-step back as Galiael the elf approaches you. 'A truly marvellous display of skill my friend, I am honoured to have competed alongside you,' he says magnanimously, lightly touching your shoulder. 'I must confess that I was sure I would regain that which was lost to us. For this bow is truly not Deva's gift to bestow. It is rather a relic of my forefathers, who formed these lands and enlightened the human-kin. The light guiding them from barbary. Though you triumphed, friend, a greater deed would be to return that which was lost from us, but is now found.' Galiael pale silver blue eyes penetrate your own, and smiling he reaches out for the Silver Bow. 'It is better for all of you that this is returned to the Elves,' he reassures you gently.

If you give him the bow, turn to 412.
If you decline to hand it over and send him on his way, turn to 274.

176

As agile as fighting dogs, and just as vicious, the ghouls dart between your blows, thrashing at you with savage swipes of their claws. You land a series of strikes, sending the victims rolling back across the cobbles each time. Despairingly, with each strike the others quickly fill the void, leaping about you with fiendish skill. One manages to tear a bloody furrow across your shoulder, causing you to yell in torment - **Lose 1 point of Fortitude.** They dance so, that you feel yourself being encircled and not a little disoriented.

If you want to fight a retreat into a narrow adjoining alleyway, turn to 134,
Or if you have a change – or a loss – of heart, and decide to flee, turn to 219.

177

Keeping out of range, you evade the Champions thrusts and lurching grabs at you. You allow yourself a satisfied smile as you see Rollo - not a young man - begin to pant, and wipe the stinging sweat from his eyes. Using fancy footwork and deceptive feints you toy with the big man. But the restless crowd begins to boo - enamored of your delaying tactics. Debris begins to reign down into the ring as catcalls threaten to descend into irritated hooliganism.

If you have the Gift of Acrobatics, and/or your Agility is 8 or above, turn to 8.
If not, turn to 344.

178

You quickly survey the area, scanning the tiled rooftops. All you can see in the gloom are outlines of chimneys, of awnings and rooftop vines. Wiping the drizzle from your eyes you curse your luck when the hairs on the back of your neck stand up. You hear a ssshhhHUNK! - As a throwing star hits you in the shoulder, sending you toppling from the rooftop. **Deduct 2 Fortitude Points.** You smack onto the cobbles, followed swiftly by a terracotta pot which smashes beside you. Dogs bark, a baby cries, and you see torches being lit behind the leather window coverings of several houses. You bite into your sword strap as you quickly dig out the morning star with your dagger, and wrap it in some cloth. You consider your good fortune it didn't kill you, and mumble a quick litany before you depart into the night – to follow the crackling blue flames over Artur Keijzer's house. Pepin soon joins up with you, white as a sheet, and clearly rattled by the night's events. Tousling the boys hair, you set a course through the dark city streets.

Turn to 464.

179

Turning on your heels you rapidly depart the tent. As you emerge with haste from one of the canvas flaps, you nearly collide with a shifty looking group of four Stygians. You mumble your apologies and set to make off from the fayre, in a half run, when you quickly realise you've seen this group of men before. When you first arrived - the men accompanying the hooded stranger! No sooner can you turn round, than the animal master steps out of the tent and exchanges a wordless greeting to the others.

'Be gone, fool. Do not linger here if you value your life!' the animal master threatens, pointing towards the city-proper. All five men turn to glare at you, and the long shadows of the morning reach out towards you. It's clearly time to leave the scruffy wasteland of the city gardens, and so you make for the relative safety of urban Deva. As you trudge through the long grass, the sun beats down relentlessly, but an uncommon chill creeps over your skin.

Shivering a little despite the blistering heat, you head back to your lodgings, turn to 361.

180

She utters a thousand kind words and embraces you passionately, intoxicating you with her scent, starved as you are of such wholesome treats aboard this stinking vessel. Concealing it on your person you notice a shaggy form enter the cabin, as the wolfhound pads back into the room.

'How did it...open the door?' you have just enough to wonder, before Captain Hessler, the bosun, and several other crew members enter the cabin. Surveying the scene, the Captain snorts with dissatisfaction, glaring at the young woman, who scowls in return. 'You and I had better have a little chat,' he murmurs to you, not taking his eyes off his prize. **Write the codeword VELVET on your adventure sheet**

If you accede to go with him, turn to 87.
If you'd rather take your chances in the confined environment and attack now, turn to 149.

181

The spectators heave a large sigh as you lose your tie - being something of an underdog, you had become a crowd favourite. After exchanging a few pleasantries with the other competitors you drift away from the archery colonnade as night draws in. Somewhat rueful about your defeat, you traipse back to the city centre. Glancing at the festival pamphlet, the final act of the evening is the retelling of Elven Sagas in the amphitheatre.

If you wish to try to gain entrance, turn to 372.
If not, you may head to the Diving Swallow for some well-earned rest, turn to 243.

182

Calculating the Elven tree is central to the nefarious plans of the Stygians, you charge through the city streets, clattering into the Piazza Arborea in the nick of time. Grey hooded acolytes are swarming from an open sewer grill, and pouring over toward a cart. They rip back its tarpaulin revealing several large barrels. The same number head directly for the tree, carrying a huge wobbling timber saw and giant lumber axes. With a huge heave, the cart begins to creak forward on the dusty cobbles towards the tree. Just as Adz opens his mouth in dumbfounded wonder, the door to the Elven tower adjacent to the square crashes open, and the two remaining Elven Sentinels burst out with frantic urgency. One cries out in what you perceive to be near terror, whilst the other hastily lets fly an arrow, sinking it deep into one of the Stygians carrying the band-saw.

You tug hard on the reigns and bring your mount to a rearing halt. With heart pounding at the chaos, you see; a spark ignite as the laden cart trundles towards the tree; desperate Elven guards screaming and hurtling toward the same. A half dead Stygian, an arrow embedded in his chest, struggling to his feet with supernatural determination; dumbfounded Devans standing uselessly with clubs and knives - one of them dropping a pot of red paint. On the periphery - a clatter of arms as the Militia approach the entrance to the square; and finally, Adz - stood slack-jawed with his massive battleaxe weeping crimson, looking at you for further direction.

If you rush to stop the Elves reaching the tree, turn to 126.
If you want to tackle the Devan locals, turn to 74.
If you decide to leap aboard the cart and attempt to put out the sizzling fuse, turn to 138.
If you want to tackle the Stygian carrying the timber saw, turn to 390.
If you decide it'd be better to take off before the Militia arrive, turn to 197.

183

The two of you rush back to the location of the orb. Galaiel fixes his gaze upon the black sphere, and begins to recant the enchanted words. His sharp eyes become glassy and unfocused as his lips move rapidly, uttering the lines with the speed and accuracy of someone born for this very purpose. The elf's body seems at times to float, and at others be dragged from side to side by some unseen hand. All the while he remains impassionate, as if in a trance.

Your disbelieving eyes widen with a cocktail of terror and wonderment as blue sparks crackle forth from his fingertips, and as he completes the words, blinding light shoots from them and soars into the black sky above, exploding in a blinding blanket of brilliant white light. You recoil onto the sodden wet carpet of the plateau, blasted by the winds of magic. With trepidation, you open your eyes and glance expectantly at the Orb. Its oily black lustre replaced with soft illumination as it glows warmly. Looking skyward you see a brilliant second sun cast upon the sky, and the pulsing light of the comet's progenitor – the fragments searching parent.

Wordlessly, Galiael steps forward, and with great care takes the Orb in his delicate palms. Much to your surprise the graceful elf offers it to you, nodding in affirmation, his silver eyes betraying no known emotion. You reach out and take it, nervously. It produces a satisfying buzzing sensation and you linger on it for some moments, before wrapping it carefully and seal it carefully in your pack. Smiling with renewed comradeship and confidence, you make to depart the plain back in the direction of the crystalline forest and of Deva. Suddenly, a large shadow sails over you at speed. You're heart fairly sinks when it's followed by an ominously huge roar. Exhaling with resignation you turn and look skyward. 'What now!' you shout pointlessly, to no one in particular. Cursing darkly, you see a bleached white **Bone Dragon** diving toward you, its ancient leathery wings flapping like torn sails in the wind.

If you possess the Silver Bow, turn to 139.
If you don't, but possess a Dragonfire Gem, turn to 421.
If you have neither of the above, and you decide to make for the near tree line, turn to 3.
If you stand your ground, preparing to do battle with this timeless foe, turn to 369.

184

Bruno growls, and goes in for a bear hug, which you duck under, counter-punching him in the kidneys. The bruiser exhales like a deflated bladder and sinks to his knees, wincing in pain. You make to knee him in the face, but he blocks your strike with his forearms and grips your leg tightly, only releasing it when you ram your boot into his chops. A small crowd forms, attracted and delighted by the spectacle by two drunks brawling. As you sink your teeth into Bruno's thigh, you make out someone shouting, 'The Watch, the Watch!' You frown, as you hear the oncoming clatter of boots and armour.

If you want to carry on with the fight, and teach these fops and their ape a lesson, turn to 419.
If you decide to flee the area, before the Watch turn up to complicate the situation, turn to 67.

185

Under a leaden sky you do battle with the thunderous creature, as it twists and stomps, chasing you like a cat chases a mouse. Its ungainly might is in stark contrast to your nimble evasion, as you strive to stay alive long enough to better the beast. You strike, time after time, trying to find a weak point, and as you do, you feel the burn of fatigue as the sodden earth extracts a toll on your energies. The injured **Bone Dragon** emits a roar of frustration, rears up onto its hind legs and throws its terrible head up to the heavens. For split second you glimpse its exposed and loosely connected thorax. Can you land the killing blow? **Add together the totals of your Dexterity and Agility, and add 3 to the total for each of the Gifts of Acrobatics and Martial Prowess.**

If the total is 15 or more, turn to 323.
If the total is 14 or less, turn to 403.

186

It's nightfall when the crowds begin to disperse. A few half-hearted cheers ring out as you hear a distant and sustained volley of arquebuses, eventually taking the beast down. Citizens begin to slope off to their homes in nervous relief. Feeling slightly abashed - you also decide to make tracks back to your lodgings at the Diving Swallow.

Only wastrels and ne'er-do-wells walk the streets at night - so is the opinion of the Watchdogs, who patrol these streets with unfettered violence. These bullies seem to be everywhere, and you can feel the palpable oppression in the night air.
Take a 'Watch Patrol' test.

If the total is 2 or more, turn to 327.
If it's 1 or less, turn to 243.

187

You attempt to drag Pepin behind a nearby doorway drape, but the boy panics and wriggles, leading out high-pitched squeal just as the footfall passes you. In the blink of the eye the drape is ripped from its fixings leaving you exposed. Three mean looking **Stygian Footpads** loom over you, menacingly.

'They've seen us now,' one says in a dead voice,

'They'll have to die,' says another - the old man you knocked over at the gate! – He spits the words from underneath a hooded cape, over the cannonade of rainfall on the cobbles. Pushing Pepin aside, you steel yourself for their attack.

If you have a pistol and wish to use it, turn to 108.
If not, and the total of your Dexterity and Fortitude exceeds 16, turn to 299.
If not, the total of your Dexterity and Fortitude is 16 or less, turn to 216.

188

Bellowing an oath to the Gods soon met, you race across the timeless flagstones toward the wobbling sickly pink sac of pus. Enraged by the total evil facing you, threatening you, threatening all you care for, your screams shatter the very air you burst through. Strangely invigorated by the terror in your soul, you leap with all your might, blade raised high aloft, towards the pulsing womb. Brilliant white light blinds you as you soar through the air. You may as well be an eagle in the sky, for all time seems to freeze.

Across the eternal sea an unseen hand scores the last words into your scroll.

Flashes of memory movements, images of lives lived, and love ones lost. Sun-cracked and shackled to an oar. Screaming in smoke filled battlefield agony, chest wracked with sobs and waste deep in Friesburg mud, pleading to your mother joining the legion others, 'Mama! Mama save me! A father dead. Swinging like a wax mannequin from the noose.

Dimly aware as though as in a dream, your blade slices through the butterfly-wing thin membrane effortlessly as you rise up into cotton clouds. Whatever was, has fallen, distantly screaming, and continues to fall for all time down the never-ending pit. For you, a mothers smile never seen, but a voice heard and gentle, a tender and reassuring caress felt. A melodic and lilting hum, soothing you as you sleep. 'Settle down little one, always kicking, so full of life!' Love felt from a life as yet unborn. Love requited, love to be felt again. The proud tousling of wayward hair, 'My beautiful boy, Siga, what a handsome boy you are!'

Your adventure ends here. The story, about to begin again.

189

Tiring of the beating you, the burly guards deposit you back into your hole. An indeterminate amount of time passes, as you sit bored and bleeding in this cell. Days seem to pass, until you're awoken by distant screams - obviously at the hands of the brutal jailers. At last the hinges creak open on your cell door. You rise to your knees about to launch a tirade at your jailers, when you think something looks odd about the stooped and panting shape in the doorway. Stiff and blinded you're unable to defend yourself against the undead horror, born of the horror assailing the city, as it leaps onto you and rips your throat out before devouring your corpse.

Your adventure ends here.

190

You reach out for a rescuing hand, and grip that of your benefactor. You hear an empty laugh, 'So, the deal is struck mortal'. I shall call for you, and you WILL do my bidding.'

A heartbeat later you find yourself submerged in liquid, tasting of salt - the sea? Lights shine high above, guiding the way. With one powerful kick you emerge from the briny depths, gasping for breath. You swim through the dark brackish waters to a nearby pontoon, realising as you do that you appear to be in the Deva harbour! Hauling yourself up onto a pontoon, you brush off the worst of the slime, and lay for a few moments to gaze up at the constellations above. In the fabric of the night sky the twinkling stars shine like Gods diamonds, unending, undying and timeless. You feel a peculiar tingling sensation coursing through your veins...how did you get...? You cannot fathom how you came escape the collapse, only that something magical has transpired. You feel invigorated, renewed. Touched by the hand of...a God? **Restore your Dexterity, Agility, and Fortitude levels to their original values.**

So much for the chaotic and pointless lives of this worlds denizens. Murdering and rutting and wriggling, grasping for wealth, for nourishment, for a hot piece. How the Gods must be ashamed of their wayward and wasteful creations. You look across the inky waters to the city of Deva; the screams punctuating the night air, the many fires burning - sending plumes of blue black smoke spiralling up into the ether. You look at the wharf side, and see the opportunistic. For already gangs of armed men wander, looting and pillaging, risking even the unseen terrors of the night in pursuit of their material goals.

As another tremor rumbles through the city the screams grow louder, accompanied with bestial howls not of this earth. Terrible danger stalks these now cursed streets. The Master, now freed from its arboreal prison, is no doubt tearing a channel through the city in ways you try hard not to imagine. The dead will be risen, and other abominations will no doubt be drawn to its baleful presence.

You look to the nearby ships, on some of which crews scurry like ants, working the rigging with a determined intensity. For a moment you consider evacuating the city, leaving behind the crucible of fire and blood...and then you remember; the Professor will be waiting for you, with your old and trusty pal Adz. Casting an envious glance at hoisted sails and raised anchors, you dive once again into the waters and swim to nearby north quayside.

Dripping wet in the moonlight, you take care to avoid the roaming bands of freebooters by hiding behind some barrels, as you ready yourself, and your gear, for the next chapter in this eventful evening.

If you wish to head directly back to the Piazza Arborea, in the hope of Adz and the Professor still being there, turn to 341.
If you think it best to cross the city to the Diving Swallow, and hole up there awaiting their return, turn to 120.

191

'The Elves? They marched up to the Duce's Palazzo, and left hours later looking aggrieved. Doesn't everyone know of this? I suppose you have more questions with which to interrupt me?' You smile disingenuously, and nod.

To ask him why there seem to be so many Stygians in the city, turn to 279.
To enquire about the Lemon Tree medallion, turn to 384.

192

You kneel on the scorching paving, and begin to rifle through the Stygians darkly rank clothing. Exclamations and angry accusations of the disgusted Devans ring in your ears, as you shake the corpse in frustration - nothing! All this would-be assassin was carrying was the blade with which to kill you. Disappointed and angry you push yourself to your feet, only to see a three man Watch patrol bustle into the square, led by an conspiring local. Your heart sinks as you see a veritable forest of indignant Devans, led by the cursing baker; their fingers pointed towards you accusingly.

If you want to explain the attempt on your life, turn to 165.
If you decide fleeing the scene is the best option, turn to 353.
If you decide to put up a fight, turn to 261.

193

You plant your feet solidly and await the unseen horror as it emerges from around the corner. You see the nails of the Ghoul first. Long filthy blacked fingernails, sharp as needles, followed by its sinewy arms and hideous humped back, matted with thick black hair. It raises its mockery of a face, and snarls at the sight of you. The **Slum Fiend** hisses wildly, and its plump purple tongue salivates with unrequited hunger. Blood of misfortunate's drips down from its freshly stained fangs.

If your Dexterity is 8 or more, turn to 113.
If your Dexterity is 7 or less, turn to 399.

194

Coming to your senses just in time, you yell loudly at the unnatural assembly of animals. The music stops sharply, and with a clatter the instruments drop the ground, sending the furry critters scurrying into the bracken. You set about them with your sword, bellowing curses and sending tufts of fur flying as the woodland creatures - now reverted to their natural state - scatter in base terror. Knee deep in the undergrowth, you thrash wildly at them partially with relief, partially with anger, to the sounds of croaking laughter peeling from the empty sky. Galiael pulls you away from the slaughter, and gestures for you to follow him to the ruined stairway. Flushed with a mixture of confusion and embarrassment, you follow, cursing.

Turn to 21.

195

The fiend gurgles with insatiable hunger as it sinks its teeth into your flesh. **Deduct 2 points from your Fortitude.** Howling in pain, you shove the stinking monster aside, swearing in anger at your own foolishness. It tries pathetically to clamber to its feet, shambling like a ghastly puppet. Grimacing, and annoyed by your brush with this ungratefully released creature, you stride towards it and decapitate it with one swift chop. Wiping the gore from your blade on its ragged clothing, you decide on your next move.

If you decide to head down the stairway, turn to 427.
Or if you'd rather squeeze through the partially collapsed doorway, turn to 317.

196

With an almighty killing blow you bring your sword down on a weak vertebra, and smash the undead beast back to the dust. The Bone Dragon collapses into a pathetic collection bones. You stand, panting with effort, face glowing with satisfaction. This is soon tempered by the sight of a stricken Galiael - his broken body limp and horribly burned, his delicate hands fruitlessly attempting to hold his intestines from escaping a gaping abdominal wound. He croaks wordlessly as you spring to his aide, ripping rags from your tunic as you feverishly attempt to bind the wound. 'No, friend,' your companion says gently as he pushes away from your medical attention, 'it is too late for me...take the Orb and bring down the comet...kill the Beast unleashed in Deva...' His eyes close with effort and his life force fades. Suddenly he lurches forward and he grips you with unnatural strength, 'But promise me this. PROMISE ME... that you will not open the Gates of The Old Ones! Forget them, Siga... but do not forget me....' You mutter an otherwise empty promise to your unlikely companion, as he smiles a last sad smile, and utters his final words. .'.my last gift to you, friend.'

Galiael lays dead as you kneel over him. Automatic thoughts of searching his body appear in your mind. Natural in the circumstances, you reason. Before you can act another shadow looms overhead.

'What *now!*' you shout as you reach once again for your blade. This time however, no foe appears, only the majestic and gracefully figure of a brilliant white Pegasus, which lands gracefully and stands proudly before you, swishing its silky mane. 'My last gift...'

If you are Unwatched or Favoured of the Gods, turn to 28.
If you are Marked of the Gods, turn to 11.

197

Adz' meaty grip pulls you to the ground, just in time to escape the worst of the deafening explosion which blasts through the square, sending timber and shards stonework flying in every direction. Sounds of screaming limbless figures resonates through the darkness. Your ears ring painfully as the smoke clears. **Deduct 2 from your Fortitude, and 1 from your Dexterity and Agility** until further notice, as your sense of balance has been badly compromised in the blast.

You can make out an elf crying, delirious with sorrow and fear...joyful Stygian chanting...Middenlander oaths, as the remaining living locals and militia drag themselves away. You cough harshly, expelling dirt from your lungs, and rub your eyes, red from the dust.

Adz grabs your collar and pulls you to your feet, saying to you gravely, 'Siga, by all the Gods, let's get out of here - don't you hear it? He stamps kicks the loosened cobbles, and from beneath it the deepest, most hollow, laugh imaginable - a demonic laugh only the blackest terror can emit. You turn to cast a glance at the tree, which is ruined. Only a charred stump remains, the formerly beautiful blue blossom falls blackened like ashes to the cracked earth. As Adz drags you from the scene you see the elf, turning to you, eyeless from the explosion, though still with some inner sight able to point a bitter, guilty finger at you. As you stumble away in horror, the entire square begins to give way from beneath, and cascades into the earth.

A shard of sickening pink light blaze skyward, filling your heart with terror, and the terrible form of the long dead Master rising up from the pit - a huge black figure, glistening with liquid darkness. You instinctively avert your gaze, so as not to catch its eye, and with booming laughter echoing round the city, the very same pink light bursts forth, first from cracks, then expanding into widening chasms opening up in the disintegrating streets.

Turn to 306.

Breathing heavily, you leave the stinking pile of Ghoul corpses in the alley outside, and stride proudly through the shattered doorway into the Orphanage vestibule. A fair chorus of screams din your ears as the children screech in terror at your silhouetted figure entering their sanctuary.

'Children,' you reassure, as quickly as you are able, as dollies, cups and broken toys rain desperately toward you. 'Don't be worried, I am like you, see.' You pull a comedic face and smile broadly. The children heave a collective and joyous sigh of relief, as you notice an exhausted figure emerge from the shadows. A mature woman of perhaps forty, approaching old age but still of graceful and kind appearance with an almost iridescent skin, clear of pox.

'Thank you Sire,' she sighs with effort. I am but a frail woman, but fragility has met its salvation here tonight. Had you not happened across us, we surely would have perished.' You are suitably impressed as she introduces herself as Aloevopia, High Priestess of Heliopia. 'I visit our all Temples, Shrines, and Houses of Innocents,' she explains softly, casting a loving glance around at Her children, 'Merciful Heliopia blessed us this night, her guiding hand giving me the opportunity to be here, in this place. I blame not the poor Watchmen who raced out terrified into the night. Most men have wits more fit for the mundanities of this world,' she muses sympathetically, before turning her gaze to you.

'Not like you, you are destined for greatness, Sigasünd.' Gobsmacked at her knowing your true name, you are about to inquire by what power she draws upon, before she makes an appeal, and tugs on your hand.   'Take this!' she urges, pushing 20 silver scuda into your hands, 'And this!' she adds, unlatching her **Necklace depicting the Goddess Heliopia**, into your hands. The necklace is indented with a dozen or so tiny turquoise gems, matching the devotee's soft eyes. 'Take these children, take these orphans, hurry them down to the docks and buy them passage of a ship...to anywhere safe. They are not safe here,' she adds doubtfully. 'I must go to my temple, people will need me. More than they have ever needed me before on this black night.'

You follow her eyes to the cracks in the shuttered windows and see the orange glow of nearby flames paint a scene of hell on the night sky, and you cannot argue against her duty. Glancing round at the children - a dozen or so ragged urchins - your heart sinks at the burden of leading them to safety, exacerbated by the tiny raven-haired girls widely optimistic eyes.

If you give in the High Priestesses entreaties, and agree to take the children with you, turn to 7.

If you protest, citing the impracticalities of such young babes on these tempestuous streets, turn to 302.

199

You tug at Pegasus' mane, and with considerable efforts, steer him away from the cemetery. The wilful beast flares its nostrils and throws back its mighty head in distress at your insistence. Doubting your decision, it occurs to you to guide the magnificent steed back to release the innocents from their turmoil, when the night sky is pierced with the unmistakable cry of gargantuan vultures, which plague the high places around Deva. You hear first the loose flapping of wings, before two of the **Giant Cadaverous Birds** loom into view. Nature turned on its head, these reanimated birds - in life so hungry for the dead - now have an insatiable appetite for the living.

To raise your blade aloft, and do battle with these carrion, turn to 172.

If you have a Calcified Horn, you may blow this now. Turn to 94.

200

Another lumbering grope, another precision strike. With a thud, the beast is felled - eliciting cheers from the relieved crowd. Wiping the blood from your hands as best you can, you offer it to the abandoned young noblewoman, who gratefully takes it, staining her porcelain skin red with the ogre's liquors.

If you have VELVET written on your adventure sheet, turn to 278.

If not, her attendants eventually return, and shoo you away, horrified, leaving you to exit the square quite alone despite your heroism.

If you haven't already visited it, you could head for the Elven saga telling at the amphitheatre. If so, turn to 372.

If not, or if you've already seen it, you have little choice but to head back to the Diving Swallow. Turn to 243.

201

You take the shield from your back, and in fluid upwards motion smash it into the Centurion's jawbone – sending its skull bouncing headlong into the depths of the cave.

Turn to 335.

202

Covering your face you plough through the wall of flame up the stairwell to the top of the tower. **Lose 1 point of Fortitude** from the flames licks. Emerging singed, you make it to the top level of the tower, into a book stuffed study, thick entrails of smoke following you, and also pouring malevolently through the beams of the floor. A finely dressed, but pallid and eternally sad looking man steps nervously backwards, and fumbles against a stair to the rooftop at the other side of the tower. You reason that this must be Ludovico Moretti, the cursed exile, one of the sorrowful undead.

You cast a quick glance around in wonder at the study, as Adz bundles up the stairs behind you, cursing and patting out small fires on his cloak. The walls are thickly laden with indexed and rare volumes, and astronomical apparatus are set into an ornate desk in the centre of the floor space. The aching floorboards burst into flames, and papers on the desk catch light, blazing into the air. With a forlorn howl Don Moretti takes a sweeping view of the burning tomes, and bolts for the roof hatch. With floorboards snapping beneath your smoking boots, you have little option but to follow.

Turn to 251.

203

You twist the handle and lean against the door, which to no great surprise remains steadfast. Set into it is a circular metal inset and a latch, no doubt the locking mechanism. Do you have a **Lemon-motif Medallion?**

If you do, you can try place this into the inset and try the latch. Turn to 107.
If not, you can attempt to force the door. If so turn to 345.
Otherwise you can explore the rear seaward side of the tower. Turn to 163.

204

You step forward bravely and easily deliver eternity to the already dying lord. Immediately his corpse bursts into brilliant flames, and you're forced away from the body, stumbling backwards onto your rump. You sit in a pool of mud and pant with effort, whilst Adz looks at you and sighs heavily, uncharacteristically shaking his head, in what you take for disappointment.

Turn to 388.

205

'Fine work for burly fellows such as us, Siga - shopping like scullery maids!' Adz complains, as you eventually set about picking up supplies at the market. Tallow, wicks, blankets, climbing ropes... you score out items on the professors list methodically, as Adz dawdles behind, kicking stones and muttering to himself. Noon approaches when you finally scratch of the last items, and the sun hangs heavily in the sky. It beats down remorselessly, fair scorching the marble flagstone of the central piazza. Most of locals have departed the market, seeking the solace of some shady corner or other for their habitual midday snooze. Across the dazzling white piazza you hear the creaking of a cart at the other side. Two black-grey clad shapes are labouring to wheel a large cart in the direction of the merchant quarter. Their wheezing and cursing resonates through the emptying market place, and their incongruous crow-like garb sets them apart - Stygians.

'Adz, look at our Stygian cousins labouring with a heavy load - should we not go and help them?' Adz pulls a sour face, and turns his palms out in confusion, before finally cottoning on. 'Oh...*help them? Why, yes of course!*'

If you want to approach them directly and see what load they're hauling, turn to 444.
If you'd rather follow them from a distance, turn to 431.

206

'We'll catch up with our friend later,' you cheerfully say to the giant doorkeep. He responds with a wide smile and a gracious nod.

'We could have taken them,' Adz complains, as you lead him away with some difficulty, suspecting your friend may be right. You sit and wait in the relative shade, underneath a thin copse of trees on a crest overlooking 'The Gates.' For what seems an eternity, you wait for the departure of Tancredi from his entwinements. Adz sits sulking on his sweating horse, making no efforts to hide his peevishness.

Mopping your own brow, you're about to completely lose patience, when finally you hear the coaches horses whinny. In a little puff of dust, Tancredi and his driver head along the along the bumpy track and back towards Deva. 'Cheer up old friend, now for action!' you say to the giant Nhortlünder, who snorts in return.

You wait until the coach is some distance away from the row of establishments, before spurring the horses toward it on an interception course. Whether spooked by the sight of two approaching riders, or by Adz' thunderous expression, the driver panics and reaches down into his footrest, drawing out a huge blunderbuss. 'By the Gods!' Adz exclaims - 'Look at the size of that!' You don't have any time to appreciate this fact, before the giant firearm is levelled in your rough direction, and fired!

If you are Favoured by the Gods, turn to 342.
If you are Unwatched or Marked, turn to 140.

207
You leave the other competitors in the tourney grounds and set off back into the city, ambling around with no particular plan. After walking for some minutes, you arrive adjacent to 'The Mezzaluna' – a huge crescent surrounded by high walls and bristling guards. The richer merchants reside here and the little square adjacent to the entrance is clogged with beggars. The desperate and dispossessed wave petitions and shake pathetic wooden cups in anticipation. Away from the main entrance, however, you see a forlorn and looking character in a ratty jerkin, sat on a bench underneath a shady cypress tree. He has the impassive look of someone used to waiting a long time, and has the same Lemon Tree insignia sewn onto his threadbare tunic, as the one you handed over to the shadowy stranger on your entrance to the city.

If you want to engage him in conversation, turn to 439.
Or, you could quench your thirst down at the Festival of Wine and Song, which runs all day into the night, turn to 420.
You could make your way to The Plain of Heroes, to witness the military display. If so, turn to 413.

208
You leave the Devans and Elves to fight it out, the clash of blades clattering behind you as you hurry after the assassin. Bursting through the dark streets you see your quarry ahead. With some surprise you make good ground on the elf, who is tumbling through the streets in an ungainly fashion. He tosses aside the bow and looks around with a terrified expression. Your pulse races as you bear down on the would-be killer, who

stumbles, yelping, over some loose cobbles. The stench of dye and boiling fat fills your nostrils as you chase the assassin into the garment making district, through bubbling pots, pits of soaking fabric and line after line of drying cloth. Like a fly caught in a spiders web the pursued figure becomes entangled, pathetically swiping at his bonds and whimpering with fear and gasping for air. Emerging from the shadows, you purposefully stride toward them, concealing your own breathlessness. Using the last of their energies the figure has strength enough to tear themselves free, and fumble inside their tunic...

Turn to 102.

209

You shove the stinking rigored form aside, before it can sink its pointed, poisonous stumps into your flesh. It gurgles pitifully as it tries to clamber to its feet, shambling like a ghastly puppet. Grimacing, and annoyed by your brush with this ungratefully released fiend, you stride toward it, decapitating it with one swift chop. The ruined doorway looks less appealing after this encounter, its tight dark confines alarms your sense of self-preservation.

Wiping the gore from your blade on its ragged clothing, you decide on your next move.

If you decide to head down the stairway, turn to 427.
Or if you'd rather squeeze through the partially collapsed doorway, turn to 317.

210

Was that the twinkling of metal on stone, as the phantom departed this realm? You scan the dark stone cavern floor, thrusting your torch into the dark cracks and recesses. There, glinting like a tiny star, you find a simple gold ring. Inspecting it closely, you can see it's inset with Elvish sigils which glisten with a magical iridescence. You recognise it, as an **Elven Ring of Kindred,** an ancient token of friendship, sometimes used to secure passage or entry. It's too slender to fit on your thick fingers, so place it carefully within a fold of cloth and secure it within your tunic. **Add it to your Adventure Sheet.**

With the hypnotic 'thub-thub' drawing you ever nearer, you make toward the light, reaching some rough-hewn steps descending further into the deep.

Turn to 438.

You collide into the far wall and feverishly pad the walls for the exit, as the world cascades down around you. Choking on dust and blinded by the same, you cry bitter tears of frustration as you find naught but stone after stone - no aperture of safety found. The dull pain of thudding stonework numbs you, as you prepare to embrace the now inevitable End of Days. An all too brief consideration, cut short as a ewe sized chunk of cornice smashes down through your skull, killing you with merciful haste.

Your adventure ends here.

Breaking off from the drunken procession you race toward the square, against the flow of revellers streaming the opposite direction. To the sounds of militia whistles and the clank of armoured mercenaries filling the square, you are amazed to see four **HOBGOBLINS,** seemingly escaped from between the bent bars of a splintered cage, which appears to have been driven into the square by persons unknown.

'Look!' Adz exclaims and pushes your head in the direction of a tiny lane leading off from the square. You just have a split second to see the satisfied smirking face of a Stygian, before he dons his cowl and disappears from view.

'Not our fight?' Adz asks, guessing at your thoughts. Without replying, his meaty grip pulls you away, and the pair of you beat a hasty exit from the square, batting any terrified revellers foolish enough to cross your path to the cobbles. Catching a look over your shoulder you see the frenzied Hobgoblins rending and tearing at the defenceless meat on offer, and spitting their plague tainted bile at the armoured forces now flooding into the square from all quarters of the city.

'What the seven hells, Siga!' Adz exclaims as you take cover, catching your breath behind an upturned vegetable cart. You look upwards into the orange sky and see the plume of grey smoke - and blue petals - rising up into it from the direction of the Elven Quarter. You look down at your hand, clasped tightly on the pommel of your sword, and your white knuckles represent exactly the feeling in the pit of your stomach. 'To The Swallow,' you decide, your friend agreeing with a thoughtful nod.

Together with Adz, you push and shove your way through the tight alleyways of the terrified city. Drunken revellers flee in every direction, their joyous masks a fearful parody against the backdrop of a city in turmoil. You squeeze through a bottleneck leading off from a tiny square, and are about to cross timber gangplanks spanning one of the cities many foetid canals when you are stopped in your tracks by a sound, deep from the bowels of the earth, 'Thub-Thub.' A pause. Then another 'Thub-Thub.' You glance down at the rotten planks of wood spanning the filthy water. It resonates with every beat, every beat of the sound, 'Thub-Thub.' The stream of ooze too, ripples unnaturally... with each 'Thub-Thub.' Suddenly, the cities rotten heart cracks with laughter. A laughter of such unfathomable depth and horror, that it causes even Adz to pale. Ever reliable to state the obvious, your big Norsiczan friend turns to you with a cheerless grin and asserts, 'I've got a bad feeling about this.'

Turn to 306.

213

You cover Pepin's mouth with your calloused hand and sink into a nearby doorway, obscured by a thick drape covering the entrance, holding your own breath. You can hear panting voices getting closer as the footfall slows down and stops, someone heavy breathing with exertion not three paces away. You make out at least three voices; one of them whinging in pain.

'Come *on!* one urges, insistent, in what sounds like a Stygian accent, 'Keep moving, don't slow down.'

'I have to slow down, you idiot,' another replies, 'I've broken my grobbing ankle, jumping out of that *grobbing window!'* Harsh and muffled laughter bounces off the cobbles,

'No you haven't, soft balls, come on, it's only a sprain... let's get back to the warehouse'. You hold fast for a couple of minutes as they set off, until you can no longer hear them, and then carefully set off again. The young lad stoops down to pick up an object, which he presents to you with a nervous smile.

'I think they dropped this?' he whispers. An **Iron Key with the number 34 engraved into it.** You pucker your lips as you inspect it, before pocketing it for future consideration – **add this to your adventure sheet.**

Turn to 464.

214

You wisely reach for a sword, a familiar weapon in expert hands. You swish the blade through the air and whistle at the Ogre.

'Hoi ugly!' you yell, grabbing your crotch in the disrespectful way of soldiers. Something in your gesture resonates with the reanimated beast, and it howls with fury before thundering towards you.

If you want to land a telling blow without delay, turn to 382.
If you would rather feint, and fool the monstrous beast to catch it off guard, turn to 17.

215

You puff out your chest and approach the guards, who regard you keenly as you stride towards them, fingers whitening around their halberds. Using the only information you know you attempt to convince them you're on urgent business for the House of Moretti, but lacking any means of convincing them, they decline to admit you, warning you in no uncertain terms they don't have the patience for tricks, sweating as they are in their scalding armour. You step back considering your options - there are lots of people around... and lots of eyes. The miserable steward is stood limply under the shade of a tree, wringing his hands. You can:

Go with him to the crossroads burial site, turn to 484.
Or, you could leave the wretch, and quench your thirst down at the Festival of Wine and Song, which runs all day into the night, turn to 420.
You could alternatively make your way to The Plain of Heroes, to witness the Military Display. If so, turn to 413.

216

Whether for the driving rain in your face, or the black of the night, you struggle to impose yourself on the motivated Stygians. Panting like an old man, you slash wildly at your darkly clad assailants. Adrenaline fills your nostrils with the stench of iron as fight to the death in the tight confines of the alleyway. Blow after blow hammers against you before you can gain the upper hand. **Lose 2 points of Fortitude,** from the punishing strikes. Eventually, your superior skills rise to the surface – much to your relief. Your blade finally glints keenly in the moonlight, dispatching the Stygian footpads to miserable deaths.

You can hear shouts, whistles and the clank of approaching armour and torches, as your sword cuts down the last of them, sending him gurgling to the reddening cobbles. You take a quick glance about you - Pepin is nowhere to be seen, he must have gone to fetch the watch, naive child! The dark cloaked old man needs that split second to bound onto a water butt with astonishing athleticism, and with one further leap clambers up onto the roof of the single story house.

If you try and follow the old man, turn to 324.
If you want to quickly search the bodies, turn to 308.
Or flee the scene by darting down an alley and make your way to meet the professor, turn to 233.

217

A blood orange noon sun burns through your eyelids and awakens you, as you stifle a contented yawn. Such a luxurious slumber you consider, you have never before encountered. Stretching your revitalised limbs you fold your palms behind head and sigh happily. Peering out through rheumy eyes, you appear to be in a beautiful rolling field. Soft grass caressed by a gentle wind, and wild flowers tumbling forth in an explosion of pretty colours. Familiar animals frolic and scamper nearby. A badger, a ferret, a fox… There is no sign of Galiael. Nor of your clothing. Nor belongings. For you are quite naked and not a little scorched tender by the sun. Quite where you are - or how you happened to arrive here is a mystery, such is the fickle nature of chaos.

You live on, in a way, but your adventure ends here.

218

The voices - Stygian in tongue - increase in volume and intensity as they approach. Fast footsteps betray the fervour of the new residents of the passageway. Upon seeing you, the wide-eyed fanatics hurl themselves at you, shrieking desperate curses as they struggle with each other to reach you in the narrow confines. Shoulder to shoulder with Adz, there is no doubting the resolution of this contest. The answer is soon laid bare; a teeming pile of filthy grey Stygians - blood and shattered bone littering the passageway.

'More voices - and fire,' states Adz sternly, and nods down the narrow tunnel. Smelling smoke and seeing the orange glow of lit torches approaching, you motion for Adz to make good your escape in the only way possible.

'Come on, quickly!' you order the big Nhortlünder, as you both scramble up and out of the false flagstone, remarkably unseen by indifferent locals. Once clear of the square, you head to the safety of the Diving Swallow, quietly informing Adz of your fears and suspicions.

Turn to 161.

219

Spinning on your heels, you sprint away from the Ghouls as quickly as you can through the tight alleyway. Over corpses of the dead, you leap, through piles of stinking rubbish and past cowering dogs. All the while the sound of hungry panting nears, as the agile Ghouls give chase. You reach a dead end; a door to who knows where which is bolted from within. Furiously you pound upon its reinforced timbers, but you see not the inhabitant inside. Wide eyed with terror, their hands clasped over their ears to your threats, to your pleading. All the while desperately hoping you would just go away and die somewhere else, ignorant and selfish to the end. Such is the want of the common man. You bellow a final curse before you are dragged like quarry to the gutter, and torn limb from limb with merciful haste.

Your life, and your adventure, ends here.

220

You can smell Deva before you can see it, the unmistakable aroma which accurses every large metropolis. The stench of shit and death. Unsavoury looking jetsam tickles the sides of 'The Boogenhofen' as you cruise into view of the huge white marble bridge spanning the harbour. The first - and best - view anyone will ever get of Deva. The great bridge a relic of a former age, built by the Elves - the founders of the city, but departed eons ago. Dead animals and broken timbers litter the brackish waters, suggesting the recent storm also hit the city and the landscape around it.

But now the blazing sun beats down remorselessly, baking the surface and causing foul evaporating vapours to hiss off the seas surface. A pilot guides the ship through the great harbour chain, and past the sea defences, and stone jetties into the massive crescent of the sheltered harbour. Collecting your belongings, you are much relieved to have arrived in one piece, and can only hope for a quieter time until you can be reunited with your master, the professor.

Turn to 95.

221

The flushed figure fumbles for a concealed weapon, and draws a knife. With a trembling hand and indistinguishable cry, he leaps toward you. Ridiculously, the man stumbles in his haste and lands with a thud onto the cobbles. Groaning, he rises wet with blood, which spreads its inevitable course over his tunic. Gawping at the knife embedded in his belly, the man stares at you idiotically before gurgling his last. Some people are truly born under unfavourable auspices, you muse. You look down at the bleeding corpse...and kick off a pair of waxwork ears...so not an elf at all. A quick search of the body uncovers nothing, except a crude tattoo scrawled on the dead man's breast, 'Brotherhood.' Anxious to put distance between you and this foolish would-be assassin, you hastily depart the scene back to your lodgings. As you move silently though the city streets your thoughts are preoccupied with thoughts of Aegnor's pleas, and whether the *two hundred and twenty eight years* of The White King's reign will soon witness another calamitous event.

Turn to 243.

222

Taking the **Famished Ghouls** by surprise, you rush into their rear, decapitating one before it can so much spit its bile at you. The other three break off their bestial attempts to breach the Orphanage, and spin quickly around to face you. Their oily rigored skin is stretched over sinewy muscle, foul and polluted blood pumping through their reactivated veins. With howls of fury they spring toward you with alarming speed, their tainted greenish claws at the ready.

Should you wish to do battle with them in the open street, turn to 176.

If you want to fight a retreat into a narrow adjoining alleyway, turn to 134.

Or if you have a change – or a loss – of heart, and decide to flee, turn to 219.

<hr>

223

Heading directly to the port, you are able to conduct some friendly negotiations with Captain Hessler - a man known to be able to acquire the required at short notice - and hire two riding horses, and also the services of a wiry, taciturn guide, who introduces himself quietly as Gallo. Through his thick Devan mumble you learn from him that it's less than an hour's ride to The Gates, but hours to the Moretti hunting lodge, along a treacherous coastal path. He urges that you should depart without delay to beat the tides. 'It's all lined up for us,' declares Adz excitedly, 'What a day's hunting we'll have!' Adz seems much cheered with the possibilities of unknown adventure, as the three of you trot your horses out of the Bractianine Gate, and along the highway. You barely leave the environs of the city when Gallo begins to grumble to himself and look repeatedly at the sun. 'We must move up the coast quickly, the sea is very fast this season,' he says, somewhat ominously. He catches sight of you staring at his thick winter cloak with more than a hint of confusion, considering the heat. 'You do not know that the coastal marshes are so thick the heat never penetrates it?' he asks, incredulously. He snorts with derision at your apparent ignorance and kicks his horse forwards.

After a short, uneventful journey, you arrive at the six league marker to see a trail leading off into a gentle valley. Adz seems eager to deviate down it, eyes wide in anticipation. Gallo meanwhile urges you onwards to the Moretti hunting lodge, muttering darkly of mists and creatures lurking in the gloom.

If you decide to head down into the valley toward Heavens Gates, turn to 479.

Or should you decide to head to the Moretti hunting lodge, turn to 132.

<hr>

224

Following the woodland trail high into the towering pines, it soon becomes apparent the beautiful agony the Woodsman was fleeing from has spread with malignancy. Evergreen shoots and leaves gradually give way to a forest of dazzling glass. Tiny shards of kaleidoscopic glass shatter underfoot with every stride. Leaves hang like priceless jewels from the crystallized trees, and your jaw drops agog with the twinkling of wings as birds soar overhead, cascading through the sky like delicate angels. Such is the wondrous prismatic majesty of the forest, you almost forget the inherent danger of such a cursed place - reaching out in wonder at a diamond-like berry hanging juicily from a nearby branch. Galiael taps your hand with the flat of his blade, and motions at you to not touch anything - immediately breaking the illusion. Suddenly there is a heavy crushing sound and an echoing roar that vibrates through the glacial tree trunks. A flash of brilliance; two heavy shapes leap into sight, refracting light with dazzling effect.

Two **Crystalline Mountain Lions** appear before you, scratching at the surface of the smooth glassy ridge. Crystals sit atop their hides like an armoured carapace, but have not served to dull their reflexes. With blazing eyes glinting like forbidden rubies, they posture to attack.

If you want to try and back away calmly, turn to 156.
If you have a pistol and wish to fire at one of the Crystalline Lions, turn to 50.
Or if you wish to hold your position and level your sword in readiness, turn to 53.

225

The Prince begins to speak, as you strain to pick out what few Elven words you understand, but the tongue is so high and arcane that it's near incomprehensible to you. All beyond the portal focus on, and address only, Galiael. Only the odd scathing glance is cast in your direction, and when they begin to speak it seems command Galiael harshly, as he bows his head subserviently. This most true form of Elvish is almost impenetrable to human folk, and even with your studies you are unable to follow the conversation, instead focussing on the Elves body language. Galiael looks somewhat crestfallen, and casts a furtive glance in your direction. Swallowing nervously, he seemingly attempts to argue, but is abruptly cut off by the Prince, dismissing any and all protestations. You're gob-smacked to hear Artur Keijzer's name, and that of Professor Kroos! Whilst you contend with this revelation, suddenly the image becomes polluted as if with ink, and tendrils of oily blackness spiral like a whirlpool. A demonic moaning sound echoes through the portal and the Elven voices fade, until nothing left in front of you but a dark pool of circling matter. Your Elven companion continues to stare into it long after the image of his homeland has faded, his jaw set firm and a quivering hand hovering stiffly over the pommel of his sword. A single tear winds a lonely path over a delicate cheekbone.

Galiael stands perfectly still, save his trembling fingers. Almost at once, you realise what he has been tasked with, but not before you former companion spins around with an agonized, yet malicious, intent.

If you have any of the Gifts of Intuition or Martial Prowess, and/or your Agility score is 8 or more, turn to 315.
If your agility is lower than 8, and you have neither of these Gifts, turn to 36.

226

You bump and bustle through the flow of traffic to the sprawling city gardens; a sprawling and unkempt area of semi agricultural common land, that leads up to the southern city walls. The fayre is already in full swing - and groups of young Devans are milling around in the sunshine, carelessly enjoying the uncut wine on offer.

Several overly familiar hawkers assail you, espousing the wonders of the different attractions. Of the more appealing options, you could – **if you have not already** - visit:

The fortune teller, turn to 59.
The wrestling contest, turn to 275.
The 'fantastic' animal show, turn to 379.

Or, you could leave the circus, and **if you haven't already**, you can:

Head to the Grand Market, turn to 376.
Head to the Festival of Wine and Song, turn to 363.

Otherwise, you may head back to your lodgings to escape the chaos, and enjoy a revitalising lunch.

Turn to 361.

227

Moments later the square begins to flood with tense looking troops. A bearded young captain, a mercenary from the Norsiczan lands, enters behind the vanguard. 'Clear the square!' he orders, and at his behest you are jostled away from the square. The soldiers look around themselves at the scenes of carnage, and glare at you with fear filled and suspicious stares. 'The City is under martial law, another attempt has been made on the Duce's life by the Elven assassins, the streets must be cleared! Anyone found outside of their homes will be summarily dealt with.' He turns his look at yourself and Adz, armed to the teeth, and covered in blood. So gob-smacked is he, that his face cracks into a smile. 'Brother, in what Gods names do you quench this thirst for blood? he asks Adz. Adz beams, and shouts loudly 'The Gods of the Nhort! The true Gods of Ice and Winds, and Storms!

In unison, the two Norsiczans throw back their heads and laugh heartily. You exchange a quick look with a worried looking solider, who evidently takes the two for maniacs, as they engage each other in animated conversation, Adz swishing his axe around demonstratively. Looking down you can't help but notice wide cracks have appeared in the square and buildings surrounding it, and several flagstones have sunk into the earth. A faint pink light emanates from one of them, suggesting something lays beneath. The surviving elf has succumbed, and lays motionless on the cold stone, eyes wide open, inert but accusing. His outstretched finger pointed toward a yawning chasm in the earth...big enough for you to fit through.

You look again at the trooper. He looks very pale and licks his lips in nervous repetition. You follow his glance to the flagstones and see rats, hundreds of rats, scurrying away in the direction of the docks. His lips quiver as you both hear the sounds of howling dogs, howling wolves, and the cries of gulls as they fly out in a giant flock, far out to sea. Staring down at your feet, you feel vibrations through the tough hide of your boots, a 'thub-thub, thub-thub', which sets your teeth on edge. The senator, his retinue, and assorted gawpers are ushered out of the square and on their way, as the troops themselves begin to file out to continue their sweep of the city.

Adz is clasping the Captain in a farewell embrace, not noticing the thousands of rats that have ascended from the sewers on their desperate race through the square. You look at the hole in the earth, at the dead elf's rigored finger. At the light seeping out of the earth, and the departing birds far overhead. With a deep sigh and a heavy heart you wander over to Adz, and pull him over to your discovery.

Turn to 31.

228

'For two hundred and twenty eight years,' you shout. Only reasonably sure of the answer you project your quavering voice into the darkness, and step forward muttering a feeble prayer. Cheeks flushed, you exhale a deep breath of relief as you step over the be-glyphed flagstones and don't hear the rumble of solid rock from overhead. From the portal beyond you see dazzling multicoloured lights shift around rapidly; a scene with both intrigues and disturbs you. From behind, the strained faces of the stone titans seem perceptibly burnished with new found hope. And so it is, with the Elven Gods renewed, that you step forth through the portal into the chamber beyond.

Increase your current Fate condition from Marked to Unwatched, or from Unwatched to Favoured, depending on your current level.

Touched by divine forces, you press on forwards. Turn to 41.

229

With some embarrassment, you regale Adz of your encounters with the fair Contessa. Rapt, Adz listens on excitedly as you describe her alluring physical attributes.

'My God, Siga, who would have thought an ugly, scarred lump like you could attract such a hot piece! My loins are stirring at the thought of it!' He lets out a booming laugh and pats you with unintended force across your shoulders.' 'We'll have to start calling you "His Eminence" soon, you giant love-struck fop.' He affects a mockery of a finely educated man, and teases you mercilessly until he runs - not before time - out of steam, still chuffed with his own humour. 'So, are you going to deliver her note then?' he asks, drafting his ale.

If you want to attempt to deliver the Contessa's note, turn to 162.
If you insist on doing as the professor says, in picking up supplies from the market, turn to 205.

230

Too quick for the lumbering - and probably intoxicated lawmen - your superior fitness sees you leave them far behind. Dashing through the streets you reach a shady square and refresh yourself with some of its cool fountain water. **Restore 1 point of Fortitude.**

Deciding to make yourself scarce, you resolve to head out of town to witness the military display. Turn to 413.

231

The guardians of glass stare down at you with strained and expectant hope, locked as they are in their two dimensional realm. The beast uncoils its deformed prehensile tail and given up of hesitantly stroking the inner membrane, now lashes it with extraordinary malevolence. The sac bulges obscenely, its thin pink skin expanding to near transparency, though it has not yet torn. Still unrevealing of its abominable face, you sense that only seconds remain before this Master of the Pit awakes fully, to claim this realm as its own.

Will you choose to run forth and slice open this foulest of wombs before The Master fully awakens? If so, turn to 188.
If you decide that your small soft body, and toy-like sword, are no match for such a creature, then you must flee this place from whence you came. Take flight, and turn to 270.

232

You step into the bizarre waterfall and immerse yourself in its tainted waters. Sensations of refreshment cool your aching bones, and for a few moments you feel relief that a thorough soaking is the worst you'll suffer. Then the burning starts. The cool water suddenly begins to boil with chaotic malevolence, the steaming spray scalding you badly. As you rush through to the other side howling in pain, you strip yourself down and tend to your burns the best you can. The tender discomfort suffered, gnaws at your every move. **Deduct 1 from your Dexterity.**

Turn to 441.

233

Not wishing to attract even more attention - even at this ungodly hour, you make haste away from the scene. Soon after, Pepin emerges smiling from behind an overflowing water butt. Grabbing the confused young boy by the wrist once again, you prod him into guiding you toward your destination.

Turn to 464.

234

Minutes seem like hours as you descend down through the crystalline forest, such is your eagerness to be well rid of this tainted scar on the earth. The crunching of crushed minerals gives way finally to the soft carpet of the true forest floor, moss and pine needles provide a soothing balm for your punished bunions. Sweating, you arrive at the location of the tethered horses, and are relieved and delighted to find them waiting for you patiently, quite oblivious of the perilous danger lurking in Deva. Before mounting, you gently pull the orb from its bag. You stare deep at the black fragment, the humming sound it emits resonates through your senses and you wonder at the unfathomable distance travelled. A tiny pin pick of light flickers magically along the surface, and you're drawn to turn your face upwards, toward the unveiled night sky. A tiny, twinkling star pulses faintly, and in amazement you sense that the orb seems to flicker in unison. A child's reply to its mothers beckoning. Almost with a sense of guilt you once again wrap up the orb and place it safely within the bag.

You race the horses down the night-shrouded hillside and through the empty fields. Only the occasion sound of barking dogs, and the hum of crickets, gives you any solace as you approach your final destination. The Appucine road leads to the Gate of the Leaping Lion- whether you will be able to gain entrance is an unknown. The river provides an alternative, if you can find a suitable vessel, and navigate through the locks. You pass by one of the mighty aquifers providing water to the parched city, from the distant hills and lush valleys. You imagine these must be locked with grills and the like. However, they may circumvent the more fortified entrances to the city. The horses can take you no further. Their hooves would only attract the attention of, well, whatever may be lurking around the walls. With a calming pat, some shared rations, and a whisper of gratitude, you send them off through the olive groves, as you consider your re-entry into Deva.

If you approach by road toward the Gate of the Leaping Lion turn to 351.
Should you wish to investigate an approach via the river, turn to 39.
Or if you want to attempt to clamber up into the aquifer, turn to 374.

235

With the amphitheatre in uproar you clamber up towards the private box, and are immediately swiped at by one of the Duce's bodyguards, **Lose 1 point of Fortitude, and add 1 to your 'Watch Test' total.** Elves and men draw swords and a blow, somewhere, is struck, igniting the kindling for a wider conflict. Sensing trouble, and that this is not your fight, you resolve to give chase to who you suppose is the assassin.

Turn to 69.

Evening is descending on the colonnaded arena, when you re-enter for the final pairings. Hundreds of torches have been lit to illuminate the targets, arranged in the effigy of a dragon's mouth. The crowd is rapt, and noticeably more attentive than the rabble of drunken young bucks from the earlier sessions. After the opening preamble, the orator hails the mighty feats of those who remain; the massed spectators hush themselves into a respectful silence. Eight competitors are still in the competition. As you regard them, you consider ways to best them. **If you have the Gift of Skullduggery, decide now whether you wish to use it.** The eight mill around with retainers, in varying states, ranging from outright nervousness - to the ice-cool demeanour of the one elf left in the running. He is surrounded by well-armed retainers, no doubt from his ship's company. These warriors whisper encouragement and oaths as he prepares his ivory bow. Drawn first, you are called to the mark.

Your first opponent is an ancient looking Dwarf, who has never stopped caressing his gilded crossbow since you first noticed him in the arena. He seems extremely focused, his steely eyes twinkling with gritty determination, bordering on fever.

You squint, and take aim. **Is your Dexterity 8 or above?**

If it is, turn to 55.
If it is not, turn to 181.

The rickety ladder splits and creaks under your weight, causing the figure to stir. In a flash he opens his wide bloodshot eyes, and instinctively kicks out a boot on your exposed head, sending you tumbling down the ladder - **lose 1 point of Fortitude.** As you clutch your face, growling and cursing with pain, Adz grabs at the very same boot and drags the Stygian from his loft. The man appears drugged. Or else a fanatic - long beyond the fear of death. Adz pulls him to a corner and pummels him into submission with his mighty fists. Soundly beaten, the figure slumps like a leaking sack whilst yourself and Adz attempt to question him. The man offers you nothing, save curses and blood filled spittle, absorbing your blows and threats.

'Kill me now!' he screams with determination, 'For I will have but hours of impatient rest before Mastru Rau destroys the tree, and I am embraced by the eternal life of The Master. Ignorant fools! This mortal body is of no consequence to me now,' he mocks, smirking. He points a grubby finger at Adz, 'And as for you, you fat Nhortlünd pig, The Master will make a quick meal of you!'

Adz growls and smashes his fist into the man's face, causing it to break like a pottery vase. Nudging the man's body with your boot yields no response.

'Sorry, Siga,' Adz apologies, turning out his palms, 'you heard what he said about me.'

Turn to 168.

238

The captain studies you carefully. A considered eyebrow raises and a thin smile breaks on his craggy face.

'Very well, good Sir,' he says. 'In which case we cannot have you wandering around the ship unescorted. I'll honour my contract with Kroos and deliver you to Deva sure enough, but you will be confined to quarters until we dock.'

Turn to 220.

Words tumble from your lips, whilst sweat pours from your brow. Time after time you feel the ground beneath your feet begin to slip away, but each time you contrive to master the elusive words, plucking them from the air and binding them with arcane mastery. The unimaginable pain of casting snakes through the very fibres of your being, as you recite the last lines blindly, gasping as unearthly forces race through your veins.

Your eyes open with a cocktail of terror and wonderment as blue sparks crackle forth from your fingertips. As you complete the words, blinding light shoots from them and soars into the black sky above, exploding in a blinding blanket of brilliant white light. Through the agony of ages, and gritted and rattling teeth of the present, you bellow out the final words, and are violently hurled backwards to the soft wet earth, wracked with pain and the tips of your fingers burnt and blacked. With trepidation, you open your eyes and glance expectantly at the Orb, its oily black lustre replaced with soft illumination as it glows warmly. Looking skyward you see a brilliant second sun cast upon the sky, and the pulsing light of the astral comet.

Blowing on your blackened fingers with cool satisfaction you approach the orb and pluck it from the air. It produces a satisfying buzzing sensation and you linger on it for some moments, before wrapping it carefully and seal it carefully in your pack. Smiling confidently, you make to depart the plain in the direction of the forest and of Deva, when a large shadow sails over you at speed. Followed by a huge roar... Exhaling with resignation you turn and look skyward. You curse darkly as you see a bleached and rotten **Bone Dragon** diving toward you; its ancient leathery wings flapping like torn sails in the wind.

If you possess the Silver Bow, turn to 139.
If you don't but possess a Dragonfire Gem, turn to 421.
If you have neither of the above, and you decide to make for the tree line, turn to 45.
If you stand your ground, preparing to do battle with this timeless foe, turn to 369.

240

You lower your weapon and quickly blurt out the sorry tale, leaving out details, but giving reassurance of deliverance to this heartbroken figure. Moretti slumps forward, sobbing forlornly, rivers of tears sizzling down his smouldering cheeks. 'My Darlings,' he cries, almost with pleasure, 'I shall be reunited with you very soon!' As he bursts into almost total combustion, Moretti struggles to deliver his final redemption. 'Maestru Rau...the Stygian leader...he said he would deliver the souls of my children...but he lied...and I was tricked...he seeks only to bring about the destruction of Deva. He will destroy the Elven Tree which binds to Master to the earth...this very night! Once this happens the only salvation... will be found at the ancient

Elven gate in the Appucine lofts beyond Deva...bring down the Heavens on the foul demon! Take what little I have.' He screeches, as he proffers you a long knife crackling with magic.

He lets out a shrill cry, as his very soul ignites and quickly utters his last words. 'Where the Giant sleeps, beyond the maiden's hair... I sought to locate this myself with my studies, and would have surely done so myself... if not trapped...in this terrible place, TERRIBLE PLA...!!!

Write the word GIANT on your adventure sheet, and add 'Ensorcelled Knife' to your Trappings.

Adz glances at you, and mutters a quick litany to his Norsiczan Gods. 'What a way to go, Siga. Please deliver me quicker, should I ever head the same way.' With a nervous laugh you offer a thin smile in return.

If still in the tower, you must leap to safety from the blazing structure into the soft mud below, before it crumbles into the tidal flats.

Either way, turn to 495.

241

Headed to the dockside warehouse, you hope not to bump into one of the many aggressive watch patrols, especially with Adz in tow - not a man known for his tolerance of such bullies. On this the final day of the festival, the activity is low down by the docks, with only a few sour faced store men mill around. Most of the warehouses appear to be securely locked up, including warehouse thirty four - which you observe from a distance. Some minutes pass and there is no sign of anyone coming or going from the warehouse. You nudge Adz, and wordlessly motion him into following you to the door, and pulling out the heavy iron key, you slot it into the lock and turn...

Turn to 78.

Together will Galiael you take cover behind a rocky outcrop, but the music still comes closer. The elf looks bemused as the notes sail ever closer, until the melodies are all around, filling the still air of the plane. You emit a joyless laugh as your brain strives to comprehend the musical assembly which shuffles in front of you. Woodland animals - beasts of the yonder forest - bow before you gracefully, and on the command of a dignified looking badger, strike another tune. You gape in wonder as ferrets, wildcats, marmots and other mammals stand before you, dressed gaily in the garb of troubadours. They smile wide toothy smiles as they shuffle on their little paws to the chords of a lilting tune. A fox reveals some cymbals and...winks at you. With incomprehension you note the fox is holding you transfixed with a devilish grin, crashing them with a hypnotic beat. Still smiling, still crashing. Giddy with delight at the cute ensemble, you feel the ground beneath your feet begin to pass away.

If your Fortitude is 8 or above, and/or you have the Gift of Iron Willed, turn to 194.
If your Fortitude is lower, and you are not Iron Willed, turn to 217.

243

Keeping to the dark places, you swiftly and softly move through the night, leaving your battles far behind. The **midnight** wolves gather on the hills surrounding the city and offer their devotions to the moon. In unison they fill the cloud-filled sky with their everlasting howls.
If you know of a meeting taking place at this time, turn to that reference, otherwise read on.

Moving through the dark streets, a band of thuggish looking Militiamen gives you what has become their customary filthy looks. You avert your gaze and hurry past them. One of them spits, calls out and laughs. A few seconds later, you hear one of them shout something you can't quite make out. Whether at you, or some other misfortune you aren't quite sure, but either way you increase your pace, and are relieved to make it back to the Diving Swallow, just as the first rain drops of the imminent rain shower begin to fall from the sky.

The kitchen porter scrapes together some leftovers, which you devour greedily - late as it is – **Regain 2 points of Fortitude.**

You consume it in solitude; the other patrons already in their beds, and once satisfied you tread heavily up the rickety stairwell to your bed. To the soft coos and chirps of the avian residents, you sink into a deep and relaxing sleep.

Turn to 125.

244

You fight the powerful Dragon the best you can, but your valiant efforts are not enough. In desperation you hack at its exposed yellowing bones. The fight is futile. Weakened as you are, you eventually succumb, and dropping to your knees you look for a few seconds into its obsidian eyes, before the beast immolates you. Thus you die, a human torch on a tainted plateau.

Your adventure, and your life, ends here.

245

The assassins star whistles past the elf, nicking an ear on the way. Galiael howls in fury and pain, and leaps toward you - his fine blade glistening in the diffused light of this tainted plain.

Turn to 312.

246

Do you have the word **SHADRACK** on your adventure sheet?

If you do, turn to 381.
If not, turn to 492.

247

Stunned, you find yourself returned to the Hall of Tapestries. With a cautionary glance you once again inspect the woven images. Not a figure stirs – the artworks are now merely mundane hangings, yet your encounter with the Deity remains clear in your mind. By equal measure wowed and irritated with the workings of these Gods, you recollect your wits and head through the doorway at the head of the chamber.

Turn to 410.

248

You land the killing blow and witness the last remnants of the tattered beast drop like rags, much satisfied with your work. But to your dismay, Pegasus begins a spiralling descent and once landed throws you from his back with a violent buck. The equine flyer holds you for a moment in its huge dark eyes, before turning his head away. You make to remonstrate with the unfathomable beast, but he gallops up into the darkness of the night sky. Abashed, you pick yourself up from the hard earth, still some four hundred paces from the South Gate. A tiny figure in the dark, and outside the city walls, you feel chillingly vulnerable and alone. Further along the road, the huge city walls rise up before you like a sheer black cliff, its timeless gate sealed shut from the outside world. To the north, five hundred paces away, the river flows into the city. You factor, it's protected by chains and locks, but in these times...who knows what lurks there.

If you wish to approach the city by road and via the gate, turn to 351.
If you favour an attempt to re-enter Deva by river, turn to 39.

249

You advance quickly into range of your opponent and unleash a hurricane of punishing blows, pounding with all your might - looking for a quick win. Through his tight guard, you can see champion winking at you. Alarmed, you seek to quickly change tack.

If your Dexterity is 8 or higher, and/or you have the Gift of Martial Prowess, turn to 58.
If your Dexterity is 7 or lower, turn to 466.

250

Together with Adz, you push and shove your way through the tight alleyways of the terrified city. Drunken revellers flee in every direction, their joyous masks a fearful parody against the backdrop of a city in turmoil. You squeeze through a bottleneck of alleys leading off from a tiny square, and are about to cross timber gangplanks spanning one of the city's many foetid canals when you stop in your tracks by a sound. A deep sound from the bowels of the earth. 'Thub-Thub.' A pause, and then, 'Thub-Thub.' You glance down at the rotten planks of wood spanning the filthy water. It resonates with every 'Thub-Thub.' The stream of ooze ripples unnaturally with every beat. Suddenly, the city's rotten heart cracks with laughter. A laughter of such unfathomable depth and horror, that it causes even Adz to pale. Ever reliable to state the obvious, your big Nhortlünd friend turns to you with a cheerless grin and asserts,

'I've got a bad feeling about this.'

Turn to 306.

251

Bursting up through the hatch, you clamber onto the roof of the tower. Ludovico Moretti faces you, leaning heavily against the crenellations and sobbing bitterly. Almost in tandem with the blazing flames, a rare shaft of light burns through the grey mist as the sun struggles to penetrate the gloom. Together with Adz, the pair of you step forward as the desperate vampire's skin begins to bubble and smoulder.

'Finally someone has come to deliver me from this place!' Moretti cries bitterly, 'Robbers! Murderers! I have no desire to depart this world with more blood on my hands!' he spits, looking over the edge of the brickwork.

If you step forward to attack him, turn to 9.
If you tell him you have granted his children rest, turn to 240.

252

The throwing star flashes towards the elf, who cries in alarm and attempts to dodge the murderous missile.

If your Dexterity is 8 or more, turn to 469.
If your Dexterity is 7 or less, turn to 245.

253

You haul yourself up onto the ledge, and begin to ease your way across it and over the inky black expanse below. Disturbed by the seismic events of the last few hours, the rock-face begins to give way and threatens to crumble into the black pool beneath. With the sounds of splintering rock filling your ears, you have no choice but to attempt to leap to safety on the other side.

If you have the Gift of Acrobatics and/or your Agility is 9 or more, you bound across. Dabbing only the merest toe of your boot in the pool, turn to 147.
If you don't have this Dexterity, and your Agility score is 8 or less, turn to 417.

254

Even with your base understanding of the astronomicum, it's clear that the comet - projected brilliantly against the night sky - has nearly concluded its journey across space to this, its final destination. Minutes remain, and the very air crackles with energy at the approach of the falling star. Invigorated both by the burden of salvation, deliverance, and the very real threat of not living to see another sun, you race through the streets. Only now, as End of Days approaches, do you begin to feel regret. So many relationships unrequited, so many wrongs left wrong, or worse still. The blood soaked streets disgust you. The poverty and misery disgust you. All around you the wailing of the living, of the dead, of the half-dead - risen again to stalk the fearful and the abject. Charging onwards through contrasting districts, from the formerly majestic to the dismal, you pay no heed to any howls, roars, or cries - but nothing can distract you from your mission.

In its bag, the fragment of the comet begins to smoulder, emitting acrid white smoke - the fires of a longing to be co-joined with its progenitor, an urge spanning galaxies and eons. The little fragment's beckoning call is being heeded, and the low hanging comet in the sky is fixed on an avenging course. As you near the Grand Piazza you dash past fighting men. They look weary and battle fatigued in dirty and sweat soaked tunics, their eyes empty of the many horrors seen. Some call out to you, in a variety of tongues - military slang -hardened fighters, no doubt prodded into the breach at the command of their paymaster. Many a fortune has been made upon the ashes of a stricken and desolate land.

Pushing up through one of the wider arteries to the square, you arrive at a manned barricade. A dozen or so men guard it with degrees of attention. Several screen for approaching fiends with enormous arquebuses. A couple are wiping their weapons free of gore, a couple more sharpening and polishing, talking quietly of a hard nights work. Two are playing dice, and drinking without an apparent care in the world, and one is even sleeping, no doubt having decided that as dawn approaches this nights ghastly games are nearly over. These are professional fighting men, not green city militia or nervous draft guardsmen.

One of the dice players glances up as you approach, and spits some chewing-leaf at a headless twitching cadaver. A couple of the others look up, and laugh hoarsely as he addresses you, 'There's nothing for you that way Princess, save your tender curls and wait until dawn. They're quietening down now. I don't want the sight of such a gilded peacock as you to arouse their rigoured cocks.'

Gritting your teeth at this last obstacle, you stare upwards towards the night sky. Day appears to have come early, as so large in the sky is the comet - that it could be mistaken for the sun. You hear the roar of the Master of the Pit, as you quickly consider your next, and perhaps final, action.

If you have the word ROLLO on your adventure sheet, turn to 442.

If not you can choose not to dally, but instead plough on alone through the massed ranks of the undead. Turn to 135.
Or try to galvanise these reluctant fighters with an inspiring call-to-arms. If so, turn to 333.
Or play to their natural inclination to greed, and bribe them with silver and other riches. If so, turn to 493.
If you think it better to wait until dawn breaks to act, turn to 472.

255

You dash through the city's dark streets after the black-clad figure, to a nocturnal accompaniment of barking dogs and howling cats. Pursuing your quarry, you feel exhilarated by the chill night air, forcing vitality from your worn muscles. The would-be killer turns sharply down a small alley and you hear a cry of frustration. Bursting round the same corner you see the narrow lane ends in a stout door inset into a sheer brickwork façade. The assassin pounds fruitlessly on the door, and attempts a failed leap to scale the wall. Sensing your presence, the lithe figure then spins around and draws twin blades from scabbards on either hip. The sudden twist causes her cowl to fall, and the release of ribbons of lustrous blonde hair - a woman! Marking your obvious surprise, the **Female Assassin** raises an eyebrow on her finely featured face, and purses her blood red lips into an alluring smile. You exhale deeply, the energy of the chase seeping from you as you stand transfixed by the beauty, crouched mantis-like before you.

'Gods be damned!' you force yourself to shout, chiding your innate weakness for the fairer sex. Soft hair, sweet smells, and welcoming curves can't mask the cold steel, or murderous designs. Immediately the woman senses your resurgent resolve, and in a baleful flash she wheels toward you - a blur of blades and the steely intent of a trained killer.

If your Dexterity is 9 or more, turn to 288.
If it's less, turn to 452.

256

You quickly fumble inside your tunic, and palming the Lozenge, bring it to your lips. With minor theatre you cough heartily, excusing yourself and slyly swallow the pill. For a moment you feel flushed, and your heart races with exhilaration. Your mind becomes acutely sharp of thought, and crystal clear. Containing the wonderment engulfing you, you scarcely manage to conceal your surprise at now being able to understand each and every Elven word spoken.

'Galiael, House of Trenagar,' the Elven Lord begins, 'we give thanks that you have found what has remain hidden for millennia. 'I give thanks to the merciful Gods,' affirms Galiael automatically. 'Read the inscription we have given to you, this incantation has been composed by the Archmage personally, invoking the celestial powers of the Lore of Ages. This will bring down the celestial comet, bound to its fragment, its beacon. This fragment will attract its progenitor from far across the galaxy, and this alone will deal with the *imminent* danger, this force of imbecile menfolk have unleashed. We have protected our wayward children for eons, and bound the evil to the earth… and it is now undone,' he says bitterly, before glancing at you.

'The human must die; the location and nature of this place must remain known only to its custodians. He must die and you must find his master, Kroos, and his troublesome cohort, Artur Keijzer. You must find them and uncover the locations of the two remaining Gates of the Eternal Ones, and then they too must die. For when all three gates are known, then it will be possible to pass through them physically. I need not lecture you on the catastrophic dangers this presents should the secrets be revealed to any but us. The humans must be killed. Mankind can guarantee nothing,' - he spits - 'Save greed, avarice, and opportunism, this is known to all as an indisputable truth.' Galiael looks awed, but crestfallen, and casts a furtive glance in your direction. Swallowing nervously, he makes to appeal on your behalf, but is harshly cut off…'You are duty bound, by your unending oath and the sworn affirmations of your ancestors to obey,' commands the Lord, dismissing any and all protestations. 'The farseers cannot maintain us much longer - the eddies of the Otherworld are powerful and we navigate through them at great risk. Act - act quickly, that we may have conclusion! Men will bring an end to this realm! I warn you, do not fail ussss...'

The image becomes polluted as if with ink, and tendrils of oily blackness spiral like a whirlpool. A demonic moaning sound echoes through the portal and the Elven voices fade, until nothing left in front of you but a dark pool of circling matter. Your Elven companion continues to stare into it long after the image of his homeland has faded, his jaw set firm and a quivering hand hovering stifling over the pommel of his sword. A single tear winds a lonely path over a delicate cheekbone.

If you seize the opportunity of surprise and immediately strike down the elf, turn to 415.
Or confront the elf with your secret understanding, and reveal you heard every word, turn to 378.

257

'The Elves? They marched up to the Duce's Palazzo, and left hours later looking aggrieved. Doesn't everyone know of this? I can see I will not have any peace here to continue my work,' the Freelander merchant says. Collecting his apparatus he departs huffing, to the sanctity of his private room.

What does the day hold for you?

There is a marksmanship contest, with early heats taking place very soon, and promises of a great prize, if that interests you - and only you still possess a pistol - turn to 68.
Or you could head to the Plain of Heroes for the Military Display. If so, turn to 413.
Or to just quench your thirst down at the Festival of Wine and Song, turn to 420.

258

You slowly reach up and lift a sparkling torch from its bracket. You afford yourself one dubious glance at the magical looking flames, before tossing it into the mass of Wraiths. As you grab the dazed Galiael's arm, and spin, tugging the elf toward the entrance, you hear an almighty whoosh from amidst the unholy congregation. The shrine fills with the sounds of agonised shrieks, as the inhabitants thrash wildly, consumed by silver fire. Seeming to sense Galiael's presence, they swoop toward him like blazing birds, and assail him with their sonic screams.

You could try and manhandle the elf toward the door; though his state of transfixation renders him near insensible. If so, turn to 383.
Or if you think it noble to dispatch these ghosts to another realm, and attack them, turn to 141.

259

As the Aquarius lumbers toward you, a patch of slimy moss causes you to lose your footing, sending you tumbling into the stream. Panic flashes through your mind as the undead fiend lurches onto you and begins to gouge at your clothing with its ragged green fingernails. **Lose 1 point of Fortitude**. Smashing your powerful fist into its hanging head causes the final tendons to snap causing the detached skull to bounce down the tunnel. With little effort you clamber back to your feet and offer a strike of deliverance, sending the abomination back to End of Days.

You rinse the gore from your blade in the cool mountain-born waters of the aquifer, and hurl the corpse of the former guardian to the rocks below, looking on impassively as it bursts like a tossed watermelon upon them. With little difficulty, you're able to squeeze past the broken grills and enter into the city. Any other protectors of these irrigating tunnels long since fled, or dead - or worse. You navigate a course further into the heart of the city. The shrieks and howls echoing through the tubes, setting your teeth on edge, as nerves begin to get the better of you. Through tiny apertures, you occasionally peer down into the streets below. Feasting ghouls stalk the blood splattered cobbles, running down those foolish enough to expose themselves alone. You wince helplessly as you witness dozens of innocents fleeing in useless terror, only to be caught, and torn asunder. You look on in horror as the pipeline runs parallel to the main square, and there, holding ghastly court, the abominable figure of The Master sits, resplendent of his perverse throne of skulls. Shuddering, you move on to seek out an exit point and presently the tunnel terminates, reaching the central pump-house, some three hundred paces from the square.

The fragment of the comet burns brightly within the confines of the bag it's stored in. Orange light creeps though the worn stitching, and the blackened bag is hot to the touch.

If you want to head directly toward the square, even though the streets are still dark, turn to 254.
Or if you choose to wait until sunrise before venturing into the open, turn to 472.

260

With a smacking of lips and animalistic grunts, the **Crypt Ghoul** awakens. Sniffing your human scent keenly, it emits a low growl, and with a flash of razor sharp teeth, it leaps atop a sarcophagus. Eager for a fresh soul to devour, it wastes no time before pouncing at you!

If you have the Gifts of Hyper Senses and/or Martial Prowess, turn to 145.
If you don't, turn to 414.

261

You pull out your knife and skilfully begin to weave through the cumbersome Watchdogs - piercing two of them - who then stagger backwards clutching their punctuations, idiotic expressions on their dull faces. You've dealt with common bullies before you think, adrenaline pulsing through your veins, as you cut a swathe through them. Sure of killing them all quickly, you unexpectedly feel a dull crack on the side of your head. You gaze in confused amazement at a common washerwoman, another cobble in hand, about to be flung at your skull. She's screaming insults at you in a language you can no longer understand, as the colours of the cityscape begin to fade, her outline disappears, and you lose consciousness for the last time.

The watch drag you bleeding down to a nearby manhole, gathering an excited crowd of urchins and beggars, who take turns to dart forward defile your now naked and tattered body. After turns to insult and spit upon you, one leans forward to cut your throat. Another anonymous foreigner is dumped like an animal, dead into the foetid sewers.

Your adventure is at an end.

262

Heading directly to the port, you and Adz are able to conduct some friendly negotiations with Captain Hessler - a man known to be able to acquire the required at short notice - and hire two riding horses. You also contract the services of a wiry taciturn guide, who introduces himself quietly as Gallo. Through his thick Devan mumble you learn from him that it is several hours ride to the Moretti hunting lodge, along a treacherous coastal path. He urges that you should depart without delay to beat the afternoon heat, and the tides.

'It's all lined up for us,' declares Adz excitedly, 'What a day's hunting we'll have!' Adz seems much cheered with the possibilities of unknown adventure, as the three of you trot your horses out of the Bractianine Gate, and along the highway. You barely leave the environs of the city when Gallo begins to grumble to himself and look repeatedly at sun.

'We must move up the coast quickly, the sea is very fast this season,' he says, somewhat portentously. He catches sight of you staring at his thick winter cloak with more than a hint of confusion, considering the heat. 'You do not know that the coastal marshes are so thick the heat never penetrates it?' he asks, incredulously. He snorts with derision at your apparent ignorance and kicks his horse forwards.

'Like old times, Siga. Me and you, and trouble coming along to make three!' You frown at Adz' simplistic excitement, who consequently looks a little crestfallen, as you inform him that this is a reconnaissance trip, and should on no account turn descend to the fine red mist of a killing spree. He sinks back into his saddle and the together with Gallo.

An hour passes slowly, as Adz recounts stories already told a hundred times, when Gallo gestures for the three of you to leave the main road and head to the coastal path. There is a palpable change in the weather once you near the marshy shoreline, and a depressing grey drizzle falls into the sea, which is as motionless as a millpond. Adz is uncharacteristically quiet as you pull your cloak tight against the chill, silently cursing the lack of warm clothing. You travel the winding coastal path for more than an hour in silence - Adz' face is a mask of thunder as droplets roll down his brawny forehead, and Gallo is also silent several spans ahead, wrapped up against this dank micro climate. A thick mist soon descends and visibility becomes poor, Gallo becoming a wraith in the near distance. Looking down onto the path, you notice with some horror that sea water is gently lapping over the stones.

You hear Gallo's horse whinny to the front, and seconds later the guide gallops past you, shouting something unintelligible in his thick brogue, causing your horse to snort nervously. Adz manages to control his mount and sidles up to you, cursing. 'This is queer place, Siga! Do you see how we are losing the path?' he says, pointing a huge finger at the submerged hooves of the horses. 'What shall we do?'

If you want to head back to the city, turn to 131.
If you want to push on along the coastal path, turn to 332.
If you want to head inland, but still in the direction of the lodge, turn to 460.

263

Under a leaden sky you do battle with the thunderous creature, as it twists and stomps, chasing you like a cat chases a mouse. Its ungainly might is in stark contrast to your nimble evasion, as you strive to stay alive long enough to better the beast. You strike, time after time, trying to find a weak point, and as you do, you feel the burn of fatigue as the sodden earth extracts a toll on your energies. **Lose 2 points of Fortitude** as you struggle to evade its fiery breath. The **Bone Dragon** emits a roar of frustration, rears up onto its hind legs and throws its terrible head up to the heavens. For split second you glimpse its exposed and loosely connected thorax. Can you land the killing blow?

Add together the totals of your Dexterity and Agility, and add 3 to the total if you have the Gift of Acrobatics. Add 4 if Galiael is still alive.

If the total is 15 or more, turn to 323.
If the total is 14 or less, turn to 403.

The horses trudge through the punishing terrain for what seems an eternity, before finally emerging once again near the coastline. Through the clogging mists, you make out the black silhouette of a tower on a rocky promontory a league or so away. This must be the Moretti hunting lodge - and indeed it looks a fine place for a miserable exile. Its circular black granite composition contrasts with the featureless pale grey gloom canvas of the sweeping estuarine bay it overlooks. There is a heavy wooden door set into the stonework at the head of the main path leading to the tower, and you also note sea-worn steps leading to a wooden platform at the rear of the tower. Its narrow windows are too high to reach and shuttered from within, and casting a sideways glance at Adz, somewhat too narrow to fit squeeze through anyway.

If you want to try to enter via the main entrance, turn to 203.
If you want to explore the rear of the tower for an alternative entrance, turn to 163.

265

The Half-Orc enthusiastically lumbers forward, club raised high. But this blow is too slow and you punch him hard in the gut, folding him in two. A swift knee to the chops leaves him prone in the dust, his spittle oozing out of his gaping jaw. Adz has bested his man, and stands proudly atop him - like a hunting dog over quarry. You smile at your friend, and dusting yourself down, prepare to enter this fine house of iniquity. **You may add the Iron Studded Club to your adventure sheet if you wish.**

Turn to 491.

You approach the unfortunate residents of the stocks. The clearly inebriated local is rambling on about some girl or other, and has obviously been involved in some drunken brawl over the same. The Dwarf, also drunk, is loudly blaming all the ills of the world and his own situation on - not untypically for a Dwarf - the Elves. All the while the old man keeps repeating, over and over again; 'The leaves will wither…The ground will awaken… The seventh day marks the coming…' as if in a trance. Your interest prompts the spiteful guard to wearily give each of the three a malicious prod with his spear shaft, paying special attention to the old man. 'Quiet, you old hound!' he says, a second prod rendering the mantra broken, and the man unconscious. 'On your way, Nhortlünder,' he growls menacingly at you. You're left with little choice but to carry on the riverside stalls.

Turn to 24.

You push your way to the front of the crowd of commoners, gathering in slack jawed expectation ahead of the evenings spectacle. A roped off area to the right of the stage houses several dignitaries and dilettantes, seated on plush furniture, fanning themselves vainly against the stifling heat. At the head of the Piazza is a raised platform, topped with all manner of scientific apparatus; volumetric flasks - bubbling with iridescent green gloop, copper coils, funnels and ornate and complex levers. Pitched at a 45 degree angle, and covered by a hessian throw, someone…or something *large,* appears to be strapped to a large wire frame. Filaments and cords creep like veins underneath the sheet, seemingly attached to whatever is under there. The crowds chat light-heartedly amongst themselves, evidently impervious to the dry mouth and twitching bowels bothering you. You find yourself pinned to the front of the barrier, jammed into position by the weight of numbers. With a certain anxious resignation you resolve to watch the show come-what-may, and finger your weapon hilt for reassurance. Years of facing dangers the ignorant are too stupid to consider, has afflicted you with a certain wariness you just can't shake. A local nudges you in the ribs encouragingly as the show begins. Unseen stage hands dim torches around the perimeter of the square, and theatrical vapour-lamps are lit from below the stage, casting eerie and harshly angled shadows across the wooden platform. The crowd listen in silent anticipation as a hidden mechanism clunks into gear, and Dr Döll rises up through the trapdoor onto centre-stage.

'My noble Lords, and most dignified Ladies,' he begins, in a suitably dread inducing manner.

'Tonight you shall behold the triumph of science over magic, of reason over superstition...it is no Heresy, for Heresy is defined by untruth, and this is...no lie. For tonight… tonight we are as Gods, and as Gods we shall conquer death!' The assembly of peasants gasp in confusion, some grinning nervously, others whimpering fearfully. The lords and ladies of Deva alternate between pious affliction and disdaining denial, so far as you can make out in the dim light. Döll commences a tedious, but necessary monologue which appears to resonate with the masses - detailing his journey, his struggle against oppression and reactionary dissenters. He regales the crowd with tails of planetary trajectories, alignment of certain constellations and alchemistic formulas...until he reaches a crescendo and strides towards the hidden figure. 'The miracle...' he booms, 'of life!'

With an extravagant swish, he whips away the sheet to reveal an impossibly large and monstrous ogre. The beast is the colour of rotten apples, an abominable patchwork of various ghastly components. Its rippling muscles are stiff with the rigours, and its abhorrent face a mask of pain. Some in the throng swoon, peasants and lords alike. Shouts ring out. Cries for the Watch, appeals to the Gods, mocking catcalls - bravado of the much imbibed. Döll is clearly lost in the moment, and with an almost possessed expression he bounds towards a large vertical lever and pulls it downwards with great intent. 'I bring... life!' he shrieks, as the lever grinds into action. The gas-lamps flicker violently, and the green liquid boils uncontrollably. Sparks scream out from tentacle like wires which slither across the stage. Suddenly the metal frame begins to resonate wildly and turns an incandescent blue. With an almighty crack, lightning smacks downwards in a brilliant arc, and energises the metal frame holding the beast. For a moment, nothing happens, and the gas-lights settle into a flickering normality. Döll remains frozen, gaping at the monster stiffly, and very intently. Boos ring out, laughter peels from the crowd, and you're about to breathe a sigh of relief, when... with a sinking feeling, you see one of the Ogres obscene claws twitch into life. Then another. The crowd gasps once more. They listen rapt, as the Ogre takes a long and wheezing intake of air - the very reversal of a dying breath. In a split second its eyes explode open wide, and filled with malevolence - it glares at the crowd. Such is the poison in its stare you notice some of the guard begin to shuffle nervously, and the rich lounging on sofas sit bolt upright, as if to flee at any moment. Then, with a soul crushing bellow, the Ogre howls at the abject torture of being reanimated from beyond the grave, and in two violent jerks breaks free of its bonds. Screams of terror peel out from the crowd and with a huge surge they begin to stampede from the piazza.

If you decide to flee with the masses, turn to 167.
If you want to assist in tackling the monstrosity, turn to 457.

268

Fumbling through your trappings, you look in vain at the contents of your bag. Even though you know items may bear ensorcellment, they stubbornly remain inert, displaying nought but drab mundaneness - something about the cloying mists must be sapping their benefits. You glance at the rancid black river, and back at the rabid skeletons about to ram your little boat. Uttering a quick prayer to any and all gods listening, you secure your possessions and dive into the chill waters.

Take your Fortitude score, adding two to the total if you are Iron Willed. If the score is 11 or more, turn to 60.
If your total is 10 or less, turn to 310.

269

In a fit of over-confidence you toy with the three drunken Watchdogs, piercing their jerkins with humiliating and painful pricks. So sure are you of teaching the bullies a lesson that you quite underestimate their abilities. Furious with embarrassment they rush you, and quite overwhelmed you find yourself face down in the dirt, and promptly disarmed. All the colours begin to fade from the night sky's dark tapestry as you're beaten unconscious by a relentless stream of violent blows. An indeterminate amount of time passes before you're awakened, bleeding and broken by the powerful scent of a urine soaked rag. You scarce have time to gather your wits before you see the swirling sea far below – and so it is that this maelstrom is the last thing you see, before your body is dashed asunder on the unforgiving cliffs.

Your adventure, and your life, is at an end.

270

An earth shaking howl - a howl born of the pit and unleashed now upon this mortal realm fills the chamber...and fills the sky high above an unsuspecting city. A howl which terrifies the Citizen, his bowels contracting over a half empty chamber pot. A howl which disturbs the Priest, mid coitus, with the confused and reticent maid, her white knuckles clenched tightly around her prayer beads. A howl which is heard far away by Princes and Kings, and which is ignored as a distant dream. But is heard somewhere...

At the far ends of the earth in the land of the Undying, the Elves hear. It is met with wails of timeless regret. Caring not for the petty cares of Priest nor king, you take to your heels and run like you've never run before. Heart near jumping through your chest, you race out, back through the entrance to the vaulted chamber, all the while feeling the baleful glare of

The Master in the back of your head. As you rapidly cover the glyph ensorcelled flagstones, the remaining roof supporting titans slowly begin to speak once again. With granite tones, they impotently mouth their challenges...'How many...' 'Cabbages!' 'Dung-heap!' 'Big stone balls!' you cry out, as you hop from one dusty slab to another, setting off in motion your most urgent of desires - the sealing of this entire tainted tomb!

Gaping cracks snake through the vaulted roof and walls buckle violently. The chambers rapid collapse ensured, chunks of gigantic masonry smash down all around you, filling the air with a thick blanket of dust. With only a rough sense of the exit, you run blindly through the pitch black toward temporary salvation.

If your Fate is currently Favoured by the Gods, and/or you have the Gifts of either Intuition or Hyper Senses, turn to 169.
If you are Unwatched or Marked, and have neither of these Gifts, turn to 211.

271

Both sets of guards snap to attention as you escort Her Ladyship up the curved marble steps to the entrance. The Devan guards regard you with a look of stony disdain - your dusty garb and blood splattered tunic in sharp contrast to your maidens fine robes and glowing skin. You smile cheerfully at them and they respond with stiff nods - scarcely concealing their true thoughts. Here you are on the arm of one of the finest ladies in all of Deva! You barely stifle a guffaw thinking how Adz is going to react to the news.

You're shown into the amphitheatre proper, and to the luxurious private stalls. The Contessa's attendants fuss around her endlessly, near enough ignoring your presence - not being quite able to comprehend the horror and having a sweaty and hairy Norhlunder in tow. You take in the vista of the sweeping arena, and are able to pick out a few key figures. The Duce is here, resplendent in his personal box - like a finely-dressed toad - jaw jutting out in constant defiance.

'My Father,' spits the Contessa — motioning at the same - causing you to choke, and spit your wine onto the row in front. Heads of several of the religious orders are here too, and many of the Council of Fifty who rule the City-state. Delicate yet powerful melodies resonate throughout the arena, as the Elven ensemble begin their passion play with a musical introduction. There's audible scoffing within the crowd, which grows into outright guffawing as the all-male warrior troupe take to the stage bedecked in various historical outfits. It seems what passes for serious storytelling in other Kingdoms, only raises hilarity in Deva. You can't discern a reaction from the proud elves - all of whom seem apparently lost in the play, wearing utterly inscrutable expressions of complete seriousness. The ages are covered, highlighting episodes of Elven intervention and guidance. The

Devans seem either to smirk or yawn in equal measure; a sideways glance at the beautiful young noblewoman betrays her as the latter - her lovely eyes are practically glazed over in a mask of indifference. Aegnor takes the stage during the final chapters, mournfully describing the flight from the Old World, and its inevitable slide into chaos and disorder. In parts dictating, in others appealing, it's difficult to track where the past ended and the present began, as the play takes on speech like qualities. A distinguished figure steps forward.

'That's Aegnor – leader of these fairies,' scoffs a drunk in the row in front. The figure steps forward and directly addresses the crowd, and in particular the Duce, who matches his steely gaze with his own. He begins,

'Never again, dear cousins; never again can we, jointly, allow evil to penetrate these lands to the extent of the past. After **two hundred and twenty eight** peaceable years of the White King's reign, we are now at the gates of Armageddon friends, and they buckle against the vanguard of darkness. Disorder needs *no* invite! No invitation to enter this world, and it does not need assistance from meddlers in the black arts. Dear friends of common cause, we watched from afar but can watch no longer. We have come to help you protect yourselves. Yes, I say this now, and I beseech you to heed my words. Only by joining as one can we hope to eliminate the threat - only as one can we hope to bolster the gates, in whatever form, and make them bulwarks against evil. Portents of the most ruinous form have been scryed in the Crystal Pools, and these are *imminent.*' Aegnor again regards the confused and mocking crowds somewhat urgently.

'Friends,' he pleads, 'we must address this without delay…we have seen that under this very city...' You sit forward to listen keenly, it becoming harder to pick out what is being said with the onset of cat-calls and booing. '…there are gates with are opening…' The boorish pig in front of you rises to toss a used flagon at the stage, but you firmly pummel him back into his seat. '…we locked the gates eons ago, they are not the playthings of men!'

It's chaos in the amphitheatre, as people rise to make off - when suddenly The Duce cries out in pain and sinks into his velvet throne clutching an arrow sunken into his breast. Suddenly one of the crowd rises and shouts, 'The Elf! There on the Colonnade!!' and points to an Elven figure making off from the scene to the north, bow in hand. Pandemonium ensues as elves and men alike try to comprehend the situation, both reaching instinctively for their weapons. As you scan the shadows high on the colonnade, you see another figure, this one black-clad, returning an unshot arrow back into their quiver before darting off to the south.

If protecting the Contessa is your priority, turn to 359.
If you give chase to the assassin headed north, turn to 208.
If you want to pursue the figure making off to the south, turn to 69.
If leap up to the private box to assist The Duce, turn to 235.

272

Blinded by the imminent arrival of the comet, once hurled, you lose the trajectory of the thrown fragment. The forest of cadavers blocking the way to The Master emit a high-pitched shriek, as they somehow seem to sense the celestial threat. White light, and a maelstrom of masonry and flesh. As if in a dream, your last memory is seeing unnatural entrails of thick dark green smoke seeping out, and upwards from The Master, and his eyes rolling in their sockets, the fires within extinguished. A brief feeling of despair tugs at the very centre of your being as the comet strikes with supersonic force.

You do not live to see the calamitous detonation, the blinding white holocaust which leaves no stone in the square unturned. For the duration of the hummingbirds heartbeat, you are entwined with The Master's corpse, melded together as one in the inferno.

But then to the Pantheon for you, and your place at the Table of Heroes. And then to the Pit for the fiend. The unnavigable, inescapable, pit.

Turn to 411.

273

Just as your spirit is about to crushed by the despondent darkness that resonates throughout the tomb, you're abruptly shaken from your maudlin thoughts by the alarming sight of a heaving Crypt Ghoul. The thing is stood, panting - apparently asleep - in near pitch black gloom at the rear of the tomb! Snapping to your senses, you instantly freeze on the spot, and breathing shallowly you consider your next move.

If you want to deal first with the tragic white coffins, turn to 260.
If you want to take the Crypt Ghoul by surprise, turn to 145.

274

Galiael regards you with a withering glare. 'Take it then, selfish human,' he hisses, 'May Menax protect you, should you ever have the misfortune to need to use it.' With a theatrical pivot he wheels away, his billowing cloak slapping in your face. Your new found friends melt away in startled embarrassment, not quite sure where to look, or what to say. 'Don't worry,' one timidly pipes up, 'The Elves will be gone soon... with any luck,' he concludes, hopefully. But you're not so sure, and so rub your chin ruefully.

Turn to 423.

275

A large and dirty pink and yellow striped tent houses the wresting ring - a small canvas circle, bound by ropes and raised up from the noisy spectator's benches. The crowd looks quite drunk and roars as you enter, just as the previous challenger is led dazed and bleeding profusely from the ring. The champion - a huge brute - lifts his hands aloft.

'Is there no man here who can defeat the mighty Rollo?' taunts the ringmaster. The system seems to be that each silver scuda you bet on yourself, you win twice as much back. Rollo prowls around the ring smirking confidently, and catching sight of you bellows,

'Ho! And what a dainty little madam we have here, all the way from the lily-livered Nhort!' With a taunt like that, you're unable to resist...

Bet however many silver scuda you want to risk, and turn to 104.

276

Looking as inconspicuous as you can - stood outside the Captain's cabin - you affect a nonchalant demeanour as a plump ruddy faced cook descends the stairwell. The ship lurches violently, struck by a powerful wave - the final wheezing gasps of last night's storm, causing him to lose grip on the tray he's carrying. The cheesecloth slides off, revealing two platters and two goblets. You both look down at the cloth, then the platters, then each other.

'Aye, then?' the cook challenges, somewhat aggressively,

'Two platters, Cook?' you prompt, raising an eyebrow conspiratorially. The cook wheezes, and squints at you,

'Aye. It's for the master's dog'

'The Master's dog?' you enquire doubtfully, 'And the wine? Does the Master's dog also take wine?'

The cook examines you with his one good eye, 'Aye. Aye, he does. When the mood takes him. For he has expensive tastes, he does.' With that, the portly cook juts out his jaw and squints at you furiously, defying a response. Grunting as he squeezes his chubby form past you in the tight corridor, he enters the cabin with the food. 'Here you go, Thorin, here's your dinner, and your *wine*' he says loudly, surely for the benefit of your ears. Leaving the room empty handed the cook scowls at you and disappears back up the stairs toward the galley, leaving you alone outside the Cabin.

If you want to try handle and slip inside quickly, turn to 283.
Or if you haven't already, call on the awkwardly aloof young man, turn to 474.
Or if you haven't already, instead pay a visit the wild-eyed extremist, turn to 451.
If you've already met both of the above, or just decide to save your energies for adventures yet to come, and return to your cabin, turn to 220.

277

You listen to the voices - and recognise them as members of the Brotherhood, no doubt bent on vandalising the walls of the Elven compound, or even the tree itself. They cast a quick glance in your direction, but don't notice anything untoward. Looking out across the square with narrowed eyes, you note the smell of drink carrying on the light breeze.

'Siga!' Adz whispers harshly, 'Do you smell it? No, not the drink - gunpowder!' Adz points toward the covered cart tied up in the square...the apparent source. 'Gods, Adz, what is going on here?'

If you want to maintain your position and see what their intent is, turn to 404.
If you want to jump up and hail them as brothers, turn to 98.
If you want to jump up and challenge them, turn to 23.

278

You lift the figures delicate chin with your callused fingers and meet her eyes. The Contessa! Words fail you - as they commonly do in the presence of beauty - and you continue to stare like an imbecile, much dizzied with carnal desire, and unfamiliar stirrings in your breeches.

'Sir,' she breathes in sweet tones, 'you have once again come to my aid. I am in your debt. No doubt you are surprised to see me on public display. A display it is indeed; to quell wagging tongues since word of my...disappearance became public.' A perceptible smile emerges from her lovely face, and she narrows her eyes as she scrutinises your face with increased interest. You can do nothing but pant like a dog, the endeavours of tackling the ogre catching up with you in ill-timed fashion.

Before you can stutter a reply, her attendants scurry over and quickly swamp her with excuses; whole-hearted promises that *they* were about the tackle the monster, and rescue her from her inevitable fate should you have not! None seem much interested in you, save to avert your gaze, and avoid brushing against you, lest they soil their silken garments. Members of the Watch reappear, throwing jealous glances in your direction.

Add 1 to your Watch Test total, as your deeds gain their unwanted attention.

The noblewoman captures you with an apologetic smile and raises her voice over her attendants incessant chatter.

'Contessa Appollina of Nias – please excuse my jailers.'

'Sigasünd...of the Seas,' you croak, digging your punishing fingernails into your thighs, hotly embarrassed by your ridiculous reply. Her Ladyship chuckles in a good-natured way, seeming not to notice your blushes.

'You must accompany me to this evening's Elven recital...it would be my honour. Call it a grateful reward for a heroic rescuer.'

If you wish to accept the offer, turn to 271.
If you decline, under the hostile glances of her retinue, turn to 243.

279

'Stygians? What should I know or care of such detritus?' He fidgets tensely, tutting and obviously annoyed by your presence. 'Well, I can see I will not have any peace here to continue my work,' the Freelander merchant says, collecting his apparatus, and departs for the sanctity of his private room. What does the day hold for you?

There is a marksmanship contest, with early heats taking place very soon, and promises of a great prize, if that interests you - and only you still possess a pistol - turn to 68.
Or you could head to the Plain of Heroes for the Military Display. If so, turn to 413.
Or to just quench your thirst down at the Festival of Wine and Song, turn to 420.

'I...couldn't help but notice your pendant,' he says, pointing at the amber gem which has crept from under your shirt. 'I'll be frank - I've been looking for a similar decoration for some time. I'm something of a collector.' Hessler empties his purse and counts the contents carefully. 'I have 40 silver scuda here...can we come to an agreement at that price?'

If you decide to sell the Dragonfire Gem, make the modifications to your adventure sheet. Either way, you bid farewell to the captain. Turn to 18.

The short journey feels like an eternity to you. Time after time some unseen figure lurches out in front of you. Whether of the living world or the dead makes a difference not, as you cleave them aside with desperate hacking blows, screams and bellows ringing in your ears each time. Breathlessly you push your way onto the wharf. The docks are alive with activity, and thick with rats. Sailors and stevedores scurry this way and that along the harbour-side, tangling with guilty looking soldiers and militia, and desperate, forlorn citizens.

A great rattle of ships anchors being hauled, mixes with marine commands barked out by bosons. This clamour is occasionally punctuated by screams, as frequent undead fiends stumbling upon the harbour side – and upon some poor unsuspecting victim. Everyone is frantic, self-absorbed in their own nightmare, no one casts so much of a glance at you as you brush past the swarming masses. You look out across the harbour at the flotilla of ships heading out through the massive Elven sea gates. It must have been so eons ago, when the Fathers of Men who constructed them also departed this place. Great frigates of the Devan Navy queue with free-booting cogs, their sailors shouting curses, and their cannons pointed threatening at one another, as they jostle for an advantageous position. Down on the surface of the water, pilots throw their arms around, gesticulating wildly and shaking their fists at their contemporaries; the legion of fishermen and pleasure boat skippers all contesting for a position away from the city, into the relative safety of the open sea.

You see 'The Boogenhofen', still at anchor, away from the wharf, but curiously not contesting for a position through the gates. Surely if Hessler was on aboard, the wily old skipper would be half way to The Daab by now? You shout for the professor and for Adz, and cast your eyes over the maelstrom but are met with no answers.

'Oi, there!' a burly sailor bellows at you, pushing past. He rushes to some crew mates, busily loading the last rowing boat for a trading vessel, a hundred paces out to water, with wares from the company warehouses. You look at the ensign and markings on the vessel - ' The Kraken.' Painted in Imperial letters, but carrying no flags of office. This ship will be likely headed far south - to a civilized land, all things considered. Its captain paces up aboard deck. His face is a mask of inscrutability, making it difficult to gauge his disposition.

Do you have a dozen orphaned children with you? If so, turn to 154.
Otherwise, you can make for the Diving Swallow, turn to 120.
Or you can seek safe passage aboard The Kraken, turn to 380.

282

Before they can react, you deftly draw your trusty pistol and aim it directly between the ears of who you presume is in command.

'Down! Slowly!' you bark at them in Midden tongue. After exchanging a nervous and almost imperceptible glance at his two brothers-in-arms, the sergeant motions with his palm to obey. They manage with some difficulty to prostrate themselves on the slippery cobbles. Confident that these human tortoises will take an age to clamber back to their feet, you dart past them, giving the ugliest looking one a firm kick in the ribs as you do.

Following the illuminated patterns adorning the watery night sky, you continue to the Keijzer house. Soon after Pepin emerges smiling from behind an overflowing water butt,

'I lost them - fat hogs!' he squeaks excitedly, well pleased with himself. You tousle his hair in congratulation...then remembering how he scarpered, leaving you alone to face the law, you give him a firm clip around the ears with the other hand. Grabbing the confused young boy by the wrist once again, you prod him into guiding you toward your destination.

Turn to 464.

283

You quickly try the handle - with mild surprise it clicks opens. Glancing about you, you stealthily enter, careful to close the door quietly behind you. Hessler's cabin is luxurious - in the circumstances and tight confines of the ship. Rich furs adorn bed, and table of charts is laden with exquisitely crafted navigation tools. A tapestry of maps covers the walls, heavily indented with the captains notes. A rich velvet curtain is pulled across the cabin, concealing the far end of the room. You freeze in your tracks as you notice a large sleeping wolfhound underneath the table, its twitching paws extending across the floorboards. It has a curiously intelligent face - bedecked with a pair of spectacles – and betrays no sign of awakening as it breathes deep and long.

If you take the opportunity to slay it whilst it sleeps, turn to 336.
If you attempt to sneak past the slumbering hound, turn to 65.

284

You hurtle toward the relative safety of the forest as fast as your legs will carry you. You splash over the sodden green carpet of the bilious plain, but the thick lichen like surface causes you to stumble and slip. Instinctively, Galiael dives to protect you, as the Bone Dragon swoops. With a mighty roar the monster consumes you pair of you in a hell-like furnace of blazing flame. **Lose 1 point of Fortitude, and 1 from your Agility** as your Elven comrade bears the brunt of the agonies. Throwing off the charred elf you turn to face the gargantuan beast which has now landed before you, poised to strike with its immense claws.

If your Dexterity and Fortitude combined total 12 or more, turn to 263.
If they total 11 or less, turn to 244.

285

Steering your reluctant mount a safe distance from the fiend filled square, you anxiously await the becalming rays of dawns early light, wishing its warm tendrils to reach out into this cursed city and push away the shadows of the dead. Howls, screams. Human and...otherwise, fill your ears as you wait - reaching a crescendo shortly before dawn. A fiery orange crust forms on the horizon as the sun awakens, and the comet looms swollen against the purple sky. The chorus of howls reaches such a pitch that something stirs within you. A nagging doubt, a sinking feeling in your soul. Have you waited too long? Tears form in your eyes, as your mind is filled with despair and regret. You belatedly emerge and set forth to the square with frantic urgency. The howls subside as you approach, and in terror you look up to see the comet form a low trajectory behind you, blistering the air as it scorches towards its child.

The sun's brilliant orange light casts long fingers of shadow upon the flagstones as you reach the square. The multitude of horrors are disappearing into the pit with their master, who has already sunk to the depths, offended by the light. With Pegasus' wings bursting with furious effort you howl with unrequited vengeance, as the clothes on you back begins to smoulder in the approaching heat of the comet. With dull realisation of the inevitable you hurl the burning orb toward the pit with all your might. Mere seconds later you are entirely immolated by the white heat of the star-shattering explosion.

Whether or not the Master is destroyed by your brave - but hesitant - actions, you will never know.

Your adventure, and your mortal soul, ends here.

286

You pull out your knife and skilfully begin to weave through the cumbersome Watchdogs, piercing two of them, who stagger backwards clutching their punctuations, idiotic expressions on their dull faces. You've dealt with common bullies before you think, adrenalin pulsing through your veins, as you cut a swathe. Sure of killing them all quickly, you feel a dull crack on the side of your head. You gaze in confused amazement at a common washerwoman, another cobble in hand, about to be flung at your head. She's screaming insults at you in a language you can no longer understand, as the colours of the cityscape begin to fade, her outline disappears, and you lose consciousness for the last time.

The watchdogs drag you bleeding down to a nearby manhole, collecting an excited crowd of urchins and beggars, who take turns to dart forward defile your now naked and tattered body. After taking turns to insult and spit at your wrecked person, one leans forward to cut your throat. Another anonymous stranger is dumped like an dead animal, into the foetid, maggot filled sewers.

Your adventure is at an end.

287

You career across the slippery drained canal, jumping from one tombstone to another, as nimble as you dare. From behind you a huge dust ball emerges from the collapsed chamber, and you rush into the Hall of Tapestries. The magical white flames illuminating the room flicker with uncertainty, as huge cracks forge their way across the ceiling and down through the walls. Your ears are filled with thunderous detonations of falling rock. With a plunging heart you note the entrance on the other side of the gallery collapsing, sending dust and debris into the air. Your lungs are burning, and your heart pounding as you search frantically for escape. There seems no way out, and you begin to resolve yourself before facing the Gods.

If you have any of the following words: MENAX, SANROMAI, or NAED written on your adventure sheet, turn to 190.
If you do not, turn to 211.

288

Under a baleful black night sky you do battle with this graceful foe. The assassin is a skilful opponent and you struggle to land a telling strike as she dodges and parries. Deftly avoiding a particularly savage - if crude - blow, she cart-wheels away like a circus performer, before reaching inside her tunic and throwing something at you. You have only a split second to avoid the glinting metallic object.

If you have the Gift of Acrobatics and/or your Agility is 8 or higher, turn to 124.
If you benefit from neither of these, turn to 452.

289

Casting an orange glow against the widening rock-face, you thrust the torch into the alcove and see that it develops into a chamber in its own right. As you step into the space, you are sure that the sobbing sound is real, but from where you cannot tell, as no other exits adorn the surfaces of the walls. You are about to turn away from the disquieting sobs when you see tendrils of ethereal essence seep from rock-face. Gob-smacked you stand rooted to the spot as a wispy figure forms before you, a ghostly Elven mirage of timeless age. Your mouth opens and shuts wordlessly as you consider hailing the phantom. Before you can decide, the figure begins itself to mutter, uttering verse like sentences in what you take for archaic Elvish, interspersed with anguished sobs. You clench the pommel of your sword tightly as you carefully regard the ghostly figure.

If you choose to attack the Phantom before it notices you, turn to 356.
If you want to attempt to communicate with it, turn to 418.
Or should you wish to leave the ethereal figure in peace, you can head back down the passageway, toward the light source. Turn to 438.

290

The sergeant and his bullies, give you another beating, taking it turns to pummel you - **lose 2 points of Fortitude**. Sure of your imminent death, the thrashing is interrupted by a nervous looking guard, who enters the room from the counter of the gaol.

'Captain...CAPTAIN!' he urges. We have...err, visitors.' He steps aside, pointing his finger hurriedly, before being pushed aside by Galiael, and a band of heavily armed Elven warriors. You smile though blooded lips, as the jailers back away from you and turn white with fear. Galiael kneels down to assist you, wiping your face with a clean cloth.

'Friend,' he says, somewhat disappointed. 'How ever did you go from being Champion, to being a common thug, incarcerated in this evil place?' He shakes his head sadly, and slides the **Elven Ring of Kindred** from your finger - cross it off your adventure sheet. 'We have fulfilled our obligations to you,' he concludes. He pulls you to your feet, and one of the other elves returns your belongs, from a stunned looking guard. You are escorted out of the gaol by the Elven band, and left to your own devices without further discussion. In the circumstances you consider the best option is to return to the Diving Swallow.

Turn to 125.

291

You drink the liquid...with some trepidation. It burns with a satisfying strength, revitalising your dry mouth and steadying your nerves. **Regain 2 points of Fortitude.**

If you decide you want to offer some prayers before you leave the shrine, turn to 56.
Should you think it best to press on down the steps, turn to 71.

292

Again and again you plunge your weapon into the roaring beast, losing grip of it entirely. **Lose 1 point of Fortitude** from the sheer fatigue of combating such a leviathan. Its fury shows no sign of abating, although you do sense its vitality is waning as it staggers clumsily before you, a listless tongue hanging from its repulsive mouth.

If you wish to press the fight with your knife, turn to 200.
Or you can choose to flee, and hope the wounded monster is in no position to pursue you, turn to 243.

293

You push Adz towards the carts, and adopt a tree-ward position away from the approaching footsteps entering the square.

'Siga...' Adz begins, but you shush him as you strain to listen to the voices.

If you have BROTHERHOOD written on your adventure sheet, turn to 343.
Otherwise, turn to 404.

294

By a hair's breadth your shot is closer to the bull! To rapturous cheers you progress. In the final round, you face the graceful Elven Champion, Galiael. His progress has been unfaltering. The elf's exquisitely crafted Elven arrows thudding home with unerring accuracy throughout. Regardless, you step up to the mark, and take aim…

Take your total from the previous round, and add three to this if you choose to use Skullduggery - if you did, you managed to sneakily nobble the fletches on the elf's arrow.

If your total is 10 or more, turn to 175.
If your total is 9 or less, turn to 181.

295

You stumble away from the unseen beast, though narrow abandoned lanes as you once again look up hopefully for your bearings. Rotten beams and stained awnings converge across the narrow passageways to blot out the night sky, and thick hot smoke fills your nostrils as you hear the roar of nearing flames, no longer drowned out by the screams of the city.

If you decide to clamber up onto the rooftops of the dwellings in the hope of getting your bearings, turn to 86.
If you persist with your journey, unseen, within the confines of the slum warrens, turn to 348.

296

With a mighty heave you push your blade though the Hellhounds soft underbelly and twist. The beast snaps at you wildly, whilst you hold it on the blade at arm's length. As its thrashing dies down its thick pelt begins smouldering, giving off acrid black smoke. Its eyes begin to fade, and with a torturous howl the fur explosively ignites, immolating the beast and sending you reeling backwards, singed by the flames.

You turn to Adz, who is dealing a final blow to the other blazing beast. Flames crackle violently up the carved panels of the tower, and tapestries are sucked into the inferno taking hold.

'Siga!' Adz coughs through the smoke, 'Which way?'

If ascending through the flames to the top storey of the tower is your choice, turn to 202.
If you decide to flee the blazing tower the way you came, turn to 43.

If ascending through the flames to the top storey of the tower is your choice, turn to 202.
If you decide to flee the blazing tower the way you came, turn to 43.

297

'If Adz could see me now,' you mumble wryly, as Galiael waits, trembling with anticipation at the tip of your sword. You lower your blade. Smiling apologetically, your fatigued mind thrashes around for momentous words befitting such a pivotal occasion.

'Embrace me, friend,' you stutter, screwing your eyes up with embarrassment. The elf doesn't share the emotion, and instead clasps you tightly, sinking his head into your chest with earnest devotion. You consider coughing sharply to halt the unseemly débâcle, but indulge the noble being in his uncharacteristically emotional display.

Galiael mutters a meandering oath into your tunic and raises his wet eyes level with yours. 'Sigasünd…the scrutiny of the Gods falls upon us. We are favoured and blessed to be chosen for such a task.' He steps backwards, and looks heavenward, as if in rapture. 'Come, brother! To the Orb, to the weapon gifted to us - to rid this land of evil. It will be an honour to die alongside you, should it be willed. I swear it!'

'Death!' you spit. 'Death has reached out for me many times before, Death is a hungry bitch,' you declare harshly, leaving your companion speechless. You briskly stomp and splash forth across the addled plateau surface, leaving Galiael in your wake. 'But I spurn her hunger each time! Come elf, make haste!'

Turn to 183.

298

Not long after you leave The Diving Swallow, Adz exclaims excitedly,

'Siga! Look, let's get some masks and join the party!' Too consumed by the festivities to await a reply, the big oaf bounds across to a shifty looking hawker, peddling garishly painted masks from a rickety stall. You roll your eyes as you see money exchanged and Adz returns with a disguise for each of you; a hideous beaked mask for himself, and a mask of lip curling sorrow for you, complete with painted tears of woe. 'Here you go, stoic friend, this suits your cheerless personality entirely,' he laughs, in good humour. You are about to protest when you look about you, indeed every person in the whole of the city seems to be masked. Disguised as mock animals, characters from fireside tales, or disturbing creatures of the night.

'This will be a long night,' you mutter to a mangy cur. Sat in the gutter, it raises an ear to you in hope of a tasty morsel.

'Hmm, what was that...a good night? Of course it will, old friend!' The big Norsiczan laughs, aiming his boot at the flea ridden whelp, which scampers away - well used to avoiding such treatment.

Much wine is being consumed by the swollen band of cavorting revellers as it snakes its way around the walls. A mass of anonymous figures scratching away the veneer of morality, as groups break off to enlighten dark corners with all manner of licentiousness. Gongs, symbols and firecrackers keep the songbirds from roosting, indeed the clamour is near loud enough to wake the dead...

Your lumbering friend is too distracted to hear it at first, perhaps because of the exposed flesh and inviting glances. But you do. The unmistakeable sound of screaming, breaking out from the direction of the main square.

'Adz! Adz, you oaf!' you shout to him bad-temperedly. Before your erstwhile friend can reply, a huge explosion rips through the clammy night air, halting the cacophony of noise emanating from the masked dandies. Screams are definitely coming from the Grand Piazza, but the explosion seemed to come from the direction of the merchant quarter...or possibly the Elven quarter.

'Who cares anyway?' slurs an inebriated party-goer, as he lurches into you, his hot of breath reeking of sour wine. The blow you strike fair bursts the man's stomach as he collapses, retching up the unsavoury contents of a day of plenty. Ripping off your mask and throwing it to the floor, your mind races. As the stray dog laps hungrily at the fresh meal produced into the gutter, you must make your mind up where to rush to.

To the Grand Piazza, and the screaming, turn to 212.
Toward the explosion, somewhere near the confluence of Merchant and Elven quarters, turn to 250.

299

The motivated Stygians take turns to lurch at you, inexpertly swiping through the driving rain. What they lack in skill they make up for in effort. Despite your superior skills, one lands a sneaky blow to your hip, causing you to roar in pain. **Lose 2 points of Fortitude.** Furious, you hack at them with chilling violence. Eventually, your blade gathers purpose, and glints keenly in the moonlight as it dispatches the Stygian footpads to miserable deaths.

You can hear shouts, whistles and the clank of approaching armour, as you cut down the last of the second sending him gurgling to the reddening cobbles. You take a quick glance about you - Pepin is nowhere to be seen, he must have gone to fetch the watch, naive child! The dark cloaked old man needs that split second to bound onto a water butt with astonishing athleticism, and with a further leap clambers up onto the roof of the single story house.

If you try and follow the old man, turn to 324.
If you want to quickly search the bodies, turn to 308.
Or flee the scene by darting down an alley and make your way to meet the professor, turn to 233.

300

You put your shoulder to the door - much to the horror of beggar - who recoils, grey with fear.

'Keep a watch!' you hiss, as you give the entrance several stiff thrusts. You curse as you see a sneaky looking citizen take note and slip round away – **Add 1 to your Watch Test total.** Once forced, you creep inside. The beggar attempts to follow, but a firm hand in the chest causes him to reconsider.

The Keijzer house is filled with gloom, the sky lights darkened by recent smoke. The rooms surrounding the atrium have been thoroughly ransacked. Experiments and mechanical contraptions lay disturbed and smashed. Clothes and mundane trappings are strewn everywhere. Silver too - you count at least 30 scuda - left scattered with the other belongings.

Whoever has ransacked this place clearly wasn't bent on common burglary. As you prod the detritus with your boot, you catch sight of the source of the burning stench. In a bed-chamber, signs of a now extinguished fire, with several papers lying burnt within the ashes. Maps, letters, scrolls, most are beyond recovery...but...one item remains mostly intact. A **Notebook**, inscribed with images of comets, dragons and owls. Measurements and compass directions are prominent – **94 degrees east, and 17 leagues distance.** Though mostly incomprehensible, there also appears to be some kind of incantation - and something draws you to carefully stow it about your person - **add the notebook, and these co-ordinates to your adventure sheet.** A melted bell-jar lies next to the fire - damp patches on the floorboards suggest the flames, once lit, were soon extinguished by the falling water filled receptacle. Perhaps this job remains unfinished...

There is no time to consider further as your erstwhile lookout squeaks a warning of approaching watchdogs! With no inclination to be incarcerated once the professor arrives in the city, you think it best to leave this place. Securing the notebook, you push past the beggar - leaving behind the Watches cries of 'halt!' - and head back to the Diving Swallow.

Turn to 75.

301

Your eyes roll with ecstasy as you batter yourself free of the bellowing oaf. You almost feel pity for the creature...as you savour the salty nectar filling your lungs. The dark waters of the sea envelop you, as you are carried into the embrace of the deep. Your last fleeting moments are filled with unimaginable bliss as your tortured soul is finally extinguished.

Your adventure is at an end.

302

You half-heartedly patch up their barricade, and offer lies of dubious reassurance to the sullen children, as you set about leaving the Orphanage for the docks - alone. Aloevopia doesn't protest, but merely watches.

'I was wrong,' she says sadly, as you step out into the alley way. 'You are not destined for greatness. Go now, save at least yourself.' You hear the little raven-haired girl sobbing with bitter disappointment as you skulk off into the night toward the docks.

Turn to 281.

303

Do you have the word **SHADRACK** on your adventure sheet?

If you do, turn to 15.
If not, turn to 492.

304

As you prepare to dispatch these wretched dead back to rest, you lose your footing on the slimy rocks - seating you painfully on the seat of your pants. **Lose 1 point of Fortitude.** As renewed tremors shake through the crumbling edifice, you hack down with urgency, keen to be free of this place lest it also become your tomb.

Turn to 54

305

Deciding not to dally, you stride forward out of the dark, going unnoticed by the ethereal figure. With a savage cleave you bring down your blade, but it merely parts the air with a cool swoosh. Braced for the expected impact of steel on flesh, you lose your balance and stumble, crashing into the rock-face. A bone chilling shriek fills the cavern, so high-pitched that you instinctively clasp your palms over your ears in agony. As you scramble to your feet in the darkness, you look up in horror as the bound spirit brings its spectral face close to yours. Its eyeless death mask seems to bore through your very being. It sniffs and tilts its death mask, seemingly inspecting you, or at least your aura. You don't breathe, don't blink. Your fingers move by atoms, towards the hilt of your dropped weapon. In an instant the phantom's mouth expands with uncommon elasticity, and it *screams*.

You bellow by return, blood running through the cracks in your fingers as your eardrums are breached. Staggering away blindly you crash along the splintered walls and toward the distant light, with only what is secured about your person - **Remove the weapon you were carrying from your list of items.**

The primal scream finally subsides, and you sink to your knees in relief and pain. **Deduct 1 from your Dexterity, and 2 from your Fortitude.** Cursing your ill-advised choice, you eventually pick yourself up and make toward the light, which emanates from some rough-hewn descending steps.

Turn to 438

306

Having reached a foetid waterway nearby to Piazza Arborea, and upon seeing the water ripple in unison with the 'thub thub' sound resonating through the city, you take stock.

'Adz, do you remember our time in Budazan?' you ask your friend, over the cacophony of screams and shrieks assailing the city. The hymns of the fearful are sung ever louder from the unusually crowded temples.

'How could I forget,' he replies, with a frown. 'When the dead walked the earth...when the gates of hell were breached. What of it?' You grit your teeth and shake your head in annoyance, wishing anything for a quiet life.

'I have a feeling we're about to have a repeat.' No sooner have you spoke than seismic quakes shake through the city, sending masonry cascading to the cobbles shattering into uncountable fragments. All around you people are screaming. Some in terror, some with fearful wounds, maimed by the merciless torrent-like shrapnel of exploding roof tiles. Another movement sends Adz tumbling into the canal, for a moment disappearing under the muddy brown surface.

'Adz!' you cry anxiously. The big man reappears through the sludge though, and you haul him out of the cloying waters which have sucked many a man to his grave. 'We have to find the professor!' you shout over thunderous noise, and see Adz nod his head in agreement, dirty blond hair plastered over his wet face. 'University?' you mouth at your friend, with the dust clouds forming. Consumed by dust, you are quickly enveloped in a bubble of near total darkness.

'Go!' he bellows by return, though you barely hear it.

Turn to 16.

307

You pull the trigger on your wheellock pistol and twist your head as the elf disappears in a plume of blue smoke. You hear a cry, followed by a wet thud, as Galiael slumps motionless to the sodden carpet of the plateau. With the invigorating stench of sulphur filling your nostrils, you step over to the corpse, and nudge it with your boot. Of the elf's finely chiselled features...practically nothing remains. Refilling the pan with gunpowder, you carefully re-holster your firearm with satisfaction.

Turn to 350

308

You begin to rifle through the corpses' belongings. Both of them smell richly of lemon – strange, as they are otherwise ragged and unkempt. On the first body you find an **Iron key, with a lemon motif and the number '34' etched into it, and 5 silver scuda.** If you wish to take these, **add them to your adventure sheet.** You can make out a metallic clanking of armour - getting closer. The watch must have been alerted by the screams.

Do you quickly search the second body? If so, turn to 490.
Or if you make good your escape, turn to 233.

The legions of the dead, drawn in thick knots by the magnetism of the master, turn with primeval instinct at the war cries of the dozen. With you at their vanguard, your band plough through the soft corpses like a scythe through ripe wheat. You can't help but wish Adz were here, to see this majestic spectacle. Despite the circumstances you're unable to stifle a wild belly-laugh at the thought of his sorrowful face when...if...you regale him of the tale. The leader of these men, Rollo, is by your side, hacking at the shambling dead as if they were straw stuffed practice dummies. He too is smiling.

'Yes, my friend!' he shouts breathlessly, as he cleaves an undead wench in twain, 'Let's enjoy these moments, if they are to be our last!' Against the odds, the dozen hack a path toward the Master.

His gaping bestial maw emits a paralysing roar - a roar of terror! In confusion and panic he lurches to and fro, trying to shift his massive bulk through the hordes of the dead, to the foul sanctuary of the smouldering crater. But despite valiant efforts, the dead are too many, and you see several comrades fall to the blood-red marble flagstones of the square. Almost unawares, you too are stricken by the many savage wounds inflicted. You feel your heart quiver and tighten - the spectre of impending death circling overhead. But your mind lives on a few more breathless moments. Drowning on the blood which is filling your lungs, you have the fortitude to claw at the drawstrings and unveil the comet fragment, a forest of cadavers still blocking your way. For a fleeting second as you twist upwards to face the heavens the child is superimposed upon the parent, and you are superimposed against the dark shape of The Master, as you hurl the beacon toward the epitome of darkness.

If by Fate, you are Favoured, turn to 272
If you are Unwatched or Marked, turn to 402.

310

You thrash mightily through the thick, stinking waters, through filth and detritus. Past corpses and bloated animal cadavers you swim - each stroke an agony as your muscles burn with fatigue. The black world disappears for a few fleeting moments as your weary head sinks behind the river. You consider surrendering yourself to its embrace, and roll onto your back, arms outstretched...when you catch sight of it. There in the pre-dawn sky, the comet. You know in an instant what you must do, and so loosening the straps on all your belongings, you allow all your weighty possessions to sink into the mud of the river bed. **Cross all your possessions off your adventure sheet**. Except for the Orb, of course.

Turn to 60

311

You feel a curious buzz from inside your backpack. Upon investigation, the source appears to be emanating from the marvellous little owl. You study the dials and complex numerals with your dirty and callused hands. Do you have Artur Keijzer's notebook?

If so, combine the two figures noted, and turn to that page number.
If not, then though curious, you cannot fathom any reasoning to it, and popping the owl back in your knapsack, you begin the long trek back to Deva. Turn to 121.

312

This Elven champion is a formidable foe; skilled in the arts of battle. Tumbling across the tainted plateau, you are locked in a contest of survival. Kill or be killed - only one can walk away alive.

Combine the totals of your Dexterity, Agility and Fortitude and add two if you have the Gift of Martial Prowess. If the total is 20 or more, you have the means by which to defeat the elf. Turn to 350.

If the total is 19 or less......Galiael bests you, and as you sink punctured and bleeding numbly into the ground, you can only hope that your deliverer can save the souls of your comrades from the impending forces of darkness.

Your life - and adventures, end here.

313

Taking the glowing orb from the bag, you hurl it down the hillside away from you. After a hurried descent you reach the wretched hamlet to find it entirely abandoned. Making haste you clamber into an ancient coracle, and with silent strokes you row the vessel toward the pine crested islet. Doubts creep into your mind. Will this too be inhabited by creatures of the night? Will there be a source of food...water even? You grimace and glance down at your blade as you consider your perilous future. At the midway point, you rest the oars to gaze in wonder as you watch the comet smash into the hillside throwing up a firestorm of pine and cypress trees. Ripples from the impact race across the surface of the sea, carrying you ever closer to the shore. From the distant city you hear the ceaseless groan of the many-dead, drifting across the black waters. But for today at least, you live on.

Your adventure – but not your life – ends here.

314

Sapped of energy, and weakened by injuries and endeavours, for a moment you think you will be engulfed in this wave of undeath. Somehow you tap your inner resolve, and grunting with fatigue you redouble your efforts to stem the tide. **Unless you are Iron willed, lose 1 point of Fortitude** from your labours.

Turn to 85

315

Open jawed as the maddened elf springs toward you, you gather your senses just in time to pivot from a violent hack, which sends **Galiael** tumbling down the steps. No doubt pained from the foul deed to be committed, your former companion has lost some of his poise and seems uncharacteristically flustered and clumsy. You quickly resolve to take advantage of the situation, and you leap down to deliver this murderous elf back to his ancestors.

Turn to 109

316

You recount the story of the Moretti family, the vampiric children, the possible link to the other events to Adz, who listens on excitedly.

'The market can wait,' he declares. 'Let's go and hunt down this fiend! If his hunting lodge is only ten leagues away we can get there and back before nightfall - come on, Siga, it'll be like old times!' You look at the giant lump, excited as a child at the prospect of a bit of adventuring, and can't help but think to humour him. You Consider that the professor, from experience, will probably take longer than a day before he's ready to set out. Adz interjects your thoughts - 'I'm sure Captain Hessler will know where we can borrow some horses and hire a guide, come on, make haste with that ale.'

If you agree to set out for the Moretti hunting lodge, turn to 262.
If you insist on doing as the professor says, in picking up supplies from the market, turn to 205.

317

You pull away at some bigger chunks of the masonry, and clear a wider entrance for yourself before squeezing through into the narrow passage way beyond. Treading carefully over the cracked flagstones, your eyes are drawn to the well preserved Elven murals on the walls - displaying momentous scenes of the Kingdoms of the Everborn. They describe pictorially the one hundred conquests of Pentarc, first of the Elven Primarchs, who swept evil from the world and for a time subjugated its avaricious kings. Viewing this artistry, you feel a degree of magnetism towards it, and resolve to remember the story it tells. **Write down the number of Pentarcs conquests - 100 - on your adventure sheet.**

It's a joy to see bear witness to such craftsmanship as you tread carefully along - and down the passage way. It develops into a marked descent, and as you spiral downwards the path is much disturbed by the recent quake. Here the murals lay shattered on the cold floor, entrances to sub-chambers and doorways are totally caved in, and impenetrable. The only way forward it to clamber over a pile of rubble blocking your way and maintain your course. Dropping down on the other side of the rubble, only the flames from your torch illuminate the darkness, and you can barely see one span in front of you. A foul odour lingers on the dusty air. The stench of death. Another footstep forwards and you tread on something soft. It gives way like a ripe peach, sending ripples through your bowels. Glancing down you see a glossy dark liquid seeping into the earth, before a low moan in front of you freezes you to the spot and raises the hairs on the back of your neck. Something is shambling toward you in the enveloping gloom! With no time to turn and climb back over the rockfall, you raise your blade, and thrust the flames forward, illuminating enough of the darkness to see a dead-eyed elf, his brain hanging out of a gaping wound on the side of its head. From behind it another, and another! With grasping hands the **Undead Elves** reach out for you with hungry desperation.

If your Fortitude is 9 or less, turn to 314.
If your Fortitude is 10 or more, turn to 85.

318

The fop squeals, and takes a step backwards breaking your grip on his ear. Flustered and fearful he exclaims, 'I am the half-nephew of The Duce, the esteemed leader of the Council of Fifty!' He looks around anxiously toward a large barrel shaped man. 'Bruno!' The young noble shouts loudly, irritated at the delay in assistance. Bruno rises wearily and rubs his stubbly chin with his sausage-like fingers.

'Yes, m'lord,' he replies automatically. Rolling his sleeves up, he lumbers over, fists clenched and shaking his head.

Do you stand your ground? If so, turn to 184.
Or do you jump over the benches and disappear into the thronged masses? If so, turn to 67.

319

You grasp the weapon in both hands and level it at the beast. 'Hoi, ugly!' you yell, drawing an infuriated howl. It thunders toward you, swinging its mighty fists with furious intent. Stabbing powerfully into its enlivened abdomen, you carve two fearful wounds into the pallid flesh. Over-stretching – or is it over confidence – you struggle to retain control of the polearm, long unaccustomed as you are to bearing one.

If your Dexterity is 9 or more and/or you have the Gift of Martial Prowess, turn to 292.
If not, turn to 42.

320

'Like I said friend,' growls the **Animal Master**, through his thick black beard, 'The show's over - for you!' His cruel whip cracks with spite as he advances toward you. You have no choice but to do battle with this menacing foe.

If your Dexterity is 7 or lower, turn to 128
If your Dexterity is 8 or higher, turn to 497

321

Shollstüg- the seventh day, MMDXXXI

The three of you return to the Diving Swallow, to catch a few hours sleep as dawn breaks. **Restore up to 2 points of Fortitude, not exceeding your starting total.**

You consider yesterday's events - the arson attack on Keijzer's house, the portentous dreams of chains and trees - the reoccurring omens of beating hearts. The elves - what's the story with the elves? What are the mysterious Stygians up to? You've had more dealings with them in the last days than in a lifetime before. And the stranger who reeked of death – what, if any, significance does the lemon tree medallion have? On balance, you decide you prefer the more familiar and less oblique dangers of being half a league underground fighting Hobgoblins, or lined up on a muddy battlefield with an obvious enemy in clear sight through cannon fire and muzzle smoke! You shake your head at the nagging complexity of the situation - how on earth is a man supposed to enjoy the festivities on with the din of such a backdrop! The warm sun pokes through the late morning haze, and three of you stir together, ascending to the terrace.

'Adz and Siga - I want the two of you to go to the market and bring these items, we need to refresh our supplies for our trip to the mountains.' He hands you a list detailing the necessities. If you have lost your sword, Adz furnishes you with another – **make a note of this on your adventure sheet.** The professor explains he needs to attend the university to study this manuscript or other, to finalise the location of the Elven gate, able as he is now to put all the pieces of the puzzle together. You think better of troubling the old man with further discussion and so he departs unawares of your troubles. Maybe Adz will be a more receptive ear and co-conspirator…

If you have both LUDOVICO and VELVET written on your adventure sheet, turn to 90.
If you have only LUDOVICO written on your adventure sheet, turn to 316.
If you have only VELVET written on your adventure sheet, you may turn to 229.
If you have neither of these, but you have an Iron Key, you can turn to the number etched on it.
If neither of these words are written on your adventure sheet, and you do not have a key, you finish your ales, and set off with Adz to the market. Turn to 205.

<hr>

322

'A Fleshhound's bastard spawn? Cabbage brained bog-sniffer? Siga - you don't really think these things of me do you?' says the grey blob in front of you. 'Siga - I am wounded to my tender soul, you know what a sensitive lamb I am,' the blob continues with a chuckle.

'Adz…is that you? What…what happened out there in the sea?' you manage to ask, through your splitting headache.

'Look what you did to me!' moans Adz, pointing to some angry red gouges on his cheek, 'I've been scratched less in a Casconqian whorehouse! You heard some soothing female voices, Siga, and typically went running for them - only this time it was the waves which were calling. Sea spirits. Luckily for you I'm not susceptible to such entreaties. You've always had a weakness where women are concerned...even long dead ones.'

Your eyes adjust to the onset of your senses and Adz comes into view, still affecting a wounded demeanour, whilst you sit agog with your mouth open trying to comprehend your brush with death.

'Thanks, friend,' you smile at Adz, 'You're not a cabbage brained fleshhound...you're my hero.'

'Idiot,' Adz says self-consciously, as he rises to his feet. 'Come on now, flea-brain, we haven't got time to waste if we're to get there and back to the city by nightfall...and if we don't we'll both need saving from these haunted marshes!'

Without further ado, you set off for the hunting lodge. Turn to 264.

323

If Galiael is dead, turn to 76.
If you did not kill Galiael, turn to 196.

324

You clamber up the drainpipe onto the roof. It's difficult to see which way the old man went on this dismal night - through the awnings, smoking chimneys and rain sodden rooftop gardens.

Take your current Agility score, and add two to it if you have the Gift of Intuition.
If the total is 8 or less, turn to 178.
If the total is 9 or higher, turn to 391.

325

You pass from tapestry to tapestry, admiring the exquisite craftsmanship and artistry comprised in each. They seem to represent labours set by each of the Elven Gods. Each depicts an act of great valour - conquering a mighty foe, reclaiming a lost treasure in the face of insurmountable conditions, or selfless sacrifice the in the face of mortal danger. You step forward for a closer look and begin to hear faintly audible sounds of clinking armour, of cries, and the stamping of boots. The stench of dying men. You watch in wonder as the woven fibres of the tapestries burst into life, and each of them becomes a moving story in its own right! From the nearest three - outstretched hands bursting forth from the pictures. You recoil instinctively, but the hands remain offered to you. Will you choose to take one of them in your own...and which one?

That of Naed The Destroyer. If so, turn to 396.
Or the hand of Menax, God of War. If so, turn to 38.
Or perhaps the smooth hand of Sanromai, Keeper of The Heart. If so, turn to 477.
If you spurn all the hands, and prefer to continue through the portal at the head of the hall, turn to 410.

326

You burst inside with your weapon drawn, smashing the marble door aside. Sarcophagi in various perilous states are strewn over cracked marble slabs, the contents looted from the empty coffins generations ago. Only two remain intact, the two small white coffins of the tragic Moretti children. The sad sight plucks at your glum heart, stopping you in your tracks. Just as your spirit is about to crushed by the despondent darkness that resonates throughout the tomb, you're abruptly shaken from your maudlin thoughts by the alarming sight of a disgusting shape, hunched high the corner of the tomb...

Turn to 260.

327

You dust yourself off, and head on your way. After turning a sharp bend, you enter a tiny neglected square, where you encounter three guilty looking militiamen. They appear to be slyly counting valuables - no doubt pilfered from the crowds escaping the Ogre strewn piazza.

'What are you looking at scumbag?' one challenges aggressively. The smallest of the three - a remarkably feral looking character - stands and reaches inside his cuirass for what you imagine to be a concealed weapon.

If you stand your ground, turn to 110.
If you think it best to flee the situation, turn to 123.

328

Taking the silver from you, and pocketing the necklace, the Bosun ushers the children aboard.

'Step aboard, my little princes and princesses,' he charms, with a deferential sweep of his arms. The gaggle of little ducklings eagerly descend the slippery green steps down to the overladen rowing boat, still holding hands tightly. Their bright faces turn to face you, wide innocent eyes burnished with childlike hope.

'Look Sire!' the little raven haired girl shouts at you with pride, 'We're all still holding hands!' Your spirits rise when the children are lead aboard, struggling with the crewmen to still clench hands. Looking on as the children are pulled aboard 'The Firefly' your heart races. For you know not of this captains nature, and whether any kindness remains in his heart. As the children wave at you, some crying, you stare hard at the captain. From the distance you can just about make out a low nod, and even in the darkness you somehow know that no harm will come of these children. A bonded affirmation taken from that most imperceptible of actions. The Gods smile upon your noble deeds, and selfless generosity, **increase your FATE by 1 step if possible, and restore up to 4 points of Fortitude.**

Your soul lifted, and re-energised of body, you face no choice but to hurry to the Diving Swallow, and the chance of being reunited with the Professor, and Adz. Turn to 120.

329

You immediately recognise the would-be assassin as one of the Brotherhood members from the meeting earlier in the evening.

'You fool!' you exclaim, shaking your head in fury. You cuff the trembling man about his face, knocking off his waxwork Elven ears. 'Don't you realise your ridiculous Brotherhood will bring ruin to the city? You want rid of the elves and seek to frame them for the attack on the city leaders? Don't you see this will result in further conflict? You think the elves will leave now? I wager, friend, that this will only serve to increase their determination to remain, as they seek to prove their innocence in this deed. When they do, be sure that the path will lead directly to your door, and the doors of your deluded friends. You will have a lot of explaining to do, and you can only hope they reach you before the Duce's watchdogs.' The pathetic figure sits gob-smacked on the dark cobbles, stunned at the true magnitude of his actions. 'I should kill you now, and spare you from your fate,' you continue, drawing your sword as if to deliver the man to his grave. He whimpers and scuttles backwards in terror, before you sheath your weapon and spit in his direction. With a boot to the ribs, you leave him curled like a baby in the darkness and head off back to the safety of The Diving Swallow.

Turn to 243.

The waning moon kisses the steel of your blade as you slice down into the lumbering fiend's neck. The monster lets out a hollow groan as the last essences of undeath escape from its severed tendons; its head hanging idiotically to one side. But some primeval force requires it to continue its automated advance toward you. You suddenly feel chill in the warm night air, for such is the unworldly horror afflicting this accursed city.

If you decide to ignore the fiend and sprint up the Avenida, turn to 118
If you choose to complete the decapitation of the monster first, turn to 366

Through grim attrition, you patiently wait for a further opportunity to level the beast – protected all the while from its volcanic emissions. The punishing effort demands all reserves of energy, and you grimace at the heavy toil. **Reduce your Fortitude by 2.** The Gem you wear seems, however, to weaken the Dragon, and the once mighty beast is soon reduced to listlessly swiping at you with its talons. Much relieved, you stride toward your foe, sword raised in deliverance.

If Galiael is dead, turn to 76.
If you did not kill Galiael, turn to 196.

'We must stick to the path, otherwise we could be lost forever...and Gods only know what's out there - in *that.*' You stab your thumb in the general direction of the interior, which is wholly enveloped with a salty mist.

'You're right, Siga,' Adz says with a grimace, 'But let's loosen the reigns a bit.' Agreeing, you break into a trot as you carry along the coastal path, relieved that the tide has seemingly reached the high water mark, and begins to recede. Cheered by the progress, and your decision to stick to the coast, you afford yourself a satisfied smile.

Just as your relieved lips curl in satisfaction, you hear a distant melody, being sung far out to sea, which causes the hairs on your neck to stand to attention. You can hear it more clearly now, a sweet lament, which resonates through the thick fog. You glance at Adz, who shows no sign of hearing it, his jaw jutted out in stoic determination.

Traveller, In my tender embrace,
Cry no tears, no more salty cheeks,

Come drink the sweet water of my waves.
Let my tender embrace wash over you.

You think to mention it to Adz, but so sweet is the music, your heart melts with sentimentality.

Traveller, Like the babe unborn,
Float in the warm sweet waters.
Traveller rest your tired bones,
Let my tender embrace wash over you.

So beautiful is it, that tears of ecstasy stream down your cheeks as you halt your mount, and jumping from the saddle you begin to wade out to sea. The warm Devan waters soothe your weary bones, and cleanse your guilty palms as you brush them through the shallow waves. You faintly hear Adz hail you from the shore, but this is nothing compared to the lilting melodies of the sea. Insignificant and distant thrashing occurs behind you, as Adz hurls himself into the waves. The oceanic choir reaches a crescendo as you stride out further, drinking in the vital wave caressing your face. The mists rise and the horizon becomes a blanket of brilliant light. Angels guide you forwards as your toes begin to lose contact with this world, and you glide into heaven...

'Siga...*Siga!*' a voice cries. You wail in agony as the vision of ecstasy begins to fade, and you struggle to release yourself from the grip of this repulsive and flawed Norsiczan. Strips of cloth are bound around his head and ears, and his foolish and ugly face is scarred with mortal desperation. You scream with exasperation as you thrash in the surf, fighting to reach your eternal salvation.

If your Fortitude is 10 or more, turn to 301
If your Fortitude is 9 or less, and/or you have the Gift of Iron Willed, turn to 459

333

'A princess you say...and what of you, earning your silver in the ruins of a spoiled land? What will you do with your riches brave fellows, how will you spend them? I came through the market, do you know what remains of it? *Nothing remains of it!* It is burnt. The city is burnt, and ensorcelled with unholy magic. It is not a pay-day, it is a tomb! A grave from which there is no escape. I have been outside these city walls. The land swims with the dead. The port is empty of ships. Likely, your paymasters have long since fled, or are dead. Or worse. In other circumstances I would seek out the noble, to carry out this mission - the noble always flock to the cause of a princess after all.' You have the mercenaries attention, and several laugh at your self-deprecating humour.

'I don't expect ignorant soldiers to know how honour feels. But then...but then you're more than that. I know you have fought for Lords and for pretty flags, and for religion, and its abhorrent defilers. You have fought for your own skin, and you have fought for your families. You're better than just chain-dogs of war. I was like you too, once, and I will not dazzle you with the twists and turns of how it came to be, but this comet fragment which I carry is - singularly and collectively - our only hope.' You pull the smouldering comet from the bag. The orb is glowing so with brilliant orange that it burns your hand, and it drops to the floor with a clunk. The bravos leap away nervously, muttering oaths and curses.

'What is this, some kind of grenade?' one asks, 'A naphtha device I'll wager,' adds another.

'You are wrong,' you explain quietly, before detailing its true origin. The blazing orb in the sky, its defining truth, and of its purpose - saving the city - and who knows, maybe the world as they know it. The men gaze in wonder at the twin sights, the parent and child. You can almost see their renewed hearts pounding beneath their armour. A bottle is passed round. Each man swigs generously from it, each man muttering an oath afterwards. As the bottle reaches your lips, you drink lustily, the burning liquid a foil for the bright little star. As you wrap it in soaked leather rags and place it once again inside its bag, you stare hard at each of the men.

'So what is it, best-of-men?. To die old, in your bed, shit-stained and decrepit. Or in the service of some cuntish lord? To die for riches, to die pointlessly for some soon to be forgotten border? Or is it to seize the chance to sit at the Pantheon's table - the Table of Heroes - and have your name written into the lists of the glorious dead! What will it be comrades, to seize this chance to be a hero today? Or to die forgotten tomorrow? With me men, over the barricades. Let's light a rocket under the arse of this ugly bastard - and send him back to pit! Tomorrow is for the dead, tonight is for The Living!'

'The Living, the Living!' the men roar, emboldened by your words. With war cries in a dozen tongues, and under a red and fiery sky, you clamber over the barriers and charge headlong into the masses of undead.

Turn to 309.

334

Muttering a prayer to any Gods happening to listen, you reach out for the Orb with a trembling hand. You scarce feel any pain; only a brief premonition of it, as your grubby finger brushes the smooth opaque surface. The celestial lightening fork strikes at you with such force that you're atomised in many times less than the blink of an eye, leaving nought on the plain but a powdery black outline. In this windless and unfathomable place, the faint trace of your life remains for eternity.

Your adventure ends here.

335

After dealing with the skeletal puppet, you turn to face Ingmar. The young apprentice staggers back, and makes to jabber some excuses. Enraged, you grab him roughly by his fancy collar and drag him outside into the dazzling light, hurling him face down onto the rocky path. He raises furiously, his red cheeks a mask of blazing embarrassment, and looks for a split second as if he might strike you. A powerful cracking blow seats him back into the dust, as you break his nose, causing a torrent of blood to soak the parched earth. Ingmar struggles to spit out curses through a mouthful of blood, as you shake your head in disdain.

'This world is already full of people who would mean you harm fool, without you resurrecting long dead murderers! Take my advice boy, cease your petty follies and concentrate on beneficial augments and healings. Worthwhile magicks, which simple people will be grateful for.' Ingmar rises once more, more contrite than previously, nervous of another cuff. He appears crestfallen, and on the verge of tears.

'All my efforts...all my studies...I should be powerful, I deserve to be powerful!...I....' He shakes his head peevishly, and you can tell from his still pinched lips that your words of advice have gone unnoticed. As you untether the passive donkey, you cast a glance at the boy, who is staring open mouthed looking into the dark abyss of the cave mouth, and you know he is already lost to the dark temptations. Digging your heels into the donkey's ribs and yelling a command, your doughty mount brays with satisfaction and carries you down the slope, and back to Deva.

Turn to 499.

336

Before the beast can react you stride across the cabin and thrust your blade into its soft underbelly, killing it instantly. Suddenly a scream rings out, a young woman has pulled back the curtain. White-faced and trembling with fear, she looks on in horror at the slain hound bleeding into the deck boards. The door bursts open, Captain Hessler and several of the crew fill the room and disarm you with ease. Hessler looks impassively at his slain companion, his steely grey eyes betraying no emotion.

'Take Him,' a simple command, one which leads the crew to roughly haul you to the top deck. Mere minutes later, hamstrings sliced and cruelly blinded, you are tossed overboard, trails of blood in the water inviting the many horrors of the deep to the ensuing feast.

Your adventure, and your life ends here.

337

You step closer to Adz, laying your hand on the pommel of your sword. Adz in turn releases the catch on his axe, which swings loosely from his thick leather belt. Five swarthy men approach, each dressed in bizarre festival fashions. They regard you with some surprise as they stall at the entrance to the Piazza.

If you have BROTHERHOOD written on your adventure sheet, turn to 277.
If you do not, but want to hail them cheerfully, turn to 98.
Or if you do not, and you want to challenge the men, turn to 23.

338

You dismount and, ignoring the protestations of the driver, rip back the awning covering the rear of the wagon. What you see causes you to step back in alarm! Several occupants are laying across one another in apparent agony, their bodies naked except for angry rashes of crystalline scales which malevolently creep round limbs and torsos alike. One small figure has almost entirely crystallised, prisms of colour sparking in the penetrating shafts of light, almost beautifully. A forlorn mouth is all that remains human, opening and closing in wordless torture.

'My family,' sobs the bereft driver. 'Please help me...help them!' he implores you, pushing his luck by grabbing your arm in desperation. You shake him off briskly as you notice signs of the same glittering scales snaking from beneath his sleeves. 'How did this happen friend?' you ask in soothing tones, temporarily calming the man.

'We knew the plateau was tainted,' he begins, 'we never go there, it's an evil place which no man returns from - so they say. But recently the forest has acted strangely, the evil from the plateau has spread, thousands of trees around it have turned to glass, animals too...and my...' he trails off and shakes his head in disbelief. 'The river passage to the cursed place has become befouled, and the waterfalls...I cannot comprehend it! he shrieks, gripping his ears and sobbing hysterically. You are barely able to get basic directions from the poor fellow, before he trundles the cart off in a mindless state, with his pitiful family in tow.

If you head off the path in the direction of the waterfall, turn to 136.
If you choose to follow the trail through the forest, turn to 224.

339

You push Adz towards the bench, grabbing a discarded bottle from the slumbering beggar.

'Siga...' Adz begins, but you shush him as you strain to listen to the voices, as five people in various garish costumes enter the square.

If you have BROTHERHOOD written on your adventure sheet, turn to 277.
Otherwise, turn to 404.

340

You lean back, panting against a water butt. Blood covers the cobbles, the dead lay twisted around your feet...what have you done? Suddenly, from an adjacent house a piercing shriek, as an old housewife emptying her bedpan catches sight of the carnage. All of a sudden it seems like the entire city is awake - dogs howl, babies scream and men shout the alarm. One burly fellow bursts out of his homestead, crude cudgel in hand. With your guilty heart beating so hard it feels like it will burst out of your chest, you shove him out of the way, and lumber off into the cover of night, the sounds of alien malevolent fury ringing in your ears.

As a public enemy, from this point onwards any **'Watch Patrol' test will automatically fail. When prompted to take a test you must always choose the option with the highest total.** Running out of options you decide to risk meeting the professor, and following the illuminated patterns adorning the watery night sky, you continue to the Keijzer house. Soon after Pepin emerges smiling from behind an overflowing water butt,

'I lost them - fat hogs!' he squeaks excitedly, well pleased with himself. You tousle his hair in congratulation...then remembering how he scarpered, leaving you alone to face the law, you give him a firm clip around the ears with the other hand. Grabbing the confused young boy by the wrist once again, you prod him into guiding you toward your destination.

Turn to 464.

341

Never are the dull in more peril of their neighbours, than when their neighbours themselves are threatened by a greater foe. Cries for mercy and screams so high-pitched that they set your teeth on edge abound from locations unknown. Temple bells peel out in warning - in hope of salvation, forming an uneasy orchestra with the whistles and trumpets of the city militia. Distant fires roar as beams snap and barrels explode. As you bound up some filth encrusted steps, you encounter a band of urchins headed the other way. They exchange some feral glances, and one looking guiltily at a blood tainted dagger.

'I got one of them, Sire,' he lies hopefully, throwing a thumb over his shoulder. 'You know, those Stygian death worshippers.'

'What is happening in the city? Tell me, quickly,' you urge. The three look at each other nervously, before the tallest, a mature boy of twelve or so, pipes up.

'People say the Master of the Pit has returned. I heard his howls, and the screams of the poor folk caught by him. But I never saw him. We did see little Matteo though.' The boys lip trembles a little, his youthful bravado ebbing away as he recounts the meeting. 'Poor little Matteo, dead with the pox just three days before. He limped from his grave all the way back to our hideout. Scratching at the door he was, moaning like. The dead are everywhere. Some say they outnumber the living.'

You look at the other urchins, one of who is gently sobbing in oversized and expensively cobbled felt boots. Another is carrying a gentlemen's money pouch, embossed with initials and the sigil of a merchant house. Turning on their heels and shouting platitudes, they scamper away, quick as rats.

'Hoi!' you cry after them, 'And what of the Stygians, who raised their Lord?' The smallest turns around and laughs heartily.

'Sire,' he shouts, much mirthed, 'They were the first to be eaten!'

Turn to 465.

Turn to 465.

342

A crack rings out through the valley and the driver is engulfed in a cloud of white smoke. You hear a swooshing sound followed by a bellow. Adz clenches his left arm, bleeding from small nick in his torn jerkin.

'He shot me! The weasel shot me!' he exclaims with incredulity.

'Adz! No!' you shout, but it's too late. The thunderous Norsiczan races his mount toward the cart. You hear the driver yelp in terror as the horse gallops across the hard earth, its rider holding aloft a huge battleaxe. Furious, Adz strikes, cleaving the driver in two, the bottom half of the unfortunate man left seated where he died - and the head and torso falling into the grass with a wet slap. The coach's door swings open and a young man jumps out, shrieking at the sight of the bloody remnants of his driver.

'You killed him!' he wails in shock.

'How much did my father pay you to drag me back to his dreary villa? Did he pay you extra for murdering my driver?' he shouts, on the verge of tears. Adz pulls a face and raises his furry eyebrow.

'You mistake me for a watchdog,' you counter without emotion, 'I am not here on your father's business, but to bring a message from your love, the Contessa.'

'Oh,' he says, and looks suddenly crestfallen, 'I...I abandoned hope of being reunited with her,' he says quietly, lips trembling. He breaks the seal and reads the note. Sighing and exhaling heavily as he pours over the words with deep concentration, before gently folding the delicate paper and securing the ribbon. He looks somewhat stunned, placing his hands on his head and puffing out his cheeks. He looks up sourly from his note. 'Will you kill me too? he challenges angrily.

Curiosity overrides any need to apologise to the young man, and gnaws away at your sense of high adventure. You wrestle the notion of enquiring about the note's contents, stealing it even. But you resist the temptation to pursue it. Considering your mandate, and other numerous obligations, you turn without another word, and head back to the way marker to reunite with your guide.

Write TOGGIA on your adventure sheet, and turn to 37.

343

You listen to the voices - members of the Brotherhood, no doubt bent on vandalising the walls of the Elven compound, or even the tree itself. Looking under the carts you count five pairs of boots, approaching cautiously, the smell of drink carrying on the light breeze.

'Siga!' Adz whispers harshly. 'Do you smell it? No, not drink - gunpowder!' Adz taps the covered cart above you and tiny granules of black powder float down through the panels.

'Gods, Adz, what is going on here?' you wonder.

If you want to maintain your position and see what their intent is, turn to 404.
If you want to jump out and hail them as brothers, turn to 98.
If you want to jump out and challenge them, turn to 23.

344

You fail to catch sight of a stout earthenware jug hurtling toward your skull - thrown by a drunken spectator. You feel a sickening thud as the vessel cracks into the side of your head, knocking you senseless. **Lose 2 points of fortitude.** Rollo's eyes widen with opportunity as you stagger blindly in a wide circle around the ring. Lumbering across it, he emits an almighty roar and swings his hammer like fist into your raw cheek, knocking you to the canvas and claiming victory. **Lose another point of fortitude.** Defeated, you spit the blood from your mouth and hand over the coin you gambled. With a splitting headache and an uneasy sense of balance, you fumble your way dizzied from the tent.

Turn to 70.

345

Together with Adz, you take turns in forcing the door with your shoulder. Heaving with effort and cursing long enduring former injuries, you make several forceful attempts on the entrance, before it starts to yield with a satisfying crack. Suddenly the hairs on the back of your neck rise, and instinctively you reach for the pommel of your sword. As you cry out to Adz, you spin round to see a repulsive **Lycanthrope** loom from the grey mists, alerted by your thudding on the door. Realising that even if you still have your pistol the powder will be dampened, you consider other strategies.

If you want to hurry away at opening the door, turn to 487
If you prefer to stand ready to fight the beast, turn to 407

346

You head into the warren of slums, resolving to head at all times to the direction of the Piazza. Pushing aside abandoned handcarts and through washing lines, you stumble blindly through the rubbish strewn passageways, the overhanging dwellings and smoke blotting out the guiding stars above. You bitterly curse your choice of route as you're soon lost in the confined spaces, with little idea of location. Cries and whimpers lay behind the many filthy awnings to improvised dwellings, as you begin to realise the claustrophobic environs will likely harbour great danger in such times. As you plough on, you stumble into a tattered leather hearth covering and fall into a mud and wicker dwelling. Drawing your sword instinctively, you come face to face with a group of children, clutching a soiled blanket in the corner of the sty, their rapid breathing and white faces paint a pathetic image of abandonment.

'Take us with you, Sire,' one squeaks pitifully. You grimace at them guiltily as you turn to leave, and hear a drooling panting sound emanating from the path you have trod, evidently following your route. A dark twitching shadow appears in front of whatever casts it. Silhouetted in the flame-tarnished orange moonlight, it appears hunched and bestial.

If you stand to face whatever fiend is about to round the corner, turn to 193.
If make haste and choose not to dally here, turn to 295.

347

The events of the last day or so have left your reflexes dulled, causing you to catch the Half-Orc's club square in the temple. The blow stuns you into a seated position and leaves you with loose teeth, and shaking stars tumbling from your addled mind. **Lose 2 points of Fortitude and the Gift of Hyper Senses - if you have it.** Pulling yourself together, you resolve to teach this ugly dullard a painful lesson.

Turn to 265.

348

Lost and utterly alone, your heart burns with shame as you listen to the terrible screams of the abandoned children, as the unseen beast enters the dwelling. You clutch your futile hands to your ears as you try to blot out the horrible sounds - none so worse as the sound of babes murdered. Trapped in a slum warren, ankle deep in filth, blood and rubbish, lungs and eyes stinging with of acrid smoke, you feel the burning wind of the approaching fire, as it effortlessly surpasses your desperate escape attempts. Whether you burn to death, transformed from a blazing torch to a charred mannequin, or whether you take your father's route to purgatory and spare yourself the worst of the hellish agonies...

Your adventure ends here.

349

A howling maelstrom erupts from within the confines of this place of hatred. A stinking fiery vortex sends prayer books and sacred texts spiralling high above you. A deafening moan accompanies the gale, sending vibrations up the blade of your sword and causing the hairs on your knuckles to stand proud. Sensing imminent doom you dart through the doors, dragging Galiael with you. The badly damaged elf yelps with pain as you shove him headlong out of the Shrine into the long grass, his mouth full of blood as he attempts to babble some words to you.

'What is it now!' you shout, struggling to understand his gesticulations. With scarce time to even catch a breath, you follow the line of his frightened eyes to the approaching melodies, and emit a joyless laugh as your brain strives to comprehend the assembly now in front of you. Woodland animals - beasts of the yonder forest - bow before you gracefully. On the command of a dignified badger, they strike a tune. You gape in horrified wonder as ferrets, wildcats and other mammals stand before you, dressed gaily in the garb of troubadours. They smile wide toothy smiles as they shuffle on their little paws to the chords of a lilting tune. A fox is crashing some symbols together, and...winking at you with a devilish grin, smashing them to a hypnotic beat. Still smiling, still crashing. Giddy with delight at the cute ensemble, you feel the ground beneath your feet begin to pass away.

If your Fortitude is 8 or above, and/or you have the Gift of Iron Willed, turn to 194.
If your Fortitude is lower, and you are not Iron Willed, turn to 217.

350

The elf vanquished, you stand over this crumbled body and set about hurriedly searching the corpse. His sword is of fine quality and as you inspect and test it you notice the pommel is partially unscrewed. Investigating this further, you gently complete the separation which reveals a **Scroll of Elven Lore** - folded neatly within the cavity. Your eyes pour over it - the secret incantation of The Heavenly Comet! Tucking this safely about your person, you may also take the stricken elf's **Fine Sword**. It's of mundane construction, though of divine quality, using this is combat will garner you a **+1 Dexterity bonus whilst wielding it in combat.** Swishing the blade through the air with satisfaction, you head off in the direction of the Orb.

Turn to 355.

351

Running under the moonlit sky, your boots pad swiftly along the cobbles as you race along the Appucine Road to the mighty gatehouse. You're dwarfed by the huge gates, each as thick as a bull's shoulders, and bang on them in frustration, sealed tightly shut as they are. Thick gouges adorn the timber of the gate, smudged with bloody hand prints. Fresh splinters of wood - clawed from the gates - litter the ground around it, blotted with thick gore. High above, the night watch tremble in the relative safety of their guard room.

If you want to shout up the guardsmen, and beseech them to open the gates, turn to 424.
Or if you decide to head off into the dark, toward the river bank, turn to 39.

352

Blitzrstüg- the eighth day, MMDXXXI

Together with Galiael, you lead your horses under the forbidding Leaping Lion gate. The embossed animal motifs appear more vicious and lifelike than previously - their hackles raised, ready for the kill. A chill resonates down your spine despite the searing heat, as you nervously glance at your implacable companion - but his face remains a mask of calm serenity. Travelling through the pastoral idyll of the rolling countryside, you consider an almost impossible contrast to the unspeakable horrors of the city. No stench of death, no bestial howls. Instead vineyards and olive groves bask in the sunshine, and wildflowers blaze down the hillsides, so far untouched by the polluting caress of evil.

After stifling progress for many leagues, the air gradually cools as you ascend through the gentle foothills. Looking into the distance you see the majestic pine forests which encircle the Plateau of Discord, a veil of mist clinging to the looming treetops. Galiael pulls the reins on his mount, and motions for you to stop and listen. An approaching rumble. The aching squeaks of worn axles heralds the arrival of a heavy covered wagon, driven by an agitated looking driver, his eyes dark with rings of fatigue. Hailing him, he somewhat reluctantly draws the oxen to a halt.

'I head for the market Sirs, in the village of Gironita, I carry only mundane produce, nothing to interest fine gentlemen such as I see before me,' he offers, nervously glancing over his shoulder at the cart. You reason the twitchy demeanour of this unsophisticated bumpkin suggests otherwise.

If you insist on looking into the wagon, turn to 338.
If you continue onto the forest trail, turn to 224.

353

Wishing nothing more than to feel the cool winds of your homeland, you turn from these irrepressible scoundrels, and flee.

If the total of your Fortitude and Agility is 13 or more, turn to 230.
If the total is 12 or less, turn to 92.

354

The malcontents lips curl sourly, and his red-tinged eyes narrow in disdain. He shakes his head in something approaching despair.

'Blind,' he mutters, 'Blind to the dangers all around. Does the world have to be ablaze with fire before man awakens? Go, friend.' He wafts his hand at you, dismissing you with bitter disappointment. You look down at the angst ridden figure, and certain you have no more business with him, you retreat from his cabin. The ship nears Deva, and with the summer storm finally having ebbed you consider your options.

To visit the strange young Casconqian, turn to 474.
To investigate the sounds from captain Hessler's cabin, turn to 52.
If you've already done both of the above, or wish to save your energies for adventures yet to come - you rest in up your bunk for the rest of the voyage, turn to 220.

You trudge wearily back to the orb, your heavy heart filled with murderous regret and feelings of trepidation at possessing the powers within it. The heavy skies seem to sink, bathing the plain in mists, causing whole areas to disappear from view - whether visually, or as you suspect with resignation, from actual reality. Thoughts of past studies return, of the texts you read, never knowing the importance that they would present at this very moment. The annotations in the margins and illustrations of blazing comets - it's now clear what these indicated and to what they described. Words tumble chaotically through your mind as you reach your destination, and stand before the opaque and intensely black Orb.

If you possess a Scroll of Elven Lore, and wish to attempt to cast the spell, turn to 88.
If you don't possess such a scroll, but wish to attempt to cast the spell, turn to 375.
If you don't, or wish to take the Orb without attempting to cast a spell, turn to 334.
If you can neither cast, nor wish to chance taking the Orb, turn to 371.

Are you carrying an Ensorcelled weapon?

If so, turn to 155.
If not, turn to 305.

Taking the hint, they slope off to annoy someone else, trailed by an exasperated looking bodyguard, who gives you a wink of thanks. Delighted, the young singer bounds down from the stage to thank you gushingly. It's his first time visiting from the provincial backwaters he regales you, and he's already seen such amazing sites; the Elven bridge, the Triple Fountains at the Temple of Volkan, and several other places he rattles off in such a blur you can't keep up. Tiresomely, he begins to list the creatures he saw in the Stygian caravan bound for the circus, and you're about to brush past him - when you hear the word 'Hobgoblin.'

'You must have been mistaken,' you say gravely, 'No one would tolerate Hobgoblins within the city walls, caged or not - not after the incursions in the East.' The minstrel gulps nervously, doubting himself, and daring not to counter you. Sensing your irritation with him, he loses his spark and tails off. Stammering tentatively, he invites you to his afternoon performance. But you decline with a sad smile, citing a preferable encounter with a blunt clawed Marsh Troll. Nevertheless, **write the word MINSTREL on your adventure sheet.**

If you want to depart for your lodgings at The Diving Swallow, and await the professor, turn to 361.

Or, **if you haven't already visited them,**

You could head to the Stygian Fayre, turn to 226.
You could visit the Grand Market, turn to 376.

358

Feeling mildly foolish, you offer silent words of devotion and respect, reasoning that assistance could be reasonably expected, given your current predicament and the catastrophic evil facing the world. An empty feeling of solitude sinks your spirits, as minutes of meditation renders the Gods mute to your plight. Disappointed by the inert, unseeing Gods, such as they exist, you leave the shrine and head down the steps, further into the bowels of the catacombs.

Turn to 71.

359

Well armed Elves quickly pour into the amphitheatre, weapons drawn and at the ready. As you grip the maiden's arm and near pull her to her feet, shouts ring out as several small fights ignite between various factions. Gathering her up, and shooing along her ridiculous entourage, you manage to bully and boot them all outside into the relative safety of the adjoining concourse. Her startled attendants insist strongly that she returns home *immediately*, and look at you with undue hostility and suspicion. Her Ladyship, smiles warmly at you,

'I have little choice, my brave champion - for my attendants think so highly of me...but so lowly of you,' she says scowling at them. 'Sadly, I must accede to their wishes, but I am forever in your debt.' She leans forward, and taking off her silk scarf, she ties it round your wrist. Its perfume intoxicates you. 'Do not forgot my message,' she whispers, before she departs, gifting you a wink, and one more winning smile over her shoulder, before leaving you to dawdle off. Giddy as a puppy, you make your way back to the Diving Swallow.

Turn to 243.

The Marshlights circle around, occasionally darting out in front to show you the way, the light within them pulsing with what appears to be excitement. The surrounding air is thick with salty coastal mists. Adz is but a dark shape not two spans away from you, so you keep contact with intermittent inane chatter. You are somewhat transfixed by the graceful floating of the orbs, and their pale glow which cuts through the gloom...but a long and deep gurgling sound, from deep beneath the horse hooves snaps you back to full attention.

'Please tell me I didn't hear that, Adz,' you ask nervously.

'Gods, Siga, I wish I hadn't,' he manages to reply before both horses begin to snort and refuse. Suddenly, the Marshlights zip into a circular formation, surrounding you. As if by command, they begin to pulse with increased illumination. Another immense watery groan rises from beneath you, and the ground begins to sink. Losing control of the horses you have no choice but to leap onto the marsh and ready yourselves, as an enormous **Bog Octopus** rises up from the mud. It smacks its repulsive tentacles into the wet mud, covering you with filth and rendering any powder you may have useless. The Marshlights buzz with anticipation, awaiting the commencement of this grisly candle-lit feast.

If you take aim for its swollen body, turn to 432.
If you decide to lop off a tentacle, turn to 144.
If you want to attempt to mount your horse and flee, turn to 478.

Making your way back to The Diving Swallow, you pass through a dusty little square, surrounded by several tall buildings - Piazza Arborea, or 'Tree square' in your Nhortlünd tongue. The square is home to a very tall and fine looking tree, with a wide canopy of exquisite and delicate blue leaves. On a plaque planted on a stake in the ground near the trunk, there is a weathered inscription which you manage to interpret:

'Through valour of lost ages'
'The roots quell the hatred that rages;
'Protecting the Everborn and Mankind'
'If on the Seventh Day doth fail, all will fall close behind'

Surrounding the curious inscription are various obscene pieces of fresh graffiti, aimed mainly at the Elves. It appears like efforts to clean up the inscription have been made, with little success. As you're pondering this message you realise a grubby and quite disgusting little man has sidled up next to you, squinting in the sun.

'Elves put to shore last week, loads of them,' he begins, 'Marched straight on up to the Palacio. The Duce near soiled his breeches...so they say.' You look down to study the stunted figure. 'Interested eh? They're not here for the festival, that's for sure. Maybe you'd like to know something else about them? A filled belly can sometimes loosen lips.' He smiles at you, and rubs his dry lips pathetically with a filthy sleeve.

If you give him a silver scuda, turn to 368.
If you usher the ghastly little beggar away, turn to 75.

362

After some friendly negotiations with Captain Hessler - a man known to be able to acquire the required at short notice - you hire two riding horses, and the services of a wiry taciturn guide, who introduces himself quietly as Gallo. Through his thick Devan mumble you learn from him that it's less than an hour's ride to The Gates, but that you should depart without delay to beat the afternoon heat. Without further ado, the three of you trot your horses out of the Bractianine and along the highway. Leading the horses down the gently descending track you enter the valley. After a short, event-less journey, you arrive at the six league marker to see a trail leading off into a gentle valley. Adz seems eager to deviate down it, eyes wide in anticipation.

Turn to 479.

Walking down to the improvised refreshment stalls by the river, you amble through a small piazza and encounter some stocks. Three unfortunates occupy a miserable position within them, exposed to the blazing sun, sweating like dogs. The first is a snoozing and bedraggled dwarf, blistered by the heat. The second appears to be a local; vomit caked on his chin, and with a bloody nose, he's alternating between giggling and sobbing quietly. The third - an old man - appears to be quite mad. He fixes his alarmingly wide eyes on you, and is repeating words you can't quite hear. A scruffy and stressed looking Watchdog is guarding them, sweating in his filthy doublet and breastplate.

If you go over for a closer look, turn to 266.
Or to carry on past these petty criminals, and slake your thirst down at the refreshment stalls, turn to 24.

Sure-footed and fighting in harmony, yourself and Adz present a formidable unit. The slimy creature moans with dull idiocy as he reaches out with childlike imprecision, grasping at your legs. Two or three savage strikes are all that are required to split the Troll in two ragged halves. Adz winks at you, and you're about to return the favour when you notice a burning sensation on your arm. In the shower of gore, some of the Troll's disgusting and corrosive stomach liquors splattered over you. You rub cooling – if stinking – mud over the sore, silently reminding yourself to be more careful should you ever have the misfortune to meet one of these creatures again. **Deduct 2 points of Fortitude** due to the burns. Soothed, you tread through the foul pantry and head on up the inner staircase

Turn to 386.

The Stygians swarm from their subterranean bolt-hole, and pour over to the cart; its tarpaulin cast aside revealing several large barrels. The same number head directly for the Tree of Life, carrying a huge wobbling band-saw and giant lumber axes. With a huge heave, the cart begins to creak forward on the dusty cobbles towards the Tree. Just as Adz opens his mouth in dumbfounded wonder, the door to the Elven tower crashes open and the two remaining Elven Sentinels burst out into the square with wild urgency. One cries out in what you perceive to be near terror, whilst the other hastily lets fly an arrow, which sinks itself deep into one of the Stygians carrying the band-saw.

You spin a full rotation on your axis as you take stock of the situation. With heart pounding, and fists stained with the blood of Brotherhood thugs you see: a spark ignites as the laden cart trundles towards the tree; desperate Elven guards screaming and hurtling toward the same; a half dead Stygian, arrow embedded in his chest, struggling to his feet with supernatural determination; dumbfounded Devan thugs standing uselessly with clubs and knives - the pot of red paint dropping in slow motion. On the periphery; a clatter of arms as the Militia approach the entrance to the square, and finally, Adz stood slack-jawed with his massive battle axe weeping crimson, looking at you for direction.

If you rush to stop the elves reaching the Tree, turn to 126.
If you want to press the fight against the Devan extremists, turn to 74.
If you decide to leap aboard the cart and attempt to put out the sizzling fuse, turn to 138.
If you want to tackle the Stygian carrying the band-saw, turn to 390.
If you decide it'd be better to take off before the Militia arrive, turn to 197.

366

You hack down on the remaining sinews and send the fiend's ghastly head bouncing along the cobbles. Like a chicken, its headless torso continues to fumble forwards, greedy filth encrusted claws reaching out hungrily. You scarce notice the scraping sound as you stare in disgust at the abominable spectacle. You have no time at all to regret dallying in such a place before you feel an agonising tear in your calf. Whirling round in shock and pain, you look down into the wide eyes of a legless corpse, its jaws clamped around your juicy flesh emitting a satisfied groan, suggesting something akin to pleasure.

'Seven Hells!' you shout in disbelief as you shake your leg wildly. With two powerful hands, you manage to prise the gnashing jaws apart long enough to be able to extract your leg and throw the monster back, summarily cleaving it in two. You boot the fiend's head mightily down the Avenida and laugh – a little too manically for comfort – as you watch it bounce like a cannon ball and out of sight. The wound doesn't look too deep, but it is painful – **Lose 1 point of Fortitude**. You've heard stories of such wounds leading to unpleasant endings...but you can't afford to dwell on that now.

Wasting no more time, you hurry along up the Avenida toward the Piazza Arborea. Turn to 118.

You move from the wagons towards the University, when you hear a distant cry. 'Adz! Siga!' - It's the professor! You look all around you, with elation and concern equally measured. Adz – always the first to pick up a trail – shouts something unintelligible to you, and bounds off down an alleyway. The ancient bell tower in the corner of the square groans and buckles, its fastenings and foundations torn loose in the violent tremors. In a cascade of masonry and dust, the failed structure crashes down into the square. In terror you manage to scramble into a doorway and protect yourself from the worst of the falling debris. The mighty brass bell bounces off the hard surface of the square, sending deafening and idiotic peels into the night, near popping your eardrums. You cry out for Adz and the professor but hear no sound. Nor can see anything other than a chaotic and broken city caked in white dust. Scrambling from the square, you reach the alleyway – or what was the alleyway – and collapse in a lung burning coughing fit. There is no sign of the two. A good sign, and searching through the rubble reveals nought. You feel a twinge of indulgent sadness, but curse yourself for being selfish. You would do the same. You would abandon Adz to drag the professor - no doubt protesting - to safety. Siga and Adz are well versed in the solo pursuit of staying alive, you muse. Devoid of reference points in the tattered cityscape, you decide not to dally. The cacophony of the falling bell has attracted the creatures of the night. Their groans and scratching claws herald an advance you dare not face. Quite alone, you make off into the night, unsure of either your present location or even your destination.

Turn to 341.

The beggar tugs at your sleeve encouragingly, as he leads you through winding alleys, eventually stopping in an incongruous street. High, but unremarkable stucco walls run the length of it, with wooden doors punctuating them - entrances to the courtyards of the individual residences behind.

'This is the Keijzer house,' the beggar says - pointing a crooked figure towards a thick and ornately carved door. There are no Elves in the street. Passing people seem to be going about their daily business, in an unsuspecting manner. A moment of awkward silence passes between you and the twisted beggar, as he continues to look up to you expectedly, awaiting your next action. You hesitate for a while before knocking - as the beggar nods expectantly. No reply. You try the handle. Locked.

Do you have the Gift of Skullduggery? If you do, turn to 458.
If not, and wish to force the door, turn to 300.

If you chose not to dally here, the beggar looks disappointed, and losing interest, releases his clutch of your sleeve. Somewhat abashed, you curtly nod to your crestfallen new friend - avoiding his eyes - and with cheeks blazing you - head off directly to The Diving Swallow.

Turn to 75.

The **Bone Dragon** swoops, and with a mighty roar unleashes a hell like furnace of blazing flame. You manage to leap aside, dodging the worst of the inferno, but are still singed as you do - **Lose 1 point of Fortitude.** With smoke billowing from its nostrils the gargantuan beast lands before you, poised to strike with its immense claws.

If your Fortitude is 8 or more, turn to 263.
If your Fortitude is 7 or less, turn to 244.

The uncommon heat must have stewed your brain. Starting a brawl in a foreign city, and continuing it on with the local law-men! As adept as you are in martial matters, you are soon outnumbered, and the sneaky outstretched foot of an unknown hero in the crowd is all it takes for you to trip and be set upon by your foes. Vengeful blows rain down upon you, and several skull-crackingly painful blows later, you are knocked insensible. To a heckling crowd, you are dragged through the filthy streets to await your fate. **Lose two Fortitude Points.**

If you have killed someone in this adventure thus far, turn to 127.
If you haven't killed anyone, turn to 473.

371

Bitter tears of a thousand regrets burn your reddened cheeks, as you depart the cursed plane. The sky ruptures all the while with mocking laughter. Driven to the point of near insanity you eventually escape its scrutiny, and stumbling through the crystalline forest you emerge half mad with remorse into the mundane forest canopy. As you descend the woody slopes you catch a sight far, far on the distant horizon of a blazing orange maelstrom. This is Deva. This is the fate of your true companions. With a deadened heart you bite your trembling lips, and turning your back on all that you have known you head blindly away to distant lands.

This adventure, if not your life, ends here.

A chance of atonement remains. Still of sound body and mind, and with the trappings of this mortal world, you live on, and should you be brave enough to someday turn around, your adventure can once again begin.

372

You reach the amphitheatre, and on this hot and thundery night the crowd jostle sweatily. Evidently this is an invitation only event, and people are being turned away in disappointment. It's difficult to force a path through the ticket-less milling crowds and aggressive hawkers, but eventually a way is cleared and you reach the ornate entrance sheltered by a huge gilded awning. There is a mix of security on detail tonight, some thuggish looking junior city officers in full dress complete with epaulettes and azure plumage, and some stoic and sinewy Elven guards - both parties regarding the other somewhat coolly from either side of the entrance.

If you have the Victory Laurel, turn to 20.
If you don't have the Victory Laurel, but have the Gift of Silver Tongued, turn to 450.
Otherwise, turn to 47.

373

You grunt with effort, but lack the vitality at this critical time, to reach the cart in time to extinguish the fizzing fuse. With a loose feeling in your bowels, you wince as the cart thuds into the tree and halts. Scampering back towards Adz with your head ducked you wait for impact...

Turn to 197.

374

It doesn't take long to locate a maintenance hatch and, hauling your tired bones up a service ladder, you pop the bolts on it and ease yourself inside the basin. To interfere with, or to trespass within a city aquifer normally warrants summary execution, but you reason no warrant carrying city officials are patrolling its length on this night. Cool water runs ankle deep within the echoing chamber. Roughly as wide as a man's span, constructed of a stone base and covered with a leather canopy, these irrigating pipelines are a lifeline to the cities of the South, carrying waters from far flung mountain ranges into the hearts of the thirsty metropolis.

You walk, and occasionally slip and slide down the pipeline as the gradient changes with the terrain. You count your paces as you pass by several other hatches to gauge when you might enter the city. Your spirit sinks a little as you pass hatch ripped from its latches, it flaps loosely in the breeze. At the same time you hear a low moaning in the near total darkness ahead. The low sounds increase in volume as the unseen threat approaches, tumbling splashes announcing its arrival. By the light of tiny tears in the leather covering, the source of the moaning emerges from the gloom into view. An **Undead Aquarius** - no doubt drawn to the Aquifer by force of habit - lumbers toward you. The fiend has a huge gash to its neck and its bloodless head lolls disturbing to one side, only connected to the spinal column by tort, stretched tendons. You have no option but to do battle with the monstrosity, in the tight and slippery confines of the pipeline.

If your Dexterity and Agility scores total 15 or more, turn to 171.
If by ceaseless attrition, your total is less than 15, turn to 259.

375

You fix your gaze intently on the Orb. Remembering passages from half read texts, and heeding examples of spellcasting witnessed on your life's travels, you think it prudent to dispense of your armour and any metal about your person. Laying these down carefully and steeling your mind tight with concentration, you reach deeply into the caverns of your soul. Clawing at lines half read and words half remembered, you begin to orate the spell with hesitation, cursing fate at never understanding the significant role they would ever play. If only you had known! You surely would have mastered them, rather than casually scrolled through them unawares of their pivotal nature.

Gusts of wind appear from nowhere and a huge hole is ripped through the mists, to the heavens above - revealing the black sky bejewelled with a thousand twinkling stars. As the winds of space roar through your soul, you near completion of the recital, both invigorated and terrified by the unfathomable forces at work.

Combine the total of your Fortitude, plus two for each of the following:
Your Fate level is 'Favoured'.
You possess the Lozenge of Tongues.
You have the Gift of Arcania.
You're carrying Artur Keijzer's notebook.

If your total is 13 or more, turn to 239.
If your total is 12 or less, turn to 463.

You follow the crowds to the Festival Market, laid out under canopies to the south of the city. There are indeed a wide variety of traders and stalls selling wares from every corner of the known world - mostly at eye-watering inflated prices. Excited haggling rings in your ears, with traders pouting in disdain, insulted, as locals make their gambits. You see a group of young Midden ladies of wealth, tittering in embarrassment at some outrageous ebony carvings from the Southlands. As you meander along through the stalls, you know not what your adventures will require, and so you've already decided against purchasing anything, when you come across a huge billowing yellow and pink striped tent erected in the centre of the Market. An opulent gold leaf sign hangs over the threshold reading 'A Cornucopia of Wondrous Delights.' Two very large Daabans stand guard outside, in ornate white armour, woven with gold thread. A queue of people are waiting in line, and the less finely attired are being turned away in disappointment.
If you want to join the queue, turn to 130.

Or, if you've had enough of the Market - and if you haven't already - you can…

Head to the Stygian Fayre. Turn to 226.
Head to the Festival of Wine and Song. Turn to 363.
Or, if you've already done all these things, or would rather just head back to your lodgings and wait for the Professor, turn to 361.

Before you can act, Adz murders the sergeant in a single stroke. The surprised corpse makes wet slap on the flagstones of the square, and ashen-faced, the two remaining whistle furiously, backing away with quivering halberds lowered. You pummel your blood-clouded friend back into sense, and drag him away, cries and shouts filling your ears. Catching sight of more Watchdogs clattering into the square, you bundle Adz through the tight warren of streets. Sweating with effort in the disorientating heat, you career down a twisting passageway. The shouts and sounds of heavy footfall seem perilously close when you notice a doorway awning open, and a small man appears. He motions for you enter, and with little other option, you pull Adz in behind you.

The two of you breathe heavily in the cool dark hovel, as you hear the Watchdogs run past and away. The owner of the hovel nods and smiles assuredly. An old man, filthy, covered in scabs and with a chaotic white beard faces you.

'I saw you when you arrived in harbour,' he says, leaving you somewhat surprised. 'I also sensed the smell of death.' You stare hard at the disgusting figure, gob-smacked. Adz holds out his palms in confusion. The old man titters and slaps his skinny thighs in mirth at your expressions. 'My accent has nearly vanished brothers, but if you listen carefully, my tones confirm me as a Man of the Nhort, such as yourselves.' He sighs and looks around his grubby home. Wistfully, he continues, 'In my younger days I was an honourable knight, a Volkan Paladin. I wanted for nothing. Petals were strewn at my feet. Maidens swooned. Yes, yes, I know it's hard to believe looking at me now.' He slumps down on his disgusting mattress sadly, staring into the dark corner of his nest, 'Alas, due to an indiscretion long forgotten, I fell into disgrace. Fate determined that I ended my days living like a pig in this foetid city. I also foresee death, in my dreams. I foresee chains broken, and my sleep is disturbed by the sounds of a beating heart, deep within the earth. The Tree! The Elven Tree! It cannot fall this night! He reaches beneath his filthy cot and draws out a fine sword, its hilt embossed with Volkan sigils. 'Swear to me, you will quench the blade in blood and satisfy its hunger,' his voice wavering.

You take the sword from the old man with gratitude. 'This blade will once again bring honour to its rightful bearer,' you confirm, taking it from him. **Write the word TREE on your adventure sheet - when requested if you have this codeword, you may turn to reference 161. Also add the Volkan Sword to your equipment list. This will bestow +1 to your Fortitude score at the commencement of each battle.**
After confirming the streets outside are safe once again, you bid the old Paladin farewell. Turn to 158.

378

'Don't do it Galiael,' you say, slowly and solidly in Elvish-tongue; sliding your sword free of its sheath. The stunned Elf freezes in surprise as you address him in his own tongue. Disarmed by the sudden revelation, he is at the tip of your sword before you continue, 'I heard every word, friend.' Gob-smacked and deflated, the elf unclenches the hilt of his weapon, and drops his arms loosely at his sides. 'Sigasünd. Friend of the Elves. You heard the orders issued to me, which by sworn I am duty bound to take...on pain of exile.' His melancholic eyes linger on the far horizon as he speaks the sad words.' Sigasünd, if I do not kill you I will never again see my homeland or my kin. If I do not kill you, my name will be erased from the scrolls in the High Temple. It will be as if I never existed. My bones will be scattered and disturbed by animals, and my shade will wander, lost in perpetuity.

You look at the proud figure stood before you, completely at your mercy. Smiling gently, you bid him to continue - never once allowing your levelled blade to drop, 'I think though, that my Prince underestimates the fabric of your being my friend,' he smiles knowingly, before continuing. 'Did you know the Everborn can see a man's soul - his aura? I see yours - and though tinged with darkness, a wonderful light emits through it. The light battles relentlessly, keeping the darkness at bay, and never allows the malignant influences to overcome its radiance. I know you are a good man, Siga, a special being destined for greatness. I see this, and on my vision I risk all. I know that we must join together to rid the world of this most imminent of threats. For this reason, I forsake my kin and my liege, and I put my trust in you. You have my word.' You puff out your cheeks and exhale slowly, taken aback by his dutiful promises and eloquent words, delivered with such finesse. With his piercing eyes burning into yours, wide with appeal, a decision of trust filters through your mind.

Should you trust Galiael, and agree to continue the quest together, turn to 297.
Or, if you see these promises as lies, and wish to take your deadly advantage and slay the elf, turn to 150.

379

The current show has nearly finished by the time you arrive for the circus, and the faded tent fairly heaves with crowds of boisterous locals, jeering and tormenting the so-called 'fantastic beasts.' Pushing your way into a good viewing position atop some sacks of feed, you view the end of the spectacle with an unimpressed eye, as a manacled bear walks atop a greased barrel being turned by two leering midgets. The performers finally bow and take the drunken plaudits of the crowd. You hail a man who looks like he's the animal master, to enquire about the next performance.

'Show's over,' he announces brusquely, as various forlorn looking animals are whipped back to their cages. **Do you have the name 'MINSTREL' on your adventure sheet? If so, turn to** 89.

Otherwise, you can visit:

The fortune teller, turn to 59.
The wrestling contest, turn to 275.

Or, you could leave the circus, and **- if you haven't already -** you can:

Head to the Grand Market, turn to 376.
Head to the Festival of Wine and Song, turn to 363.
If you've already done all these things, you head back to the Diving Swallow, turn to 361.

Turning your back on the maelstrom and on those you hold dear, you hail the captain, requesting safe passage to unknown shores. The flames from the wharf side dance in his black eyes as he ruminates on your plea. With a flick of his head he accedes to you boarding, and two eager crewmen beckon you into the row boat. Leaving behind the flames the pair row you through the pitch black waters to the vessel. Neither makes eye contact with you, both smirk and snicker. Harsh features and black and gold teeth turn your stomach, either with distaste or foreboding.

As you climb the greasy ladder to the deck, shipmates cease their industrious labours and turn to stare, as does the captain, who looks you up and down more than once, before his face breaks into a humourless smile. Your heart races with uncertainty, and feeling the leering shipmates edge forward it begins to sink.

'More booty for my scurrilous lads!' shouts the captain, raising a malevolent cheer about the sailors. Despite protestations, pleas and fierce resistance you're roughly stripped, coshed around the head and tipped overboard into the drink. Whether you drown, or awaken destined for the feast - to be devoured by the creatures of the night, your shade only knows.

Your adventure ends here.

You elbow a ravenous beggar in the throat, to create some space around you - just in time to catch a glint of steel in the midday sun. A ragged black-clad Stygian raises a dagger and takes a murderous leap towards you through the scrum.

If you have the Gift of Martial Prowess and/or Intuition, turn to 408.
If you do not, turn to 157.

You plunge the sword in the Ogres pallid chest, hilt deep, extracting a woeful cry of misery. It fails however, to level the beast, and it angrily swipes at you with its massive hands. Alarmed at your failure to land a killing blow, you hack at it with all your might, sending bits of the reanimated fiend flying far and wide. Again and again you plunge your weapon into the roaring beast, losing grip on it entirely. **Lose 1 point of Fortitude** from the sheer fatigue of combating such a foe. Its fury shows little sign of abating, although you do sense its vitality is waning as it staggers clumsily before you, a listless tongue hanging from its repulsive mouth.

If you wish to press the fight with your knife, turn to 200.
Or you can easily flee, with the wounded monster in no position to pursue you, turn to 243.

You head for the shrine doorway, grabbing the dazed Galiael's arm as you do. Tugging the elf toward the entrance, the chancellery begins to fill with the sounds of agonised shrieks. Seeming to sense Galiael's presence, the Wraiths swoop toward him, assailing him with their spiteful accusations.

Turn to 349.

'It's a merchant's passport, you need one to get into the Mezzaluna. You know, the Mezzaluna? The Merchant's Quarter!' He shakes his head at your ignorance. 'The Lemon Tree belongs to the Moretti family. Ludovico is the head, but I haven't seen him for at least a year, I think his wife died and he left the city. Anyway, you don't need to know any of that,' he barks at you somewhat impolitely, annoyed at his own candour. Through gritted teeth you thank him cordially for the information. If at **any time during daylight hours of this current day**, when you are given options of locations to visit, you can once opt instead to **Turn to reference 81** to go to the Mezzaluna. **Write this down on your adventure sheet.**

'I can see I will not have any peace here to continue my work,' the merchant says, collecting his apparatus, and departing for the sanctity of his private room.

What does the day hold for you?

There is a marksmanship contest, with early heats taking place very soon, and promises of a great prize, if that interests you - and only you still possess a pistol - turn to 68.
Or you could head to the Plain of Heroes for the Military Display. If so, turn to 413.
Or to just quench your thirst down at the Festival of Wine and Song, turn to 420.

385

The sergeant takes the Silver Bow, all your other weapons, all the coinage you are carrying, and any other items you have about your person. **Make a note of this on your adventure sheet.**

'If we see you again, you will end your days in the sewer, with the other rats!' He gives you an unnecessary blow to the stomach - **lose another point of Fortitude.** If you are still alive, you hobble back, beaten, bleeding and dispossessed to the Diving Swallow.

Turn to 125.

386

You head up the stairs to the second level of the tower, which reveals a bedroom chamber, richly decorated with furs and tapestries. Carved wooden panelling encases a large bed; made up, but thick with dust. You glance at the hunting scenes displayed as Adz touches the mattress, and mouths the word 'cold.' Pursing your lips, you search the chamber in the low light; the silence once again punctuated by occasion stifled sobs from the towers upper levels. Turning out richly embroidered clothes from a fancy travelling case you rifle through the pockets, finding a letter. Motioning Adz toward you, you read it to him as quietly as you dare.

Ludovico Moretti, paradigm of mercantile benevolence, and charitable to the poor.

I, Maestru Rau, of the scorched and scattered Stygian bloodline, am most humbly blessed and delighted to make your acquaintance. I received your loyal messenger with profound and sympathetic interest. I confess to a state of transfixation as your tragedy was unveiled unto me, I, as a man who has known great loss, could not refuse your offer. My heart painfully wept upon news of the passing of your beloved. A cruel world in which the chance passing of unseen miasmatic essences can steal a life held dear. I know not how you found me, but found me you did - and with what fortune! For we have reasons enough to visit Deva, myself and my retainer, that to meet with you, and engage your offer of safe lodging at your apartments, and use of your business interests forms a perfect synergy to our vanguard plans.

The journey back from the Black Sea of Ending is fraught with untold agonies, but safe passage is guaranteed. Your message indicated that you have prepared yourself for what awaits you, as part of this exchange.

I reflect with compassion upon the loss of your beloved and beautiful wife, currently... but not eternally, departed to End of Days.

Rau

Creeping toward the sound of the sobs, you make your way upwards, turn to 428.

387

Pointing out the many times the Elves have come to the assistance of the race of Man, you swiftly de-construct his arguments, using logical and reason, as the flustered demagogue becomes only redder in the cheeks - his knuckles clenched in white fury.

'Traitor!' he spits angrily 'Elf Lover! Fox in the coop!' He rises trembling, his wild red-ringed eyes flashing dangerously. Unable to contain his passions he lurches toward you, screaming insults and strikes at you in amateurish fashion. A little surprised by the wholly hostile reaction, you have no option but to put him on the seat of his pants, sending him crumpling to the floor, clutching his broken nose.

The door swings open and Captain Hessler enters, leading some of the crew to the source of the audible disturbance, as the bleeding malcontent continues to curse you through wet sobs of pain. Ignoring your pleas of relative innocence with an irritated demeanour, Hessler shakes his head dismissively and confines you to quarters. Bad enough the ship spent the last night rolling like a cork without passengers brawling amongst themselves. Given no other option, you resolve to save your energies for adventures yet to come.

Turn to 220.

388

Squelching through the mud flats to the rocks of the shoreline, you pull your heavy bodies to safety, and turn exhausted to see the final dying embers of Don Moretti as his charred corpse is consumed by the tidal sands. As the last traces of him - and indeed his secrets - are sucked into the earth, the tower gives out a huge crack and crumbles blackened and utterly demolished into the mud. A twinge of regret gnaws away at you, at learning little on this detour. Your hopes for further information sink along with the remains of the tower, as that too is sucked into the depths. Left with little option, you saddle up the horses and journey back to Deva, hoping to return before nightfall.

Turn to 495.

389

'No!' Galiael cries as you move to step into the circle, but not soon enough. A blistering spasm of white heat soars through your body, and with an immense cracking sound you're thrown a great distance back onto the plain. **Lose 5 points of Fortitude.** If still alive, you stare at your smoking boots in terror, and instinctively beat them into the sodden carpet of the plain. When the coolness of the damp weeds has extinguished the burning sensation in your feet, and the smoke subsides, you hobble miserably back to the elf, who continues to stare, rapt, at the unearthly black orb floating unsupported on the air.

Turn to 400.

390

You race over to the Stygian saw bearers and hack one down with a single powerful blow, and once again the saw clatters to the cobbles. Adz, for this part, has just cleaved in twain an axe wielding acolyte - who you are amazed to behold still attempts to drag his legless corpse toward the Tree with an idiot grin.

'By God, what are you doing, you fools!' screams the elf in total horror, as he struggles to get past you. You look beyond him, as he hurtles desperately towards the fizzing gunpowder laden cart. With a loose feeling in your bowels, you wince as the cart thuds into the tree and halts, the fuse crackling to completion...

Turn to 197.

391

You quickly survey the area - scanning the tiled rooftops, when you hear a shhhhHUNK! You duck quickly as a morning star embeds itself into a washing pole a hairs breath away from your head, and can only watch as the **Stygian Leader** nimbly dances from rooftop to rooftop, disappearing into the gloom. Knowing you have little to no chance catching such a foe, you dig out the **Throwing Star** with your dagger and wrap it in some cloth before pocketing it – **add this to your adventure sheet.**

You consider your good fortune, and mumble a quick litany before climbing down a nearby pipe, and follow the flames, into the night and bound for Artur Keijzer's house. Pepin soon joins up with you, white as a sheet, and clearly rattled by the nights events. The young lad is holding an object which he presents to you with a nervous smile.

'I think they dropped this?' he whispers. An **Iron Key with the number 34 engraved into it.** You pucker your lip lips as you inspect it, before pocketing it for future consideration – **also add this to your adventure sheet.**

Turn to 464.

392

Under a leaden sky you do battle with the thunderous creature. Sensing your immunity from its fiery breath, it resolves to simply thrash and stomp after you - chasing you like a cat might chase a mouse. Its ungainly might is in stark contrast to your nimble evasion, as you strive to stay alive long enough to better the beast. You strike, time after time, trying to find a weak point, and as you do, you feel the burn of fatigue as the sodden earth extracts a toll on your energies. The **Bone Dragon** emits a roar of frustration, rears up onto its hind legs and throws its terrible head up to the heavens. For a split second you glimpse its exposed and loosely connected thorax. Can you land the killing blow? **Add together the totals of your Dexterity and Agility, and add 3 to the total if you have the Gift of Acrobatics and / or Martial Prowess.**

If the total is 15 or more, turn to 323.
If the total is 14 or less, turn to 403.

Your frayed tendons scream for mercy in tandem with your burning lungs, as you sprint through the flame licked city streets. All about you lay piles of the dead...and the dead-ish. In the moonlit night it's difficult to tell the two apart, not that you dally to investigate - with the howls and booms of insidious laughter from The Master's host still resonating in your ears. Through dark alleys and down treacherous steps you bound breathlessly, heading to your goal. With soaring masts in sight you race down the main thoroughfare to the wharf, past abandoned warehouse and tumble down taverns. Persistent criminals emerge from these dark and broken buildings, their arms full of loot, carrying ridiculous arrays of useless burdens - when do these fools imagine they can sell these you ponder, for Deva will not see a market for seasons to come.

Suddenly, screams peel out from a side street, the screams of children, and the cries for mercy, for deliverance, from a female voice. Pausing momentarily, you see a small but squat building besieged by a handful of ghouls. The undead fiends push hard at the door, scratching deep gouges into the timbers, and tug feverishly at the window shutters - enraged at the resistance from within. Pity fills your heart as you read the stone carving etched above the threshold: 'Most Merciful Heliopas Home for Orphans.' Being this close to the docks marks the refuge out as a home for children orphaned by the tragedies at sea. A fate which connects with your past deeply. Leaning from a first story window, a small rosy cheeked girl with jet black hair catches sight of you gawping at the desperate struggle.

'Sire, Noble Sire! Please save us, please Sire!' she appeals, in a tiny but piercing voice. You hear a crack, as a hinge pops in the splintering door frame, and a corresponding escalation in screaming from within...as resistance begins to give way to futility.

'For the love of Mistress Heliopia!' squeals the pathetic figure in the upstairs window, arms outstretched toward you. You numbly shake your head at the proposition; being burdened with a gaggle of orphans on a night such as this?

If you decide to press on to the docks and diminishing flotilla of still-moored ships, turn to 79.
Or should you decide to attempt to save these doomed children, turn to 222.

394

You struggle quickly through the thick tidal mud flats after your howling quarry, now licked with flame. The shaft of sunlight expands and illuminates the bay, electrifying the white mists. Moretti stumbles and splashes into a shallow gully thrashing desperately and sobbing all the while. Treading carefully, you trudge as close as you dare, weapons drawn.

If you decide to finish him off so can search his body before it's consumed by flame, turn to 204.

If you want to tell him how you granted rest to his children, turn to 240.

<hr />

395

It doesn't take much to intimidate the nervous young man into fleeing. One swish of your arm is all it takes. Sneakily, the leader takes the opportunity to land a sucker punch to your temple. **Lose 1 point of Fortitude.**

'It's like that is it!' you bark at him, causing him to pale.

Turning your attention to your assailant, you rain blows down upon him. Turn to 445.

<hr />

396

You reach out to grasp the hand. All goes black. All goes silent. For a fleeting moment you imagine this is the passing to End Of Days, when you suddenly feel a chill. A cold wind blowing into your face. Upon opening your eyes, you find yourself on a small chunk of rocky ground overlooking a millpond-flat lake of obsidian darkness. Impenetrable mists cling to the edges of the small island and obscure the horizon on all sides. The sky - if it is the sky – is black as pitch. No stars nor moons shine. Before you sits a tired looking Elven noble, clad from head to toe in dusty black garments, his blond hair stuck fast to his scratch-marked face. His chair - a parody of a throne - is battered and charred, and wobbles uncertainly on the rocky surface of the islet. He sighs heavily, as he stares into the nothingness of the void.

'I am Naed, the eater of worlds, and I leave not one stone set upon another,' he says laconically, without looking up. 'I will save you, and I will call for you, and you will heed me - this is my bargain. My labour is finding a world in which order reigns, that I might destroy it.'

Your mouth opens and closes in silent wonderment, are you truly in the presence of a God? **Write the name NAED on your adventure sheet.** The figure snorts with derision, and without regarding you further, flicks his wrist.

Turn to 247.

You troop down the Ancient Way with the returning Devans, frazzled by the sun's punishing rays. Once inside the city you head back to your lodgings and retire to your bunk to escape the stifling late afternoon heat. You eat, and doze a little while - **regain 2 points of Fortitude.**

Awakening refreshed, you learn from Evassa that there is still no word of the Professor, so after revitalising yourself with a quick dip in the water trough, you hit the streets again. According to the grubby pamphlets, there are two main events this evening, the options being:

Doctor Döll's Scientific Wonder show. If you wish to head here, turn to 267.

The Elven saga telling at the amphitheatre. If this is your choice, turn to 372.

Or

If you have the word 'TARGET' on your adventure sheet, you can continue, if you wish, in the Archery Tourney, turn to 236.

You mark out a lieutenant - his black hair stuck fast to his flushed face. With a leap, you cling to a buttress poking from the wall, and pull yourself up above the crowd.

'Ho Sir!' you cry, above the din below. 'You must open the gates, the Master of the Pi..' Crack! Blood fills your nostrils and you fall backwards into the crowds below, who bellowing curses at you, and aim a few kicks in your direction as you pull yourself to your feet, eyes streaming and nose broken. **Lose 2 points of Fortitude.**

'Get down from the wall, Nhortlünd scum!' The soldier shouts at you, before aiming a violent prod of his pike shaft at some other rioter. Looking more stressed than before he turns his attention to the gates below as the crowd cry a 'huzzah!' Their overwhelming numbers, and probable help from within, have managed to breach the gatehouse and release the mighty bolts and latches securing it in place.

You follow the river of people out into the darkness of the countryside beyond the towering walls. The rural landscape is a marked contrast to the heaving maelstrom of the city. Once outside, the willing refugees seem uncertain of their next action, and mill about in small groups. Arguements and appeals ring out under the stars of the black night sky. Small groups begin the futile journey down the Ancient Way. Others begin hiking across the tilled fields and through olive groves to family smallholdings, and distant villas. A stranger in these lands, and with everyone you know likely to still be within the city walls, you glance around for inspiration from these dubious sources, whilst wiping the clotting blood from your top lip.

'Look, they're coming back already,' scoffs a guardsman, as he points an accusatory finger toward some dark figures lolloping through the furrows of a nearby field back onward the city, almost totally enveloped by the night. From behind you, a clank of metal and thunder of chains as the cursing city militia prepare to close the gate once again.

If you decide to head back into the city, before the gates are closed shut, turn to 142.
If you follow the majority, and strike out down the Ancient Way, turn to 97.

399

You strike with primitive blows in the dark confines of the tight alley. No finesse is required in this contest of the living and the dead. At times close enough to smell its stinking breath and feel its bristling hairs, you thrash about wildly, bouncing off walls and into barricaded doorways. With a dizzying thud your skull smashes into a low hanging beam, rendering you near insensible.

If you have the Gift of Hyper Senses, remove this temporarily until you are directed to restore it. The innate sense of self preservation eventually wins out, and you finally break the beast, hacking it into myriad parts – leaving nought but a bloated steaming sack, leaking its liquors into the gutter. After sending this slave of the night back to the pit, you decide - through a pounding headache - that clambering to the rooftops is your only hope of navigating a course to the Piazza.

Turn to 2.

400

'Seed of the comet!' he whispers, somewhat mysteriously. 'This has travelled far across the heavens, far beyond the reach of the Ancient Ones, perhaps even beyond the realm of the Gods.' You squint at the elf, and his poetic ambiguity.

'What is it? How do we harness its power?' you challenge, voice thick with practicality. Galiael simply stares outwards across the plain.

'I do not know friend, I only know we must press on to find the answer. For certain we cannot simply reach out and take it.' He allows himself an almost imperceptible smile - possibly at your ignorance - and shakes his head in wonder as you troop off, leaving the orb behind.

Turn to 475.

401

The barrel-shaped ape careers across the cobbles, slamming into you with a mighty impact. Your weapon comes down heavily onto the enraged primate, but its armoured carapace is enough to dull the strike. **Lose 1 point of Fortitude from the collision.** It roars and beats its mighty fists against its chest, as it once again charges. Eager not to feel another of its tender caresses, you prepare to leap aside - and try for a strike to the rear.

Turn to 26.

402

The legions of the dead, drawn in thick knots by the magnetism of the master, turn with primeval instinct at your battle cries. As you plough through the forest of soft corpses like a scythe through ripe wheat, you can't help but wish Adz were here, to see this majestic spectacle, and despite the circumstances you're unable to stifle a wild belly-laugh at the thought of his sorrowful face when...if... you regale him of the tale.

Despite your valiant efforts, the dead are too many, and you fall to the blood-red marble flagstones of the square, as you are stricken by the many savage wounds inflicted. You feel your heart quiver and fail - the spectre of impending death circling overhead. But your mind lives on a few more breathless moments. Drowning on the blood which is filling your lungs, you have the fortitude to claw at the drawstrings and unveil the comet fragment, a forest of cadavers blocking your way. For a fleeting second as you twist upwards to face the heavens the child is superimposed upon the parent, and you are superimposed against the dark shape of The Master.

Alas, as you make to hurl the beacon toward the epitome of darkness, your body fails you, and the comet drops to the flagstone and is lost behind the pack of fiends which pounce, leaping and tearing upon your still live body.

The subsequent explosion kills many, many of the undead followers. But not the Master... Lucky indeed for you to die in this way, and not share the fate of your comrades to come.

Your adventure, and your mortal soul, ends here.

403

Leaping into the air you bring your blade down across the Dragon's thorax, seeking to sever its head from its torso. With despair, your strike lacks the necessary accuracy, and scores merely a glancing blow. You tumble back down into the sodden carpet of the plateau, rolling quickly to avoid a thunderous stomp.

**Do you possess the Dragonfire Gem? If so, turn to 331.
If you do not, turn to 244.**

404

One of five gang members has brought with them a pot of red paint, and together they hastily begin daubing nasty slogans and threats on the wall beneath the Elven compound, hurrying each other along. A shout rings out from above, as an Elven guard leans out from a third storey window and shakes a fist at the five vandals. The five quickly finish up their daubings, as footsteps echo down the tower steps, to the doorway separating it from the square.

Suddenly, you hear a grating noise as flagstone rises up between the carts and the tree, and slides over the cobbles, closely followed by the emergence of a stream of crow like Stygians.

'Siga!' Adz cries out.

'I see them!' you reply urgently. The five thugs also turn at the sound of the scraping flagstone, and stare in nervous confusion at the new arrivals on the scene.

Turn to 365.

405

Even though the Keijzer house is halfway across the city, you can clearly see the orange glow lighting up the night sky, punctuated with crackles of brilliant blue, deep vermilion explosions, and screaming yellow rockets blazing moon-ward. No doubt the old explorer stored many wondrous concoctions and potions in his city home, and this dark night they're providing a violent departing spectacle above the silhouetted roof tops. You wind your way through the dark and drizzly streets up towards the merchant quarter, led by the messenger boy - who introduces himself as Pepin.

'Most reliable messenger in all of Deva, you need a friend like me,' he boasts. Chancing his arm after a few more strides, the scamp adds, 'For my fee, of course.' He grins cheekily, most satisfied with himself. You're about to give him a clip around the ear for his impudence, when you hear footsteps rapidly moving towards you through the dingy gloom, slapping on the wet cobbles.

If you hold your position, turn to 160.
If you drag the messenger boy into a doorway to hide, turn to 129.

406

Leaving the ground in your wake, you soar over the battlement embellished city walls, and fly high above the sharp outlines of rooftops far below. Feasting ghouls stalk the blood splattered cobbles, running down those foolish enough to expose themselves alone. You wince helplessly as you witness dozens of innocents fleeing in useless terror, only to be caught, and torn asunder. You look on in horror as you make out the distant Grand Piazza, shrouded in darkness, and straining to see, you make out a figure holding ghastly court. The abominable figure of The Master sits resplendent on his perverse throne of skulls, surrounded by a legion of fiends. Shuddering, you carefully draw out the bag containing the orb. The fragment of the comet burns brightly within the confines. Orange light creeps though the worn stitching and the blackened bag is hot to the touch. With the comet fast approaching you cast a glance at the burnished glow creeping over the distant horizon, and wonder if you will live to see another day dawn.

If you urge your mount directly toward the Master, turn to 498.
If you urge Pegasus to circle, awaiting the dawn, and possibly an easier route to the Master, turn to 285.

407

With uncommon speed the Lycanthrope lollops over the boggy ground, catching you quite by surprise. With a howl and a thrash, it rakes its claws across the both of you, penetrating through your cloaks. Alarmed and angered, the pair of you turn and make short work of the creature, raining down a torrent of savage strikes. It's not until the beast is dead and returned to human form that you stop to consider your injuries. Adz has a minor looking cut on his shoulder, and you have a nick on the back of your neck. Blood, however, has been drawn. Adz glances at the moon, then gives you a funny look. You return it with interest, frowning.

Eventually the door begins to concede defeat. Turn to 107.

408

Deftly parrying the violent stab of the **Stygian Assassin,** you seamlessly draw your weapon to face him. The would-be killer looks devoid of poise. Isolated as the crowds part and shouts ring out. Regardless, he seems anxiously determined you shall not see the day out. You snarl, affronted by this cowardly act. Kill, or be killed.

If your Dexterity and Agility combined total 14 or more, turn to 115.
If your Dexterity and Agility combined total 13 or less, turn to 80.

409

Adz listens with increasing disappointment, rubbing his knuckles ruefully at missing out on all the action.

'Gods! I should have loved to have been in these scrapes with you, Siga. Let's the both of us head down to this warehouse and turn out this nest of vipers. With your sword and my axe, this band of scarecrows won't be able to resist deaths embrace.' Adz looks at you appealingly. 'Come, old mate, for old times - you and me.'

If you think better of it, and coax Adz to the market, turn to 205.
If you want to investigate the warehouse with Adz, turn to 241.

410

Proceeding through the entrance, you tread down a short passageway of increasing ruin. The broken pathway lurches down a steep gradient into the embrace of the foetid and brackish water, polluted with disinterred skeletons and half-submerged and broken sarcophagi. Broken flagstones tumble into the water with the merest prod of your boot and sink into the darkness. A large illuminated entrance sits across the water. Frowning, you scan the cavern for a way across this unwelcoming pool. High above there is a ledge which looks like you may be able to shuffle across it over the water, though it too looks to be crumbling from the shifting earth. Two unwanted cards in your deck, you muse, as you are forced to take an uneasy decision.

If you decide to wade through the black waters to the other side, turn to 437.
Or if you risk easing your way across the high ledge, turn to 253.

You loll, presumably dead, upon a tiny row-boat, lost in the unfathomable blackness of the ocean at night. No moon nor stars to comfort you. Of The Master of the Pit, there is nothing. Nothing lights the way in this endless space, and yet your vessel is guided by an unseen source. Tears stream down your face as you cry bitterly at your life's regrets, your heaving chest heaves with sobs. Death has wrapped her arms around you, you reason, frustrated at the retention of your senses in the hereafter. The lack of peace, of sleep, of rest. No Ending of Days, just existence as a pinprick of light set against a universe of inky liquid darkness. Howling into the void you collapse and begin to beat your head furiously against the bottom of the boat, when you hear a voice. A honey rich and loving voice. A voice you have longed to hear always - all the maddening years you walked this confused path upon the earthly realm. But a voice taken from you at birth.

'It's not time, my darling,' it says softly, as you listen, rapt and terrified in equal measure. 'We will meet, my beautiful baby. I watch over you now, and will forever more...but this is not your time.' You sit clutching your chest, daring not to speak, daring not to believe.

'Mama?' you stammer weakly, heart breaking with longing and hope. 'Please, I didn't mean to, I mean.. I wasn't...' you whimper, tears cascading down your cheeks.

'I know, my darling, Siga...I have always known.' An apparition appears before you, beautiful and ethereal, unmistakably the figure of your mother as you remember her from the long lost locket.

'Oh, Gods of heaven,' you sigh in wonder, as you reach out with charred and bloody fingers.

'It's not your time,' the vision smiles, as she begins to fade. 'It's not your time....'

'No...no...please. I don't want to go back,' you whimper helplessly, as the black void brightens. As the light fills the entire universe, it fills your heaving chest with a sickening nausea. You feel blood pulse through your veins, causing you to vomit with disgust and dismay, as you continue your weak utterances, 'no...no...'

'Siga!'

You hear your name, shouted by a gruff and familiar voice. The intrusion makes you suddenly aware of the pain racking your broken body.

'Thank the Gods!' it continues. A familiar voice. Familiar voices, even.

With some effort, you blink through gore encrusted eyelids, blinded by the light of the midday sun blazing through the slits in the shutters. You look up into the relieved faces of the Professor - grave with worry, and of Adz, his eyes still encased in bandages. Of Hessler too, who looks impressed as he leans over you.

'Seems like you're a hero, the saviour of the city,' he says.

'And the destroyer!' shouts the Devan voice of the Duce, 'He's wrecked half the city with that meteor!'

'And saved your fat arse!' shouts Adz angrily, blindly lurching forward to defend your character, with tightly clenched fists.

'Siga,' says the professor gently over the ensuing din, 'what do you remember?'

You close your eyes, and grimace. Tired with the effort of listening, you sink off once again into a deep sleep.

Turn to 488.

412

Galiael smiles winningly and bids you thanks, 'This fine man,' he orates at a commanding volume, towards the rapt crowd, 'is not only a champion in skill, but also in heart!' A little embarrassed, you kick at some dust, whence he places his hand on your shoulder. 'Friend of the Elves,' he says, and presses an exquisite **Elven ring of Kindred** into your palm. 'My houses sigal.' You only have to ask the ring and we will endeavour to assist, wherever you are. It's too slender to fit on your thick fingers, leaving you fumbling like an oaf. **Add it to your Adventure sheet and also write down the word ELFKIN.**

You exchange some further pleasantries with Galiael, before he and his party depart, leaving you surrounded by stunned onlookers. Not being of an attention-seeking bent, you carefully wrap the ring up, and once out of view conceal it about your person.

Turn to 423.

413

Following streams of Devan locals, you meander out the South Gate and along the Ancient Way to the Plain of Heroes. A huge levelled parade ground surrounded by raised earthworks and gentle slopes, it affords commanding officers - and today the public - unrestricted views of troop manoeuvres. Taking your place near the highest hill, you work yourself a comfortable space in which to view the spectacle. Richly gilded commanders put their charges to the test with a series of drills, forming squares, ranks and columns. Newly conceived formations are highlighted, mixed ranks of halberdiers and gunners, of cavalry and skirmishers. Cannon fire and arquebus smoke fills the sticky summer air as different mercenary factions trying to outdo each other, in this shop window. Luminaries within the council of fifty sit absorbing the display, never short of a refilled cup or a cooling waft of a palm.

For more than two hours men scurry across the dusty plain, kicking up dust and generating smoke. So much so that your stinging eyes compete with your parched throat for foremost attention. As the demonstrations begin to subside, you notice at the very pinnacle of the hill, Captain Hessler of 'The Boogenhofen' looking intently through a large telescopic apparatus, his bizarre dog at his heels. Hessler is rubbing his chin thoughtfully and appears to be mumbling to himself. It's a hot day and the shade of the city inns are singing their siren song...

If you decide to clamber up the slope to talk to him, turn to 164.
Or if you choose to head back within the walls of the city, turn to 18.

414

In the dank and confusing confines of the tomb, you fail to avoid the ghoul's leap. You howl mightily as it sinks its rotten teeth into your shoulder, collar bone deep. **Deduct 2 points of Fortitude.** A sudden and almost overwhelming feeling of melancholy runs quick through your views. Even as you instinctively shake off the hissing beast, your mind struggles to focus through dismal thoughts, as a depression grips your soul.

If your Fortitude is 10 or more, or if you have the Gift of Iron-Willed, turn to 145.
If you benefit from neither of the above, turn to 455.

415

Reduce your FATE by 1 level

Hardening your soul against the cold-blooded act, you step forward with malevolent intent. Caught entirely unawares, Galiael lets out no more than a shallow gasp as you bury your blade hilt deep, stabbing upwards beneath his ribs. Minutes pass, and presently you release the elf's head which slumps forward in heavy confirmation, and slowly retract the reddened steel, crimson-kissed with murder. Staring down at the lifeless figure, you numbly recollect distant memories of prior crimes; the victims of your brutality less deserving but no less calculating. Your companion dead by your own hand, and alone on this soul wrecking and desolate plateau, you slump down sighing heavily with fatigue. Old injuries reappear like unwelcome guests, bearing gifts of aches, pain, and sorrow. Now aware that the only realistic salvation of Deva likely opens a door to your own condemnation, you consider once again your fleeting existence. To answer the call of the sea, and run from this place - to start again? A familiar exit, but one that guarantees uncertainty and promises nothing. Or to seize this celestial Orb, and invoke the magic bound within it. Reckless and almost certainly deadly, but the only chance to save the Professor and Adz. Under a baleful and unearthly sky you must make your decision.

If you return to the Orb, with the intention of using it in salvation of Deva and your friends, turn to 355.
Should you decide to flee this place, and live to see adventures yet to come, turn to 371.

416

The sergeant takes the Victory Laurel, all your weapons, all the coinage you are carrying and any other items you have about your person.

'If we see you again, you will end your days in the sewer, with the other rats!' he spits, giving you an unnecessary blow to the stomach - **lose another point of Fortitude.** If you are still alive, you hobble back beaten, bleeding and dispossessed to the Diving Swallow.

Turn to 125.

417

You leap with great effort...but drop like a stone into the chill depths of the pool below. **Lose 1 point of Fortitude, and 1 of Agility** as you crack your knee on a submerged rock. Clenching your teeth in pain, you roll your eyes downwards and stare with horror into the inky black waters. Something akin to fingers are winding a course up your leg...

Turn to 51.

418

'Spirit,' you command, tightly clenching the hilt of your weapon. 'Cease your babblings. I regard you from the here and now, and I would converse with you, that you might assist me.' The phantom halts its mutterings and transports its ethereal form so that its very face is pressed within a hairs-breadth of your own. Its death-mask features ripple like the wind on a pond. Nervously you continue, 'An evil lurks here, in the depths. I expect you know of this,' you add, somewhat pointlessly. The wispy figure floats inertly, imprisoned between realms it appears to not heed your utterances. 'Spirit, I care not for your shade. I am a man, of flesh and blood, and if you can help me then do so. The evil that lurks here is probably bigger than me, more powerful than me, and in all likelihood will rend me limb from limb, so if you can help me, then do so!'

Your hot breath melds with the spirits vapours and seems to bind its attention to this mortal plane. Proffering its ghostly hand towards you, you see an outstretched finger bearing simple gold ring, glinting beautifully. You carefully secure it between finger and thumb and inspect it closely. It's inset with Elvish Sigils which glisten with a magical iridescence, and you recognise it as an **Elven Ring of Kindred.** This ancient token of friendship was sometimes used to secure passage or entry. It's too slender to fit on your thick fingers, so you place it carefully within a fold of cloth and secure it within your tunic. **Add it to your Item List.** The ghost dissipates with a gasp of...relief. Of pleasure? Of deliverance from statis, and the dispatching of a tortured soul? You chide yourself for dallying in contemplation, when the hypnotic 'thub-thub' is drawing you ever nearer to your fate. You set off, making toward the light, and reach some rough-hewn steps which descend further into the deep.

Turn to 438.

419

You hammer down blow after blow on the stricken bodyguard, to cheers from the drunken crowd. But your exhilaration is short lived, as you glance up to see the Duce's half-nephew gesticulating to the newly arrived militia. Rolling away, you guard yourself against encirclement, drawing your dagger. The watchdogs close in around you, weapons drawn, accompanied by a bleeding and rather angry looking Bruno, who has struggled to his feet.

Turn to 370.

420

You beat a path for the riverside Dens, idling away the time taking in the jugglers and bards, watching the comedies, and enjoying the myriad tastes and smells. Flushed and sleepy from sampling the many refreshments on offer - **deduct 2 silver scuda** - and from the soporific summer heat you set yourself down yourself under the canopy of a nearby tree for a snooze - until a nagging feeling pricks your consciousness. Are you wasting your time? You can picture the Professors expression - always bewildered, and slightly pitying in the face of sloth or self-indulgence.

Picking yourself up wearily, you decide to exit the Festival, wafting dawdling revellers aside - when a hooded figure crashes into you, sending a tray of freshly baked pastries spilling to the flagstones of the piazza you were passing through. A moustachioed baker in a large hat begins to gesticulate angrily at you - whilst simultaneously attempting to beat away the rush of the hungry and opportunistic scrambling for a free meal.

If you assist the baker in gathering up his wares, turn to 303.
If you leave both him - and the scrum - to it, turn to 246.

421

You feel a warm sensation within the hidden compartments of your tunic, and initially think it nothing but a fearful symptom. But on closer inspection, the **Dragonfire Gem** is glowing brightest amber. You clench it tightly as the **Bone Dragon** swoops, and with a mighty roar it consumes you in a hell like furnace of fire. You scream in anticipation of a flaming tomb, but the power contained within the Gem protects you from the firestorm, which immolates the ground surrounding you, blackening the earth for a huge distance. Cursing its sulphurous stench, you shake yourself to your senses.

If you want to flee to the tree line, turn to 45.
Should you decide to stand fast and do battle with the beast, turn to 392.

422

'I'll take my chances on slaughtering an innocent,' you reply briskly, before delivering the killing blow. The woman mouths a disbelieving gasp, and slides from your blade to slump wide-eyed into the dust. You wipe her blood from your blade and set to work searching the body quickly, before others arrive on the scene. Rifling through the assassin's dark garb reveals **a throwing star, a freehand map of the city - with a cross marked on it denoting Piazza Arborea.**

Add these items to your adventure sheet and also write the word TREE on your adventure sheet. When requested, if you have this codeword, you may turn to reference 161.

As you move silently though the city streets your thoughts are preoccupied with thoughts of Aegnor's pleas, and whether the *two hundred and twenty eight years* of The White Kings reign will soon witness another calamitous event.

Turn to 243.

After exchanging a few pleasantries with the other competitors you manage, eventually, to drift away from the archery colonnade. Elated with your victory, you briskly walk back to the city centre as night draws in. Glancing at the festival pamphlet, the final act of the evening is the retelling of Elven Sagas in the amphitheatre.

If you wish to try to gain entrance, turn to 372.
If not, you may head to the Diving Swallow, turn to 243.

'Shut up, you fool!' hisses the guardsman, levelling his crossbow at you, 'You'll bring them back!' A dread sensation runs the length of your spine, and your spirits sink as you hear the crunch of footsteps on the dry earth behind you. An unsteady procession of figures emerge from the gloom, groaning with infernal torment.

If you stand and fight the Massed Undead, turn to 25.
If you choose to make a run for the river, turn to 39.

'Stygians - what should I know or care of such detritus?' He fidgets, tutting, and is obviously annoyed by your presence. 'Do you have any more questions? he asks, somewhat testily.

If you enquire about the Lemon Tree medallion, turn to 384.
Or to push him on the subject of the arrival of the Elven ship, turn to 257.

You set off down the Avenida toward the Piazza. Citizens of Deva run past you in various states of terror, some naked, some gouged of flesh and painted red with gore. Some drag sacks and carts containing the trappings and meagre embellishments of small pointless lives. Perhaps without a care, or perhaps in acknowledgement of the End of Days, sounds of rapine can be heard down dark alleys, punctuated with stifled gasps and screams. You glance to a dark corner, behind a pile of broken urns. In disgust, you see a charred corpse being gnawed by two figures, only compounded with the realisation the rewarded diners are half starved members... of the living. Turning away from this repulsive spectacle you see a large figure wandering down the road toward you, silhouetted against the moonlight.

'Adz?' you call out, doubtfully, 'Is that you?' The figure heads directly for you, and yearn to embrace you old friend. A sick vision of dead hope. The figure is no friend, no Adz, but the recently killed and risen figure of a **Lumbering Watchdog.** As its jaws open with a dull moan you can easily determine the hungry intentions.

If you want to dodge the risen Watchdog, and run up the Avenida, turn to 118.
If you decide to slay the fiend where it stands, with swift deliverance, turn to 330.

427

Signs of violent displacement display themselves in the warped flagstones and perilously bowing ceiling, as you tread down the last rubble strewn steps into a circular antechamber. The silence and stillness is penetrated only by the metronomic thumping sound from the deep, and the quickness of your breath. Freshly lit torches - only hours old judging by the remaining wicks - flank the walls of the chamber, which itself appears to have been spared any significant damage. Carefully entering the room, it's clear this is a shrine of sorts. To your left; the pantheon of Elven deities adorn a brightly painted fresco on the wall, above a richly dressed table, on which sits burned incense, fresh flower garlands and a goblet of iridescent ichor. To your right; a finely carved, and open double doorway appears to lead on, down another flight of steps. You reflect in the quiet calm of the room for a few moments, steadying yourself as you consider your next action.

If you wish to pray at shrine, turn to 56.
If you want to drink the ichor, to help steel your nerves, turn to 291.
Should you choose to leave the shrine undisturbed and unheeded, you head through the doors inset to your right. Turn to 71.

428

Ascending the stone flagstones leading to the third storey, you freeze as you hear low growls and the patter of heavy treading paws from above.

'We have company, Adz!' you hastily utter, as a shadow of a giant hound looms on the wall of the bending stairwell, swiftly matched by another. Adz makes to speak, but halts as two **Hellhounds** descend, their leering jaws full of pin sharp teeth, and demonic red eyes twinkling in the torch-lit gloom. With an angry, twisted snarl the first beast leaps toward you, intent of ripping you apart. The other growls, and springs at Adz.

If your Dexterity is 8 or less, turn to 174.
If your Dexterity is 9 or greater, turn to 296.

429

Not knowing the answer, but unable to turn back, you step forward muttering a feeble prayer. So sure are you of imminent death that your bowels nearly loosen, when suddenly, and inexplicably, the diadem you're wearing begins to glow with a brilliant sheen. You close your eyes tightly and step forward. Cheeks flushed, you exhale a deep breath of relief as you step over the be-glyphed flagstones and don't hear the rumble of solid rock from overhead. From the portal beyond you see dazzling multicoloured lights shift around rapidly; a scene with both intrigues and disturbs you. From behind, the strained faces of the stone titans seem perceptibly burnished with new found hope. And so it is, with the Elven Gods renewed, that you step forth through the portal into the chamber beyond.

Increase your current Fate condition from Marked to Unwatched, or from Unwatched to Favoured, depending on your current level.

Touched by divine forces, you press on forwards. Turn to 41.

430

Accompanied by a small group of sneering guards, you're led through a warren of tunnels, and up endless narrow stairwells until you can taste the warm night air on your tongue. The stench of misery, blood, and excrement melds with tantalising smells of baked bread and fermenting wine, as you are led to the gaol gate, and the freedoms beyond. A hunchbacked lackey labours across the courtyard clutching a soiled sack of goods, and dumps in unceremoniously at your feet. The guards snort with disdain as you reclaim your possessions, brushing from them the filth and lice. Naturally, badly paid and over taxed city officials such as this vanguard of heroes need to supplement their meagre incomes - **deduct all silver you were carrying and choose two items at random from your**

equipment. This has been pilfered - erase them from your character sheet.

To catcalls and promises of re-acquaintance, you are shoved from the gate into the empty street beyond. Evidently the city has been in the grip of a thunderstorm, as pools of brackish shit filled water lay on the cobbled, and streams of meandering filth roll down the gutters. A young page stands nervously opposite the gate, apparently in wait for you. He coughs nervously, before addressing you, eyes wide with excitement,

'Your master, Kroos, has sent me. Your freedom is bought. I'm to take you to him straight away. He's at the Keijzer house. It's burning.'

Turn to 405.

431

Your collective shadows reach out to the feet of the hot and bothered looking Militia, who squint harshly in the afternoon sun, lips curled in disdain.

You see a flicker of acknowledgement between the Stygians and the Watchdogs. Adversaries turned allies by the persuasive nature of coin. The Stygian smirks at you as the Watchdogs' posture suggests a previous transaction between the two parties.

'Begone from the Market square, crows!' the sergeant says automatically, wafting an ineffectual hand at the Stygians, 'Back to your caravans.'

'Certainly, fine sir,' wheedles one of the crows, bowing his head in deferment. As the Stygians push their cart away from the square, Adz grips your arm and blurts

'And we'll be going too...' The Watchdogs lower their halberds, and glare at you.

'Hold fast, Nhortlünd savages,' one sneers, his eyes narrowing with faint recognition.

Test for the 'Watch Patrol'
If your 'Watch Patrol' total is 2 or less, turn to 158.
If it's 3 or more, turn to 377.

432

Together with Adz, you hack wildly at where you imagine the beasts organs may be. As you rain down blow after blow, you are fair covered in mucous and slime, as the Octopus' jelly like body is macerated like a ripe peach. You glance at Adz, who is laughing manically, swinging his mighty axe like a man possessed. Steam rises up from your sweating brows and melds with the mists, as you both stagger back to a dry patch of land. Observing the obliterated creature fills you with tired satisfaction, and Adz offers you a draft of his flask - the warm liquid is a fitting toast for a job well done. Eventually, you manage to remount the horses, and after a little while manage to decipher a course to your destination.

Turn to 264.

433

You level the firearm and pull the trigger. In a puff of blue smoke the **Hobgoblin** disappears from view. The explosive boom quietens the square for a few seconds, before chaos resumes regardless. You walk a few paces and nudge the disgusting creature with your boot. This Hobgoblin will bark no more. Your attention attracted by the far larger explosion across the city, you decide to grab Adz and make good your exit from the square and head to its source.

Turn to 306.

434

'It's a merchant's passport, you need one to get into the Mezzaluna - you know, the Mezzaluna? The Merchant's Quarter!' He shakes his head at your ignorance. 'The Lemon Tree belongs to the Moretti family. Ludovico is the head, but I haven't seen him for at least a year, I think his wife died and he left the city.' 'Anyway, you don't need to know any of that,' he barks at you somewhat impolitely, annoyed at his own candour. You thank him cordially for the info - if at **any time during daylight hours of this current day**, when you are given options of locations to visit, you can opt once to **turn to reference 81 to go to the Mezzaluna.**

The merchant's attention returns to his abacus. What else do you want to ask him?

Ask him why there seem to be so many Stygians in the city, turn to 279.
Push him on the subject of the arrival of the Elven ship, turn to 257.

435

You make it back to the Diving Swallow, hot and bothered, to check whether your master has arrived. Evassa welcomes you warmly, but shakes her head explaining the Professor hasn't yet returned. She offers a refreshing sherbet and some honey cakes, fresh from the oven, which a not unattractive serving girl takes up to the roof terrace for you.

As you sit down, sweating like a mule in the uncommon heat, you stuff some cake into your mouth. **Restore 2 points of Fortitude** from revitalising yourself on refreshments. The girl leans in close to wipe away crumbs on the table, her lustrous hair tickling your stubbly cheek. You blush, intoxicated, and fairly burn with unrequited lust in the sultry breeze atop the city spires. You wheeze and splutter as the delicious honeyed treats lodge in your windpipe, and violently, you struggle to cough up the errant morsel. The girl chuckles and gives you a playful pat on the back, and rubs your shoulders playfully as you look around the rooftop garden. It's festooned with rare plants and herbs, and brilliant birds of paradise sit nonchalantly, chirping merrily. A taciturn man emerges from the stairwell onto the terrace, sits at a remote table, and offers a stilted nod with the serving girl. 'Freelander merchant,' she whispers to you. 'Not very talkative, or generous, and entirely inexpert in matters of the flesh,' she winks, departing down the wooden stairwell into the inn with, leaving you alone to nurse your sherbet, and curse your reawakened loins. There seems little point sitting and waiting at the Diving Swallow for the Professor, and glancing at the tatty pamphlet, you reason trouble is a good antidote to lust.

If you want to spark up a cheroot and engage the Freelander in conversation, turn to 483.

If you don't care to chat…

There is a marksmanship contest, with early heats taking place very soon, and promises of a great prize - if that interests you - and if you still possess a pistol - turn to 68.
Or you could head to the Plain of Heroes for the Military Display. If so, turn to 413.
Or to just quench your thirst down at the Festival of Wine and Song, turn to 420.

436

You swing time and time again, but your flimsy blows bounce harmlessly off this creature born of the hardest minerals. As it careers chaotically about the chamber, it knocks you from your feet several times, seemingly without intention, as it spirals out of control and oblivious to your presence. You stagger towards the stairwell protecting yourself the best you can. **Lose 1 point of Fortitude** – from being repeatedly bashed to the floor.

Crawling to safety, you eventually reach the steps leading downwards. Turn to 438.

Heart beating fast with trepidation, you slide yourself into chilling pool - relieved when your boot touches the bottom, with the water chest high. You steer yourself through it as fast as you dare, ancient gnarled bones gently bobbing on the ripples as you disturb the stillness. Halfway across the water deepens to neck level and you quell a desire to panic and thrash wildly for the other side. Using your free arm to paddle gently forwards you near the relative safety of the other side when you freeze - something is gripping onto your foot deep below. Rolling your eyes downwards you stare into the inky black waters, as something akin to fingers wind a course up your leg.

If you have a Ring of Kindred, turn to 443.
If you do not, turn to 51.

The stairway winds down into a long gallery; brightly lit by torches that burn with curious white flames. Adorning the walls on either side of the chamber are a number of magnificent painted tapestries, each depicting a near life-size landscape containing what you take for a hero of yore, undertaking a challenge of some form. The booming heartbeat thumps out ever louder now, 'thub-thub, thub-thub', and the tremors it causes sends faint ripples dancing through the delicate fabric of the paintings. From the opposite end of the gallery, a wide and finely carved open doorway leads into a dark cavern.

If you want to take a closer look at the paintings turn to 325.
If you would head through the gallery and through the doorway, turn to 410.

You sit down beside the withered old man and greet him cordially. His eyes sparkle faintly into life, and almost without hesitation he begins to orate his life's troubles to you, with complete and unencumbered candour. You consider this is a good example of a man who has waited a long time to get something off his chest.

'What do I care who knows my troubles,' he begins ominously. 'I'm an old man and death waits for me with declining patience. I was a good servant; I worked in the Moretti household for 40 years, and served all the Masters,' he continues proudly. 'It was a tragic turn of events that so afflicted my last, I should say my current, Master - Don Ludovico. His harlot of a wife, Donatella…oh, she was too adventurous that one. I blush when I think of the scandal she brought upon us. The way she cavorted at her get-togethers - you can't imagine my pain and degradation having to serve under such conditions. But even these infamous couplings weren't enough to sate her depravity...and she soon advanced to pursuit of the black arts...and ever-lasting pleasure'.

'I don't know exactly how it happened, but my Master must have reluctantly acceded to her whims, hopelessly and blindly devoted to her as he was. For two weeks they screamed and writhed in agony around the house, shutters fixed tightly, until finally they emerged from their ordeal changed people. The mistress became a caricature of her worst self, even more ruthless and fickle, whilst the Master emerged a broken and remorseful shadow. What happened to the children - the twins - was the worst. My Master was so bereft that he spirited them away and consigned them to an old family tomb, and using some magicks unknown to a simple man like myself, forbid entry to Donatella. I never saw him again. I suspect he may have withdrawn to his hunting lodge out on the Mirror Marches, leagues from here, for a penitent existence'

'The lady Donatella was wild with fury at the denial of her children. I was convinced I would die that very night she rose to find out what had happened, and was much relieved and shocked to finally see day break. I have not returned to that place since, though I had often looked on through the gates, and recently have seen hooded strangers entering the house. Please, brave Sir, I beg of you one favour...the twins.'

The old steward looks on the verge of tears as he begins his sad request.

'The poor innocent twins...at night their shades come to taunt me...tapping on my window whilst I cower in my cot...oh, the horror! What are the Gods doing to allow such infamy! Please, consign these soulless orphans to a restful sleep...I can show you where, and I have these...' He unravels a tattered cloth to reveal several sharpened stakes. 'I...lack...the bravery,' he sobs, finally breaking down. Taking his story into account, will you:

Go with the Steward to the burial site, turn to 484.
Try and bluff the guards and seek entrance to the Mezzaluna, turn to 215.
Or leave the man to his own issues and head out of town to witness the military show. Turn to 413.

440

You descend back to the cellar wearily, every step an effort.

'So it's settled then,' the professor says hopefully as you reappear, with twinkling eyes. 'This partnership of Elves...well, Elf, and Man, will join together for the salvation of the city. It has an epic ring to it.' he muses.

'A tragic comedy more than like,' says the Commander dubiously, 'I still think this befits a military detail! We have companies of well-trained troops who...,' Captain Hessler cuts him off.

'Companies of well-trained men that at this moment, if not shambling around in states of undeath, are either fleeing, panicking, raping or looting. Military control has been lost and will not be regained until the cellars are dry and the sun comes up - whichever happens first.' The Commander's mouth opens wordlessly, and then puckers in a tight grimace.

'Seven hells, I should go myself then!'

'And neglect the defence of the city?' Hessler teases. 'Who else will restore some discipline to this shambles?'

'You push me too far, pirate!' fumes the Commander, before the Professor, assisted by Aegnor and his retainer, restore order.

'The good captain speaks sensibly, Commander, if not a little provocatively,' the professor soothes. 'Your men need you, as Prince Aegnor's men need him. Men without a master are reduced to the base instinct of beasts in times of strife'. The professor sweeps a hand round toward Hessler, and continues his appeal, 'Hessler, like myself, is too old, and the others...the others are too young, too untested. The gallant Galiael, and the experienced and capable Sigasünd will form an excellent alliance. None can argue this pair is our best hope.'

Galiael remains laconically impassive, but to your discerning eye it's clear tiny amounts of burning pride poke through cracks in his façade. Hessler smiles conspiratorially and lights the great pipe of his. Aegnor's hands open and close slowly. Looking about himself, looking at you, with chaos raging in the streets, examining you, and finding no answers.

'So I say again,' concludes the Professor, 'It is settled, this fine pair will set forth to the Appucine lofts to locate the Seed of the comet. Steel and sweat seem to match for the Beast which has arisen. Celestial magic is our only hope. With this seed Galiael will invoke the words known only to him, and draw down this purifying energy to cleanse the city.' With nods of affirmation, the bond is sealed, and the quest agreed. You offer no argument and abandon yourself to the fate decided for you.

You prepare your kit whilst Pepin readies your mounts and stuffs supplies into the saddlebags. If you have a pistol, someone presses some dry powder into your hand as you strap on your gear. Dawn breaks over a broken city, and long shadows of the blackest night retreat into dark places. When the streets quieten, and the city takes a sick mans breath, you depart with Galiael for the Gate of the Leaping Lion.

Turn to 352.

Breathing with exertion as you ascend the rough trail through the canopy of the high tree line, each step becomes a labour. Old wounds, pulls and strains flare up without invitation. You plough on as Galiael scouts in front, seemingly unmoved by neither fatigue nor altitude, which serves only to darken your mood.

Hours pass, and so sweating and muttering you eventually leave the forest behind and emerge though sun wreathed misty fog onto the high plateau - a massive, sweeping plain, flat as a millpond, and bathed in pale and unnatural light. The bilious green moss and earth hugging foliage squelch wetly underfoot like a sodden carpet. Foliage aside, this land appears completely featureless and utterly silent - neither birdsong nor the sounds of animals can be heard in this warp-polluted place. Together with Galiael you walk onwards - more in hope than expectation, and frequently glancing at the composed elf you hope he has a better idea of your destination that you.

Some way in the near distance a most bizarre vision appears. As Galiael motions for you to halt, you both regard the sight of a black sphere, the size of a large orange and perfectly smooth, floating in the air at eye level. Around this lays crumbled masonry which is sunken into the ground and mostly concealed with tall grass and pretty wildflowers - a stark contrast to the otherworldly garish and sweating green carpet of the plain. This more natural flora extends for several paces around the orb, which is in the direct centre of the oasis. As you creep forwards with your companion, you're both careful to halt your toes at the rim of the circle.

'Our objective,' whispers Galiael, eyes wide with enchantment and fingers twitching, 'the Seed.'

If you choose to step into the circle of order and seize the orb, turn to 389.
If you wait for the elf's next reaction, turn to 400.

As you clench your knuckles in frustration at the delay, one of the fighters atop the redoubt turns in recognition. It's none other than Rollo, from the wrestling tent.

'Best of men!' he says loudly to his comrades, in some awe. 'This is only the man who has bettered me in the circle, a finer more stout man I have never met!'

Conversations quieten; the grinding wheel is halted - waking the snoozing man, who peers at you through rheumy eyes. 'And you!' the wrestler commands, lobbing a rock in the direction of the sneering dice player, 'Have some cocking respect!' This mirths the men, and with a new found spirit, they fix you with an attentive gaze.

Whether he can read it in your strained features, or by some other innate sense, the wrestler's voice rises above the other Bravos.

'You look like you've got a good story to tell Master Sigasünd,' he smiles.

Turn to 62.

As the bony hand tugs on your leggings, you overcome the desire to chop the unseen assailant with a violent swing of your blade - it's apparent that whatever lurks below is merely seeking to grab your attention. A bleached hand emerges from the black pool clenching a **Bronze Diadem**. Once aloft, it's tipped towards you in a gesture of offering. You reach out and take the unexpected gift, its cool surface shimmers iridescently and the fine engravings mark it as an item of some importance. Holding it above the waters until you cross to the other side, you turn to see the skeletal hand perceptibly wave before sliding back to its watery grave.

Turn to 147.

You approach the Stygians - striding across the piazza flagstones with purpose - who turn, and with a flicker of recognition, stop pulling and tug the awning tightly over the cart.

'Ho, friends, may we help you with your load?' you soothe, as you walk around the cart slowly, patting the load beneath the leather tarpaulin. Adz holds the two Stygians in his steely gaze.

'Thank you, cousin,' one begins nervously, 'But it is our burden to carry...and now we must be on our way.' He motions to the other, and together they strain as the heavy cart creaks back into motion.

With a nod at Adz, you rip the awning back on the cart, in defiance of the protests of its teamsters, whom Adz pushes away as you inspect the cargo. You whistle in surprise as you regard the load; a half-dozen or so heavy band-saws, the same amount of lumber axes, and 4 barrels of - you inhale the familiar pungent aroma - gunpowder.

'Which mountain are you demolishing today friends, with this little lot?' you ask the two dumbstruck fellows.

'It need not concern you,' one begins, '...We're just chopping down...some trees,' he babbles, and winces. The other Stygian aims a quick poisonous glare at him, before piping up himself,

'We'll be off now, this is our business and we bid you continue with yours.' You curse, as from across the piazza you can see a market trader, with a watch patrol, pointing toward you for some reason or other.

'Adz - Watchdogs!' you urge quietly.

If you want to hold your ground as the Militia approach, turn to 431.
If you decide to quickly depart the vicinity, and head back to the Swallow with your supplies, turn to 158.

445

As you pummel the leader, the other steps back nervously, uncertain of himself. Suddenly, you hear a grating noise as flagstone rises up between the carts and the tree, and slides over the cobbles, closely followed by the emergence of a stream of crow-like Stygians.

'Siga!' Adz cries out, and steps closer to you, parrying blows from the thugs.

'I see them!' you reply urgently. The Brotherhood members break from combat, and turning at the sound of the scraping flagstone, gawp in nervous confusion as the black clad wanderers scurry from their underground bolt-hole. Four or five swarm over to the cart and rip back its tarpaulin, and the same number head directly for the Tree of Life, carrying a huge wobbling band-saw and giant lumber axes.

Turn to 365.

446

With the scent of blood feeding its frenzy, the powerful **Hobgoblin** is a formidable opponent. The crowds look on in a mixture of fear and awe as you tumble to and fro across the square. **If the combined total of your Dexterity and Fortitude is greater than 12, you come away relatively unscathed: lose only 1 point of Fortitude. If it is less, lose 2 points of Fortitude.**

Eventually you manage to land the telling blows, and disembowel the disgusting creature. Your attention attracted by the far larger explosion across the city, you decide to grab Adz and make good your exit from the square and make a beeline for its call.

Turn to 306.

447

The Watchdogs give you a cursory glance, and one of them mutters a rude regional joke at your expense. Laughing in a humourless and vaguely threatening manner, they shove you out of the way and clank down the street, to no doubt ruin someone else's day. Relieved to escape further attention from the law, you are able to proceed on your way.

Turn to 435.

448

You step through the gravity defying waterfall. The invigorating waters electrify every atom of your being, and for a few moments you can almost feel the torn fibres of your worn out body knit back together in harmony. When you emerge you do so utterly revitalised. Looking at Galiael, his brows knitted in concentration, you doubt he's been blessed with the same restorative benefits.

Restore 4 points of Fortitude. If this takes you higher than your original total, amend your original total to this new high.

Turn to 441.

You weave your way through the early morning crowds, and after asking several disinterested locals the way in your thick Nhortlünd brogue, you finally stumble upon 'The Diving Swallow,' a three story building occupying a dusty corner near the Grand Piazza. Brushing aside the brightly coloured fly screen, you step inside to escape the rapidly rising heat. The taproom is a ramshackle affair filled with mismatching furniture, gay tapestries and wall hangings. Most remarkable is that all manner of avian fauna, some caged, some flying free, fill the Inn - squawking loudly to one another as they flit around the rafters. The proprietor of the lodgings leans across the bar and greets you warmly.

'The professor told me to expect you,' she says knowingly. 'Shush now, my beauties,' she urges the birds, which unerringly cease the cacophony, and quieten down to a low chirp.

A mature woman of thirty or so years, though not unattractive, she introduces herself as Evassa, as she tousles her long black hair, gaily decorated with exotic feathers. When asked about the professor, Evassa shrugs, and passes on the message that he left a few days ago, but should be back today or tomorrow, and wasn't specific about where he was going.

'Oh, but he mentioned you may arrive early, and he has made provision for you to stay here until he returns,' she concludes, before giving you the key for room. Thanking her for the help, you troop up the stairs to the top floor, and dump the heavier of your kit in the room. You toy with the outrageous idea of wearing your pistol and sword, but wisely settle for carrying only a concealed dagger. Securing the room, you set out to explore the city. Dunking your sweating face into the water butt as you exit, you glance at the pamphlet to see where to head first. **You may only visit each location once during the festival.**

If you wish to go to the Stygian Fayre, turn to 226.
Or perhaps visit the Grand market to see if you can pick up a bargain, turn to 376.
Or Maybe the Festival of Wine and Song, for a cool drink and pick up on the local gossip, turn to 363.

450

You dazzle the sentinel on the door with naked lies. Boasts of connections and tacit threats of recourse should you be denied entry. The confused guard clearly decides it best to err on the side of caution and ushers you inside, red of face.

You take in the vista of the sweeping arena, and are able to pick out a few key figures. The Duce is here, resplendent in his personal box, like a finely-dressed toad - jaw jutting out in constant defiance. Heads of several of the religious orders are here too and many of the Council of Fifty who rule the City-state.

Delicate yet powerful melodies resonate throughout the arena, as the Elven ensemble begin their passion play with a musical introduction. There's audible scoffing within the crowd, which grows into outright guffawing as the all-male warrior troupe take to the stage bedecked in various historical outfits. It seems what passes for serious storytelling in the Elven world only raises hilarity in Deva. You can't discern a reaction from the proud elves - all of whom seem apparently lost in the play, wearing utterly inscrutable expressions of complete seriousness. The ages are covered, highlighting episodes of Elven intervention and guidance. The Devans seem either to smirk or yawn in equal measure. Aegnor takes the stage during the final chapters, mournfully describing the flight from the Old World and its inevitable slide into chaos and disorder. In parts dictating, in others appealing, it's difficult to track where the past ended and the present began, as the play takes on speech like qualities. A distinguished figure steps forward.

'That's Aegnor – leader of these fairies,' scoffs a drunk in the row in front. The figure steps forward and directly addresses the crowd, and in particular the Duce, who matches his steely gaze with his own. He begins,

'Never again, dear cousins; never again can we, jointly, allow evil to penetrate these lands to the extent of the past. After **two hundred and twenty eight** peaceable years of the White Kings reign, we are now at the gates of Armageddon friends, and they buckle against the vanguard of darkness. Disorder needs NO invite! No invitation to enter this world, and it does not need assistance from meddlers in the black arts. Dear friends of common cause, we watched from afar but can watch no longer. We have come to help you protect yourselves. Yes, I say this now, and I beseech you to heed my words. Only by joining as one can we hope to eliminate the threat - only as one can we hope to bolster the gates, in whatever form, and make them bulwarks against evil. Portents of the most ruinous form have been scryed in the crystal pools, and these are *imminent.*' Aegnor again regards the confused and mocking crowds somewhat urgently. 'Friends,' he pleads, 'We must address this without delay…we have seen that under this very city…' You sit forward to listen keenly, it becoming harder to pick out what is being said with the onset of cat-calls and booing, '…There are gates which are opening…' The boorish pig in front of you rises to toss a used flagon at the stage, but you firmly pummel him back into his seat. '…We locked these gates eons ago…they are not the playthings of humankind!'

It's chaos in the amphitheatre, as people rise to make off - when suddenly The Duce cries out in pain and sinks into his velvet throne clutching an arrow sunken into his breast. Suddenly one of the crowd rises and shouts,

'An Elf! There on the Colonnade!!' and points to an Elven figure making off from the scene to the north, bow in hand. Pandemonium ensues as elves and men alike try to comprehend the situation, both reaching instinctively for their weapons. As you scan the shadows high on the colonnade, you see another figure, this one black-clad, returning an unshot arrow back into their quiver before darting off to the south.

If you give chase to the assassin headed north, turn to 208.
If you want to pursue the figure making off to the south, turn to 69.
If leap onto the up to the private box and assist the Duce, turn to 235.

451

You knock loudly on the cabin door, contesting against the crashing of waves pounding into the ship. The door opens with a creak, and the occupant peering round it, rubbing the red eyes of a man who doesn't sleep very much. He welcomes you in and offers you a liqueur which you take politely, whilst he begins to ramble on in the usual Middenlander manner. It's not long before the subject turns to Elves, a word which he appears to struggle on, spitting it out with some effort, through clenched teeth. No matter how you attempt to deviate the stilted conversation, it immediately returns to the subject in hand. Speaking with total conviction, the twitching malcontent lists a litany of misdeeds and ill fortune that he attributes directly to the Elven cousins.

'Did you know it was THEY, who collaborated with the forces of darkness in the attempt on the life of the King of the East? I have seen proof that this is so...with my own eyes!' he continues, fidgeting excitedly. 'Did you know that, brother?' he asks, nodding his head madly.

'No, I did not know that...brother,' you reply, removing the incredulous tone from your response. He stares directly at you and transfixes you with his bloodshot eyes,

'What say you - about these cunning liars and usurpers?' How will you respond?

Declare your love of all things Elven, turn to 387.
Remain non-committal in face of this deranged diatribe, turn to 354.
Spit with disgust at the merest mention of the pointy-eared fiends, turn to 84.

452

You roar in pain as you clumsily fail to avoid the assassin's attack. **Lose 3 points of Fortitude.** Cursing yourself, you advance in with renewed resolve. Tonight is not a night to die. The steel in your eyes seems to resonate with the assassin, who attempts a desperate lunge directly toward you.

Turn to 124.

You thrash wildly at the inky waters of the black pool, chopping at the skeletal hands iron grip. After considerable effort, and a lung full of foul liquid, you free yourself of their grasp and drag yourself to the other side.

Lose 1 point of Fortitude, due to your efforts. Cursing, you also realise you have lost an item in the struggle. **Deduct 1 non-monetary item of your choice from your Adventure Sheet.** Looking back into dark waters, you do not at all fancy the odds of retrieving it.

Turn to 147.

You push your way through the tight knots of fleeing citizens to the gates themselves. Encouraging and berating in equal measure, you assist in whipping the masses up into a frenzy.

'Heave friends! Push with all your might!' With an almighty surge the people push forwards, causing the gates to creak and bow. The crowd cries, 'Huzzah!' as their massed force - and probable help from within - manages to breach the gatehouse and cause the release of the mighty bolts and latches securing it in place.

You follow the river of people out into the darkness of the countryside beyond the towering walls. The rural landscape is a marked contrast to the heaving maelstrom of the city.

Once outside, the willing refugees seem uncertain of their next action, and mill about in small groups. Arguments and appeals ring out under the stars of the black night sky; small groups begin the futile journey down the Ancient Way, leading many leagues to the south. Others begin hiking across the tilled fields and through olive groves to family smallholdings, and distant villas. A stranger in these lands, and with anyone you know likely to still be within the city walls, you glance around for inspiration from these dubious sources whilst wiping the clotting blood from your top lip.

'Look, they're coming back already,' scoffs a guardsman, as he points an accusatory finger toward some dark figures lolloping through the furrows of a nearby field back onward the city, almost totally enveloped by the night. From behind you, a clank of metal and thunder of chains as the cursing city militia prepare to close the gate once again.

If you decide to head back into the city, before the gates are closed shut, turn to 142.
If you follow the majority, and strike out down the Ancient Way, turn to 97.

Lacking the necessary vitality to fend off the fiend, and with your soul devoid of hope as its energy sapping saliva courses through your veins, you lay down wearily in the dust. Bitter with regret about all that befell you in your violent and tragedy afflicted life, you bawl your eyes out as the ghoul begins to devour you.

So heartbroken and consumed with despair are you, that you don't even move a muscle as two beautiful and abominable creatures slide back the lids on their coffins and creep out to greedily join the feast. Staring motionless at the tattered fresco of the tomb, you consider for a moment that this is also your final resting place and with a huge sigh you exhale your final breath.

Your adventure ends here.

During the mysterious and unannounced stop at Aedes, you stumbled from your bunk, woken by the dawn chorus of insects and mewing Billy-goats. Peering out through the mists of early morning you saw two other passengers boarding, both fairly unremarkable. The younger; pale of complexion with his cheek entirely stained by a wine-blotch birthmark, and the older of the two - a man of thirty years or so; anxious and nervy.

Also hauled on board, along with long hungered for fresh supplies, was a large chest - apparently of undistributed weight, judging by the swearing and stumbling of the miserable stevedores labouring beneath it. Only now, as the red skies streak overhead and sea birds circle listlessly, are you able to leave the confines of your stinking vomit stained cabin.

You engage the relieved bosun in casual conversation, and are gratified with the ease of which he imparts his views on the two new shipmates. The young man; 'A Casconqian - and a great strutting cock,' according to his astute eye, and the older man; 'Raving nutcase...one of those 'Brotherhood' extremist troublemakers.' You chuckle along with the bosun, broadly agreeing with his judgement and clapping him on his back good-naturedly as you stroll to the foredeck. But something else tugs at your memory. Midnight screams ringing out as you drifted in and out of consciousness, contesting with the shrieking winds, and crashing waves. Female screams...from the Captain's cabin. Though surely no sailor would dare dice with such ill-starred omens as to bring on board a woman...

With only a day's sailing until you arrive at Deva you resolve to not spend that time inhaling the regurgitated rum, liberally dashed around your foetid little cabin.

If you call on the aloof young man, turn to 474.
If you choose to pay a visit to the 'extremist' turn to 451.
Or try to gain entry to Captain Hessler's cabin to investigate the cries, turn to 52.

Batting some stragglers aside, you leap over the rope and up to the stage. Dr. Döll can only stare in frozen horror as the Ogre lofts him high above its head, and hurls him onto the flagstones with a sickening crunch. Glaring around for the next victim of its furious vengeance, it rests its bloodshot eyes upon the terrified dignitaries not yet fled. Its blood-curdling roar scatters the attached bodyguards, who clank away ridiculously in their unblemished armour. You follow a line from its twisted leer direct to a now abandoned young noblewoman, face buried into a sofa. With a wry smile you pick up one of the many dropped weapons littering the emptying piazza, and gauging its balance with a few swipes through the thick night air, you leap into the fray.

If you pick up a sword with which to fight the ogre, turn to 214.
If you'd rather use one of the halberds, turn to 319.
If you'd rather get in close and use your trusty knife to land a killing blow, turn to 468.

458

You pull out your dagger - much to the horror of the beggar - who recoils, grey with fear.

'Keep a watch!' you hiss, as you angle the blade and deftly make the necessary twiddlings to free the lock. With a satisfying click, the door slams ajar, filling your nostrils with must and ash. You slip inside; the beggar attempts to follow, but a firm hand in the chest causes him to reconsider.

The Keijzer house is filled with gloom, the sky lights darkened by recent smoke. The rooms surrounding the atrium have been thoroughly ransacked. Experiments and mechanical contraptions lay disturbed and smashed. Clothes and mundane trappings are strewn everywhere. Silver too - you count at least 30 scuda - left scattered with the other belongings. Whoever has ransacked this place clearly wasn't bent on common burglary.

As you prod the detritus with your boot, you catch sight of the source of the burning stench. In a bed-chamber, signs of a now extinguished fire, with several papers laying burnt within the ashes. Maps, letters, scrolls, most are beyond recovery...but...one item remains mostly intact. A **Notebook** inscribed with images of comets, dragons and owls. Measurements and compass directions are prominent– **94 degrees east, and 17 leagues distance**. Though mostly incomprehensible, it appears to be some kind of incantation - and something draws you to carefully stow it about your person - **add this to your adventure sheet.** A melted bell-jar lies next to the fire - damp patches on the floorboards suggest the flames, once lit, were soon extinguished by the falling water-filled receptacle. Perhaps this job remains unfinished...

There is no time to consider further as your erstwhile lookout squeaks a warning of approaching watchdogs! With no inclination to be incarcerated once the professor arrives in the city, you think it best to leave this place. Securing the notebook, you push past the beggar - leaving behind the Watch's cries to halt - and head back to the Diving Swallow.

Turn to 75.

459

Tearing and spitting, you are dragged to shore by the hulking Norsiczan, as you desperately reach for your mistress, the sea. Red in the face and burning with hate, you hurl the worst of insults at your friend, who simply grins - as you would towards a child - before pummelling you with his massive fists. Your fury only subsiding as you sink into unconsciousness...

Turn to 322.

460

'We'll surely drown if we stay so close to the coast,' you declare as you turn the horses inland, into the soft marshland. The tidal shore is thick with sodden reeds, and laced with gulleys and seawater pools. The horses sweat with nervous effort, as you endeavour to navigate a course through it.

'This is worse that fighting that rearguard action against Bausthauser's Bastards in the Budazan Fens - do you remember?' Adz reminds you with a smile, seemingly cheered by memories of atrocities that would make others shudder. 'Look! Marshlights come to guide us,' Adz points, motioning towards the approaching spheres.

You halt your mount as the Marshlights circle around you. Delicate orbs of pale illumination, these fickle ethereal spirits have been known to save lost travellers...but it is also said that on a whim, they may lead the unwary to a watery demise.

'Do you see?' asks Adz, 'They want us to follow them - we're saved!' Blowing out your cheeks, and shaking your head slowly at Adz' easy optimism, you need to make a decision.

If you want to follow the Marshlights, turn to 360.
If not, and you want to keep to what you believe was the correct course, turn to 264.

461

Edging yourself into the recess of the drained passageway you slip and slide down the gentle gradient. Marooned and cracked sarcophagi, empty of patrons, are now beached upon raised sections of the floor. You spiral found a bend, the way illuminated by a distant pinprick of light somewhere far below. In the near total darkness you can make out dim shapes moving ahead. Not quite white...but rather the bleached bones of the restless dead. Woken by the necromantic radiance of the risen Master, and freed by the tremors from their tombs, these **Unearthed Skeletons** emit a soundless, but fury-filled screech, through their gaping-wide jaw bones. With tumbling catastrophe bringing down the catacombs behind you, there is little choice but to dispatch these reanimated horrors back to whichever Gods lay claim to them.

If your Dexterity and Agility combined total 14 or more, turn to 54
If they total less, turn to 304

462

Your frayed tendons scream for mercy in tandem with your burning lungs, as you sprint through the flame licked city streets. All about you lay piles of the dead...and the dead-ish. In the moonlit night, it's difficult to tell the two apart, not that you dally to investigate - the howls of the Master's host still within earshot. There is no more dangerous place than a crowded city in turmoil, you reason, as you flee through the streets, shoving aside the desperate and the panicking.

As you near the South Gate you run into a thick knot of bedraggled citizens trying to force open the sturdy portal into the countryside beyond. It's a chaotic scene; the guardsmen on the walls atop the portal are bellowing at the people to push back, as they attempt to re-secure the now unlatched gate - encouraged by some bad-tempered prods of their pikes. All around you, the seething masses pull and push, trampling over their fellow citizens in a desperate attempt to exit the city, each carrying an assortment of frivolous trappings ill-suited to a sojourn into the countryside in the lands beyond.

You see no senior officers, and it's evident the guardsmen are rudderless. Confusion reigns, as they trade insults with the crowd, evidently unsure whether the city is under a general attack.

If you clamber up toward the guardhouse, tell them all you have seen and appeal with them to throw open the gates, turn to 398.
If you think it better to blend in with the crowd, and encourage their efforts, turn to 454.

Stumbling through the arcane Elven incantation you feel yourself slipping from concentration. Beads of sweat pour down your face as you wrestle with the unimaginable forces of magic, struggling to bind the words which tumble uncertainly from your lips. The ground beneath your feet begins to give way and, for a second, you feel the complete unadulterated joy of floating in the empty space between Realms. Ecstasy is however quickly displaced by terror as the horrors of the netherworld bind their claws around you, dragging you into the black-hearted void - their tortured plaything for all of eternity.

Your Adventure ends here, your existence of unimaginable suffering begins.

Winding your way through a warren of streets, Pepin eventually leads you to Keijzer's house, only to bear witness to a smouldering pile of charred timbers. Lingering spirals of blue-grey smoke - and occasional multicoloured fizzes - are all that remain as a lifetime of work is snuffed out.

Irritated city Watchdogs - frayed of nerve - and curious onlookers, occasionally hop out of the way of sparks nipping round their boots. You give the boy a pat on the head, and approach your waiting mentor, Professor Kroos. Gently taking his arm, you greet him.

'Hello, old friend…such a pity,' he says, enveloping you in a tight embrace. Adz is also present, his Norsiczan bulk stood impassively watching the embers.

'Siga, my friend, thank the Gods we get to meet again.' You return the greeting warmly, and together the three of you survey what remains of the Keijzer house.

'All those years of collecting. All those irreplaceable treasures which must have been stored within - gone up in smoke, just like that.' You console the Professor, knowing as you do how deeply he cares for the unique, and for the treasures of the ancients. 'He was my friend you know,' he begins. 'But once he found that piece of the Triptych, it corrupted him - he was so driven to find the other two pieces of it, he neglected all his other work - not to mention his friends. I have not seen him now for….oh, more than a year. He set off for the southern tip of the Forgotten Kingdoms…he was definitely on to something, he was so excited when I briefly saw him last…but how can this be?' The professor sweeps his arm across the charcoal remnants of the property. 'It was raining hard this evening, how would a fire take hold?' You exchange a quick glance with Adz, and grimace. 'Yes, yes, I feared this would happen,' the professor muses, before turning to you anxiously. 'There is foul play afoot,' he whispers, 'and, if I'm correct…there is a grave threat to this city.'

As the illuminations wane, the militia and a small group of locals who gathered to watch the flames gradually start to melt away, leaving the three of you quite alone. As the rain tails off, a brilliant, blazing orange sun rises in the far off Appucine lofts, as another day dawns.

Turn to 321.

465

Judging by the maelstrom of screams originating up the road, you think the Avenue Arborea will take you directly to the piazza, and the forlorn Elven Tree of Life. People are scurrying to and fro, and there is no little blood being shed on it, judging by the wounded and the terrified running up and down it. The narrow maze-like warren of harbour-side slums might wind a path to the Piazza, though in the dark there is every chance of being lost within. Glancing upwards, you may be able to take an elevated route across rooftops, dangerous and energy sapping as that would be, in your soaking gear across the trepidatious tiles and thin thatches and coverings. From nowhere a repulsive old maid bounces into you, her toothless mouth gaping in terror, and her gormless face splattered with gore.

'The Master of the Pit…he has returned!' she babbles, bespittling you with pink foam. She grips your collar with whitened knuckles, and with eyes wide as a King's serving platters, she whispers, 'I saw his face!'

You push the idiot woman to the cobbles and kick her away, much disturbed, as she rolls in the sewer channel giggling mindlessly. As the crescendo rises you make your decision.

To follow the Avenida toward the Piazza Arborea turn to 426.
To clamber up onto the rooftops, above the seething streets, turn to 2.
To conceal yourself in the warren of slums, turn to 346.

466

With deceptive skill, the champion catches one of your incoming blows, and brings his fist down on your outstretched arm. You bellow with intense pain as your elbow is forced into an unnatural angle. **Lose 1 point of Dexterity, and 2 points of Fortitude.** Wounded, you expel a motivated cry and lurch toward Rollo. You grasp his stout legs with hydra-like speed, and send him toppling to the canvas. Sensing your chance, you clench the big man's neck in the crook of your elbow and squeeze with all your might. The bulging-eyed champion's purpling tongue hangs limply from his drooling mouth…but your arms are aflame with fatigue.

If your Fortitude is 11 or higher, turn to 77.
If your Fortitude is 10 or lower, turn to 112.

467

Before you can do so, the sergeant steps forward, silhouetted against the driving rain of the night sky. He glares menacingly, and snarls,

'I am *sick* of you foreigners coming into my city, waving your swords around. Tonight my friend, is not your lucky night.' He motions to the other two thugs, who step up to close ranks alongside him. Reluctantly, you steel yourself in readiness for the brutish attack from the **Watchdogs**.

If your Dexterity is 8 or more, turn to 340.
If your Dexterity is 7, turn to 494.
If your Dexterity is 6 or less, turn to 269.

468

Confronting the brute with your knife, you feint and dance, attempting to extract an opening. The Ogre merely watches you with a venomous stare. Sensing a chance, you dart forward and stab it in the belly, but it simply swats your blow aside with a painful blow to the wrist. **Lose 1 point of from your Agility total.** You realise a degree of distance is needed, and so you scoop up a nearby halberd. Grasping the weapon in both hands, you level it at the beast.

'Hoi, ugly!' you yell, drawing an infuriated howl. It thunders toward you, swishing its mighty fists with furious intent. Stabbing powerfully into its enlivened flesh, you carve two fearful wounds into its pallid flesh. Over stretching – or is it overconfidence – you struggle to retain control of the polearm, long unaccustomed as you are to bearing one.

If your Dexterity is 8 or more and/or you have the Gift of Martial Prowess, turn to 292.
If not, turn to 42.

469

Your mark is too accurate to be avoided, and the razor sharp assassin's tool embeds itself in the elf chest. You hear a cry, a gurgle. A wet thud, as Galiael slumps motionless to the sodden carpet of the plateau. With the invigorating stench of blood filling your nostrils you step over to the body. Of the elf's finely chiselled features...a mask of agony. Frowning, you kick the corpse onto its belly, so to avoid its accusatory death stare.

Turn to 350.

470

If you have BROTHERHOOD written on your adventure sheet, turn to 277.
Otherwise, turn to 404.

471

The path behind the waterfall is too narrow for the horses, so you carefully tether them before continuing. Sensing the worst and fearing the inevitable, you clasp your mouth tightly shut and hold your breath. With a grimace of expectation you step hesitantly forward and immerse yourself under the cascading waters of the upper Devani river.

If your Fate status is Favoured, turn to 448.
If your Fate status is Marked, turn to 232.
If your Fate status is Unwatched, turn to 57.

472

Concealing yourself from the terrors of the night a safe distance from the fiend filled square, you anxiously await the becalming rays of dawn's early light, wishing its warm tendrils to reach out into this cursed city and push away the shadows of the dead. Howls, screams. Human and...otherwise, fill your ears as you wait, reaching a crescendo shortly before dawn.

A fiery orange crust forms on the horizon as the sun awakens, and the comet looms swollen against the purple sky. The chorus of howls reaches such a pitch that something stirs within you. A nagging doubt, a sinking feeling in your soul. Have you waited too long? Tears form in your eyes, as your mind is filled with despair and regret. You emerge from your set, and race to the square with frantic urgency. The howls subside as you approach, and in terror you look up to see the comet form a low trajectory behind you, blistering the air as it scorches towards its child. The suns brilliant orange light casts long fingers of shadow upon the flagstones as you reach the square. The multitude of horrors are disappearing into the pit with their master, who has already sunk to the depths, offended by the light. With lungs bursting with furious effort, you howl with unrequited vengeance as the clothes on your back begins to smoulder in the approaching heat of the comet. With dull realisation of the inevitable, you hurl the burning orb toward the pit with all your might. Mere seconds later you are entirely immolated by the white heat of the star-shattering explosion.

Whether or not the Master is destroyed by your brave - but hesitant - actions, you will never know.

Your adventure, and your mortal soul, ends here.

473

Beaten and bleeding, you are dumped in a dank cell for a period of time you can't fathom. Sitting foolishly in your own filth, and stripped of all the possessions you were carrying, despair begins to gnaw at your being. As the hours - or is it days - pass by, the maddened howls and shrieks diminish your ebbing spirits. Just as you emit a huge sigh of resignation, a splinter of light penetrates the darkness, and the heavy door is forced open with a dull clank. A repugnant gaoler thrusts a torch into the gloom,

'It's your lucky day,' he says, a smirk spreading across his cruel face. 'Get up. Someone has bought your freedom - at a pretty price, too,' he says rubbing his grubby fingers together. He carelessly prods you with the shaft of his pike, and ushers you out of the dungeon, much mirthed by his ill-placed humour.

Turn to 430.

474

The door is opened by a pallid young man, with lank, dark hair and an unhealthy complexion; deathly white on one half of his face, the other stained red with an ill-omened birthmark. He frowns at you for a few seconds, before grudgingly bidding you entry. With the cool air of a privileged fop used to giving orders, he introduces himself as Ingmar Kops. You attempt to engage him in conversation, but all roads lead to himself. As he drones on, you gather this fool regards himself as the new wonder of the age, whilst haughtily dismissing any attempts by yourself to add to the dialogue.

It transpires this moneyed young Casconqian fancies himself as a powerful wizard, and it appears, through rambling boasts, that he is travelling to Deva in order to do...something. You can't quite make out what, such is his fanciful dialogue. He breaks off theatrically, and rudely thrusting his palm toward you, he boasts,

'Watch and marvel.' With a confident air, he begins to mutter lore, and strokes his fingers through the air. Sweating with effort, his eyes widen as a minute ball of flame forms and splutters in the air above him. The flickers transform into a cracking sprite, as the Casconqian pants with fatigue from his incantations. The tiny fire sprite wheels above him for a few chaotic seconds, the amateur sorcerer's face a strained mask of concentration, as he struggles to bind it. With a high-pitched whine, and a puff of black smoke the image dissipates into its realm of origin. The young Casconqian protests, excuses tumbling from his sour lips. You raise a hand to stop him making an even greater fool of himself.

'Take some advice from me, friend, stick to conjurers' tricks and sleight of hand. The less you know, the easier you'll sleep.' Face flushed with anger, he retorts,

'I don't require observations from the likes of you. One day...one day you *will* know my name!' His shrill voice wavers with youthful embarrassment. He glares at you, muttering, as you turn to leave, his thin lips pouted peevishly. You close the door, stifling a snicker, as you consider what other surprises this ship holds.

To call on the wild-eyed extremist, turn to 451.
Or if you want to try to gain entry to Captain Hessler's cabin and investigate the cries, turn to 52.
If you've visited both the above or simply wish to leave the fellow passengers to their business and retire to your cabin, turn to 220.

475
You cast several looks behind you at the Orb, the thing you came to find, as you move away from it into the endless plain. It's truly a desolate place - the flat terrain gradually becomes punctuated with ruined Elven masonry laid forgotten, covered in thickly knotted bracken. Bleached skeletons of sheep and goats poke through the unhealthily tinged weeds.

Galiael looks lost within himself, bereft at the decay and the fallen monuments of his ancestors. For a place of considerable altitude there is not a wisp of a wind on your skin. Instead the plain seems perfectly still, almost as if suspended. As you press on you encounter numerous statues, cast in lead. The towering figures litter the plain - enormous warriors, two heads higher than you, covered in a curiously powerful armour, their helms almost beaked, holding bizarre short-muzzled arquebuses, or with enormous metal fists, frozen in time.

From the direction of the forest far behind you, you can hear approaching music. A band of sorts - playing out a lilting ode. Galiael says nothing, as if the sound is inaudible to him, but the incongruous melodies send a chill through your soul.

As you plod onwards the ruins become more prominent and frequent - evidently this was a settlement of sorts. From nowhere you see a small - but gleaming and immaculate - Elven temple, and in the distance a spiral stairway to...nothing. The tall weeds immediately around it bend in a breeze of uncertain origin. You glance at your companion and recognise signs of fear: the white knuckles and slight tremble of hands.

'I am afraid of this place,' mutters Galiael, doing nothing at all to allay your own fears. The elf turns and opens his mouth wordlessly, appearing to be at a loss at what action to take, he repeatedly looks across to the pristine temple.

Should you choose to investigate the temple, turn to 83.
If you choose to wait for the approaching music to come closer, turn to 242.
If you want to take a closer look at the stairway, turn to 21.

476

Cornered, you hold your arms outstretched, and whilst dropping to your knees, you are summarily arrested, maintaining your innocence all the while. Disregarding your protestations, one of the guards manacles you with careless violence, and presses your face into the dust as you feel your possessions torn away from you. Have you killed a Watchman or a member the Militia since the beginning of your adventure?

If you have, turn to 127.
If you haven't, turn to 473.

You reach out for the hand. Your head swims with blood and you feel your pulse halt. All goes black, all goes silent. For a fleeting moment you imagine this is the passing to End Of Days, when you suddenly smell the mineral smell of blood, and the pernicious heat of flames.

Upon opening your eyes, you find yourself in the midst of a battle, and have to fling yourself to the ground as galloping warhorses career past, foaming with terror and rage. You reach for your sword, and just have enough time to unsheathe it before a huge ruby-barded destrier kicks up sods of wet earth, blinding you. As its hooves thunder down on top of you, all you can do is curl into a ball - sure of deadly impact - and expecting a skull-crushing braining. But the hooves pass through you, indeed the stallion passes through you - and charges off into the massed ranks of faceless men.

You lay back, panting with fear and confusion on the muddy battlefield, when suddenly a fire in your heart is kindled. A figure approaches. A woman, exquisite of stature and clad in an ethereal pale blue dress finished with ringlets of white flowers. Even through your stressed and bemused condition, you become acutely aware of the stench you give off. Of the muck and the filth spoiling you, of the clots of blood clinging like parasites on your unshaven face. Embarrassed under the kind scrutiny of this woman you timidly wipe your face with the clean - cleanest - bit of your hand, and stiffly straighten your tunic. The figure simply smiles. A wonderful smile which stirs your instincts.

'I am Sanromai,' she coos, soft as spring blossom. 'By my nature, I love all who have ever loved, and I love you, Sigasünd. For you have been touched by my caress and in that I am joyous.' You exhale, blissful in the presence of this beautiful Deity. Your wounds and worries seem to fade from reality, when the figures face becomes tight, and the Goddess pouts her lips, becoming peevish. 'Though I am not of this world, I am still a woman, and like women you have known, I am jealous. For knowing me, you shall know no other, and when the time comes you shall choose me, over her you truly love. This is my bargain. **Write the name SANROMAI on your adventure sheet.**

Turn to 247.

You grab at the reins as your panicking horse foams and bucks wildly, its eyes wide with terror. Adz cries out over a squelching chorus, but it's too late. One of the Bog Octopus' thick tentacles smashes down on your collarbone, sending you toppling face down in the stinking mud. **Lose 2 points of Fortitude.** Another tentacle wraps around your ankle and you feel yourself pulled towards its gaping maw with irresistible force.

Wriggling only serves to encourage the foul beast to tighten its grip. Your eyes close and you consider what End of Days may be like, before it shudders and relaxes. You look up to see Adz smiling lustily, retrieving his mighty axe from the jibbering mound of dead blubber.

'Where were you off to princess? Did your bowels have an urgent appointment with the privy?' he teases, at your attempted flight. Much abashed you offer your apologies as he looks on with contentment and good humour. **In the struggle you have lost your pistol, cross it off your adventure sheet. If you did not have a pistol, cross off a non monetary item of your choice.** Eventually, you manage to remount the horses, and after a little while manage to decipher a course to your destination.

Turn to 264.

Leaving Gallo at the league marker, you set off down the trail with Adz and the horses. It's not long before you see the Gates. Far from a heaven, it's little more than a baked mud bridle way, with drinking dens and rude shacks either side of it, held aloft improvised raised platforms. Gaudy bunting hangs limply from well worn lines, and painted women loll outside, tranquillized in the stultifying heat. Your ears burn with risqué invitations and mocking catcalls, but you ignore them, keeping an eye on Adz - whose eyes have already widened in anticipation.

'Remain strong, old friend,' you encourage your companion, 'Our quarry is in sight.' Adz follows your gaze to the largest and finest of all the establishments, a plush coach sits parked outside, pulled by two fine white horses. You tether your own sweating horses beside the coach, taking note of the insignia and crests carved into the enamelled panelling; The House of Toggia.

Your shadows cast a long reach across the dusty baked earth, stretching to steps of the whorehouse. A medium height, but powerfully built local sits on a stool at the entrance, taking considered sips from a large mug. Without looking up, he notices the shadows approach, and puts down his mug. Beside him, and snoozing in the midday heat, a huge figure - a half-Orc bastard - is folded near in two, dribbling and murmuring in its sleep. As you approach, the shorter of the two rouses his companion with a sharp kick, causing the creature to wake and rub its sunken eyes free of sleep. The burly looking fellow rises and steps in front of the entrance. His ruddy face breaks into a warm grin as he slowly shakes his head in apology.

'Alas brothers, today the house's curtains are drawn shut. A private affair is being conducted within.' He fixes your gaze and widens his grin, revealing a row of yellow teeth punctuated with empty spaces. You feel the looming presence of Adz beside you, his twitching fist muscles jumping with anticipation, waiting for the merest sign.

If you wish to stay Adz' hand, turn to 146.
Should you want to give Adz the wink - to deal with the bouncer, turn to 159.

'Best of men,' you engage assertively, never blinking as you transfix the doorkeep with a steely gaze. 'I am sent of Don Toggia, the wayward master's perplexed and bitterly disappointed father. My lord bids me to return the frolicking young hare back to his hutch, lest he accidentally sires a bastard by way of youthful over-exuberance and inexperience.' The half-orc guffaws loudly and spits into the dust, whilst stocky man blinks and purses his lips as he considers your gambit. 'For as you know,' you continue, taking a half step toward him, 'The young master is betrothed to the fair lady Magda of Mannonia, in the Nhortlünd. It would be shameful to cast disgrace on these two noble houses. I need not remind you of venerable and powerful institutions they represent.' The doorman snorts with derision,

'I care not of such games,' he says, breaking your gaze and looking down at the steps. 'Take your quarry back to his father.' He places his scarred hand on your arm 'But no trouble,' he says, then looks at Adz doubtfully, '...And don't touch the girls.'

You brush past the man, with Adz snickering to you in whispers...

'Magda of Mannonia - the ancient spinster? Siga, the lies you tell. Ha!'

Turn to 491.

481

The moans increase with every rock hurled aside as you hurry to free the wounded figure beneath them.

'Don't worry, friend, I'll have you out in a moment,' you reassure them, redoubling your efforts. The person must be seriously wounded, for they don't reply to your calming words, instead only moan louder, and with a more desperate pitch. With dust cloying against the roof of your mouth, and sweating a little from your labours you free them of the last bits of entombing masonry.

Kneeling down to turn them gently - with the due care required of the crushed, an all too common smell permeates your clogged nostrils - the stench of death! You recoil in sudden realisation that the person whose aid you have come to is already ranked amongst the dead! With a sickening twist of its long-broken neck, the cadaverous face of a zombie elf snaps toward you, bloody stumps of broken teeth gnashing desperately.

If you benefit from the Gifts of Intuition or Martial Prowess turn to 209.
If not, turn to 195.

482

Uttering a rapid prayer, you thrust the stake through the first child. It emits a piercing shriek and its cherubic face transfigures into a mask of evil before withering to dust. You recoil, shocked, just in time to see a tiny clawed hand on the side of the other coffin. Bounding over, you kick off the lid, and stake the child-vampire before it can fully rise. As it dissipates into dust you stagger backwards and with a nervous laugh. At the door awaits the steward, white with terror.

As the pair of you make your way back to the city it soon becomes apparent that the poor old man has now entirely lost his wits. The imbecile babbles on, over and over, whispering,

'I must tell my Master Moretti, Don Ludovico will need to know about this, he'll know what to do....' You attempt to restore him to sense, but he is thoroughly broken by what he has witnessed, and somewhat reluctantly you are forced to abandon him shortly, before his jabberings raise attention.

Taking pity on the man, you give him 5 silver scuda, which you press into his clammy grip. In return, he offers you **a Lemon-motif Medallion**, incoherently talking about a tower. **Make a note of this on your adventure sheet, and also record the word LUDOVICO.** Free of the old man, you consider your next move.

You could make your way to The Plain of Heroes, to witness the Military Display. If so, turn to 413.
Or you could just quench your thirst down at the Festival of Wine and Song, which runs all day into the night. If so, turn to 420.

483

You bid the Freelander good day in his native middle-tongue.

'Hmm, good morning,' he replies, not looking up from his abacus and ledgers. Undeterred, you take a seat at his table, displaying your desire to engage him in conversation. Sighing rudely, he slams his ledger shut with a dusty thump. Sensing this will be a stilted one way conversation, you quickly cut to the chase. What do you ask him?

Ask him why there seem to be so many Stygians in the city, turn to 425.
Enquire about the Lemon Tree medallion you saw upon entering the city, turn to 434.
Push him on the subject of the arrival of the Elven ship, turn to 191.

484

The ragged old steward leads you wordlessly through the bustling streets, his face etched with trepidation. In the blazing heat, you eventually head out of the South Gate. After a short plod along the dusty road, he motions for you to follow him down an overgrown track, knotted with parched scrub. The skies above - deep blue a short while earlier - have suddenly filled with looming grey clouds, which seem to hang threateningly low. You trek for some while, onto a promontory lapped by the oceans waves.

Behind a rusting perimeter fence, of some antiquity, sprawls a desolate cemetery, sorrowfully decrepit. Carrion birds wheel heavily in the thick air, which is electric with the onset of imminent thunder. The tombs seem long abandoned and in some places bones have risen to the surface. Treading carefully, the Steward points the way, though he no longer takes the lead...now he's four steps behind you. It's not long before he guides you to the Moretti crypt, a large marble dome engraved with scenes of hunting and lemon groves. Reading the names on the plaques it seems that the last official interments here took place 100 years past. The old Steward shuffles towards you awkwardly and hands you a stake with a cringing smile, pointing a crooked finger towards the entrance.

You take the stake, chiding yourself for allowing the old man to put you in this position. Turn to 106.

485

Pegasus lands close by, and rears up wildly, throwing you from his back. He pounds the hard ground with his hooves and shakes his mighty head to and fro, mouth foaming and sweating profusely. Picking yourself up you numbly walk into the cemetery. It's a forlorn and desolate place, endlessly sad, even before the diabolical events of these last days. The overgrown weeds teem with hissing babes. From the never-born to the unblessed, tiny infants crawl through the dirt with the tired red eyes of the restless dead. A hand no bigger than your thumbnail pokes pathetically through the hard earth, grasping at the chill night air. Hell, you imagine, must look like this. Tears stream down your face, stinging your reddened cheeks. Your sword hand trembles with such rigours that you need first to punch the earth to still it.

You curse the blind Gods above, the unseeing pitiless Gods! How can any Just Deity allow this, allow this sick contortion of nature to be? You slay the first like a green recruit, clumsily, with multiple weak hacks of your blade. Crying with frustration and boiling over with anger, the next is dispatched. Praying for their poor little shades, you set about them quickly, so as not to comprehend your actions. Like an unfeeling automation you cover the cemetery and deliver the innocents of this evil, all the while choked with tears, your heart bursting with sadness.

Grim task complete, you kick the rotten wooden door to the Shrine to Mortus from its hinges. You enter and quickly find some torches and oil and waste no time in consecrating the ground with cleansing fire. As you sit on the dry earth sobbing, swearing vengeance for terrible deed, Pegasus trots over to you. The noble beast lays his huge sweet smelling head on your shoulder, nuzzling you with sympathy. Wiping the tears from your eyes, the pity in them is replaced with steely determination. The bitter taste of fury in the roof of your mouth has never been more powerful.

Climbing atop mighty Pegasus once again, you roar as he soars back into the night sky and over the crenellations of the Devan walls. You roar for shades of the innocents, you roar for vengeance!

Increase your FATE level by 1 if possible. For unbeknown to you, the mute Gods look favourably upon your actions.

Turn to 406.

486

The Animal Master slumped dead to the floor, a trickle of blood emerges from his popped ears and stains the sawdust red. The animals are subdued, and cease their cries, cowed by fear and the spectacle of death. Leaning against the axle of a wagon you catch your breath, listening anxiously for footsteps. Satisfied there are none, you make to creep out of the tent, when you hear chattering and scratching behind the tarpaulin. Remembering that old familiar smell, you approach and rip back the cover of the cage... HOBGOBLINS!!

Raising your sword you attempt to skewer the hated and vile creatures through the bars of their cage, but the two pestilent creatures dance back out of range of your thrusting blade spitting and barking furiously. Suddenly you can hear lots of voices from outside - and getting nearer. Considering the expired body of the Animal Master, you decide to make good your escape. Cursing, you attempt one more dutiful but futile attempt at slaying the Hobgoblins, before dashing from the tent.

As you cover the ground quickly through the long grass of the City Gardens, you glance over your shoulder, and notice four men exit the tent after you. Bitterly regretting they have caught reasonable sight of you, but thankful they don't follow, you finally reach the cobbles of the city-proper, sweating and wheezing of lung. **Note down the name SHADRACK on your adventure sheet.** You decide it's best to stay as far away from the circus as possible.

Where next?

Head to the Festival Market, turn to 376.
Head to the Festival of Wine and Song, turn to 363.
If you've already done all these things, or would rather just head back to your lodgings to chat to Evassa, turn to 361.

Together with Adz, you pound away at the stout door, seeking to force it open wide enough for you to both squeeze through. With uncommon speed the Lycanthrope lollops over the boggy ground, catching you quite by surprise. With a howl and a thrash, it rakes its claws across the both of you, penetrating through your cloaks. **Lose 2 points of Fortitude.** Alarmed and angered, the pair of you turn and make short work of the creature, raining down a torrent of savage strikes. It's not until the beast is dead and returned to human form that you stop to consider your injuries. Adz has a nasty looking gash on his shoulder, and you have a tear on the back of your neck. Adz glances at the moon, then gives you a funny look. You return it with interest, frowning.

Eventually the door begins to concede defeat. Turn to 107.

Blinding light and white heat sears every fibre of your being. The everlasting vision of the Master of Pit - gazing up in terror as the vanquishing ball of fire bore down upon his repulsive being. Feelings of elation, feelings of release. But then...then tinged with confusion, as you half-remember black tendrils of oily miasma seeping out from the Master's form. You struggle with memories of coils of black smoke snaking their way across the flagstones of the square before the comet struck, and wonder whether they are figments of imagination, or the residue of your fears brought to life.

You awaken from this disturbed sleep, your bedclothes sodden with sweat, which trickles like ice down your fevered spine. You uneasily descend the familiar stairs of 'The Diving Swallow', and are greeted with great and warm cheers from your friends, who leap up from their chairs to embrace you. Bells peel out in the streets beyond, and the sounds of singing and laughter. The sounds of relief and victory. You shake free of your sleep clogged mind, and allow the memory of your haunting vision to fade, as your face breaks into a smile.

'We're heroes, Siga!' shouts Adz. 'We're made! Our lives of struggle are over!' Everyone in the bar room hugs, and laughs with careless abandon. Through the shattered streets you encounter scores of ecstatic citizens. Some sobbing with relief, others on their knees praying to resurgent Gods. Others dispense flowers to the re-emerged city militia and share drinks with passers-by. The party continues long into the night, as the flames subside and the blood of the dead is washed from the streets.

Turn to 500.

You step gingerly between the myriad nubile shapes reclining on the cushions and sofas, and ascend the stairs to the upper chamber. Coughing roughly rouses the handsome, but distracted young man, causing him to break off his carnal negotiations. Sandwiched on a round bed between two Daaban maidens, he blinks in surprise and smile broadly.

'Gentlemen,' he greets you, 'You seem to have me at a disadvantage.' He nods down to his loins and winks. Covering his obvious excitement, he climbs down from bed and smothers the protesting maidens with kisses, and honeyed promises. Pulling on his breeches, he looks up. 'How much did my father pay you to drag me back to his dreary villa?' he asks. Adz pulls a face and raises his furry eyebrow.

'You mistake me for a watchdog,' you counter, 'I am not here on your father's business, but to bring a message from your supposed love, the Contessa.'

'Oh,' he says, and looks suddenly crestfallen, 'I...I abandoned hope of being reunited with her,' he explains, casting a guilty look at the two young girls lolling playfully on the bed. 'I mean, I would never come here...to this, if I had known...' Pressing his palms together he rests his chin on his hands, and looks up sorrowfully. 'Pass me the note, please,' he asks politely. He breaks the seal and reads the note. Sighing and exhaling heavily as he pours over the words with deep concentration, before gently folding the delicate paper and fastening the ribbon. He looks somewhat stunned and sits back, placing his hands on his head and puffs out his cheeks, before turning toward you. 'Thank you,' he says earnestly. 'I really mean that. I am in your debt, for this,' he motions toward the note.

Curiosity gnaws away at your sense of high adventure, but you wrestle the notion of enquiring about the notes contents, and resist the temptation to pursue it. Considering your mandate, and other numerous obligations, you say farewell to a grateful man. **Write TOGGIA on your adventure sheet,** as you head back to the way marker to reunite with your guide. Gallo is waiting for you, his sullen pockmarked face shaded from the afternoon sun with a wide brimmed hat.

If you have the word LUDOVICO on your adventure sheet, turn to 132.

If you don't, but have an Iron Key you may head back to the city and turn to the section denoted by the number etched onto it.

If you don't have either, then you have little choice but to depart with Adz back to Deva to join up with the professor. After waiting for Gallo to sit out the worst of the heat, you eventually begin the return journey.

Turn to 131.

490

Sweating with haste, and sodden from the rain, you rip the cloak from the second body in two violent jerks as the militia storm around the corner, slipping all the while on the bloody cobbles. Three stand menacingly - looking damp, vexed and malintentioned.

'Lay down your arms!' one commands aggressively.

If you do you do as he says, turn to 467.
If you spring up and attack them, turn to 93.
Or if you wish to threaten them with your pistol – if you have one - and take flight, turn to 282.

491

You enter the open-plan parlour, your nostrils besieged by all manner of perfume and powder. Adz bundles through after you and violently emits an elephantine sneeze, causing conversation to cease, as the stunned occupants turn and gawp at the two uninvited guests. A polished middle aged lady in a tight blue dress totters through the silk cushions and porcelain dolls to meet you at the door. You brush past her before she can utter the merest sound of protestation. When she begins to berate you, Adz holds her back tightly and presses one of his cudgel-like fingers against her lips,

'Hush now, finest of ladies,' he urges. 'Driver!' you demand of a semi-naked figure, frozen in time between two beauties, 'Where is he?' The compromised figure designs to feign ignorance, then glances at Adz. With a worried frown, he immediately sees the futility of argument and points and uncertain finger towards a gaudy stairway to the rear; the carved angels in the banisters leading the way...

Turn to 489.

492

You eventually manage to push away the jabbering baker, and cosh a few of the rabble around the ears, freeing yourself from the unseemly scrum. Reflecting that being bumped along by jam-packed revellers isn't the most productive way to spend a day - especially in light of what you've encountered since you arrived in Deva – you decide on a change of plan. Considering your options you decide to seek relief from the teaming streets and head off outside the city walls, to the Plain of Heroes, to witness the great Military Display.

Turn to 413.

'Put your trinkets away, my little princeling, nothing you have is worth the ultimate price,' says a grizzled sergeant, rubbing the pink scars criss-crossing his worn face.

'Go sell yourself down the docks and bring us the rewards, then we might reconsider,' taunts another. A ripple of callous laughter trickles through the group, and most turn to once again face the barricade. Several men continue to stare hard at you, with a mixture of pity and contempt emerging from their bloodshot eyes. Rebuffed, and rendered ridiculous in the eyes of these fighting men, you are forced to march to your destiny alone.

You steel yourself to plough on alone through the massed ranks of the dead, turn to 135.

The three watchdogs launch themselves at you, attempting to overcome you by strength of numbers - but your skills are superior and one sinks to his knees with an opened throat in just one swish of your blade. The second adopts a ridiculous expression as you bury your weapon deep inside his ribcage. The third, terrified by now, slashes you wildly and scores a superficial strike – **lose 1 point of Fortitude** – before you round on him. Walking slowly towards him, the man soils himself upon seeing his own death reflect in your cold eyes.

Delivering the final telling blow, you consign the three bullies to End of Days. Turn to 340.

After brushing mud from your clothes, you quickly remount, and race back to Deva. Working the horses into a lather, you push hard to reach the city by nightfall – reaching the Bractianine highway as the sun fades. Following the eternally lit roadside torches leading to the city, you spur on your flagging mounts and clatter through the massive gates into the city.

Do you have either - or both of - the words GIANT or TREE on your adventure sheet? If so, turn to 182.
If not, turn to 131.

496

Feeling mildly foolish, you offer silent words of devotion and respect, reasoning that assistance could be reasonably expected, given your current predicament and the catastrophic evil facing the world. An odd feeling envelopes you. An unseen force nudges your cheek so that you turn to face an object on the table you hadn't seen previously. A rough clay icon sits amongst the more refined likenesses of the other dozen deities. You rise and approach it, drawn as if by a magnetic force you cannot resist. As you look closely at the crude statue, barely resembling a humanoid figure, you are swept by feelings of deepest awe, and something in your souls tells you that represents the thirteenth and oldest of all the Gods, the Creator whose name is not known. Taking the figure, and carefully wrapping it in some linen you tear from your tunic, you leave the shrine and head down the steps, further into the bowels of the catacombs.

Make a note of the number 13 - the *true* number of Elven Gods - on your adventure sheet, and if possible, adjust your FATE ranking one step upwards.
Turn to 71.

497

You struggle with the burly and thickly muscled animal master in the tight confines of the pens. A cacophony of howls, roars and chattering explodes as the animals go wild with fear at the violent struggle. Eventually prising the whip from his sausage-like fingers you draw it across his neck and wrap the leather tightly around. A dry purple tongue protrudes from his gasping mouth as he desperately claws at your arms, but you are too strong, and holding fast - you finally witness the last vapours to disappear from his empty lungs.

Turn to 486.

498

Sending Pegasus twisting to the earth in a near vertical descent, you scream a blood-oath with every fibre of your being, holding your blade aloft. The gaping maw of the Master opens and emits a paralysing roar - a roar of fear! In confusion and panic he lurches to and fro, trying to shift his massive bulk through the hordes of the dead, back to the safety of the underworld.

Despite your valiant efforts, the dead are too many, and you fall several times to the blood-red marble flagstones of the square. Stricken by the many savage wounds inflicted, you feel your heart quiver and fail - the siren-song of impending death lilting in your ears. But your mind lives on a few more breathless moments. Drowning on the blood which is filling your lungs, you have the fortitude to claw at the drawstrings and unveil the comet fragment. For a fleeting second as you twist upwards to face the heavens, the child is superimposed upon the parent, and you are superimposed against the dark shape of The Master, as you hurl the beacon toward the epitome of darkness, before stumbling away insensible with a riot of emotions.

You do not live to see the calamitous detonation, the blinding white holocaust which leaves no stone in the square unturned. For the duration of the hummingbird's heartbeat, you are entwined with The Master, melded together as one in the inferno.

But then to the Pantheon for you, and your place at the Table of Heroes. And to the Pit for the fiend. The unnavigable, inescapable pit.

Such is the whim of the Gods.

Your adventure, and your mortal soul, ends here.

Turn to 411.

499

You faithful mount carries you back to Deva in good time, and you reward the old fellow by setting him loose outside the city walls into someone's bountiful vegetable garden. Once inside the city and back at your lodgings, you enquire after the Professor, but there is still no word. After beating the dust from your clothes, and refreshing yourself with a cleansing dip in the water trough, you hit the streets of Deva again. There are two main events this evening:

Doctor Döll's 'Scientific Wonder' show, turn to 267.
The Elven saga telling at the amphitheatre, turn to 372.
Or
If you have the word 'TARGET' on your adventure sheet – and you still have your pistol - you can continue if you wish, in the Marksmanship Tourney, turn to 236.

You barely hear the urgent cries through the joyful celebrations. At first you mistake them for revelry - for shouts of victory and boasts of martial prowess. You step away from the impromptu festivities and strain to listen. Someone on the wall is shouting, shouting loudly! You push through the crowds and hurtle towards the warning exclamations, seeing a lone watchman looking out beyond the city into the gloom of the countryside. Agitated beyond measure, the fellow is jerking around like a condemned animal, his wild eyes full of fear. You fly up the steps, leaping up them in two strides, and skid to a stop by the terrified man.

'What is it?' you command, glancing down to the base of the wall. 'Answer me fool!' you demand, gripping him by his collar.

'They're not down there,' he whispers hoarsely, ashen faced. He slowly turns his tortured gaze to the crest of the nearby hills and gapes in horror. 'They're over there.' You follow the line of his dirty crooked finger to the fading orange glow of the setting sun. There, on the horizon, the tramping boots of thousands upon thousands of skeletal legionnaires, moving relentlessly toward the city.

'Hessler! Hessler - bring your looking glass!' you bellow over the hushing chatter in the square below. Captain Hessler is by your side in moments, and hands you his telescopic device. You shake your head with quiet horror, as you soak up a macabre carnival of death. Its reanimated slaves dance awkwardly forward, clad in the ancient armour of long forgotten warriors from yonder Belisarian Valley. As you wordlessly scan the massed abominations, you hear the watchman begin to sob softly. Hessler swallows nervously.

It's at that moment you catch sight of the master of these puppets. There, on a high ridge and illuminated by the waning light, the unmistakable scarlet-stained face of the young would-be necromancer, Ingmar Kops. As you stand transfixed you stare hard at the figure. Now shorn of his callow youth and infinitely more menacing than mere days ago, you don't have any time to consider his rapid transmogrification from Initiate to Master, before he somehow picks you out, and even though many leagues away, hidden by the veil of darkness and these deep crenellations on which you stand. He turns his unearthly gaze towards you. And he smiles.

Handing the looking glass back to Hessler, you struggle to fight the tremors in your hands as you reach for your sword...

The End